I0619423

Nomad's Ruin

Chronicles of Alcabaza Book 3

Morgan Lee Clasper

Published by Morgan Lee Clasper. For any inquiries, please contact:

morgan@morganclasperauthor.com

or visit: https://www.morganclasperauthor.com/

Cover Design by Fabrice Bertolotto

Illustrations by Marina Baskakova

Edited by Darcy Werkman at The Bearded Book Editor

Proofread by Darcy Werkman

ISBN: 978-0-473-61415-7

Books also by Morgan Lee Clasper

The Frostwing Quadrilogy

Frostwing: Dragonbond

Frostwing: Firebreath

Frostwing: Permafrost

Frostwing: Reaver's War

The Chronicles of Alcabaza

Dragon's Mark

Raider's Oath

Nomad's Ruin

Alchemist's Order

Contents

Sunstone

CLOUDS OF DUST BILLOWED FROM THE DARKNESS, invading Ramah's nostrils and forcing tears to his eyes. Flames crackled to his right, eating through the wad of resin stuck to his torch. He coughed, his voice echoing off the cramped, pitch-black passageway.

Ropes coiled into the air behind him, hugging the edge of a sheer chasm. The faint voices of his comrades wafted down from the soft glow of torches above. Ramah waved his light ahead of him, casting flickering shadows across the rough-cut sandstone.

This ruin is the one, he told himself. Sand filled the creases in his overalls, and his bald head shone slick with sweat. His heartbeat quickened as the tunnel plunged deeper into the Badlands rock. *I can feel it.*

He'd said that about every ruin they'd looted, but this time he knew he was right.

His footsteps crunched on the uneven floor. Smoke pooled on the ceiling, forcing him to suck at the musty air for breath. He tried to forget how many men had descended these maze-like tunnels never to return.

Quit scaring yourself, he scolded. He doubled over to breathe the clearer air beneath the smoke. *The fumes will kill you before gorgons will.*

The tunnel descended deeper, until the torches of his comrades faded behind him. Ramah became aware of the mass of rock above him. It filled him with a familiar thrill.

The passageway came to an abrupt stop. A doorway beckoned him. Its decorative blocks betrayed a burial chamber. Ducking to enter, Ramah swept his torch over the interior.

Sandstone sarcophagi filled the room, stacked against each other head to foot. Gold jars and artefacts surrounded them, along with dusty old paintings and disintegrating piles of books. Ramah ignored it all.

A plinth dominated the centre of the room, intricate carvings snaking up its side. Finger-like blocks of stone wrapped around like a fist, holding a slab of gold in its grip.

Ramah's hand wobbled. Embers leapt from his torch. He hardly felt them burn into the flesh of his forearm. He gasped at the air, but his lungs seized up. He put a hand to his mouth and yelled down the passageway in a strangled voice.

"I found it!"

Movement sounded from higher up in the tunnel. Ramah forgot about his friends and, lowering his torch to the ground, approached the golden slab. It formed a broken quarter of a disk, its edge smooth as if purposefully cut. A web of lines and markings snaked across its surface, too many for his eyes to take in.

Ramah carefully took the slab in his hands and prised it from the plinth. The sandstone fingers crumbled as he tugged it free. Torchlight flickered across its warm gold surface, shining brighter than any treasure he'd ever pulled from the depths of ruins. He grunted as the weight dragged him down.

"Ramah!" a voice called. Footsteps sounded along the passageway. "Hold up! Be careful with that thing."

Ramah cradled the golden slab. He felt its power course through his arms, alive with pulsing heat. His crewmates skidded to a halt in the entryway of the burial chamber. A grin spread across the lead man's face.

"There it is," he said. "A piece of the Sunstone." The crewmate unfurled a blanket. "Wrap it up. Careful not to scuff it." He looked at his companions. "Head to the surface and tell the others. Abaddon will want to see this."

Ramah set the Sunstone fragment down and bundled it in the material. The other crewmate clapped him on the shoulder and laughed. "How many ruins have we looted to find this beauty?" He let out a low whistle. "Only one more to go now."

Ramah tried to speak, but the words refused to come. The magic of the Sunstone lingered in his veins, dormant yet powerful.

Once they'd found the final piece, the Sunstone would finally be complete.

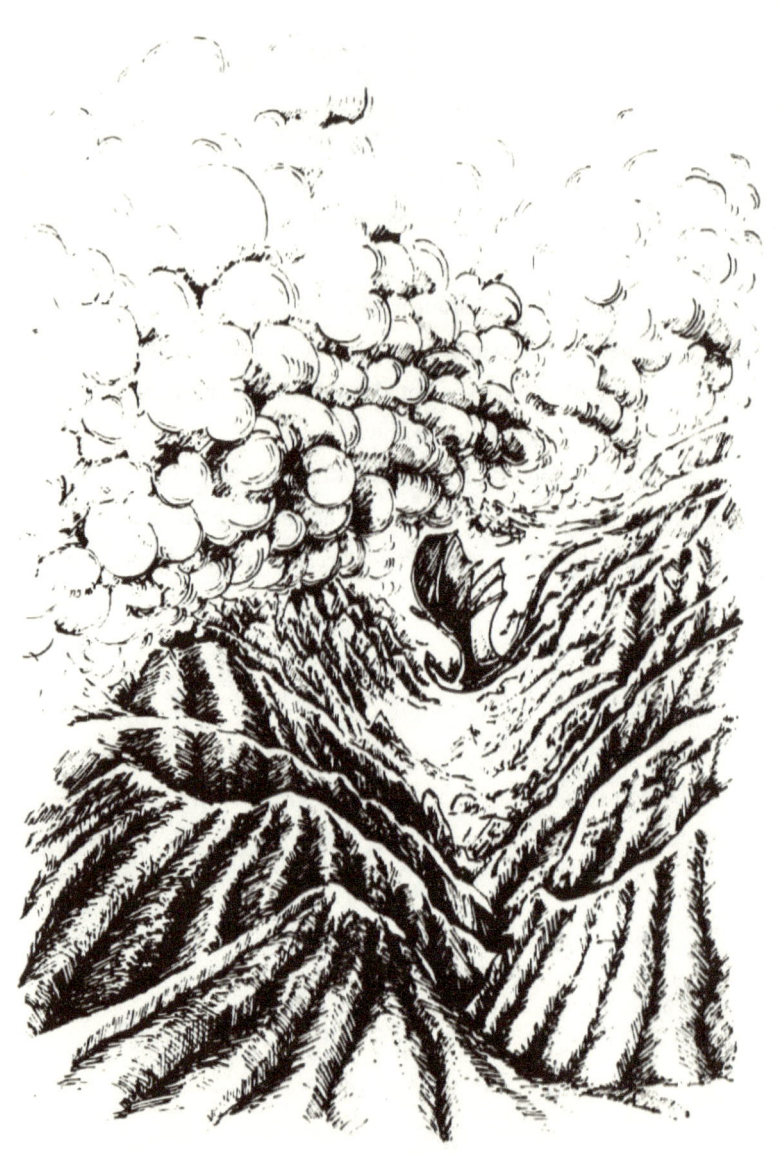

Highlands

THE SHRILL CRY OF A WILD EAGLE SPLIT the air as Aegon's shadow passed above. The bird erupted from its perch amid a cluster of craggy buttes, puffing up its neck in fright. A group of hatchlings huddled in their nest, watching as Aegon arched her back and soared higher into the sky.

Tessa crinkled her nose. "You're scaring them."

"It's just a bit of harmless fun," Isiah replied. "How am I supposed to remember where all the eagles are nesting?"

The eagle circled its nest, its beady eyes fixed on Aegon as she pulled away. Ahead of them, a jumbled maze of spires and gullies formed the rose-red labyrinth that made up the highlands.

Isiah put a hand to his forehead and squinted against the twin suns' harsh glow. A brilliant blue-white orb hung in the sky above them, its smouldering reddish cousin lurking off to the side. The sunlight played across the painted rock of the Badlands, giving life to sparse foliage and casting thick shadows across its many winding passageways and ravines.

Aegon's muscles rippled as she flew. Her vibrant purple wings extended down her sides, snaking to the tip of her tail and flaring out over her hind legs like a trailing cloak. Isiah adjusted his weight on the crest of her back, feeling Tessa's arms locked around his middle.

"We're straying far," she said. "I don't recognize these spires."

Aegon tilted on her wing and swept around a lone pillar of rock. It jutted into the sky, no more than a stack of boulders resting precariously atop one another. A trio of fat vultures scattered as Aegon let out a shrill roar. Her twin rows of jaws glistened.

Isiah laughed. "Someone's enjoying her exercise." He nudged Tessa. "We can find our way back, can't we? Your sense of direction is second to none."

Tessa's stern expression flickered for a moment. "I'm concerned about getting stuck out here, is all," she replied. "You know this is the season for dust storms."

Isiah patted Aegon's mane. A frill snaked along the top of her serpentine neck, rippling in the warm Badlands air like a sail. "Let me try a few more things with her."

Focusing, Isiah directed Aegon to break away from the spire and soar across the Badlands. The dragon responded to his thoughts, shifting her course. Her thin tail trailed behind her as her wide, leathery wings carried them into the sky.

Isiah nodded to himself. He let the sunlight warm his face as he closed his eyes. While Tessa and the Raiders needed saddles and reins to fly their eagles, his bond with Aegon let them fly together with their thoughts alone. It was a symbiosis, Solomon had said.

The thought of Solomon sent a sudden pang through Isiah's chest. He swallowed, shoving the sensation away. Aegon wobbled in the air. Her eel-like head swivelled around to check on him. Isiah stroked her flank to reassure her.

Tessa coughed. "We should head back to the Hidden Citadel."

"I still want to try a few things," Isiah said.

"No." She pointed to the horizon. "Look at that."

Isiah followed her gaze. A hazy cloud loomed in the distance, a dirty yellow-brown. It stretched as far as he could see in both directions.

"It's a dust storm," Tessa said. "And it's our sign to leave."

"It's miles away," he replied.

"They move faster than you think." She brushed her long, dark hair out of her face. "The wind is picking up."

"I only need a short while," Isiah insisted. "I don't want to miss this chance."

He tried to clear his mind so he could focus on his connection with Aegon. He narrowed his eyes, searching for the distinct feeling he encountered whenever their minds were one.

Isiah directed her into a number of manoeuvres. Aegon responded with a series of sharp turns, twisting her body and folding her wings. Tessa's grip tightened around his middle.

"Isiah . . ." she warned.

"I know, I know." He focused harder. He sensed their mental connection slipping. Aegon's movements became shaky as she lost his direction. Isiah pushed harder, but the more he grasped, the more his control slipped away. He felt Aegon's muscles tense as she became unsure of what he wanted her to do.

"You can try again tomorrow," Tessa said. She twisted around to glance over her shoulder. "We need to go."

Isiah sighed. When he checked the dust storm, it had doubled in size. He squinted, trying to figure out how fast it was moving, but the otherwise clear skies made it impossible to discern its speed.

He nudged Aegon and she swivelled in the direction of the Hidden Citadel. Lowering her head, she carried them across the broken terrain below. As they flew, the wind picked up, stirring Tessa's hair and tugging at the edges of their colourful robes.

Aegon stretched out her wings and glided on the updrafts. Tessa shifted her weight behind him. She kept checking over her shoulder.

"It's getting closer," she said.

Isiah checked. She was right—the dust storm towered behind them, a billowing wall that steadily rolled across the sky. He willed Aegon to fly faster. Her breathing grew heavier, twin plumes of hot air erupting from her nostrils.

Isiah scanned the ridges and buttes ahead for any sign of the cliffs that encircled the Hidden Citadel. The Badlands rolled ahead, empty. Particles of sand began raining onto his shoulders as the storm approached. Isiah wiped his sleeve across his eyes and pulled his collar to cover his mouth.

Tessa coughed. "We can't outrun it. We'll have to land and wait for it to pass."

Isiah searched the Badlands below for any sign of a cave or overhang where they could shelter. The seemingly solid wall of dust loomed a few hundred feet behind them, stretching into the heavens and out on both sides. Eagles landed in their nests and sheltered their hatchlings with their wings as it swept over and engulfed them.

A hollow caught Isiah's eye. "We can shelter there."

He urged Aegon toward it. She folded her wings and dropped to the Badlands below. The wind made his cloak flap around him, pelting him with dust and small rocks. Murky yellow shadows swept across the Badlands as the dust storm blotted out the twin suns.

Isiah relaxed as Aegon's hind legs hit the ground and she lumbered into the opening. The cave—no more than a narrow crack—

snaked into a cliffside. Isiah and Tessa slipped from Aegon's back as the storm caught up to them and stole the outside world from view.

Tessa huffed. "That's just great." She folded her arms. "Who knows how long we'll be stuck here now."

Isiah shielded his eyes from the sand billowing through the opening and leaned against the wall. Aegon sat with her back to the cave mouth, wings drawn around herself protectively. Beyond was nothing but a swirling mass of yellow.

"It could take hours for this to roll over." Tessa brushed herself off. "Lazaro will be worried sick about us."

Isiah slumped against the floor with a sigh. "You were right about the storm," he said. "I'm sorry for dragging you out here."

Tessa's expression softened. "Hey. We ought not to fight." She came and sat next to him. Isiah turned his head away from the stinging sand that blew in from outside. Aegon lay with one eye lazily open.

"I wonder if I'm pushing her too hard," Isiah said suddenly.

Tessa cocked her head. "What do you mean?"

"I don't know . . . it's just, we've been training together for so long. I still keep losing our connection."

"You're overthinking it." Tessa put her hand on top of his. "You're out here every day. What more could you ask for?"

Isiah threw up his hands. "I just don't know where I'm supposed to go from here. Even in Paradon, we had dragon-trainers." He glanced at Aegon. Her flank rose and fell as she slept. "How am I supposed to get better without a teacher?"

Tessa adjusted her seating. "Well . . . maybe you don't *need* one. Can't you figure it out yourself?"

Isiah hardly heard her. Learning about dragons from Ward in Paradon felt like a lifetime ago. Solomon had promised to teach him more about Aegon, but after they'd discovered the truth about him and what he was doing . . .

Isiah shook his head to clear the thought. "Let's just drop it."

Tessa shrugged. She shuffled onto her side and rested her head on her arm. "Wake me when the storm has passed."

Isiah let his head rest on the smooth stone behind him and tried to let his mind wander. Yellow-tinged shadows masked the cave interior as the dust cloud billowed outside. Aegon's steady, rhythmic breathing echoed around him.

Without anyone to teach him, how would he ever master his bond?

* * *

As the skies cleared and the wind fell to a whimper, Isiah and Tessa took to the air and flew Aegon in the direction of the Hidden Citadel. A thick haze still obscured the twin suns, muting their intense glare and settling on the Badlands like a kind of fog as the last traces of the dust storm floated slowly to the ground.

Sand settled on the mesas and in the valleys, powdering the rock with a fine layer. Eagles dusted themselves off and basked in the renewed sunlight.

Isiah let Aegon drift lazily on the air currents, watching the Badlands roll past below. He turned his attention inward, focusing on the mental link between them. While they were flying, he felt Aegon's movements as if they were his own. He became aware of each of her muscles, all working together in unison. Every twitch of her wings echoed through his mind. But Isiah knew if he tried to push any further, their link would dissolve.

They kept flying, until the Hidden Citadel appeared on the horizon. It caught Isiah's attention with a flash of green and blue, vibrant and piercing against the hazy red backdrop. At the sight, Aegon flew faster. A few dots circled in the sky above. As they drew closer, Isiah made out Raiders on their eagles.

One of the eagles turned on its wing and powered toward them. Myla sat tall and waved as she approached. "Isiah!" she called.

A grin spread across Isiah's face. He cupped his hands to his mouth. "What are you doing up here?"

Myla tugged on her eagle's reins and guided the bird to fly alongside them. "I wanted to keep an eye out for you. That dust storm was a big one."

Isiah puffed up his chest and gave her a sly smile. "It's nothing we can't handle." He laughed as he heard Tessa huff behind him.

Once they reached the Hidden Citadel, they passed over the cliffs that encircled it, and Isiah made out the sandstone town that nestled inside. A vibrant blue lake sat inside the basin, ringed by lush greenery. People milled about along the streets and past rows of crimson tents.

Isiah directed Aegon to land atop one of the cliffs, alongside the troop of eagles that the handlers cared for. She touched down and he dismounted. Myla landed beside him. Her eagle flapped its wings to steady itself and she hopped off, her curly hair bouncing with a life of its own.

"Did you like my landing?" she asked.

Isiah smiled. "You're a natural."

11

Myla beamed. "I've always wanted to be a Raider."

Ever since Solomon's death, Darla and Helen had shown Myla how to fly an eagle. In place of the overalls she wore when she was an eagle handler for Solomon, she now sported the vibrant robes and body harness of a Raider.

"I figured you'd wait out the dust storm," Myla said. "Darla said they're too dangerous to fly in."

"They are," Tessa replied. "Eagles lose their sense of direction and crash." She raised her eyebrows at Isiah. "It's risky to make long flights this time of year."

"I know," Isiah admitted. "But I need to do it. It's the only way I'll learn."

As handlers hurried over to tend to Myla's eagle, the trio left the cliffs and began down the narrow, rocky trail into the basin itself. The path gave them a sweeping view of the sandstone town, from the rows of tents at its edge to the half-built tower that housed the old ex-Raider Edith.

Isiah's gaze dropped to the lake. After flooding the tunnels beneath the Hidden Citadel and drowning Solomon's Raiders, the water was level with the gaping hole the explosives had blown. Sheer cliffs dropped sharply to the water's surface. Every time Isiah looked at it, it reminded him of Solomon's gut-churning operations.

He felt Tessa's hand curl around his. When he met her gaze, she gave him a reassuring smile.

"I can always tell what you're thinking," she said.

Isiah brushed her off. "It's no big deal." He lowered his voice. "I just can't believe I was duped like that."

It had taken a long time for the townsfolk to come to terms with what Solomon had done. Isiah still wasn't sure if some of them fully believed it. But after Edith and the rescued labourers had told their story, Lazaro and his gang had become the new protectors of the Hidden Citadel.

They reached the basin floor and passed the lake, heading to the main town. Clotheslines hung between the various buildings, and their flat-topped roofs afforded private gardens to their residents. Market stalls filled the main plaza as townsfolk shared out the produce they had farmed and gathered.

As they neared, a commotion went up from one of the stalls.

"I thought you guys shared everything out!" a voice yelled. "We traded with the nomads for this stuff, don't you know. It belongs to us!"

As they came closer, Isiah made out Aron arguing with an old shopkeeper. The boy held a sack, but the old shopkeeper had him by the arm.

"I see you pickpocketing!" the man snapped. "You don't need more food!"

"Lazaro sent me to stock up for him," Aron said. "You don't want to annoy the Raiders, do you?" When he caught sight of Isiah and the others, he pointed. "See? They're already here." He tried to wrestle free, but the man refused to let go.

Tessa laughed. "Old habits die hard, don't they?"

Aron's face reddened. "Sharing things out like this feels weird," he said. "We never did that back home."

"It's supposed to foster bartering and cooperation," Myla replied. "Raiders bring supplies from outside, and in return, we get whatever the community produces." She shrugged. "At least, that's what Edith says."

Aron pulled a face. "If Solomon isn't using them as skin donors, that is."

Isiah grimaced at the mention of Solomon. He scratched his Mark.

"Where's Lazaro?" Tessa asked, trying to distract them.

"He's in our house," Aron replied. "He really did send me out here on errands—honest!"

Myla stepped forward. "We'll bring you something from our next raid, okay?" she said to the shopkeeper. "He won't bother you again."

The man hesitated for a moment, then released Aron with a scowl. Aron dusted himself off and rubbed his arm. He nodded at Myla. "I owe you one."

They wandered away from the markets and toward the back of the town, where buildings hugged the cliffs that encircled them. Near Edith's tower, a sandstone façade protruded from the cliff wall.

Aron grinned. "It's a much nicer place than that old shack you guys had in Alcabaza, isn't it?"

Tessa pulled a face. "I liked that shack."

Aron raised his hands in mock surrender. "I'm just saying we've got a pretty sweet spot here, don't we?"

"Lazaro still misses Alcabaza sometimes," Tessa said. She shifted her weight. "He thinks I don't know, but I hear him talking to Helen."

Aron shrugged. "Hey, it's not like we can go back, anyhow. And after what they did to us? I'd rather be top dog here."

Isiah punched him playfully. "Top dog? You don't even have an eagle to fly."

"I will soon," Aron insisted. "As soon as my hatchling's big enough to carry me, we'll start lessons. Right, Myla?"

Myla giggled. "If you say so."

They approached the Raider house. Darla and Antony stood leaning against the outside of the building, talking to some townsfolk. Marie was with them. Darla had taken the timid girl under her wing after they'd accepted her into their gang. Darla broke away as they approached.

"That was a mighty dust storm," she said. "As soon as it hit, all the townsfolk scurried inside and barricaded their windows. I've never seen them move so fast."

"It gets bad this time of year," Myla said. "The dry winds carry them across the highlands. Sometimes they last for hours."

Darla nodded. "Old Edith says the nomads in these parts call them haboobs."

Aron snickered.

"You'd better watch yourselves, flying with Aegon like you do," Antony said. "I wouldn't want you to get stranded out there."

Tessa shot a sly look at Isiah. "Too late."

"We're careful," Isiah said, ignoring her. "Aegon can handle it, anyway."

"Even so," Antony warned, "it pays to exercise a bit of caution." He gestured to the cliffs. "You never know what might be lurking beyond the horizon out there."

Abaddon

"Heave the sails!" a gruff voice yelled. "Ride the wind!"

Ropes creaked as sails unfurled. Valves hissed, with hidden pipes channelling air into the belly of the skyship. Pulleys squealed as long wooden arms swivelled, their sails catching the dust-laden air and driving the craft forward.

Abaddon marched along the deck. Crewmates barked orders and waved their arms. Youths, some barely older than children, scurried along the ropes, grappling with the sails as the wind filled them. The deck creaked with the constant pounding of feet.

Abaddon reached the bow of the skyship and shielded his eyes with a weathered hand, inspecting the blood-red, desolate landscape. A tower of tattered sails rose above the skyship, casting dabbled shade across the deck, while more sails spanned either side of the vessel like a multitude of wings. A haze hung around them as the sandy wind pushed the skyship toward their destination.

"Keep those sails under control!" a crewmate barked at the youths. "Nice and steady. Maintain altitude until the captain gives the signal."

Abaddon dusted off his deep-red robes. Particles of sand caught in his thin beard and the headscarf wrapped around his head. A sabre hung at his side, its hilt embossed with gold.

He frowned at the constant creak of sails. Holes pitted the canvas, and the skyship's hull was bleached with sunlight. Its deck stretched only a few dozen feet wide and less than a hundred long—no more than a scouting vessel. The ship's prow, carved as an eagle with outstretched wings, seemed to slice the air as the craft picked up speed.

"How much further?" Abaddon asked. He towered several heads taller than the other crewmates.

"Beyond this mesa," a second crewmate replied. He gestured to a wide, flat mound of rock ahead. "That's where we found the entrance."

Abaddon scowled. "If you can keep this vessel airborne long enough to make it."

The crewmate gave him an apologetic look. "I run a tight ship, Captain, but the journey has taken a toll on all of us."

Abaddon returned his attention to the landscape. He gripped the railing and waited as the skyship cleared the mesa and their target came into view. Two more ships—both small scouting vessels—floated in the shadow of the mesa. Dozens of ropes descended from their sides to the ground below, where a sandstone archway was cut into the rock.

"It's a big ruin," Abaddon remarked. "Their entrances are usually better hidden than this."

"That's why we checked it first," the crewmate replied. "We wanted to know if anyone beat us to it."

He raised an eyebrow. "And?"

"They didn't. It's too remote and inhospitable for treasure-hunters to bother visiting."

"Lower the vessel," Abaddon ordered. "Bring it in close."

The crewmate hollered a string of commands. Pulley boys and other youths struggled with the sails as they slowed the skyship. Air

17

hissed as the vessel descended. The crewmates helped guide it parallel to the mesa's sheer wall. They neared the ground and the ship stopped with a lurch.

Crewmates uncoiled armfuls of rope and lobbed them over the railing. Abaddon took one and slid to the ground below. Years of sailing had honed his movements to a near-perfect precision. His boots met the Badlands soil and he stepped away.

A line of crewmates belonging to the other ships dragged crates out of the ruin. Others then tied them to ropes and hoisted them up to the skyships floating above. A few barrels of explosives were piled nearby. The gleam of gold caught Abaddon's eye.

"Captain!" one of the excavators called. Sweat glistened on his bald head, and his overalls were coated in sand. "You made it."

"How big is your haul, Ramah?" Abaddon asked. "Your messenger told me you found something important."

Ramah failed to mask his smile. "This is an old ruin," he replied. "An original burial site, by my reckoning. I knew it would be the one."

"Where is it?" Abaddon asked.

Ramah gestured to a pile of crates. "Tucked away, awaiting transport."

Abaddon marched past him. "I want to see it."

The other crewmates stepped aside as he reached the crates and pried the lid off one. Golden goblets and plates filled it, surrounding a cloth-clad object. He pushed the goblets aside without a second look.

The cloth fell away, revealing his treasure. A flicker of a smile up-turned Abaddon's lip.

"The Ancients hid it in some kind of maze," Ramah said. "Now we're only missing one more piece."

Abaddon reached out and ran his fingers across the Sunstone fragment. Ridges and bumps covered its surface, forming an intricate pattern of diagrams and symbols.

"What do the symbols do, Captain?" one of the crewmates asked. "It can't be for decoration."

Abaddon's nose crinkled. "The people who built this didn't *decorate* it," he said curtly. "They're instructions." He straightened up. "But we need all four fragments for it to work."

The dust in the air grew thicker, masking the twin suns in a thick haze. The skyships drifted from side to side as the crewmates fought with the strengthening wind.

"Do we hunker down here or risk returning to the fleet?" Ramah asked.

"Tether the ships and retract their sails," Abaddon said. "Bring the Sunstone fragment to my quarters. I don't want it out of my sight. We'll return to the main fleet once the weather is clear."

Ramah saluted. "Aye aye, Captain." He paused. "One last thing. Some of the crew on watch duty reported spotting another group of nomads. We think it won't be long before we'll have to make contact."

Abaddon scoffed. "Nomads can't interfere with us. They scurry under the nearest rock and hide the moment they see our fleet."

"Of course, Captain," Ramah said. "But where there are nomads, Raiders are never far behind."

"Then it's of utmost importance that we add this Sunstone fragment to our collection—and then locate the final missing piece." Abaddon waved him away. "Have your men load up the last of the ruin's goods. If the ships are too heavy, dump the crates overboard. The Sunstone is far more important to us than gold."

Abaddon marched to his skyship. The crewmates carried the Sunstone fragment after him. He waited as they secured it to a network of ropes, then raised it to the waiting ship. He turned his gaze to the earth at his feet, where the ruin's labyrinthian passageways snaked deep below.

"You hid them well, Ancients," he said quietly. "But you can't keep them from Abaddon."

Canyon

ISIAH SHIELDED HIS EYES FROM THE HARSH GLARE of the twin suns. It baked his shoulders, scorching the arid mesa he stood on and making sweat drip down his forehead.

The highlands sprawled around him. Aegon stood off to his side, resting in the shade of an overhang. Tessa had stayed behind in the Hidden Citadel, leaving him to practice alone.

Isiah wiped a hand across his face and closed his eyes, focusing on his bond. He reached out with his mind, trying to summon Aegon to him. She'd done it once before, when he and his friends were being threatened by Raiders outside a ruin. Solomon had told him . . .

Enough about Solomon. Isiah forced the thought from his mind. Solomon was a monster. Solomon was dead.

Isiah beckoned Aegon. "Come on. Let's see if we can find somewhere better to rest. The sun is getting too hot for me."

Aegon lumbered over and Isiah climbed onto her back. She launched herself from the edge of the mesa and the ground fell away. A few hulking, scaly beasts scattered in a valley below. A swathe of scraggly bushes clung to the hollows and crevices of the highlands, the only colour against the reddish backdrop.

"There must be water nearby," Isiah said. He pulled the waterskin off his belt and took a swig. A few drops of warm, sandy water met his tongue.

They flew further, each wingbeat carrying them deeper into the highlands. The horizon wrapped around them as a perfect circle, hazy with rising heat from the Badlands. A pang of unease tugged at Isiah's chest. This was the furthest he'd ever ventured from the Hidden Citadel.

A glimmer of blue snaked through a valley below. Isiah straightened up and peered over the side of Aegon's flank to get a better look. A thin river wound through a canyon, its waters lapping against sandy shores. Isiah nodded to himself.

Aegon descended toward it. As they cleared the canyon walls, she folded her wings and glided to the water. The rock hemmed them in on both sides, but it afforded Aegon enough space to land. A thin layer of water bounded across the rocks, carving a path through the highlands and giving life to thick mats of bushes and acacia trees.

Isiah popped the cap off his waterskin and knelt by the stream. Aegon lowered her head to drink.

"Tessa doesn't know what she's missing," he said. "Wait until she hears about this place."

He finished filling his waterskin and leaned against the canyon wall. A flock of birds sat in the branches above, and a handful of lizards warmed themselves in the sun. Isiah parted his robe and poured some of the water across his shoulders, sapping the heat from his Mark. His warped, candle-wax skin couldn't sweat, and the midday heat had left it an angry red. If he didn't keep himself cool, it would burn and blister.

Aegon raised her head from the stream and swivelled her head toward the sky. She let out a low rumble.

"What is it, girl?" Isiah asked. He followed her gaze.

A blip hovered on the horizon, dark against the pale blue sky. Isiah squinted, trying to make out what it was. He half-expected to see Tessa or Myla. *But it's coming from the wrong direction,* he thought.

The shape seemed to float in place, too big to be a wild eagle. Isiah climbed onto Aegon and directed her to take flight. She awkwardly clambered out of the canyon. Once she cleared the narrow walls, she stretched out her wings and caught the updrafts. Isiah put a hand to his forehead and tried to make out the shape in the distance.

"Slow down," he said. Aegon stopped flapping and let herself drift on the air currents. Beyond the shape, Isiah saw several more similar shapes. As the first blip emerged from the Badlands' haze, he made out long wings and giant crests. The image of a dragon crossed his mind.

Don't be stupid, he told himself. No dragons would ever fly so deep in the Badlands.

Aegon flew low to the mesas, trying to avoid the attention of the strange objects. She closed the distance and the wooden hull of a ship materialized. The wings Isiah had seen were sails, stretching out on both sides of the vessel. Isiah's head swam as he took in the sight. "What the . . ."

Aegon swivelled her head around to look at him, waiting for instruction. Isiah hesitated. They came within a few hundred feet of the skyship, and the figures of people became visible scurrying about on the deck. Wooden arms swivelled as the skyship adjusted its course.

I should find Tessa, Isiah thought. He suddenly became aware of how alone he was.

A loud pop sounded in the direction of the skyship. An object flew toward them. It arced in the sky for a few long seconds. Isiah's eyes widened as he realized what it was.

Aegon lurched to the side in panic as a chain whipped past Isiah's ear. It struck a nearby hoodoo and the rock exploded in a cloud of debris. Aegon hissed in alarm and pulled away from the ship. Several more pops sounded as the skyship fired on them.

Isiah gripped Aegon's neck. Another chain whizzed past overhead. Three metal balls were attached to it, making it spin as it flew. The rhythmic whirring noise echoed in his eardrums. He willed himself to do something, but his muscles felt frozen.

He managed to find his voice. "Fly!"

Aegon responded by diving toward the earth and racing over the Badlands. Another chain struck a mesa to their right. A glance over his shoulder revealed the skyship above and behind them, its sails outstretched and filled with wind.

Isiah tore his eyes away from the vessel. Aegon's huffing breaths swirled in his eardrums. The skyship kept pace with their flight. Isiah wrestled to quell the panic building inside him. He tried to direct Aegon to weave between spires, but she ignored him. The ship loomed behind them, closing fast.

Aegon lurched in the air and let out a pained shriek. Her left wing crumpled and she pitched toward the ground. Isiah's heart flew into his throat as the earth rushed to meet them.

Aegon collided with the ground and skidded. Isiah was thrown from her back and tumbled through the air. A stab of pain erupted through his ribs as he landed a few feet away.

He barely came to a halt before he scrambled to his feet, clutching his side and coughing dust. He cried out in a hoarse voice. "Aegon!"

Aegon flapped her wings and tried to stand. The chains had tangled her left wing, crushing it together and preventing her from unfurling it. Wheezing, Isiah hobbled over to her. Each movement tore at his aching lungs, but he gritted his teeth against the pain.

He grabbed the ball and chain and tried to work it free. He forced himself to slow his fumbling hands. Aegon swivelled her head around and launched a blast of fire at the skyship. The ship yawed away, hovering just out of her reach.

Isiah managed to pull one of the metal balls free. Aegon flapped her wing, shaking the weapon off. A spurt of sand and rock exploded as another one hit the ground nearby. Isiah swallowed his growing panic.

The weapon slipped free and Aegon regained control of her wing. Isiah looked up and saw that the skyship had circled around to cut off their escape. He could make out the crew loading a fresh barrage of chains. He quickly searched for some kind of escape.

The mouth of a canyon was open nearby. Piles of boulders and craggy buttes surrounded it, cluttering the skyline. An idea flashed into his head.

"Come on!" Every word forced a pained breath from his aching chest. Aegon stared the skyship down, her neck coiled and her flanks puffed up. Her chest glowed a deep red as she readied another fireball. Isiah threw an arm around her neck and tugged. "Aegon. Let's go!"

The skyships launched another volley. Aegon released a stream of liquid fire that arced through the air, but it fell short of the vessel. Isiah staggered away and covered his head. The rhythmic whir of the spinning chains rose above the yelling of crewmen. He braced himself for the projectiles to land.

Aegon lumbered after him. Isiah jumped in fright as a chain landed to his left, spitting a cloud of earth and sand. Another struck a hoodoo and showered him with sharp chunks of rock. He kept his head down as it pelted his shoulders and rained onto Aegon's body. The mouth of the canyon seemed to beckon them.

Every step sent throbbing pain through Isiah's ribs. He ran doubled over, gasping at the air. Aegon's thundering footsteps echoed behind him. Metal chains struck boulders and skidded across the ground. One of them ricocheted toward him.

Isiah launched himself at the canyon. The spinning chain flew over him, missing his head by mere inches. He braced himself as he hit the ground and slid down a scree-covered slope into the canyon. The scree cut his arms and filled his face with dust. Aegon slid behind him with a shower of earth.

Isiah hit the bottom and dragged himself to his knees. He spat the dust from his mouth and blinked away the tears gathering in his eyes. Sand filled his hair and invaded his nostrils. He hobbled deeper into the canyon, praying it would shelter them from the skyship.

Aegon's huffing breaths sounded behind him. "Keep going," he urged. His voice came out pained and weak. His eyes stung from dust and sand, making it impossible to see where he was going.

The shadow of the skyship passed overhead. Aegon huddled against the wall of the canyon, and Isiah clung to her. He wrestled his waterskin free and dumped its contents onto his face to clear his vision. He watched as the skyship climbed in altitude.

The rock formations atop the narrow canyon walls sheltered them from the ship's weapons. The skyship circled a few times, then pulled away and drifted out of view. Isiah slumped against the canyon wall, his breaths ragged and deep.

"What *was* that?" he managed to say.

Aegon's throat quivered as she gave him a reassuring rumble. The sound made his insides tremble. He leaned against her and waited for the pain in his ribs to subside. Aegon flexed and unflexed her left wing. The chain had tangled it, but the impact had left her unharmed.

Isiah's gaze dropped to a metal sphere laying on the slope nearby. He shakily stood and limped over to it. Three round, smooth balls were connected by chains, each one the size of his head. Isiah stooped and lifted it.

"Who would *do* this?" he asked. He cast a wary glance at the sky in case the ship returned. He gathered up the weapon and slung it over his shoulder. He waited until they had caught their breath, then he turned to Aegon. "Tell me you can still fly?"

Aegon stood. She stretched her wings and steadied herself on her hind legs. Isiah swallowed. "We need to warn Tessa."

* * *

Isiah let his shoulders drop as the Hidden Citadel materialized. They had escaped the canyon and cautiously flown across the highlands, steering clear of wherever the skyship may have disappeared to. It had been the longest flight of Isiah's life.

Aegon slowed her speed and came to rest on the eagles' cliffs. Isiah carefully dismounted—still clutching his throbbing side—and waited for the adrenaline to fade. A few handlers muttered among each other as he staggered away from Aegon and down the path to the Hidden Citadel. The ball and chain the skyship had fired at him was slung over his shoulder, rattling with every step. As he reached the town, Myla came running out.

"Isiah!" she called. "What happened to you?"

"I was attacked," he blurted out.

Myla skidded to a halt in front of him. She studied him with wide, concerned eyes. "You're hurt. Let me see."

Isiah winced as she touched his ribs.

"Let's get you to Edith," Myla said. "She'll know how to help you."

Isiah tried to push her away. "No—I need to talk to Tessa."

Myla caught his arm and guided him toward the tower. "Tessa is still practicing her magic with Edith. We can catch her there if we're quick."

Her words sent a new spurt of determination through him. He quickened his pace toward Edith's tower. It loomed above the surrounding buildings, sporting the wooden crane that he'd jumped from when Enrik had captured him.

They reached the front door and Myla threw it open. "Edith!" she called, cupping a hand to her mouth. "Isiah's hurt."

Footsteps thudded inside the tower. Tessa appeared from the kitchen doorway. She gasped when she saw Isiah. "What happened?" she asked.

"Let him sit," Edith said, appearing behind her. "Take him into the kitchen."

Myla helped Isiah past the cramped bookshelves that filled Edith's tower.

"It's okay." Isiah tried to brush her away. "It's nothing serious. I'm just winded."

"Let's hope you're right," Edith replied. "But I'm still going to take a look at you."

They helped him into the kitchen and he sat at Edith's table. The hunched woman shuffled over and adjusted her brightly coloured shawl. Isiah dumped the ball and chain next to him as Edith inspected his ribs. He winced as she probed him. Tessa and Myla crowded around.

"It feels like a fracture," Edith said. "How did this happen?"

Isiah recounted the story of being attacked by the skyship. The girls listened with wide eyes.

"They shot Aegon down using these," he said, gesturing to the ball and chain. "It tangled her wing and we fell. If we'd been higher up, we might have died."

Tessa studied it with a furrowed brow. "I've never heard of anything like this before."

"I have," Edith said gravely. "The nomads call them bolas. They use them to hunt wild animals . . . but I've never seen them used against dragons before."

"We should tell Lazaro about this," Myla said. "He might know what to do."

"How far into the highlands were you?" Tessa asked.

Isiah shifted in his seat. "I don't know. I didn't recognize the place. But the skyships move fast. It could keep pace with us."

Tessa stood. "Then we'd better warn people."

"Don't act too hasty," Edith said. She unwound a bandage and popped the lid of a jar of ointment. "We don't want to panic the townsfolk."

"I'll put some handlers on lookout duty," Myla said. She slipped from the table and ran from the tower.

Edith finished tending to Isiah's rib. She tied the bandage tightly and nodded in satisfaction. "That will keep it from getting worse," she said. "You should rest to let it heal. Flying again will only make it sore."

Isiah thanked her and they left the tower. They hastened in the direction of the Raiders' houses. Isiah limped after Tessa. Each breath made his side burn, even with Edith's remedy. They found Lazaro with the rest of the gang outside.

Lazaro raised an eyebrow at Isiah. "What's wrong with you, boy?"

"He was attacked," Tessa replied.

Lazaro stiffened. "By who?"

Tessa quickly recounted what Isiah had told her. Isiah glanced over his shoulder instinctively. He relaxed to see Aegon with the eagles on the cliffs.

"A flying ship?" Darla said. "That's a funny sight. Are you sure you didn't fall off Aegon and see a desert mirage?"

Isiah dumped the bola on the ground between them. "Then how did I get this?"

The Raiders exchanged glances. Lazaro stroked the stubble on his chin. "What in the Badlands did you stumble onto out there?"

"Do you think they're from the highlands?" Darla asked.

"Solomon said nothing about it," Lazaro replied. "And in all my years of being a Raider, I never heard anything about flying ships."

"The winds are strong this time of year," Antony said. "It'll be blowing these skyships straight toward us."

"Then we'd best be ready for them to stumble onto us," Lazaro replied. He scooped up the bola. "I don't know what you saw out there, boy, but nobody pushes around *my* Raiders."

Skyships

THE DAYS DRAGGED PAST AT THE HIDDEN CITADEL. Isiah stuck to the confines of the basin walls, anxiously awaiting any sign of the skyships he'd seen. The handlers kept watch from the nearby spires, but they reported nothing. He spent many hours in his tent, resting until his ribs no longer ached when he drew breath.

Tessa brought him more ointment whenever she went to study with Edith. Her illusion magic had grown stronger since their arrival at the Hidden Citadel. While recovering, he had ample time to replay the events of his fateful flight in his mind.

If only I had a stronger bond, he thought. If he hadn't panicked and lost control, Aegon wouldn't have fallen. The dull throb in his side served as a constant reminder. He gritted his teeth. As soon as he was healed, he'd get right back out into the highlands with her.

Isiah climbed out of his hammock and wandered into the hall. Muted sunlight filtered through the narrow windows. The cliffside the house was built into afforded them protection from the sun, rendering it a cool chill even in the heat of the day. Isiah left the building and emerged on the street outside.

A crowd milled about the streets, reminding him of his time at Alcabaza. A few eagles circled lazily overhead, drifting on the air currents. Further away, families lowered buckets attached to ropes into what remained of the lake, drawing out the water that sustained their settlement.

Movement caught his attention atop the cliffs. An eagle landed with a flurry of wingbeats and a figure jumped from its back. Handlers scurried about as the figure sprinted down the cliffside path.

Isiah hastened toward the edge of town. His side ached in protest, but he ignored it. A cold dread welled inside him as he made out Myla running toward him.

"Isiah!" she called. She skidded to a halt and doubled over, panting. "Where's Lazaro?"

"What's wrong?" Isiah asked.

Myla gulped down a breath. "I saw something."

Isiah froze.

"It's the skyships," Myla said. "They're heading this way. We have to warn the others." She pushed past him and ran toward their house. Isiah went after her as fast as he could manage. When he arrived, Lazaro and the others were already marching out.

"Get your eagles ready," Lazaro ordered. His sabre rattled at his side. He nodded to Isiah. "And bring Aegon into the basin."

Tessa ran up to Isiah. "Do you think you're well enough to fly?" she asked.

Isiah rubbed his side. "I can do it."

Lazaro and the others were already sprinting to the cliffs. Isiah and Tessa fell in behind them. Townsfolk watched them go, muttering among themselves.

"Do we warn them?" Tessa asked.

"Not yet," Lazaro replied. "The last thing we need is a panic."

They climbed the narrow trail to the cliffs and Isiah reunited with Aegon. She lumbered over and nuzzled him with her snout. Despite his fluttering heart, Isiah grinned. "I missed you."

Myla pointed to the skyline. "There they are."

Isiah followed her gaze. Sure enough, three dark blobs hovered on the horizon.

Lazaro tightened the straps on his eagle's saddle and climbed on. "Stick together and wait for them to get closer."

His eagle launched itself into the sky. Darla and Antony followed suit, along with Luca and Helen. Isiah scrambled onto Aegon's back and took a deep breath.

With Tessa and Myla on their eagles, they flew above the Hidden Citadel and joined the rest of the gang. The skyships loomed closer, near enough for Isiah to make out their sweeping sails and sleek hulls. Lazaro pulled out a spyglass and put it to his eye.

Darla let out a low whistle. "Isiah was right."

The ships neared the Hidden Citadel. Lazaro tensed. The eagles flexed their claws in apprehension. Aegon gave off a throaty rumble as she fixed her dark eyes on the approaching vessels. Isiah stroked her flank.

The skyships began to descend.

"What are they doing?" Helen asked.

Lazaro scowled. "Landing."

The skyships cleared the basin walls and dropped in altitude. Townsfolk pointed and retreated into their houses. Lazaro and the Raiders dropped to the basin floor and landed beside the lake. Isiah spurred Aegon after them.

The three skyships hovered a few dozen feet off the ground. They dominated the basin, looming over the buildings and casting thick shadows across the lake. Ropes dropped from their sides and figures slid to the ground.

Aegon landed beside the eagles. Isiah hurriedly joined Lazaro and the others. Tessa had her hand on the hilt of her sabre. Marie stood on tip-toes, peering between them with wide eyes.

A troop of men and women in overalls gathered beneath the skyships. The steady creak of ropes and sails echoed across the basin. Aegon puffed up her chest and hissed at the floating behemoths. Isiah patted her neck to calm her.

A man appeared at the head of the crowd. He stood taller than the rest of his crew, sporting purple and red robes. The men and women stood aside as he marched toward them. Lazaro's eagle stood to attention, surveying the newcomers with beady eyes. Townsfolk peered through gaps in their shutters at the skyships.

Lazaro cleared his throat. "What do you think you're doing here?"

The man in the lead stopped in front of them. "Who's in charge of this settlement?" he asked.

Lazaro frowned. "I am."

The Raiders exchanged glances. Isiah wrung his hands. He waited for the flash of a weapon being drawn.

The man studied them. Each second seemed to last an eternity. "I didn't expect to find a town in such a remote corner of the Badlands," he said. "Are we intruding?"

"You attacked one of my people," Lazaro replied.

The man turned to Isiah and Aegon. "I see. I never thought I'd run into a dragon so far from Paradon."

35

Isiah swallowed. The air felt heavy to breathe. The man's smooth, level tone made his skin crawl.

Like Solomon.

The man extended a hand to Lazaro. "My people call me Abaddon," he said. "I'm the captain of this fleet."

Lazaro hesitated, then shook it. Abaddon's hand dwarfed his own. He introduced the Raiders.

"I apologize for my crewmates being trigger-happy," Abaddon said. "When they see a dragon, it sends them into a panic. Rogue dragon riders have given us trouble in the past."

Tessa stepped forward. "I've never seen ships like this before. Where do you come from?"

"We're not from these parts," Abaddon replied. He gestured to the way they had come from. "We hail from far beyond the highlands." He paused. "But I know Raiders when I see them. You must visit my flagship."

Lazaro narrowed his eyes. "We don't trust strangers around here."

"I can understand that." Abaddon smiled. Isiah caught the emptiness in his eyes. "But I insist. We must have an opportunity to work out any *hostilities* that might lie between us."

The crewmates closed in.

"The fleet is moored not far from here," Abaddon said. "You can take your eagles with you."

Lazaro crossed his arms. "We will."

The Raiders climbed onto their eagles. Aegon coiled her neck and growled at the skyships.

"Your dragon had better stay," Abaddon said.

Isiah hesitated. "Why?"

"You've seen how dragons and my fleet mix," he replied. "I would hate for there to be an accident."

Tessa folded her arms. "If they're not going, then I'm not going either."

"It's fine." Isiah brushed her away. "I'll fly with you instead."

"But—" Tessa started.

"I said it's fine," Isiah repeated, louder. He lowered his voice. "Aegon is still spooked after last time."

Tessa looked hurt for a moment, then her expression dropped.

"Excellent." Abaddon motioned to his crewmates and they hurried back to their vessels. Isiah climbed onto Vyrro behind Tessa and they waited to follow the skyships back to the rest of their fleet. Isiah turned to Aegon, who watched him with a quizzical expression.

"You stay here," he told her. He looked at her apologetically. "I won't be gone long."

* * *

Vyrro flew in the shadow of the skyships. The vessels cast dark shadows on the Badlands beneath them as they floated against the wind. Wooden arms creaked and clunked as teams of youths adjusted them to catch the updrafts.

Further away, Lazaro and the rest of the gang flew. Aron sat behind Antony, while Marie flew with Myla. Their eagles strained against the wind.

Up close, Isiah took a better look at the skyships. Large cylinders protruded from their decks, attached to an assortment of pipes and valves. Crossbow-like contraptions were mounted to the railings, fitted with more of the bolas that he and Aegon had been attacked with.

They flew in silence. The muffled yell of a crewmate rose above the whistle of the wind as he barked a string of orders. After a while, more dark blotches appeared on the horizon. Isiah counted over a dozen. One loomed over the others, dwarfing them. Isiah strained his eyes against the Badlands haze to make out the details.

"That must be their flagship," he said.

Tessa grunted. She kept her eyes fixed on the horizon.

The skyships grew closer. Abaddon's vessels slowed, drifting towards the massive flagship. Isiah ran his eyes over it and his breath caught in his throat.

Four towers of sails protruded from the mighty vessel. One adorned it like a frill, while two more extended outwards like wings. A fourth hung beneath the ship, dozens of small canvases suspended from a network of wooden masts. As Abaddon's smaller ship drifted to its side, Isiah became aware of how large the vessel was.

A golden prow glinted in the sunlight, shaped like a dragon with gaping jaws. A pang of guilt tugged at Isiah's chest for leaving Aegon behind. His eyes dropped to the assortment of weapons bristling on the flagship's deck. He gulped. *Maybe it was for the best.*

They flew into the shadow of the flagship and Lazaro's eagle landed on its deck. Crewmates tethered Abaddon's vessel to the side of the flagship and lowered a wooden bridge between them. Isiah braced himself as Vyrro landed beside them. Lazaro and the other Raiders climbed off their eagles and strode onto the deck.

"Leave your birds here," Abaddon said. "There's plenty of room for them."

Darla let out a low whistle. "This is a mighty fine ship you've got here."

Isiah leaned against the low wooden wall that formed the railing. Several smaller ships floated further away, all seemingly dormant. Despite the golden prow and spotless sails of the flagship, he made out the tatters and holes pitting the canvases of the scouting vessels. A few pitched to one side, their hulls warped and sun-bleached.

"I must show you around," Abaddon said. He beckoned them. "Come."

Lazaro and the other Raiders left their eagles near the front of the ship and followed Abaddon along the deck. Isiah spied more of the air-filled cylinders protruding from the deck in places.

"How does this thing stay in the air?" Aron asked.

"The balloons keep us buoyant," Abaddon replied. "We control the gasses inside them like ballast."

Crewmates wandered about on deck, running errands and checking their sails. More of the youths Isiah had seen clambered through the rigging above.

"But why keep them inside the ship?" Aron asked. He clicked his fingers. "It's to protect them, isn't it?"

Abaddon smiled. "You're a quick one." He gestured to the ship. "We've faced Paradon and their Royal Guards many times. Sails are easy to replace, but the most vital organs of our ships must be protected from fire."

"Wait—you've fought Paradon?" Isiah asked.

"More times than we can count," he replied. "Their borders extend far . . . too far."

Tessa grunted. "Tell me about it."

Abaddon turned to Isiah. "That's why my people attacked you. They must have mistaken you for someone else."

"But there are no dragons this far in the Badlands," Lazaro cut in. "Not even wild dragons wander this far."

"There is *one* dragon," Abaddon said. "And a rider, too. I suspect he's a spy, sent by Paradon under cover. He dresses like one of you."

Isiah's ears perked up. "You mean . . ." His mind whirred as Abaddon's words sank in.

"Dragons are lurking where you least expect them." Abaddon scowled. "We can never seem to get away from them. I almost envy you, in a way, with your bond." He tapped the railing. "But our skyships level the playing field."

They ascended a flight of stairs towards the rear of the ship. More decks formed several tiers, with doorways leading into the various quarters inside the vessel. The wind carried a chill through the rigging above.

Isiah paused on the stairs to look out across the Badlands. A couple of skyships hovered further away, above the surface of the Badlands. He squinted, trying to see what they were doing.

A hand grabbed his arm and made him jump.

"Hey," Myla whispered. "What do you say we take a little look around here by ourselves?"

Isiah hesitated. "You mean, sneak off?"

Myla shrugged. "This place is cool. I want to explore."

Isiah glanced at the others. Abaddon led them on, engrossed in conversation with Lazaro and the Raiders. Tessa walked behind them, still ignoring him.

"That Abaddon guy gives me the creeps," Myla said. She leaned in and her breath tickled his ear. "There's no harm in slipping away for a while, is there?" she asked innocently.

Before he could reply, she took his hand and pulled him away from the group.

Isiah hurried after her. "What will happen when the others see us missing?"

"Relax," Myla replied. "Where's your sense of adventure?"

They passed one of the flagship's masts. It towered above them, its sides smooth and sheer. Sails were attached to it, stacked atop one another and waiting to be unfurled. Myla ran on ahead.

"Slow down," Isiah whispered. He checked to make sure no crewmates were around. One man stood mopping the deck further away, but he had his back to them.

They continued along the length of the ship, then climbed another flight of stairs toward the stern. Isiah caught sight of several youths who operated the sails. He shrank away as a crewmate marched past.

"Keep working," the man barked. "Just because we have visitors is no excuse to stand around." He shoved one of the boys. Isiah's stomach churned as his gaze dropped to the long whip in the crewmate's hand.

The boy flinched, then mumbled an apology.

"Get out on the sails," the man ordered. He brandished the whip. "Don't make me use this again. Abaddon wants this ship ready to fly by noon."

The youths scurried away. Isiah and Myla retreated further up the stairs. More youths emerged from the hull of the ship and clambered up the rigging. Their rag-like clothes reminded Isiah of when he was a labourer.

Myla leaned in. "See? I told you Abaddon gave me the creeps."

Isiah rubbed his arms. "Let's go back to the others before someone finds us."

They hurried toward the stern of the ship to catch up to Lazaro. As they passed an open doorway, he paused.

"Wait up a moment," Isiah said.

Myla stopped. "What is it?"

Isiah approached the doorway. It seemed to draw him in with a magnetic pull. He reached it and peered inside. Sandstone blocks lined the walls, engraved with intricate markings.

"It almost looks like a ruin . . ." he started.

A stone plinth dominated the centre of the room. Tables were scattered around it, strewn with maps and charts. Shelves full of old books and scrolls filled every space not taken up by the sandstone blocks. The soft glow of gold illuminated the room. Isiah's breath caught in his throat.

"What is it? Let me see." Myla pushed in beside him. Her words died in her throat.

A golden disk sat on the plinth, wider than Isiah's arm span and adorned with hundreds of carvings. A quarter of the disk was missing, and thick lines were visible where the remaining three pieces fitted together. Isiah stepped into the room.

"What *is* that thing?" Myla asked.

Isiah stood before the disk. It seemed to shimmer with a life of its own. His mind transported him back to the cramped cavern where he discovered the oasis. Without thinking, he reached out a hand and touched it.

A warm energy coursed beneath his fingers. The disk hummed, sending vibrations deep through his bones. His eyes flitted over its hypnotic surface.

Myla cocked her head. "It looks like magic. What do you think it does?"

Footsteps sounded outside. Isiah pulled his hand away from the disk and spun around. Abaddon stood beside Lazaro and the others.

"I see you got here before we did," Abaddon said.

Tessa furrowed her brow at Isiah. He looked at her apologetically. He waited for Lazaro or one of the others to scold them for wandering off. Before anyone could, Abaddon led the others inside and gestured to the disk.

"I can tell you're wondering what it is," he said.

Myla listened intently. Isiah's eyes kept drifting to the disk.

"You're Raiders, and I won't patronize you by describing the ruins," Abaddon said. "Nor will I bore you with the stories of the Ancients who used to rule the Badlands long before you built your settlements."

"It's magic, isn't it?" Isiah blurted out.

The corner of Abaddon's mouth upturned. "Indeed it is—and magic stronger than anything that has been retrieved from a ruin in hundreds of years." Abaddon placed his palm on the disk. "It's called a Sunstone."

Lazaro and the others exchanged glances.

"The Ancients used these weapons to protect themselves from Paradon and their dragons," Abaddon said. "It harnesses the power of the twin suns, reflecting their fire—stronger than any mirror—to lay waste to anything it touches."

Isiah shuddered. Abaddon traced one of the Sunstone's grooves with his hand. "Imagine it—dragons, shot from the sky. Entire armies burned alive. Scorched earth, melted flesh, the sky split in two." A cruel smile crossed his face. "Paradon never stood a chance."

Tessa slammed a fist into her palm. "If only we had one at Alcabaza. The Royal Guards would never bother us again."

"What happened to it?" Myla asked.

Abaddon's smile dropped. "The Ancients feared the Sunstone's power, so they carved it into fragments. Most have been lost to time. The few that remain are scattered, buried inside temples and tombs." He lowered his voice. "Only one piece remains to be found before this one is complete."

Lazaro cleared his throat. "And what exactly do you plan to do once you've finished it?"

"That's what I brought you here to discuss," Abaddon said. "Follow me. My crewmates have prepared a meeting room for us."

Lazaro and the others filed after him. As Isiah started after them, he glanced over his shoulder at the Sunstone. Abaddon's words echoed in his head. He tried to ignore the thought of how many of his people had been cut down by the weapon.

"Are you coming?" Myla asked.

"Oh." Isiah snapped out of his trance. He swallowed. "Of course."

He hastened away from the Sunstone and followed Myla into the belly of the flagship.

Meeting

ABADDON LED THEM INTO THE HULL OF THE FLAGSHIP, then through a doorway and into a meeting room. Slits in the wooden hull let light filter into the room, no more than gaps between the boards. A large table covered in maps and diagrams dominated the room, with chairs set around it. Abaddon gestured to them. "Take a seat."

Isiah obeyed. He sat next to Tessa and Myla. Abaddon sat at the head of the table in a large chair, with Lazaro, Darla, and Antony nearby. The rest of the gang found their own seats.

"Now that you've had the opportunity to marvel at our Sunstone, it's time to discuss why I brought you here." Abaddon placed his hands on the table's worn wooden surface. "I want to work with you."

Lazaro leaned forward. "I'm listening."

"You know we're not from these lands," Abaddon said. "We know little about your landscapes. What maps we have are outdated, long since rendered imprecise by shifting sands. We're left to hunt for the remainder of the Sunstone through brute force."

"What do you mean?" Darla asked.

Abaddon gestured to the outside. "My crews hunt for ruins. We've scoured the highlands, pulling the treasures from the earth. But Sunstone fragments are well-hidden. I still lack the final piece."

Antony and the others exchanged glances. Isiah studied the maps strewn on the table. His mind drifted back to what Abaddon had said earlier. *There is one dragon, and a rider, too.*

"You know," Aron said, "I swear I've seen that Sunstone before somewhere."

Abaddon's head snapped to look at him.

Aron scrunched up his face. "I just can't remember where."

"Could it have been on a mural somewhere?" Myla suggested. "Ruins have lots of artwork inside them, right?"

"Maybe . . ." Aron trailed off.

Antony coughed. "This sounds soulless," he said. "Using raiding crews like this. You'll empty the Badlands and leave no ruins behind for anyone else."

Abaddon shrugged. "We're no different to you Raiders, only more organized. Besides, I'm not interested in treasure."

Lazaro stroked his chin. "What do you want us to do?"

"You know the lands and the people here better than we do," Abaddon said. "You know how to find ruins, and which ones have already been looted. Your knowledge would be invaluable."

"Hold up," Darla cut in. "Just what do you plan on doing once you've assembled this Sunstone of yours?"

"I see I can't pull the wool over your eyes." Abaddon laughed. Isiah caught the emptiness in his voice. "My people have been at war with Paradon for generations. Their dragons have become skilled at bringing down our ships. We've been forced to ride the dust storms to your corner of the Badlands. A *tactical retreat*, you might call it."

"That still doesn't answer our question," Lazaro replied.

"My duty is to my people. These ships are all we have left." Abaddon straightened up. "A Sunstone will give us the power we need to protect ourselves from Paradon as we settle and create a new kingdom."

Some of the Raiders exchanged glances. Isiah saw the gears turning in Lazaro's head.

"The other Raiders won't be happy if they find out about this," Tessa said.

"The Raiders are back-stabbing traitors," Lazaro replied. "They sold us out on a whim."

"She has a point," Darla said. "The ruins belong to us."

"The ruins belong to whoever gets there first," Abaddon cut in. He gave them a sly look. "Isn't that part of your Raider's Oath?"

"The Raider's Oath is dead," Lazaro said. "They proved how much they cared about it when they exiled us."

"Then help me complete my Sunstone," Abaddon urged. "You'll never have to fear Raiders again. Such a weapon will not only allow us to destroy Paradon, but it will make the rest of your people think twice before they start any fights."

Isiah wriggled in his seat. *How does he know about the Oath?* He got a distinct feeling that Abaddon knew more than he was letting on.

"If this Sunstone is as powerful as you say it is, how can we trust you?" Lazaro asked. "Why do you want *our* help?"

"Nomads are toothless and weak." Abaddon almost spat the words. "They have no interest in helping us, and most Raiders are too thick-headed and short-sighted to see things from our view."

An uneasy silence descended on the room. Aron coughed. Isiah tried to distract himself by studying the maps.

47

"You said you wanted to settle," Lazaro said. "Where?"

"The Badlands is a big place," Abaddon replied. "There's plenty of room for our fleet. Owning a Sunstone is just our form of protection. It will stop Paradon from pursuing us."

Lazaro raised an eyebrow. "Or angry Raiders?"

"My duty is to protect my people from *all* threats." Abaddon's voice grew louder. "Help me find the last piece of the Sunstone, and I'll pay you your weight in gold."

Aron's ears perked up. "Our whole weight, you say?"

"Are you sure about this?" Tessa interrupted.

"We should talk about this privately," Antony said. "As much as I despise the Raiders for what they did to us, they're still our people. With all due respect, Abaddon, we hardly even know you."

"He's right," Lazaro said. He pushed his chair in. "We need to talk—alone. Take us back to our eagles."

The other Raiders stood. Abaddon looked like he was about to protest, then sighed. "As you wish. I'll leave you to consider my offer." His voice took on a harder tone. "But I *will* find the missing fragment, whether you assist me or not."

Isiah hastened after Lazaro and the others. They exited the hull and remerged on the flagship's deck. The crewmates yelled orders as the sails unfurled and filled with air. The flagship began to slowly drift on the wind. Vyrro gave a shrill chirp as he noticed Tessa approaching. Lazaro and the others mounted their eagles.

As Isiah surveyed the horizon, he couldn't stop thinking about what Abaddon had said. "One more thing," he blurted out. "You said there's a dragon rider living around here, right?"

Abaddon nodded. "We noticed him when we entered the high-lands. He must have been tailing us since we set out." Abaddon waited until Lazaro wasn't paying attention, then leaned in. "I'll warn you not to fly again in these parts, boy. I can't guarantee my crewmates won't *mistake* you for somebody else."

Isiah shuddered. Something in the man's tone made his skin crawl.

"Isiah," Tessa called. "Let's go."

Isiah seized the distraction and hastened away from Abaddon.

"We'll meet again," Abaddon called after them. "I trust you'll make the right decision."

Lazaro ignored him. He spurred his eagle and the bird launched itself from the deck. Vyrro and the other eagles followed suit. They glided away from the flagship and set out across the Badlands.

Isiah watched as the skyship fleet faded into the Badlands haze. The memory of the Sunstone's dull, humming power made his stomach turn in knots. He tried to shake the feeling that refusing Abaddon was a terrible mistake.

* * *

When they returned to the Hidden Citadel, a crowd of townsfolk were waiting for them. They left their eagles with the handlers and trekked into the town, followed by a throng of people. The crowd bombarded Lazaro with questions, each voice rising higher than the last.

"What were those ships? Who do they belong to?" a woman asked.

"What did they want?" another cut in.

Lazaro waved them away. "They're visitors," he told them. "From beyond the highlands. They won't trouble us."

The townsfolk began to disperse when they realized Lazaro wasn't going to answer any more questions. Isiah followed his friends to their house, and they all filed inside. He let his shoulders drop and breathed a sigh of relief.

"I don't trust Abaddon," Lazaro said. "There's something wrong about him."

Tessa nodded. "If the Sunstone *is* as strong as he said it was, what does that mean for the Raiders? He could do whatever he wanted and nobody would be able to stop him."

"Forget the other Raiders," Lazaro replied. "What about us? He'd use our help and then backstab us like the rest."

"What are we supposed to do about all of this?" Darla asked. "Do we just sit back and let him find the last piece? We'll be sitting ducks."

Lazaro stroked his chin. "I'm tempted to try and build one of our own."

Antony cocked his head. "How are we going to find one? You heard how well they're hidden."

"Maybe Edith knows something about it," Tessa piped up. "I'll ask her." She looked at Isiah. "Are you coming?"

Isiah took off after her. They left the house and ran to Edith's tower. Myla, Aron, and Marie came after them. When they arrived, they found Edith peering out of the shutters.

"Were those flying ships that visited?" she asked.

Tessa nodded. "It's a long story." She took the old woman's hand. "I'll tell you all about it."

Isiah and his friends filed into the kitchen as Tessa told Edith about their trip to the flagship. Edith listened with a thoughtful expression. When Tessa had finished, Edith nodded to herself.

"I've heard about Sunstones before," she said.

Myla perked up. "Really?"

"The highlands aren't the only place you can find them," she explained. "The other Raiders didn't know what to do with them. Most got sold off to merchants or melted down for their gold." She scoffed. "Fools, the lot of them. They don't appreciate magic like I do."

Isiah remembered his search for the oasis. Enrik had been the only other Raider who believed the place existed.

"The last time I saw a Sunstone fragment was in Alcabaza," Edith continued.

"What?" Isiah snapped from his trance.

"It was many years ago now." She scrunched her face up. "A couple of fragments were pulled from the ruins nearby. It was a plentiful site for looting, in those days. That's how the city started."

Aron clicked his fingers. "I *knew* I recognized the Sunstone from somewhere." He grabbed Isiah's arm. "Didn't I tell you guys?"

"Where did they end up?" Tessa asked.

"They were put in an observatory," Edith said. "The city's astronomers thought they had something to do with the stars. I guess they were right."

"And are they still there?"

Edith shrugged. "It's been a long time since I visited Alcabaza . . . but I don't see why not. The astronomers wouldn't let the pieces go without a fight."

Isiah nodded to himself. "Then maybe Lazaro's plan isn't as crazy as it sounds."

"Don't get ahead of yourself, boy," Edith replied. "Nobody has ever finished a Sunstone before. If they had, word would soon spread through the entire Badlands."

"Maybe we *should* give it a shot," Myla piped up. "If we don't, Abaddon will beat us to it." She shuddered. "There's something weird about him."

Isiah recalled the way Abaddon had spoken to him before leaving. He gulped. "You're right."

Edith lowered her voice. "I never told anyone about this," she whispered, "but I guess now is as good a time as any."

Isiah and the others all looked at her.

"I brought a fragment with me when I arrived at the Hidden Citadel, when Solomon and his Marked Raiders first settled here." Edith paused. "I thought it might hide some magic that had to be decoded."

"What did you do with it?" Tessa asked.

"I studied it, at first—but when I learned what the Sunstone was capable of, I panicked. I hid it away to keep it out the hands of someone who might misuse it." She lowered her voice. "Someone like Solomon."

Isiah cleared his throat. "Do you still have it?"

Edith stood. "It must still be somewhere in this tower—if only I can remember."

"We need to make sure Abaddon doesn't find out about this," Tessa said.

"I'll find it for you," Edith replied. "With this fragment and the pair at the observatory, you would only be missing one."

Isiah's mind buzzed as he put the pieces together. "Just like Abaddon."

"It's the best shot we have," Tessa said. Her expression hardened. "Imagine what we could do to Paradon if we had a weapon like that."

"I'll help you look for it," Marie added.

"Me too." Isiah tried to ignore the glee in Tessa's voice.

"Even if we found it, we'd still be lacking a fragment," Edith explained. "It must be hidden away in a ruin somewhere. Maybe the local nomads know something about it."

Tessa scoffed. "Lazaro has never trusted nomads. You heard what Abaddon said about them."

Aron stood. "I'll tell Lazaro about this. The least we can do is give the other Raiders a heads-up about Abaddon's fleet."

He ran from the room. Part of Isiah urged him to go and check on Aegon, but he pushed it away. He dreaded to think what Abaddon would do if he completed his Sunstone.

He sighed. "Where do we start looking?"

Hidden Citadel

ISIAH STARED AT THE CEILING. THE ROUGH MATERIAL of his hammock made his skin itch. The hot Badlands air filtered through the open windows, stirring the curtains and making his hammock rock gently. Isiah tossed, trying to find a comfortable position. He willed himself to sleep. The events of the previous day flashed across his closed eyelids.

They had found the Sunstone fragment that Edith had spoken about hidden in a sealed crate in the corner of her tower. When Isiah had touched it, it hummed with the same ominous power that had coursed through the one on Abaddon's flagship. Aron and Tessa had wrapped it up and stored it in Lazaro's room for safekeeping.

Isiah swung one leg out his hammock and stood. He walked to the window and placed both hands on the sill, looking out across the Hidden Citadel. A stuffiness had settled on the basin, a break in the summer winds leaving a heavy warmth in its place. Isiah tugged at his collar. Beads of sweat clung to his skin.

I need some air. Isiah abandoned his bedroom and, feeling his way down the darkened hall, made it to the main doors and emerged outside. He tilted his head back and sucked in a breath.

"Couldn't sleep, huh?" a voice asked.

Isiah jumped. He turned to see Tessa leaning against the wall, dressed in a thin nightdress. Isiah scratched the back of his neck. "Yeah."

Tessa pushed away from the wall. "Me neither."

Silence lay on the town. Shutters were closed and windows were dark. A sliver of moonlight afforded a faint glow, basking the street. A couple of figures—labourers they'd rescued from Solomon's cavern—talked in low voices. Solomon's harvesting had left their skin so fragile they could only emerge in the dark.

"I was going for a walk," Isiah said quickly. "I guess I picked up your habit." He paused. "Did you have that nightmare again?"

Tessa nodded. "It's always the same thing." She bit her lip. "It's getting worse."

She sat on the step leading to the front door. A breath of wind helped lift the stuffiness from the street. Somewhere, an eagle's shrill call cut the night's calm.

Isiah racked his brain for something to say to comfort her. He awkwardly put a hand on her shoulder.

Tessa lowered her head. "I want them to stop."

Isiah shifted his weight. "Maybe you should talk to Lazaro about it—"

"I can't go to him anymore," she said, cutting him off. "I'm too old to keep running for his help." She balled her fist. "I need revenge."

Isiah hesitated. Tessa wiped a hand across her eyes.

"I have to make the Royal Guards pay for what they did to me," she said. "It's the only way I can avenge them. It's the only way I can set things right."

"Tessa," Isiah started.

"It's the only way I can make my nightmares stop," Tessa cut in, ignoring him. "I've got to find whoever killed them."

She fell silent. The force of her words weighed on Isiah's shoulders. He tentatively put a hand on top of hers. She didn't react for a moment, then leaned against him.

"I keep thinking about what Abaddon told us," Isiah said after a minute. "About that dragon rider. Do you really think there could be someone out there?"

Tessa shrugged. "I guess so."

Isiah took a deep breath. "I want to find him."

He felt Tessa stiffen. "Why?"

"I want to find a teacher," he said quickly. "I'm not getting anywhere on my own."

"That's not true."

"It is," Isiah insisted. He sighed. "The only reason Aegon got hurt by the skyship is because I panicked. I lost my connection with her. It's my fault we were shot down."

"Do you think a teacher can show you how to fly better?" she asked softly.

"I know it. At least when Solomon . . ." He caught himself.

"What were you going to say?" Tessa asked.

Isiah kicked the ground. "When Solomon was alive, he was going to teach me. Now I've got no one."

"You've got us."

He shook his head. "Flying eagles isn't the same, Tess." He stopped. "Sorry. I didn't mean to call you—"

"No." She cut him off. "You can call me that too."

Isiah gave her a weak smile. "I think it suits you better."

Tessa seemed not to hear him. She stared at the sky.

Isiah leaned forward. "What is it?"

Her brow furrowed. "Something's moving."

Isiah followed her gaze. A dark shape blotted out the stars near the cliffs. As he watched, several more materialized. They drifted across the sky like dark, imposing clouds. Cold dread gripped Isiah's gut as he realized what it was. "Abaddon."

Tessa sprang to her feet. "Get Aegon," she said. "I'll warn Lazaro."

Isiah ran out into the street. The skyships drifted toward the Hidden Citadel, almost invisible against the night sky. His blood ran cold as his gaze dropped to the cliff where Aegon and the eagles were sleeping.

He burst into a sprint down the main road. Behind him, voices broke out in the Raider house as Lazaro and the others awoke. Isiah lowered his head and quickened his pace. The skyships cleared the cliffs and drifted over the town. Shadows swept across the streets as the vessels blotted out the moon.

A flash of orange illuminated one of the ships. Isiah skidded to a halt as a barrel dropped from the side of the skyship, sparks trailing behind it. Time seemed to slow. Isiah's blood ran cold.

The barrel hit the roof of a house and exploded. A plume of brick and dust billowed into the air. Screams erupted from the building. A second barrel dropped. Isiah flinched and covered his head as it landed across the street with a gut-wrenching boom.

Isiah sprinted in the direction of Aegon. More explosions shook the basin as barrels hit their targets. Isiah swerved to the side as a nearby house shattered. Its wall collapsed, pelting him with sharp rock. Each blast sent tremors through his bones.

He cleared the town and ran toward the cliffs. Eagles erupted into the sky with shrill, panicked cries. Townsfolk poured from their houses and scattered into the night. Flashes of orange lit the undersides of the skyships as fuses burned.

Sharp rocks stabbed Isiah's bare feet as he ran up the cliffside trail. He cupped his hands to his mouth. "Aegon!" He searched for their mental link. Aegon lumbered to the side of the cliff and spotted him.

Eagles circled above the skyships. Isiah searched for Vyrro among them. He ran up to Aegon and scrambled onto her back, gripping her mane. Explosions cut the darkness with bursts of fire. Aegon kicked off the cliff and soared towards the skyships.

A barrel struck a rooftop and it erupted in a cloud of debris, showering the main square in rock and dust. Isiah scanned for any sign of Tessa, his heart hammering against his ribcage.

An orange light welled in Aegon's chest. She lowered her head and launched a torrent of fire at the nearest skyship. The flames washed over the sails and caught hold. Aegon pulled up, soaring over the top of the vessel and leaving a trail of fire in her wake.

Isiah didn't have time to celebrate. More barrels fell, blowing chunks from buildings and collapsing walls. The explosions reflected off the lake's surface, painting it with bursts of red and orange. Aegon wheeled around for another attack.

A series of loud pops rose above the chaos. Isiah's breath caught in his throat as bolas whipped past. Aegon twisted aside to avoid the spinning chains, then released another blast of fire.

Crewmates scattered. Aegon's fire bathed the deck. It erupted across the sails, sweeping them up in an inferno. Isiah remembered Abaddon's words. *Sails are easy to replace, but the most vital organs of our ships must be protected from fire.*

More bolas whizzed past. Isiah craned his neck, searching for Tessa in the carnage below. Every scream cut like a knife through his head. He prayed none of them belonged to his friends.

The Sunstone piece. He froze. If Abaddon found it, there'd be nothing stopping him from finishing his weapon. Aegon fixed her eyes on the skyship. She readied another fireball.

"No—" Isiah scrunched his brow, trying to concentrate. He directed Aegon to dive.

The dragon hesitated, then folded her wings and soared toward the town. A volley of bolas arced above them. Aegon threw out her wings and glided over the Hidden Citadel. Isiah aimed for their house.

Movement caught his eye. A flood of townsfolk were running into the cliffside. The flash of another explosion revealed Lazaro. Aegon changed course and flew toward them.

Aegon landed and Isiah slid to the ground. Edith stood waving her arms, ushering the townsfolk into a tunnel opening.

"What's going on?" Isiah asked.

"We're getting the people to safety," Lazaro said. "There are some tunnels that the lake didn't flood. The skyships haven't noticed us yet."

Isiah pushed the hair off his face. Sweat coated his forehead. "What about the Sunstone?" he stammered.

Darla appeared at Lazaro's side. "We have it." She raised a cloth sack.

"I can't fight them," Isiah said. "The ships are too strong. They'll shoot Aegon down."

Lazaro swore. "I should have planned for something like this."

"Isiah!" Tessa shoved through the crowd. Dust streaked her face, and her robes were haphazardly thrown on. Myla and Aron stood beside her. Myla gazed at the skyships with a vacant expression.

Isiah breathed a sigh of relief. "Where's everyone else?"

"They're rounding up our eagles," she said. "Once we get the townsfolk to safety, we'll escape. We can't let Abaddon get his hands on this Sunstone fragment."

"Where are you taking it?" Isiah asked.

"To Alcabaza," Lazaro cut in. He scoffed. "I'm sure they'll be happy to see us again."

Another explosion ripped through the town, closer. Isiah cast a wary glance over his shoulder. The skyships loomed above. Flames consumed the sails of one vessel, making it glow like a torch.

"I want to find the dragon rider," Isiah said quickly.

"What?" Tessa exclaimed. "Now isn't the time, Isiah."

"He can't be far away," Isiah insisted. "How are we going to locate the last Sunstone fragment otherwise? Maybe he knows something about it that we don't."

Tessa bit her lip. Isiah took her hand. "Come on, Tessa," he said. "Abaddon won't expect us to be looking for it. If we go to Alcabaza, we'll be surrendering the highlands to him."

Tessa's expression hardened. "Fine. But I'm going with you."

The explosions grew closer. One of the skyships turned its prow towards them.

"I'll come too," Myla stammered. She tore her gaze away from the town.

"Tess," Lazaro started.

"There's no time to argue," Tessa said. Isiah braced himself for the man to object.

"Who said anything about arguing?" Lazaro wrapped his arms around her. "Be careful out there."

Tessa smiled and returned his embrace. "I will."

Edith ushered the last townsfolk into the tunnel and shut a wooden door. "You should slip out of here before Abaddon finds you," she urged. "I'll make sure the people here are safe."

Tessa hugged the woman. "Be careful."

Isiah climbed onto Aegon, then helped Tessa and Myla after him. Lazaro and the others took the Sunstone fragment and slipped away from the town. Aegon kicked off and flew into the night.

"Our eagles can't be far from here," Tessa said. She gripped Isiah's middle. "The explosions will have spooked them."

Aegon gave the skyships a wide berth, keeping to the safety of the shadows. A few eagles perched on the cliffs surrounding the Hidden Citadel. Tessa straightened up and pointed. "There!"

Isiah directed Aegon to land. They found Vyrro and Myla's eagle, and the girls reunited with them. Tessa wrapped her arms around Vyrro. "I worried about you."

Myla stared at the Hidden Citadel. The fire from explosions reflected in her eyes. Isiah coughed. "Are you okay?"

She seemed not to hear him.

"She's in shock," Tessa said. She pulled the girl away from the sight. "Come on, Myla. Your eagle is waiting for you."

Myla regained herself long enough to climb into the saddle of her eagle. She gripped the reins with trembling hands.

"Where do we go now?" Tessa asked.

Isiah twisted around to look at the skyships. The explosions had ceased. The echo crackled across the heavens like thunder. Ropes dropped from the sides of the vessels and figures slid down them into the ruins of the Hidden Citadel. Plumes of smoke rose from burning buildings, obscuring the skyships in a billowing cloud. "Far away from here."

He spurred Aegon into motion. She took off and the eagles followed in her wake. They ascended into the night, each wingbeat carrying them further from the burning town. Isiah fixed his eyes on the horizon—half in fear of looking back, half in anticipation of what lay ahead.

Somewhere out there, he'd find the dragon rider.

'Big Place'

Isiah groaned. He sat up, rubbing his aching back. His legs were numb from sleeping on the hard rock. He raised a hand to his forehead and squinted against the dawn light.

The Badlands rolled around them. The watery skies were deserted. A light wind whistled across the top of the mesa, ruffling the feathers of the sleeping eagles nearby.

Isiah stretched, wincing at the pain in his stiff body. After fleeing the Hidden Citadel, they had flown deep into the night for as long as they could, until Aegon had tired and they'd been forced to stop and rest.

Tessa shifted beside him. She winced and rolled over. Dust coated her cheek, and her hair was wild and matted. She cracked one eye open.

"How are you?" Isiah asked.

She gritted her teeth. "I feel like I barely slept."

"Me too." When Isiah swallowed, he became aware of the dryness in his throat. "You didn't manage to bring anything with you, by any chance?"

Tessa shook her head. "We left in such a rush, I didn't have time."

Isiah became aware of Myla sitting further off. She had her back to them, with her knees pulled to her chest. Isiah shuffled over.

"Hey," he said.

Myla seemed not to notice him. She stared at the horizon in the direction they had come from. Isiah tentatively touched her shoulder.

"Are you okay?" he asked.

"I can't believe it's gone," Myla said, her voice so quiet Isiah had to strain to hear it. "They destroyed our home. How *could* they?"

Isiah ran a hand through his hair. "You don't know that." He tried to sound reassuring.

"Abaddon blew it up." Myla's voice grew louder. She sniffed. Her eyes were red, and Isiah could see she'd been crying. "I lived there for *years*."

Isiah forced himself to speak. "Edith will look after it. The townsfolk are safe in the tunnels. They can rebuild."

Myla gripped her knees tighter. "What do you think Abaddon is going to do to them?" Her words hung in the air.

Myla leaned against him. Her curly hair tickled his nose. Further away, Aegon shifted. She stood and shook, letting off a cloud of dust. The eagles preened themselves in the morning sunlight. The bright blue-white sun hovered above the horizon, beginning its journey across the heavens. Isiah knew that soon the Badlands would begin to heat up.

"We have to stop Abaddon," Myla said. "We can't let him finish his Sunstone."

"You're right," Isiah replied. He squeezed her hand. He tried to shake the feeling of emptiness inside him. The events of the previous night lingered in his mind.

Tessa dusted herself off and straightened out her robes. "How are we going to do that?" she asked. "We don't have any supplies."

"We'll find a way," he said, more to himself than anyone else.

"We have no food, no water, and no tools." Tessa gestured to him. "You don't even have shoes."

Isiah looked at his bare feet. In the panic, he hadn't had the chance to get dressed.

"We have a dragon," he said. "And your eagles. If we can just find the dragon rider Abaddon was talking about—"

"And then what?" Tessa cut in. "Ask him to take us in?" Her voice grew higher. "We don't even know if Lazaro made it out safely!"

Isiah threw up his hands. "This is the best chance we've got!" He caught himself. "I'm sorry," he said, softer. "There must be water nearby. Aegon can help us search for food. Maybe we'll even find some nomads who can help us."

Tessa turned away. "You're right. I'm just worried about Lazaro."

Isiah surveyed the landscape below, searching for the reflective shimmer of a highlands stream. Green scrubland filled the crevices and valleys below, along with clusters of acacia trees.

"What's your plan for finding this dragon rider?" Tessa asked.

Isiah sighed. "I don't know—but he has to be close. Abaddon said they think he's a spy. He must be in the highlands somewhere."

"The highlands is a big place," she replied. "How are we supposed to spot him?"

Isiah racked his brains. He became aware of how desperate their situation was. "Aegon can help us," he said. "She can track it by scent, or attract it with her call, or . . ." He trailed off.

"Then what?" Tessa asked. "What about the Sunstone?"

"We can search for it," Isiah replied. "But we have to find the dragon rider first."

Tessa sighed. She beckoned Vyrro and he plodded over. "As long as we avoid Abaddon's skyships."

Isiah turned to Myla. "Are you ready?"

Myla stood. She wiped her eyes on her sleeve. "Mm-hmm."

Isiah reunited with Aegon. He waited for Tessa and Myla to climb into the saddles of their eagles, then he spurred Aegon forward.

Cruel World

Broken chips of sandstone crunched beneath Abaddon's boots. He strode down the ruined street, arms behind his back. His crewmates flanked him, sabres and boarding pikes in their hands.

Townsfolk huddled in the charred remains of houses. Abaddon swept his eyes over the remains of the town. Buildings sagged with collapsed walls and crumbling roofs. Holes pitted the road, the slabs buckled and filled with cracks from explosions. The acrid smell of black powder lingered in the air, making his eyes water. He stepped over a crumpled body and kept walking.

Crewmates stood around a four-storey tower, left undamaged by the explosives. An old woman, hunched and dressed in bright colours, stood with her arms folded as more crewmates filed through her door with armfuls of books.

"Empty the archives," Ramah ordered. "Search every corner."

Two burly crewmates, armed with hooked boarding pikes, stood on either side of the old woman. She glared at Abaddon as he approached.

"You're a scoundrel," she spat. "The townsfolk did nothing to you."

Abaddon gave a cold, empty smile. "I couldn't take any chances." He turned to Ramah. "Load anything of interest onto a scouting vessel and transport it to my flagship."

Ramah saluted him. "Of course, Captain. There's so much here, we're bound to find something of use."

Abaddon stepped aside as a pair of crewmates brought out a crate full of old scrolls. The dust irritated his nose.

"You have quite the collection," Abaddon observed.

"I respect magic," the woman replied. "Unlike your thugs."

"Don't dismiss us so quickly," Abaddon said. He leaned over so his eyes were level with the stooped-over woman. "If I didn't respect the magic, I wouldn't have dedicated my life to unearthing the Sunstone." He extended a hand. "What's your name?"

The old woman turned up her nose.

Ramah leaned in. "Edith."

"Edith," Abaddon said slowly. "I had a sister with that name. Do you want to know what happened to her?" His smile melted. "She was burned alive by one of Paradon's dragons."

Edith folded her arms. "We're no friends of Paradon here. You only want the Sunstone for its power."

"Please," Abaddon replied. "Don't act like you Raiders wouldn't use it for your own selfish ends. It was built to be a weapon."

The skyships hovered overhead. The odour of burnt wood and charred sails hung thick in the air, leeching from the vessel Aegon had attacked. Crewmates drove gangs of youths on with whips, forcing them to replace the ruined material.

"It's a shame Lazaro and his gang slipped away," Abaddon said. "I would have liked to add the younger ones to my crew."

"They're already on their way to warn the other Raiders," Edith replied. She gave him a smug smile. "What do you think the cities will do once they hear about this?"

Abaddon laughed. "As soon as I've completed my Sunstone, they won't be able to *do* anything. My fleet will have the power to destroy anyone who stands in our way—" he snapped his fingers "—like that."

Edith's smile faded. Abaddon paced in front of her.

"Your cities are impossible to conquer through sheer force alone," he said. "You crush one, and another springs up somewhere else. Paradon gave up trying to control you a long time ago. I won't allow my people to be dragged into an endless and futile war with Raider gangs."

He turned on his heel. "But if I had a Sunstone, well, one display of power is all it would take to scare them into submission." Abaddon balled his fist. "The Badlands will be ours . . . and I'll be able to take revenge on Paradon for what they did to us."

Edith eyed him. "What are you planning?"

Abaddon stopped in front of her. "My people are homeless. We've spent months surfing the haboobs in search of a new home." His face twisted into a snarl. "Paradon slaughtered my people and scorched our homeland to cinders. This fleet is all we have left. Time is running out for us, Edith, and I won't let my people die like this."

He grabbed Edith's shoulders. "The Badlands is going to be our new home—and the Sunstone will stop Paradon from hurting us ever again!"

Edith staggered away. "You're mad."

"Is it madness to save my people?" Abaddon asked. "Don't tell me you wouldn't do the same."

Ramah cleared his throat. "The crew is almost finished here, Captain. No sign of anything on the Sunstone."

Abaddon scowled. "Where are you hiding it, Edith?"

Edith folded her arms. "You're too late. Lazaro took it all with him. I've been pushed around by one monster in my life. I won't be bullied by another."

Abaddon straightened up. "No matter. There are still more ruins to loot."

"What are your orders now, Captain?" Ramah asked.

"Search the town for supplies, and drain their lake for our water reserves. We'll show them the same kindness Paradon showed to us."

Edith's face paled. "What about the people here?"

"What's the matter?" Abaddon asked. "Do you mean you *care* about your people? I guess we have something in common after all."

The crewmates snickered. Several long pipes snaked from the deck of a skyship and sank into the lake. Townsfolk looked on in horror.

"It's a cruel world, Edith," Abaddon said. "And it's every man for himself."

Fool's Errand

A DEEP EXPLOSION CRACKLED ACROSS THE BADLANDS. Aegon wobbled and let out a hiss of alarm. The noise rumbled across the sky like thunder, shaking Isiah to the bones.

"What was that?" Tessa asked.

Isiah knew what it was. He straightened up, scanning the landscape. "Fly low. We don't want to get spotted."

Tessa and Myla obeyed, directing their eagles to skim over the tops of mesas. Isiah directed Aegon after them. He adjusted his robes, keeping the harsh sun off his skin. His Mark itched. When he felt it, it was hot to the touch.

Another boom sounded somewhere to their right. Aegon's head snapped around. A plume of dust and debris spurted into the air. Isiah narrowed his eyes. "They're close."

Aegon spread out her wings and glided to the rocky ground below. Tessa raised an eyebrow, then followed him once she saw what he was doing. They landed amid a cluster of misshapen hoodoos, and Isiah climbed from Aegon's back.

"Why are we stopping?" Tessa asked.

"I want to get a closer look," Isiah said. "They'll spot us if we fly overhead."

Leaving Aegon and the eagles behind, they crept through the rocky terrain toward the source of the explosions. They reached the edge of a cliff and crouched behind a cluster of boulders.

A skyship hovered in a valley, squished between twin walls of rock. Ropes dangled from its side, and crewmates milled about beneath. Several carried more of the explosive barrels they had attacked the Hidden Citadel with.

"So *this* is how they excavate ruins," Tessa said.

The crewmates placed a barrel against a hole in the rock, then lit the fuse and bolted. Isiah tensed as the fuse hissed. Moments later the barrel detonated. Even from so far away, the force of the shockwave washed over him.

As the dust cloud cleared, the crewmates advanced, clutching pickaxes and torches. The explosives had revealed a tunnel that descended into darkness. Isiah knew where it led.

"That will keep them busy," Tessa said. "Let's go while they're distracted." She paused. "Unless you want to attack their ship?"

Isiah shook his head. "It's too risky."

"Come on, Isiah." Tessa folded her arms. "We're running out of options. How long have we been looking for this dragon rider of yours?"

"It's only been a couple of days . . ." he started.

"Vyrro can't keep flying like this," she said. "And if we get stranded in another haboob, we could die of thirst before we find our next water source."

"You didn't see what the skyship's bolas can do," Isiah replied. "I can't risk Aegon like that."

Below, the crewmates disappeared into the ruin. Several stayed behind on the floating skyship. The ropes Isiah had seen earlier tethered the ship to the ground.

"If we don't find something soon, we'll have to abandon our plan," Tessa said.

Isiah opened his mouth to protest, then fell silent. Their robes were crumpled and stained with dust from nights spent sleeping in the wild, and scratches crisscrossed Isiah's feet. Once they ran out of Badlands streams to follow, he dreaded to think where they'd find water.

He left the boulder and hastened back to where they'd left Aegon and the eagles. Tessa and Myla followed behind in silence.

"Let's find the next river, okay?" he said. "I know there's one nearby."

Tessa grunted.

"I'm with you," Myla said tentatively.

Aegon kicked off and rose on the updrafts. Tessa sighed, then the pair of eagles took flight. They hastened away from the skyship, heading toward a glimmer of water on the horizon. Isiah scanned the landscape for any sign of the dragon rider.

They reached the river and landed on its sandy bank. The water snaked through a wide canyon, with smooth, painted walls and lush foliage. Aegon and the eagles took the opportunity to drink. Isiah cupped the water in his hands and brought it to his mouth.

"Maybe we should split up," he said once he had finished.

"Are you crazy?" Tessa turned up her nose. "If this dragon rider of yours *is* from Paradon, who's to say he won't kill us? Raiders and Royal Guards don't mix."

"We *would* cover more ground that way," Myla said.

"Don't you side with him." Tessa crossed her arms. "You have to admit it, Isiah. We're on a fool's errand."

"The dragon rider *has* to be here," Isiah insisted. "You heard what Abaddon said!"

"But we won't find him if we die out here," Tessa shot back. She slumped against a boulder by the waterside. "Vyrro is getting tired. He'll be too weak to fly if we don't find food soon."

Isiah rubbed his temples. He fought to suppress the welling sense of hopelessness. "This is the only chance we've got."

They sat in awkward silence. Tessa played with a curl of her hair. Myla traced lines in the sand with her foot. Aegon raised her head from the river, water cascading from her chin. Her shimmering scales had lost some of their lustre.

Isiah's Mark prickled with heat. He grimaced and splashed a handful of water onto his shoulders. The warped skin shone an angry red. His empty stomach rolled with nausea.

He gritted his teeth and scratched his Mark. His skin burned. He frowned. That only used to happen before he'd bonded with Aegon . . .

Isiah staggered to his feet. "There's a dragon nearby."

Tessa frowned. "How do you know?" She got up and put a hand against his forehead to check his temperature. "Are you getting heat-stroke?"

"It's my Mark," Isiah said. "I can feel it." Without waiting for her, he took off upstream.

Tessa called after him, but he ignored her. He willed his fatigued muscles to move faster. He scanned the sky above for the reflective glimmer of dragon scales. If it flew overhead, he couldn't afford to miss it . . .

A throaty bellow made him skid to a halt. A burst of fiery pain rippled over his Mark. Isiah gasped and clutched his chest. He twisted around to the source of the noise.

A dragon emerged from a cave on the cliffside. It unfurled its wings and fixed him with a cold stare. Isiah stumbled away. He raised a hand out to the beast.

"I'm not your enemy," he stammered. He hoped the beast could understand him. His foot hit a rock and he tripped, landing on his back in the river. The cold water shocked his skin.

The dragon rose to its full height and slithered out of the cave. The sunlight reflected off its brilliant scales, and its outstretched wings shone a deep purple. Scree crunched as the dragon advanced, neck poised to strike. Isiah raised an arm to shield himself. He reached out with his mind to Aegon . . .

A roar echoed through the canyon. The dragon's head swivelled around. Aegon lumbered toward them, kicking up waves of water as she went. Tessa and Myla stumbled along behind.

The dragon twisted its body to face her. Its growl made Isiah's bones rattle. He scrambled to his feet and staggered to Aegon as she skidded to a halt a few dozen feet away from the new dragon.

Aegon coiled her neck and cracked open her jaws to let out a bellow. Twin rows of jagged teeth glistened with strings of saliva. Isiah stroked her flank, trying to calm her. Aegon's tail twitched, and her hind legs tensed like springs. She ignored Isiah's desperate tugging on her neck.

"What's going on here?" a gruff voice called.

The new dragon broke away. Isiah turned to see a man in nomad's robes striding down a dusty path. A turban adorned his head, and his skin was a deep tan.

Aegon's rumbling ceased. The man waved his hand at the second dragon. "Calm down, you. There's no need to be territorial." He turned to Aegon. "You're a long way from Paradon."

"You're the dragon rider?" Isiah blurted out.

"You've got that right—but it's clear I'm not the only one," the man replied. He nodded to Aegon. "That's a fine dragon you've got. Sorry about Enzo. He's never been social."

Tessa and Myla hurried to Isiah's side. The man popped a cap off a waterskin and filled it. Enzo lurked further away, watching Isiah out the corner of his eye.

"Are you from Paradon?" Isiah managed to ask. After spending so long searching, his words deserted him.

"I was." The man took a swig. "But I haven't heard that name in a long time."

"Wait," he said, "you mean you're not a spy?"

The man cocked his head. "Who gave you that idea?"

Isiah told the man about Abaddon and the skyships. The man's nose crinkled.

"I noticed them enter the Badlands a few months ago," he said. "I've tried my best to keep out of their way." He paused. "Why have you been looking for me?"

Isiah exchanged glances with Tessa and Myla. "I want you to teach me."

"Teach you?" the man repeated. "You flew here on a dragon. What more do you need?"

"No—" Isiah collected himself. "Nobody ever showed me how to bond." He grabbed his collar and pulled it down to expose his shoulders. "I failed my Ceremony."

The man leaned in to inspect Isiah's Mark. "That's impossible."

"I saved Aegon from the Raiders," Isiah said. "She bonded with me because we helped each other."

The man straightened up. "Come with me to my base camp," he said. He started up the trail. "The name's Gaelon, by the way," he called over his shoulder.

Isiah hastened after him. Gaelon led him out of the canyon and into a maze of gorges and basins. Shrubs and small trees clung to the rock, snagging Isiah's clothes. He winced as sharp stones bit into the soles of his feet.

"You said you were from Paradon," Isiah called after him. "Why are you living here?"

"I left," Gaelon replied. "The Badlands has been my home for years. I can guess why *you're* here."

Isiah nodded. "They banished me for my Mark."

"And yet you managed to prove them all wrong," Gaelon said. He craned his neck. "We're coming up to my camp now."

Ahead, two pillars formed a tight passageway, hidden by bushes. Gaelon slipped through. Isiah followed and emerged in his camp. A large tent, made from a weatherbeaten canvas stretched over long sticks, stood before a firepit. Various ceramic pots and jugs stood scattered about, along with a dusty rug and several tanning racks.

"Your dragon can make itself at home," Gaelon said. "Enzo is used to eagles, too."

Aegon flew up over the pillars and sat atop a ledge. Enzo lay in the shade, while Tessa and Myla coaxed their eagles into the camp. A smile stretched across Isiah's face, melting the fatigue away. It made his face hurt.

Gaelon put out a hand. "Stop moving."

Isiah froze as Gaelon reached out and plucked something from his shoulder. He dangled a fat, black scorpion by the tail.

"These are dangerous," he said. "It must have fallen on you as you came in." He grabbed a small ceramic pot and, popping off the lid, dropped the writhing arachnid inside. "The local nomads grind them up for medicine."

Tessa pulled a face. Isiah shuddered and rubbed his shoulder instinctively.

Gaelon placed the pot on a low table. "What brings you three here?"

Isiah recounted the story of the attack on the Hidden Citadel. "We need your help," he said. "We don't have any supplies."

Gaelon scratched his chin. "They say charity doesn't get you far in the Badlands . . ." He paused. "But the locals helped me enough when I landed here." He turned and disappeared inside his tent. "I'm sure I have a spare pair of shoes you can use."

Isiah took the opportunity to sit by the firepit and take in his surroundings. Myla met his gaze and smiled. Tessa had lost her scowl. Gaelon emerged from the tent and passed Isiah a worn-out pair of nomad's shoes.

"These should fit you for now," he said.

Isiah thanked the man and slipped them on. They gave his feet too much room to move, but he didn't complain. Gaelon sat on a wooden bench. He had the broad shoulders and tall stature of a Royal Guard, and a warm face that reminded him of Ward. Wrinkles around the man's eyes and on his forehead betrayed his age.

"I want you to teach me how to master my bond with Aegon," Isiah blurted out. "You've spent a lot of time flying dragons, right?"

"I have . . ." Gaelon said slowly.

"Then you must know something that can help me." He looked to Aegon. "If I'd passed my Ceremony, I would have been given training, but I've been abandoned to figure things out on my own."

"A bond is a deeply personal thing," Gaelon said. "You can't teach it any more than you can pass the Ceremony *for* someone."

"You *have* to show me." Isiah's voice grew more desperate. "There must be something you know that can help me."

Gaelon hesitated. "I guess I can show you a few things while you're staying here," he said at last.

A flood of relief washed over Isiah. "Thank you."

Gaelon stood. "Start the fire, will you? We'll cook up some food and then I'll take you flying."

Gaelon

ISIAH WATCHED THE SMOKE CURL FROM THE burnt-out firepit. Tessa and Myla sat in the shade of the tent as the twin suns reached their highest point. Their bowls—empty—lay in a pile beside them. Further off, the eagles picked over a carcass of a dead gorgon they had found. Not even the sickly stench of its decomposing flesh had put Isiah off his food.

"I wanted to ask you," Isiah said to Gaelon. "What made you leave Paradon?"

"I got tired of it," the man replied. "The same old thing, over and over. Constantly putting your dragon in danger. They always tell you that being a Royal Guard is such an honour, the chance to protect our kingdom and its people from harm." He shook his head. "That life isn't for me anymore." He dusted off his hands. "If you've recovered from your trip, I want to take you flying."

Isiah sat up. "Now?"

Gaelon shrugged. "Now is as good a time as any. Get your dragon. I want to see what you're capable of."

Isiah jogged to Aegon's side. Enzo slithered out to meet Gaelon, and the man climbed onto the dragon's broad back.

Tessa stood. "I'll come too."

She called Vyrro away from the half-eaten carcass and climbed into his saddle. Myla volunteered to stay behind, and the three of them flew out of the camp and into the Badlands sky. Isiah scanned the horizon for any sign of Abaddon's skyships—or haboobs.

"Your bond shouldn't be possible," Gaelon said. "You've been both rejected by the dragons *and* accepted by them. Enzo doesn't know what to make of it."

Isiah adjusted his robes. His Mark tingled as the dragon's eyes washed over him. The magic buried deep within his flesh let off a burning sensation. He forced himself to focus on his mental link with Aegon.

"Tell me everything you know about dragons," Gaelon called.

Isiah ran over everything Ward had taught him . . . and Solomon. They flew in circles above the camp, catching the updrafts and cutting effortlessly through the sky. Tessa followed further behind on Vyrro. She watched Gaelon with veiled suspicion.

"Now show me how you fly," Gaelon said.

Isiah obeyed. His mind flashed back to when he flew with Aegon near the Hidden Citadel, before he and Tessa had been caught in the haboob. He directed Aegon into a series of tight turns and spirals. She pitched hard on one wing and he slid to one side. He opened his mouth in shock and grabbed her neck instinctively.

"What happened?" Gaelon asked.

"I felt myself slipping," Isiah replied. He waited for his heartbeat to settle, then kept going. He strained, trying to maintain his connection with Aegon. He sighed as it faltered and dissolved.

"You *know* what you're supposed to do, boy," Gaelon said, "but you don't *feel* it."

"What do you mean?" Isiah asked.

"You don't trust her." He motioned to Aegon. "Something is holding you back."

Isiah frowned. "That's not true."

Gaelon directed Enzo to land atop a mesa. Aegon and Vyrro went after him.

"I can sense a blockage," Gaelon said as Isiah reached his side.

"I just need a teacher," Isiah insisted. "Nobody showed me how to improve."

"Nonsense." Gaelon waved him away. "Our earliest heroes *had* no teachers. When they first tamed the wild dragons of Paradon, they learned from the dragons themselves."

"They were different," Isiah said. "They weren't Marked."

"Aegon trusts you," Gaelon replied. "She doesn't care about your Mark, else she'd have killed you a long time ago. Why can't you trust her?"

"I *do* trust her," Isiah insisted.

Gaelon paused. "Let's try something." He pulled a strip of fabric from his pocket. "Put this over your eyes."

"What?"

"Trust me," Gaelon said. "Aegon won't crash if *you* can't see where you're going."

Isiah tentatively took the blindfold and wrapped it around his head. The material blocked out all light. He wobbled, suddenly aware of his precarious perch atop Aegon's shoulders. "Now what?"

"You're going to fly," Gaelon replied. "And I want you to feel the connection. You can't see, but if your bond is strong enough, you'll learn how to see *through* her. Her senses will become your own, and you'll fly in tandem."

Isiah hesitated. He gripped Aegon's neck and cautiously spurred her forward. The sound of Aegon's wings unfurling met his ears, then his insides lurched as they ascended into the sky.

Isiah forced himself to take a deep breath. *Okay, don't panic*, he told himself. Without his sight, he became aware of every tiny adjustment of Aegon's wings, along with the subtle twitch of her tail. He tried to turn his focus inwards, seeking out their bond.

"Relax your shoulders," Gaelon called from somewhere beside him. "Trust in your bond."

Isiah gripped Aegon tighter. "I'm going to fall off!" he cried.

"No you won't," Gaelon replied. "Direct Aegon to follow me. She'll do the rest."

Isiah obeyed. The rush of wingbeats sounded in his ears as Aegon fell into pursuit of Enzo. His heart climbed into his throat as they dropped toward the ground, then soared over unseen terrain.

Isiah clung to Aegon's neck for dear life. She made a sharp turn, then another. Every part of his brain screamed at him to rip the blindfold off. Aegon picked up speed. Her huffing breaths swirled in Isiah's eardrums. She soared upward, nearly vertical, and gravity pulled Isiah backwards.

Isiah panicked and yanked the blindfold free. Bright sunlight stabbed his eyes. Enzo's serpentine form glided through the sky above. Aegon pulled away and flew back down to the mesa.

She landed and Isiah dismounted, panting. He leaned against her and waited for his heartbeat to steady. It hammered against his ribcage, making him lightheaded. Enzo landed nearby and Gaelon walked over.

"Do you see my point?" he asked. "You're still unwilling to give up control."

Isiah slumped against Aegon. She nuzzled him and gave him a re-assuring rumble.

"She flies fine on her own," Gaelon said. "But when you're controlling her, then you start having problems." He leaned in. "You're overthinking it."

Wingbeats sounded as Vyrro landed and Tessa jumped off. Her face was flushed. "That was crazy!" She laughed. "You should have seen how fast you were going. Vyrro could hardly keep up."

Gaelon smiled. "Dragons are called the rulers of the skies for a reason," he replied. "And with a strong enough bond, no so-called sky-ship is a match for us."

Isiah slumped his shoulders.

"Don't be so hard on yourself," Gaelon said. "A bond doesn't grow overnight. Royal Guards train for years."

Tessa turned up her nose. "I suppose you got a lot of practice when you were patrolling the Badlands."

Gaelon shook his head. "The only patrolling I do now involves checking my camp for scorpions and snakes." He summoned Enzo, who lumbered to his side. "Now, are you ready to give flying another go?"

Alcabaza

"WE'RE NOT FAR NOW," LAZARO CALLED. "I recognize these landmarks."

Aron clung to Antony's waist as they flew across the Badlands. Lazaro was in the lead, and Marie shared Helen's eagle as they followed nearby. Aron exchanged glances with the girl.

Excitement buzzed in his gut. He wiped his sweaty palms on his robes. He hadn't seen Alcabaza since being sold to merchants and smuggled out of the city. The thought of returning made him giddy with a mixture of apprehension and unease.

"We should avoid the roosts," Antony called over the rush of wind. "We don't want to attract any unwanted attention."

"You're right," Lazaro said. He scowled. "They won't be happy to see us."

A sack hung from the saddle of Lazaro's eagle, containing the Sunstone fragment they'd rescued from the Hidden Citadel.

"What are we going to do once we arrive?" Aron asked.

"We sneak up to the observatory and see if what Edith said about the Sunstone is true," Lazaro replied.

They flew on for a few minutes in silence. The rocky, arid terrain rolled past. Aron recognized the buttes and valleys. His heart fluttered as Alcabaza materialized on the horizon.

The great mountainside city loomed over the surrounding plains, hugging the side of a lone mountain. Three terraces, bursting with sandstone buildings, climbed up its slope, with a lattice of wooden beams forming the elevators and scaffolding that connected the city to the ground below.

The silhouettes of eagles circled the mountain's peak. It was flat and smooth, as if sheared off. Circular landing platforms jutted from the eagle roosts a few hundred feet below. As they drew closer, Aron frowned.

"Something's wrong," he said.

At the foot of the mountain, brightly coloured merchant camps sprawled across the fields. Makeshift muddy tracks cut between them, with dozens of people wandering about. A few nomad groups trickled in from the surrounding Badlands.

"Why aren't they going inside the city?" Helen asked.

"It doesn't matter," Lazaro replied. "Remember to keep your heads down."

Their eagles glided toward Alcabaza. Aron studied the merchant camps as they passed overhead. "I've never seen them do anything like that before."

More Raiders wheeled above the city atop their eagles. Some landed on the roosts, while others descended to the lower levels, disappearing behind buildings. He frowned. "Raiders never land inside the city."

"At least we won't look suspicious," Antony said.

They guided their eagles toward the first of the three terraces. It was the largest, and it connected to the elevators that lifted merchants and nomads into Alcabaza. Houses perched precariously on its edge, held aloft by wooden supports. The crowd scattered as their eagles landed on the main street.

Aron swung one leg off the saddle and slid to the ground. Despite himself, a smile broke out on his face. He stretched and sucked in a deep breath of the hot, aroma-laden air. "Alcabaza, how I missed you."

The vibrant smells of incense and burning wood drifted over from a nearby bazaar, mingling with the pungent odour of donkeys and sweat. Despite the beggars slumped in doorways and the constant din of haggling merchants, being in the city again made Aron's heart swell.

Marie hopped off Helen's eagle and wrapped her arms around herself. She surveyed the crowds with wary eyes. Aron clapped her on the shoulder. "It's quite the sight, isn't it?"

"I've never been to a city before," she said quietly.

Aron grinned. "Trust me, you'll love it here."

Lazaro dusted off his hands. "I want to visit our old home," he said.

"Good idea," Helen replied. "Luca and I will look after the eagles while you're gone."

"You don't want to visit with us?" Aron asked.

Helen brushed him off. "It brings back too many memories."

Leaving their eagles behind, they wandered deeper into the city. Aron let his shoulders fall back. Despite the weight of their exile, the familiar side alleys and hidey-holes called out to him. He recognized the faces of merchants and shopkeepers as he passed. Marie walked beside him, so close she was almost in his pocket.

"There's something wrong here," Antony said.

Aron looked closer. Many of the merchant stalls were empty, and the crowds were thinner than he remembered. Several eagles soared overhead and landed behind a row of houses. Aron spotted a makeshift wall—made from piles of furniture and stone slabs—blocking off access to a street.

"Aron!" a voice called. He twisted around to see a girl running toward him.

Lazaro tensed. His hand gravitated to his sabre.

"It's okay," Aron said quickly. "We're friends." He recognized her as Heather, one of the Scavengers he used to know while he was part of Enrik's gang.

Heather skidded to a halt in front of him. "I didn't expect to see you back here," she said. "I thought you were banished."

"We are," Aron replied. He became more serious. "What happened while we were gone?"

"After your exile, the Raider's Oath broke down," Heather said. "We thought that after the attacks stopped, we'd have a chance to end the tensions and suspicion between the Raider gangs—but instead they broke out into a turf war for control of the city."

Heather took Aron's arm and guided him away from the blocked-off street. "Mauriel's gang seized control of the roosts, so the others have taken over different parts of the city," she said.

"That explains the eagles," Aron replied. "What about the merchants?"

"One of the other gangs destroyed the elevators to cut off the supply lines," Heather explained. "Their plan was to starve Mauriel and her allies into submission."

"And it hasn't worked, I take it?"

Heather rubbed her arms. "They're tearing the city apart."

Lazaro cut in. "Let's keep going to our old house. We can rest there and lay low until we figure out our plan."

88

Heather caught Aron's sleeve. "Why did you come back?"

Aron shot a glance at the sack containing the Sunstone fragment. "We've got some important business." He broke away and hastened after Lazaro and the others.

"Don't go into the walled-off areas," Heather called after him. "The Raiders are on high alert."

Aron hurried down the main road, weaving through the crowd. He tugged on his collar. The deserted bazaars and empty merchant stalls suddenly made sense. A cloud of flies swarmed around a beggar, no more than a bundle of rags. Aron crinkled his nose at the sickly odour of death.

"With the Raiders fighting over Alcabaza, it will make the perfect cover for us to slip into the roosts," Lazaro said. "With any luck, they'll all be too busy with each other to notice us."

Aron cast a glance toward the roosts. A few eagles circled above the mountain peak. "Mauriel is up there somewhere."

Lazaro balled his fist. "Maybe we'll get a chance for some payback after what she did to us."

A figure darted across a rooftop. Aron frowned. A nomad boy, no older than seven or eight, crouched atop the flat roof of a building. Aron paused. "What's he doing up there?"

"He's probably just a pickpocket," Darla replied. "You heard how desperate they're getting."

Aron squinted at the boy. A spyglass dangled from his belt. Several others appeared on buildings nearby.

Darla gave Aron a playful punch. "Are you worried they're going to rob us?"

They turned down a side street and quickened their pace. The boys on the rooftops kept up with them. Aron glanced over his shoulder and a Raider stepped into the street behind them. His blood ran cold.

Several more Raiders materialized ahead, cutting them off. The man in the lead folded his arms.

"Don't move," he growled. "I've no qualms about spilling more Raider blood."

The other Raiders closed in from behind. Aron searched for an escape route. Sheer walls hemmed them in on either side. If someone gave him a boost, he might be able to scale one . . .

"Lazaro," the lead Raider said. "I didn't expect to see your face around here."

Lazaro glared at the man. Aron tensed his muscles, waiting for a fight to break out. The other Raider gang outnumbered them.

"I thought I'd drop back in and see how my old city was doing," Lazaro said in a steady voice.

"You're banished," the Raider replied. "Returning means death."

Darla and Antony exchanged glances. Marie whimpered and clutched Aron's robes. Each second dragged on.

"But times have changed," the Raider continued. "As I'm sure you've noticed."

"Mauriel wasn't strong enough to hold the Oath together, was she?" Lazaro asked. "No surprises there."

"We're no friends of Mauriel." The Raider scowled. "But we ain't no friends of yours, neither." He put out his hand. "Give us your weapons. Valerie will want to meet you."

The Raiders closed in. One reached forward and pulled Aron's sabre free from its scabbard. The others forced Antony and Darla to hand over theirs. The lead Raider confiscated Lazaro's blade and shoved him.

"Start walking," he ordered.

The Raiders marched Aron and his friends out of the side street and along the main road. The thought of escape played on Aron's mind, but he decided against it. Even if he made it back to Helen and Luca, they couldn't do anything against the much stronger Raider gang.

"How did you find us?" Lazaro asked. "Haven't you got your hands full as it is?"

The lead Raider nodded to the nomad boys on the rooftops. "No eagles pass by unnoticed with our sentries on duty. A few coins each and they practically work for free."

The Raiders escorted Aron and the others deeper into the city, then through a gate in their makeshift wall. A Raider stood watch in a rickety wooden sentry tower. The crowds thinned, reduced to a mere handful of people.

Ahead, a break in the buildings revealed an open plaza. Strips of canvas were strung between the houses, creating a kind of open-air tent.

"It keeps the prying eyes of eagles away," the lead Raider said, noticing Aron staring.

Raiders worked in the covered plaza, carrying resources into a bazaar and sharpening their blades on grinding stones. Raiders stopped and stared as Lazaro passed.

"Where's Valerie?" the lead Raider called. "I've got someone she'll want to meet."

A group of Raiders parted to reveal a tall woman with piercing eyes.

"Lazaro." She cocked her head. "Do you have a death wish?"

"I'm here on my own business," he replied coldly.

"You have quite the nerve to show your face again here," Valerie said. "This city has enough trouble, without you adding to it."

"I'm not here to start a fight."

"Too bad. There's been nothing *but* fights ever since you were banished." Her eyes flitted over the group. "I'm half-tempted to sell you to Mauriel. She's still furious about you sabotaging her hunting party."

Lazaro's nostrils flared. "I thought you weren't Mauriel's friends."

"We're not." Valerie's voice took on a hard tone. "She allied with the biggest Raider gang and they took over the roosts together. We have most of the bazaars in our territory, so we cut the elevator cables to try and starve her out." She paused. "But if I arrived on her doorstep with *you*, she'd owe me a couple of favours."

Lazaro matched her gaze. Nobody spoke. The tension in the air made the hair on the back of Aron's neck rise. He sidled closer to Marie in case a fight broke out.

"So tell me, Lazaro," Valerie said slowly, "why shouldn't I?"

"Because I have an offer for you." Lazaro slung the sack containing the Sunstone fragment off his shoulder.

"Lazaro," Darla hissed. "What are you doing?"

Lazaro marched to a table and placed the sack down. Valerie and the others crowded around as he pulled the covering off and revealed the Sunstone.

One of the Raiders let out a low whistle. "Is that thing solid gold?"

"It's a piece of a weapon," Lazaro explained. "One strong enough to destroy Paradon—or anyone else who gets in our way."

Valerie's eyes flitted across the Sunstone fragment's surface. "I'm listening."

"It's useless on its own," he said. "There are four pieces. One is here, and two are inside the observatory in the roosts."

Valerie gave him a smug smile. "Then what's to stop me from taking this to Mauriel and cutting you out of the picture entirely?"

Lazaro leaned in. "Because the rest of my gang are looking for the fourth." He tapped the fragment. "And without *that*, this is nothing more than a fancy hunk of gold."

"Well, look at you, Lazaro," Valerie said. "You've returned a skilled negotiator. What happened to you while you were gone? I expected you to start throwing punches."

"I've learned a few things," he replied. The corner of his lip upturned. "But don't push it."

Valerie stepped away. "What do you need us to do?"

"Help us find a way to overthrow Mauriel and take this fragment to the observatory."

"We've been trying to put an end to her since the moment you left." Valerie clapped Lazaro's hand and shook it. "Well, Lazaro, you're a wild card no more. Welcome to my gang."

Soul-searching

"THERE YOU ARE." TESSA GRABBED ISIAH and pulled him inside Gaelon's tent. The large structure had become their home for the past few days. Several blankets on the earth formed their beds, and the material above kept the sun off in the heat of the day.

Isiah pulled away from her. "What is it?"

"I've been looking for you," Tessa said. "You keep disappearing to fly with that Royal Guard."

"He's not a Royal Guard anymore," Isiah insisted.

"Whatever he is, I've barely seen you." She checked that nobody was listening and lowered her voice. "When are we going to start looking for the missing Sunstone piece?"

"Soon," Isiah said. A pang of guilt tugged at his chest, but he pushed it aside. He'd searched for so long to find a teacher. "I'm finally making progress with Aegon."

"You were already making progress before we arrived."

Isiah shook his head. "I'm *learning*, Tess."

Tessa folded her arms. "Who said you could call me that?"

"I thought you did . . ." Isiah started.

"Whatever." Tessa threw up her hands. "Look. We're not going to finish the Sunstone if we stay here. Abaddon is still searching for the last piece, and you know what will happen if he beats us to it."

"I know," Isiah said. "But we don't know where we're supposed to start looking. Abaddon has an entire fleet."

"Doing *something* is better than nothing," Tessa replied. "Right now we're just waiting for him to complete his Sunstone and terrorize everyone. The Badlands belongs to *us*."

Isiah put a hand on her shoulder. "I'll ask Gaelon if he knows anything about it today, okay?"

Tessa pulled a face. "Are you sure we can trust him?"

"He seems nice," Isiah replied.

"You said that about Solomon."

Her words cut into him. He looked away before she could see his expression.

"Wait, Isiah—"

"I'll ask Gaelon," he repeated. "You're right. I shouldn't be so selfish."

"I didn't say you were selfish . . ."

Before she could say anything else, Isiah exited the tent and hurried across the camp.

You shouldn't have said that, a voice in his head told him. *She's right about the Sunstone.*

"Isiah," Myla called. She bounced over. "Are you going flying?"

"Maybe," Isiah replied.

"Great," she said. "I'll come with you this time."

Since arriving at Gaelon's camp, Myla had begun to brighten up. The loss of the Hidden Citadel weighed on their shoulders, but Isiah felt it slowly lifting.

Gaelon stood in front of a tanning rack, stretching a gorgon skin with twine. A pile of claws, along with the beast's long fangs, were in a basket nearby.

"Are you ready to go?" Gaelon asked. "I saw Aegon somewhere nearby. She's settling in well."

"I wanted to ask you something," Isiah said. He took a deep breath, then told Gaelon about the Sunstone. As he talked, Tessa joined the group and stood off to the side. She avoided Isiah's gaze.

"I've heard about the Sunstone before," Gaelon replied when he'd finished. "Of course, I never had any reason to go looking for it."

"We were wondering if you had any idea where we should start searching," Isiah said.

Gaelon scratched his chin. "I do have *one* idea," he said slowly. "But it's not something to be taken lightly."

Gaelon grabbed a stool and sat down. Isiah listened intently as he continued. "The local nomads have ways of discovering things," he said. "Their rituals have been passed down for thousands of years, long before Raiders and merchants first settled in the Badlands."

"What sort of rituals?" Myla asked.

"They know how to concoct a brew," Gaelon explained. "It puts you in a trance—lets you see things. The shamans use it to guide their clans to find resources in the Badlands." He turned over one of the gorgon fangs in his hands. "I learned how to make it while living with them. I used it a few times for soul-searching." He inhaled sharply. "But it's dangerous."

Isiah exchanged glances with the others. "How dangerous?" he asked.

"The brew itself is made from a mixture of toxic Badlands plants," Gaelon replied. "You drink it and then allow yourself to be stung by a specific type of scorpion. Only then will you slip over to the other side."

Myla leaned closer. Gaelon kicked over a stone and a tiny scorpion scuttled out.

"From the outside, you look sick," he said. "Sweating, convulsions, fever. That alone can kill you. But inside—" he grabbed his head "—you wander a different world altogether."

"And can this help us find the Sunstone?" Isiah asked.

"I warned you, boy, it's not to be taken lightly," Gaelon said. "Sometimes people get lost in there. Once you go inside, you can't always come back again. Sometimes people make it back only to be changed forever."

Isiah's expression hardened. He pushed away the sense of unease. "I'll do it."

"Wait." Tessa grabbed him. "Don't feel like you have to do this, Isiah. There might be another way."

Isiah brushed her away. "You were right. We have to find the last Sunstone fragment before Abaddon does."

"I can find the ingredients nearby." Gaelon stood. "Our dark sun will crown the sky two nights from now. The shamans believe it brings good luck."

"Two days," Isiah repeated. He hoped they weren't already too late.

The Roosts

ARON SLIPPED THROUGH THE CROWD. HE TIGHTENED the hood around his head and peered beneath its rim. Marie walked beside him, trying her best to blend in. They followed the roads away from Valerie's headquarters, heading in the direction of the roosts.

"What will we do if somebody recognizes you?" Marie asked. She clung to Aron's side, nervously checking over her shoulder.

"Hopefully it would only be a friendly Scavenger," Aron said. "They don't have any reason to sell us out."

Lazaro and Valerie had discussed how they were going to overthrow Mauriel and drive her Raiders from the roosts. Aron had volunteered to scout the place and look for weaknesses.

"And if it's a Raider?" she asked.

"Then we run."

Marie whimpered.

"Hey," Aron said. "I know all the alleyways in the city. Stick with me and we'll get away no problem."

Ahead, a stone staircase led to the second level of the city. More makeshift palisade walls marked the edge of Valerie's territory. While settling in, Aron had a chance to learn more about the situation in Alcabaza.

"There are half a dozen big Raider gangs," Valerie had told him. "They've carved off parts of the city and turned them into base camps.

Nomads and civilians and the likes can pass through without much difficulty, but Raiders arouse suspicion. With all their sentries, not even eagles can fly past undetected."

Aron tightened his collar as they passed a Raider on watch duty. The man stood atop a platform, arms folded. Aron felt his gaze wash over him.

He hastened up the staircase and melted into the crowd. Ahead, further up the mountain, wooden landing platforms jutted from the roosts. Aron steadied his breathing as he ran over his mental plan.

"All we need to do is check it out," he told Marie. "Valerie said none of the other Raider gangs are happy with Mauriel for stealing the roosts. If someone found a weakness to exploit, her control would collapse."

They passed the smithing district with its burning forges and the steady grind of sharpening stones. Another bazaar stood off to their right, little more than a ghost town. A couple of beggars slumped against the wall, weakly raising cups to passers-by—who all ignored them.

Aron scratched the back of his neck. "I'm starting to wonder whether destroying the elevators was such a good move." He'd never seen the place so empty.

Before he could dwell on it, they reached the roosts. A series of staircases climbed the mountainside to the third terrace. The crowd thickened, pushing and shoving each other as they climbed. Aron took Marie's wrist and they joined the crush of bodies.

At the top of the stairs, more palisade walls greeted them. Raiders stood on raised walkways behind it, watching the crowd as it was funnelled through a narrow gate and into the roosts. A few tattered flags flew from the wall.

Mauriel has built herself a makeshift fortress, Aron thought.

Tightening his hood, he lowered his head and slipped in with the crowd. They made it past the Raiders standing guard and entered the roosts.

"Where is everybody going?" Marie asked.

"I don't know," Aron said slowly. "Normally only Raiders use the roosts."

The crowd carried them along like a current, past rows of eagle pens and landing pads. Aron caught sight of several more Raiders blocking off streets, herding the crowd along. He stumbled as someone pushed him.

The crowd slowed as they reached a plaza, like the one Valerie had turned into her base. Taverns and Raider houses bordered it. A storehouse stood in the centre. Aron recognized the place as being where the Raiders kept food for their eagles. The smell had prevented anybody from living close to it.

People stopped as a fence barred the way forward. They stood packed against one another, watching the storehouse expectantly. Aron frowned. *What's going on here?*

"Line up, nice and orderly," a Raider called. He marched along, brandishing a sabre. People scattered out of his way. Aron noticed that many of them were clutching empty cloth bags and wooden bowls.

The storehouse stood in the centre of the plaza, surrounded by empty space. The fence that held back the crowd wrapped the entire way around it. The crowd stopped muttering and jostling, leaving the roosts eerily quiet.

Wingbeats sounded above. Aron ducked as an eagle soared low overhead. It threw out its wings and glided to the storehouse, landing on the flat roof. A Raider threw one leg off and dropped onto the building. The crowd leaned in.

"Don't cross the fence!" the sabre-wielding Raider barked. He marched in front of them. Aron averted his gaze to avoid drawing attention to himself. He felt Marie's fingers digging into his arm.

The Raider on the storehouse opened a hatch and disappeared inside. A few moments later, he emerged with several sacks. He tried them to his eagle's saddle and then flew over the crowd. People turned and raised their hands as if trying to catch the bird.

It soared overhead and its rider cut the sacks free. The crowd surged toward them. Aron craned his neck to see what was going on. People grappled with each other for the sacks. Others plunged cups and bowls inside to scoop out the contents. Grain spilled and scattered across the street.

They were waiting for food, he realized.

The eagle returned to the storehouse and the Raider gathered a second load. Voices yelled and fights broke out as people fought for their share. Some dropped to their knees to scoop up the spilled grain.

"This doesn't make any sense," Aron said. "Why aren't there more Raiders guarding the storehouse? This fence won't stop a crowd so desperate."

The eagle flew overhead and the Raider released another bundle. People climbed over each other to reach them. A merchant grabbed one and tried to drag it away. Someone cried out amid the crush of bodies.

"Let's get out of here," Aron said.

Keeping Marie by his side so she didn't get lost, he fought his way to the edge of the crowd. He dusted himself off and sucked in a breath.

"Why do you think Mauriel is doing this?" Marie asked.

"She must be feeding the civilians," Aron said. "Maybe she's trying to keep the last semblance of order alive." He furrowed his brow. "But how can she stop them from storming the storehouse? It doesn't make any sense."

"We should tell Lazaro," Marie replied. "The storehouse could be a weakness, right?"

"Something doesn't sit right with me." Aron looked about. He spotted a cluster of sandstone buildings with a vine growing up on one side. "I want to stick around for a while longer."

He darted to the house and, checking that none of Mauriel's Raiders were around, climbed to the roof. Marie awkwardly clambered up after him. Aron caught her hand and helped her over the low wall that surrounded the rooftop.

"Now what?" she asked.

Aron leaned against the wall and watched the storehouse. "Now we wait."

* * *

"Aron, wake up!"

Aron stirred as Marie shook him. He snapped to attention. "What is it?"

"Look." Marie pointed.

The streets stood deserted, shrouded in darkness. A few lights glowed further off where Raiders revelled in taverns. Aside from a few sentries—no more than dark silhouettes on rooftops—the city was deserted.

The moon cast a silvery light across the storehouse and the empty plaza. Without the crowd from earlier, it felt like a ghost town. Aron scanned for guards. Nothing.

"I saw something," Marie said.

Movement in an alleyway caught Aron's eye. He squinted. A figure emerged on the edge of the plaza, dressed in the rags of a beggar. A long beard swung as he walked. The beggar checked that nobody was watching, then ducked under the fence.

"He's going to steal food," Marie said. "Where are the Raiders?"

Aron ignored her. The beggar tiptoed towards the storehouse. He carefully placed a foot on a sandstone slab, then twisted his body and stepped on a slab further away. His arms wobbled as he tried to keep his balance.

Marie tilted her head. "What is he *doing*?"

The beggar cautiously lifted his foot from the first slab, then paused to assess his next move. He lowered his foot and waited. Satisfied, he took another step.

An explosion split the night.

Aron jolted in shock. The beggar screamed and fell backwards, clutching his leg. A plume of dust and sandstone erupted from the slab he'd been standing on moments before. His agonized screams pierced Aron's head like a knife.

Movement sounded on the street below. A Raider swore. He sprinted over, keeping to the other side of the fence.

"Thought you could pilfer our stores, did you?" he spat. He produced a long, hooked pike. The beggar wailed, holding his stump of a leg as it oozed blood.

The Raider used the pike to hook the beggar's rags and drag him out of the plaza. Marie covered her face as the Raider drew his sabre and brought it down. The screaming ceased.

Silence returned. Aron's gut churned as the Raider buried the hook into the beggar's flesh and dragged the corpse away. He knew what would happen to it. *Eagle carrion.*

Aron slumped against the low wall. The beggar's screams echoed in his eardrums. Marie gagged.

"Mauriel booby-trapped the plaza," he said. "That's why they don't have guards." He felt sick to his stomach.

"What are we going to do now?" Marie asked.

"We'll have to wait here until morning," he replied. "The crowd will give us an opportunity to slip out."

"Do you think this is the weakness that Lazaro is looking for?"

Aron checked the plaza again. The dust settled, revealing a hole in the sandstone street. "I bet if we found a way to destroy the storehouse, it would push the civilians over the edge." He shuddered.

If we can avoid being blown up ourselves.

Spirit World

GAELON PULLED OPEN THE TENT FLAP. "It's time."

Isiah climbed off the blanket that made his bed. A few feet away, Tessa and Myla stirred. Isiah gathered his things and pushed out of the tent.

A sliver of moon hung in the sky overhead. The smouldering sun, separated from its bright cousin, smothered the landscape in reddish shadows. An eerie hue hung over Gaelon's camp. Vyrro ruffled his feathers, sensing their unease.

"I've finished gathering the ingredients," Gaelon said. He carried a sack slung over one shoulder and a belt of ceramic pots tied together. "Now we fly to the ritual site."

Isiah broke away to get Aegon. The dragon lay sleeping on the edge of camp. She raised her head and rumbled a welcome as Isiah approached. Isiah stroked her nose and took a deep breath.

Tessa and Myla readied their eagles. With Gaelon in the lead on Enzo, they took off and flew into the night. A cold wind stirred Isiah's robes, chilling his skin. Enzo sailed through the empty sky, a silhouette beneath the reddish sun. Isiah put a hand on his chest to quell his heartbeat.

They flew for several minutes, then Enzo dropped to the ground. As Aegon landed, Isiah made out a large stone circle in a valley. They dismounted and gathered around.

Gaelon knelt before a large metal bowl, wider than Isiah's arm span. Rust clung to its edges, and in the eerie light, Isiah made out the markings etched around its rim. Gaelon lit a fire inside it and the flames crackled to life.

"Take a seat," Gaelon said.

Isiah found a place to sit on the edge of the circle. Pointed boulders stood at intervals around it. Tessa and Myla sat either side of him.

"I'm going to prepare the brew." Gaelon took a pot and placed it over the fire, then filled it with water. "Once it's complete, the ritual can begin."

They sat in silence as Gaelon worked. He dumped the contents of several bags inside the pot. Isiah recognized some of the plants, but others he didn't. Gaelon brought the pot to a boil and stirred it.

Isiah jumped as Tessa took his hand. She leaned in. "Are you *sure* about this?" she whispered.

Isiah forced himself to sit tall. "It's what I have to do." He tried to ignore the chorus of doubts swirling about his head.

"When you drink the brew, you'll fall into a sleep," Gaelon explained. "We'll care for your body on our end, but once you cross over, you're on your own. I can't tell you what you'll see, or what you'll need to do to find the Sunstone fragment."

Isiah forced himself to take measured breaths. He realized how tightly he was squeezing Tessa's hand.

"There are dangers in there," Gaelon warned. "The nomads forbid anyone other than shamans to drink this brew. As soon as you find what you're looking for, get out."

Isiah forced himself to speak. "I will."

Gaelon lifted the pot off the fire and emptied its contents into a bowl. He passed it to Isiah. "I must warn you, it's not pleasant."

Isiah tentatively took the bowl. He winced as the heat scorched his fingers. Myla watched him with wide eyes. Isiah raised the bowl to his lips.

The bitter liquid slid down his throat, searing hot. Isiah fought the urge to gag. The pungent smell brought tears to his eyes. He drained the bowl and coughed.

"Do you feel any different?" Tessa asked.

Isiah grimaced. He rubbed his hands. His fingertips felt numb.

Gaelon produced a ceramic pot and popped off the stopper. "Put out your hand."

Isiah did as he was told. Colours lingered at the edges of his vision. The air filled his lungs like syrup. When he tried to think, his skull felt too small for his brain. Gaelon took his hand and tilted the pot. A fat, black scorpion slid onto his palm.

Isiah tensed. The scorpion bared its claws. Its tail twitched in warning. Gaelon prodded it with a stick, and it sank its barb into Isiah's skin.

A pained gasp escaped him as liquid fire coursed through his veins from the sting. The scorpion scuttled off and Isiah pitched backwards. Tessa caught him.

"Is he going to be alright?" she asked. Her voice sounded distant and murky.

"He's slipping into the trance now," Gaelon replied. His voice grew faint. "It's up to him now."

The muscles in Isiah's arm clenched as the scorpion's venom seeped through his system. His skin flushed red-hot. He opened his mouth, but no sound would come. Darkness crept across his vision.

His head rolled back and the void consumed him.

* * *

Isiah sat up. His lungs gasped for breath. He clutched his burning arm and a fit of coughing overcame him. He blinked the tears from his eyes and propped himself up on his elbows.

Wisps of murky white fog surrounded him. Shadows loomed from it, revealing twisted hunks of rock. Isiah waited for his coughing to subside, then cautiously stood. The pain in his arm faded to a tingling numbness. When he looked down, the site of the sting shone an angry red. Black lines radiated out from it like a spiderweb of veins. Isiah spun around, trying to take in his surroundings.

The fog limited visibility to no more than a hundred feet. He glanced up at the empty sky above. There was no sign of the smouldering sun, or the moon—or anything.

Isiah clutched his chest. *Calm down*. His heart thundered against his ribcage. An eerie silence cloaked whatever place he found himself in, making each echo seem to reverberate for miles.

Isiah started to walk. Buttes and piles of boulders materialized from the fog. He found the tallest and hurried over to it. Placing one foot against it, he began to climb.

"That won't get you very far," a voice said.

Isiah jumped. He spun around to see a boy. His own face stared back at him.

"W–what are you?" Isiah managed to ask.

"What am I?" the boy asked. "I'm you." He shrugged. "Kind of. You won't last long in here without a guide."

Isiah waited for his pulse to settle. A million questions flooded his head. "What is this place?" he blurted out.

"It's not somewhere you can reach by walking, that's for certain," the guide replied. "It's hardly a physical place at all."

"That doesn't answer my question."

"It's another plane," he explained. "One that's just under the surface of your world."

Isiah looked up at the sky.

"Not like that," the guide said. "You can't access this place through your senses, not while you're tethered to the regular world." The guide spread out his arms. "We walk a thin line between your comfortable home and the beyond."

Isiah rubbed his temples. "I–I don't understand."

"Call it the spirit world," the guide replied. "But it doesn't matter where you are. What matters is *why you're here.*"

Isiah's Mark burned. He winced and scratched it.

"Magic is stronger here," the guide said. "This is where it draws its strength from. It's all connected, see?"

Isiah stretched out his arm. "And what about this?"

The guide inspected it. "That's your timer," he replied. "Once the venom runs out, you'd better be out of here."

Isiah shifted his footing. "And if I'm not?"

"Then you'll become trapped." He sighed. "How a bunch of scorpions ended up with magical properties, we'll never know."

"I need to find a Sunstone fragment," Isiah interrupted.

The guide tilted his head. "Since when did playing with magic turn out well for you?"

"It's important," he said. "Can you help me find it?"

"I can do one better," the guide replied. "I'll show you where it is."

He stepped forward and grabbed Isiah's head. Isiah's body jolted and a burst of light stabbed his vision. Isiah reeled away.

"What was that?" he yelled. A dull, throbbing pain gripped the base of his skull.

The guide pointed. "I did what you wanted."

Isiah turned. A golden beam of light split the fog, rising in the distance.

"The spirit world is a mirror of the physical one," the guide said. "Follow that light, and you'll find where the nearest Sunstone fragment is hidden."

Isiah put a hand to his forehead and squinted at the light. "Can't we just fly there or something?"

"It won't work," the guide replied. "You're still tethered to your body. We'll have to walk." He set off. "You'd better move quickly. Your time is ticking away."

Isiah looked at his arm. He could have sworn the black liquid in his veins had grown smaller.

He pushed the thought out of his mind and ran after the guide.

Awakened

"I HAVE TO WARN YOU, RETRIEVING THE SUNSTONE won't be easy," the guide called over his shoulder.

Isiah's lungs heaved as he climbed up the slope. He grabbed the trunk of an acacia tree for balance. It stretched into the empty sky, reaching for sunlight that didn't exist. "Gaelon warned me there were dangers," he said.

"There are," the guide replied. "The Ancients left a few surprises behind."

Isiah slipped on the loose scree. The Badlands materialized from the fog as he walked. The piercing beam of light towered in the distance ahead, and it didn't seem to be getting any closer.

"What kinds of surprises?" he asked.

"They broke up the Sunstones and buried the fragments for a reason," the guide said. "They knew how powerful they are. The last days of their empire were spent tearing down anything that could help their emerging enemies gain a foothold in the Badlands."

"And who were they?"

The guide laughed. "Paradon, of course." His voice echoed into the empty sky.

Isiah wiped the sweat from his brow. He shrugged off the relentless burning sensation of his Mark.

"The Ancients were the ones who first discovered the magic," the guide explained. "They traced it back to its source." He spread out his arms. "To the chaos that underlies the world. They learned to manipulate it and mould it so that it would become useful to them."

Isiah's head swam. He tried to make sense of what the boy in front of him was saying.

"Sometimes the magic takes a living form." The guide's voice took on a grave tone. "And like your Mark, all magic is stronger in here." He craned his neck and grinned. "We're coming up to something. You won't want to miss this."

The guide ran on ahead. Isiah hastened after him. He reached the crest of a hill and a valley stretched before him. A stone circle sat at the bottom.

"Is that . . ." he started.

"It sure is."

Isiah looked behind him. "But how—"

"It's an illusion," the guide said. "The line between your mind and reality becomes blurred here. After all, we *are* still inside your head."

Isiah hardly heard him. Figures sat in the circle below. He took off at a run.

"Wait up!" the guide called.

Isiah reached the bottom of the valley and ran to the circle. Gaelon sat before the fire, with Tessa and Myla facing him. They had a washed-out appearance—as if made of the same fog that surrounded them.

Isiah waved his hands. "Can you hear me?" he called.

"They're not real," the guide said. "It's your mind, remember?"

Isiah whirled on him. "Then what *is* real?"

The guide gestured around them. "The landscape, for one. But your mind will spin it whatever way it chooses. The shamans are masters of walking the spirit world." He paused. "But because everything is woven through this plane, you *can* use it to your advantage."

"How so?" Isiah asked slowly.

"Touch their heads," the guide said. "You'll get a glimpse into their minds." He pointed to the beam of light. "Like what I did when I showed you that."

Isiah backed away. "I can't do that!"

"Why not?" The guide gave a mischievous grin. "Don't you want to learn more about Aegon? All that knowledge is locked away inside Gaelon's head. Why not take a peek?"

The apparition of Gaelon sat by the fire, motionless. Tessa was nearby, her knees pulled to her chest. Isiah's stomach rolled. He brushed off his arms as if clearing himself of the thought. "I can't. It's wrong."

"Gaelon will never know," the guide said. "You'll become a master at flying Aegon overnight. Isn't that why you found him?"

Isiah hesitated. After his failure with the blindfold, the allure of mastering his bond with Aegon played on his mind. He took a tentative step toward the man.

"What will I see?" he asked.

"Only what you need to."

Part of Isiah's brain screamed at him to stop, but the thought of Aegon drove him on. He grasped Gaelon's head and closed his eyes. Nothing happened for a moment, before an explosion of light swept across his vision.

Isiah's body fell away. Colours flashed past, forming memories that flitted across his mind. He saw Gaelon flying with Enzo across the Badlands. The scene faded, replaced by a shot of Gaelon in Paradon as a young Royal Guard. Pain rippled in the base of Isiah's skull. He gritted his teeth as his head felt about to burst.

The images flew past. He saw Gaelon patrolling the Badlands with a squad of Royal Guards. Raiders flew on the horizon. The dragons closed in, unleashing their fire. Burning eagles dropped from the sky.

Isiah tried to let go, but his fingers were glued to Gaelon's head. An eagle spiralled to the Badlands below. It hit the ground in a plume of dust. As it faded, he saw a woman trapped beneath it.

Enzo landed and Gaelon jumped off. Isiah tried to tear his eyes away, but he couldn't. Gaelon approached the Raider woman and drew his sword. Out the corner of his eye, Isiah noticed the girl cowering in-side the eagle's gutted corpse . . .

Isiah screamed and pulled away. His hands came loose and he fell onto his back. A searing pain rippled through his skull. He kicked up the dirt, scrambling away from the apparition of Gaelon.

"You tricked me!" he stammered. His chest heaved with laboured breaths.

The guide chuckled. "You wanted to see it."

Heat flared in Isiah's chest. He jumped to his feet and launched a punch at the guide. His fist went straight through the boy.

"You have nobody to blame but your curiosity," the guide said. "What did you see?"

Isiah regained control of himself. "I saw . . . him killing Raiders." His insides felt hollow as the shock subsided. He knew who Gaelon had killed.

Tessa's parents.

"Is it true?" he asked. "The things I saw, I mean. How do I know it's not my imagination?"

"The visions don't lie," the guide replied. "There's a reason shamans forbid eavesdropping."

Isiah swung another fist at the boy.

"Relax." He raised his arms. "We'll go find the Sunstone fragment now."

Isiah's glared at the guide. He cursed himself for not listening to his gut. *How am I going to tell Tessa?*

"You don't have to," the guide said.

"Did you just . . ."

"I told you, I'm *you*. You can't keep secrets from me."

Isiah waved the boy away. "Whatever. Just take me to the Sunstone fragment."

"You got it." The guide took off.

Isiah gave the apparition of Gaelon one last look, then hurried after him.

* * *

The pillar of golden light loomed beyond a ridge. Isiah craned his neck to follow it as it disappeared into the endless sky. The steady crunch of his boots on the rocky earth rang in his eardrums.

He tried to shake the visions he'd seen. The dull throbbing in his skull had subsided. A cold emptiness gripped the pit of his stomach. He shook his head, trying to clear the visions.

It can't be real. I must be imagining things.

The guide coughed.

"Don't say anything," Isiah snapped. "I don't want to hear it."

He returned to his thoughts. *Gaelon isn't like that.* He tried to convince himself that the visions weren't true.

You were wrong about Solomon, a voice in his mind said.

"We're getting close," the guide announced, snapping him from his trance. "You'd better be careful."

"What is it now?" Isiah asked. "Do you have any more tricks?"

"I wish I did," the guide replied. He reached a boulder and crouched behind it, peering at the beam of light. "Remember when I told you the Ancients left behind some surprises?"

Isiah nodded.

"We're coming up to some."

Isiah hunched over and picked his way across the rocky terrain to where the guide was crouching. Ahead of them, the crest of a hill blocked the source of the beam. A few loose stones clattered beneath Isiah's feet.

"What's on the other side?" Isiah asked.

"The Ancients called them the Awakened," the guide replied. "They're the guardians of the Sunstone fragment. Abaddon's crewmates had a fun time discovering that fact for themselves." He chuckled. "Some of them still blame the gorgons for all their missing men."

Isiah peered over the boulder to try and get a better look. The crest was empty. "Where are they?"

"Oh, they're around here somewhere," the guide replied.

Isiah checked his arm. The black venom had shrunk to half its size. "What do I have to do?"

"Touch the ruin entrance," the guide said. "Gaelon was just practice."

Isiah rubbed his temples. "Why can't I just leave now?"

"Then you won't form a connection to it." The guide tapped his head. "You have to link yourself to the Sunstone's magic, then you can find it in the real world." He stepped away. "I brought you here, like I promised. I'm not pushing my luck with the Awakened. From here on out, you're on your own."

"Wait—" Isiah started.

The guide turned and melted into the fog. Isiah swore. He pressed himself against the boulder and looked for any sign of movement. When he found nothing, he cautiously crept to the top of the ridge.

A deep canyon lay beyond, its sides rough and rocky. A river cut through it, stopping at a waterfall on the far end that poured over the canyon wall. The beam of light erupted from somewhere behind it.

Isiah squinted. No sign of life. He emerged from cover and began to pick his way down the canyon's side. Boulders gave him ledges to stand on, and he hugged the sloping wall to keep his balance. The river snaked below, tantalizingly close.

He reached the bottom of the canyon and sucked in a breath. From inside, the twin walls blocked off the outside world, leaving only a narrow crack of foggy sky above. The faint roar of cascading water met his ears from the other end. The rest of the canyon lay eerily silent.

Isiah followed the canyon wall, keeping to the cover of craggy boulders and clumps of bushes. A fine mist billowed from the waterfall, covering everything in a thin layer of moisture.

Isiah swallowed. He became aware of how parched his mouth was. The long hike had left his throat scratchy and dry. He cast a glance at the water. The bank was empty, devoid of rocks or bushes that would give him cover.

Forget it, he thought. *I'll be out of here soon.*

He kept moving. The mist in the air seemed to mock him. His body cried out for water. He stole another look along the canyon. No sign of life. The beam of light was still a few hundred feet away.

Fine. Keeping low to the ground, Isiah crept to the water's edge and knelt by it. The middle shone a deep blue, cutting into the rock to form a strong current, while the edges lapped against the deserted, sandy bank. Isiah plunged his hands into the cold water and took a drink.

Rocks crunched.

Isiah jumped. His head snapped around as he scanned for the source of the noise. More rocks clattered somewhere to his right. Isiah froze like an animal caught in panic. A million possibilities passed through his head. The footsteps came closer—slow and heavy.

Isiah tore himself from his trance. If he tried to make it back to the bushes and find a place to hide, whatever it was would reach him before he got there. His gaze fell to the river.

He took a deep breath and plunged beneath the surface. The cold shocked his skin. He ignored the sensation, diving into the middle of the river and grabbing the rocks at its bottom. A stream of bubbles rose around his face.

A shadow fell across him. Isiah risked peering up. The water blurred his vision. A tall, dark shape walked along the riverbank. It lurched with each footstep, arms swinging in an awkward, distorted gait.

Isiah pressed himself against the riverbed. The current tugged at his robes, trying to dislodge him. He followed the towering figure with his gaze. It slowly strode past where he was hiding.

Isiah gritted his teeth against his burning lungs. Floating particles of sand stung his eyes. He prayed the rising bubbles wouldn't betray his position.

The figure carried on down the canyon. Isiah waited as long as his screaming lungs would allow, then kicked off the river floor. He broke the surface and sucked in a breath, gasping.

Without waiting to catch his breath, he scrambled out of the water and ran to the cover of the nearest boulder. He paused, waiting to see if the figure would return to investigate the noise. Nothing appeared.

Isiah held a hand to his chest. Water streamed from his sodden robes, and his hair was plastered to his forehead. He pushed it out of his eyes. The guide's words rang in his ears. *The Ancients called them the Awakened.*

Isiah picked his way across the few hundred feet that separated him from the waterfall. As he approached, the roar of gushing water intensified, spraying him with mist. He hoped the noise would mask the sound of his movements.

Another figure moved in the fog on the other side of the bank. Isiah blinked the water out of his eyes and squinted. It stood twice his height, partly stooped and sporting long, disjointed limbs. Isiah gulped.

He cautiously advanced to the beam of light, keeping the waterfall between him and the creature. Behind the waterfall stood a tall stone door. Part of it had collapsed, leaving a gaping hole in its wake. Thick cracks crisscrossed the remainder.

This is the place, Isiah thought. The darkness seemed to beckon him, reeling him in with the same magnetic allure that he'd felt from Abaddon's Sunstone.

Isiah wiped his palms on his robes. He prepared himself for what he was about to do. A quick glance at his arm revealed the venom slowly fading, his time slipping away . . .

He placed his hands on the ruin's door. An electric shock coursed through his body and the world faded to white.

Images streamed through his mind's eye, flashing past faster than he could take them in. A towering city, ringed by huge obelisks and looming over the desert dunes. Scores of eagles, seeming to blot out the sky.

Isiah clenched his teeth as a searing pain gripped his skull. More images flooded his brain. A golden disk, adorned with intricate carvings. It caught the light of the twin suns and shone with a radiance so bright it forced him to squint.

Isiah wobbled. His hands felt glued to the ruin door. The visions continued. Thousands of soldiers marched in unison, adorned with gleaming plate armour. Dragons wheeled overhead through the Badlands sky. The proud banners of Paradon fluttered in the breeze.

A cold dread welled in Isiah's chest. Soldiers yelled as a blast of light erupted from the horizon. It struck their ranks and swept through them. Hair singed. Flesh melted. The ground cracked and buckled. Their screams stabbed Isiah's head like white-hot knives.

The beam split the sky in two, arcing across the heavens. Dragons exploded into flame and dropped like falling comets. The clouds seemed to catch alight.

Soldiers broke rank and scattered into the wilderness. From atop its perch in the city, the Sunstone seemed to sing.

Then the pain grew too much and Isiah slipped beneath its grip.

Highland Nomads

TESSA CREASED HER BROW. "Is he going to be okay?"

She sat with Isiah's head on her lap. Beads of sweat formed on his pale face, and his forehead was hot to the touch. He kicked in his sleep and mumbled.

"The venom is working its way through his system," Gaelon said. "All we can do is watch."

Overhead, the first traces of dawn hung on the horizon. Tessa's legs ached from sitting on the hard ground, but she hadn't been able to get a moment of sleep. Myla sat further off, watching with a concerned expression.

"Why is he not back yet?" Tessa asked. "How long is this supposed to take?"

"Time moves differently in the spirit world," Gaelon said in a calm voice. Tessa caught the twitch of his hands as he fiddled with his turban.

Isiah groaned. His back arched as he convulsed again. Tessa grabbed his arms to try and still him. Aegon watched Isiah out the corner of her eye.

"Even Aegon can tell something is wrong," she said. "You didn't tell us it would be like this!"

Gaelon pulled off his turban and ran a hand through his hair. "He *is* taking his time . . ."

The smouldering red sun had long since set, disappearing beyond the horizon on its course to rejoin its brighter cousin. Myla's head lolled, but she snapped herself awake. The fire glowed with dull embers.

"Isn't there anything we can do?" Tessa asked. She checked Isiah's temperature for the hundredth time. Her hand came away searing hot. Sweat rolled down his pale skin.

Gaelon glanced at the emerging sun. "If he hasn't returned soon, we'll find help."

"Help? What kind of help?"

"I know a nearby camp of highland nomads," Gaelon said. "Hopefully they haven't packed up and left yet. If Isiah can't find a way out, a shaman will be able to go into the spirit world and retrieve him."

They waited, but still Isiah didn't wake. The soft colours of dawn strengthened to morning. Tessa folded her arms. "That's it. I'm tired of waiting."

"You're right." Gaelon summoned Enzo. "His condition is deteriorating."

Gaelon and Myla helped secure Isiah to Vyrro's saddle. He lay sprawled across the eagle's back, head rocking limply. Tessa bit her lip.

"Hang in there," she whispered in his ear. She hoped he could still hear her. She climbed into the saddle and took Vyrro's reins. Aegon slithered over and looked at her inquisitively.

"Aegon can follow us," Gaelon said. "The local nomads are used to dragons, so she won't spook them."

With Enzo in the lead, they took off and left the ritual site behind. Isiah kicked in his sleep. His unconscious body strained against the bonds holding him to the saddle.

They flew across the empty terrain. Gaelon leaned over Enzo's shoulders, scanning the ground. In the pale light, a few coils of smoke rose on the horizon. Tessa urged Vyrro toward it.

As they drew closer, she made out the nomad camp. A cluster of large tents, similar to Gaelon's, stood among a field of low bushes and acacia trees. A watering hole sat nearby, vibrant blue like the lake in the Hidden Citadel.

Enzo let out a bellow. The nomads below emerged from their tents and raised hands to their foreheads. Gaelon circled the camp, then descended. Aegon went after them.

Isiah groaned. Tessa hurriedly tugged on Vyrro's reins. The great bird stretched out his wings and landed amid the tents. She scrambled off and fumbled with Isiah's binds.

Myla ran over. "I'll help you."

They untied Isiah and carried him away from Vyrro. Gaelon stood by one of the tents with the nomads. Their dusty brown cloaks trailed to the floor, while strings of tooth and bone adorned their necks.

"It was foolish of you to agree to make him the brew," a woman scolded. Her dark skin was leathery and weathered, and she was missing several teeth. "I warned you how dangerous it is to the inexperienced."

"I'm sorry, Sybil." Gaelon hung his head. "I thought he would be fine."

"There's a reason only shamans drink the brew," Sybil replied. "It's to stop things like this from happening." She noticed Tessa and waved. "Bring him over here."

Tessa anxiously carried Isiah to the old woman. Sybil parted the cloth of her tent and stepped inside.

"Gaelon, get a fire going," she said. "And fetch my herbs." She turned to Tessa. "Now, let's take a look."

Tessa stepped into the tent. The sweeping material muted the sunlight from outside, rendering the interior in dim light. A few rugs lay on the dusty floor, with several dozen crates and ceramic jugs. A wide bowl, similar to the one Gaelon used at the ritual site, stood in the centre.

Myla helped her lay Isiah on one of the rugs. Sybil knelt and placed a palm on his forehead. Tessa made out her gold earrings and the rough-cut precious stones decorating her bony hands.

"He's gone deep into the trance," Sybil said. She scrunched up her face. "So deep that he might not be able to climb out on his own."

Tessa wrapped her arms around herself. "Can you help him?"

"I can pull him out," Sybil said slowly. "What's he doing there in the first place?"

Tessa wobbled. She wasn't sure how much to tell the shaman. "He's looking for some magic."

Sybil's nostrils flared. "Greed, is it?" She shook her head. "Raiders are all the same."

Before Tessa could protest, Gaelon appeared with an armful of pots. He placed them by the bowl and started a fire beneath it. Sparks flickered, then a wisp of smoke curled up to the hole in the tent's roof.

"I'll have to go inside and bring him out myself." Sybil scowled at Gaelon. "I would make you fix this mess yourself, if I didn't think you'd do more harm than good."

Myla tugged on Gaelon's arm. "I thought you said you were experienced!"

"He trained with me." Sybil waggled a finger at him. "And you're still my student."

"I warned him about the dangers," Gaelon protested. "And their reasons are important."

"Your reasons are just like all the others," Sybil said. "I've seen those skyships. We know that they're building a Sunstone. I'm guessing you just want to find the pieces before they do. You'll be bringing on a whole heap of troubles on yourself, no matter who finds it first."

Gaelon brought the ingredients to a boil and poured them into a bowl. He handed the brew to the shaman. Sybil took it and turned to Tessa.

"I want you to come with me," she said.

Tessa froze. "Me?"

"He'll recognize you," Sybil replied. "A familiar face will make the extraction easier."

Tessa hesitated. The sight of Isiah's pale, feverish form made worry claw at her insides. Her expression hardened. "I'll do it."

Sybil took a swig of the brew, then passed the bowl to Tessa. She did the same. The bitter liquid made her eyes prick with tears. Gaelon popped the stopper off a pot and dumped a scorpion onto Sybil's hand.

"I'm going to send you through first," Sybil said. "Wait for me once you wake up."

Tessa clenched her jaw. Sybil took her arm and pressed the scorpion against it. She winced as its barb sank into the soft skin of her forearm. Sybil let the scorpion sting herself, then dropped it back into the pot.

"Lie down before you pass out," she instructed.

Tessa found one of the rugs to lie on. Her head swam. Fiery pain coursed through her arm, but she held back her gasps of pain.

"Good luck," Myla said, kneeling over them. "Bring Isiah back for us."

Tessa let her head fall back, and darkness consumed her.

* * *

When Tessa awoke, the foggy, empty land of the spirit world greeted her. Her arm throbbed where the scorpion had stung her. She groaned and held her head.

"Sybil?" she called. She shakily stood and looked around, squinting into the fog. Her voice echoed across the desolate landscape.

"Over here," Sybil said.

Tessa hurried in the direction of her voice. The old shaman materialized from the fog.

"Where are we?" Tessa asked.

"A different plane of reality," Sybil replied. "Stick close. I don't want you to get lost as well."

Tessa wrapped her arms around herself. The eerie silence made goosebumps form on the back of her neck. "Where's Isiah?"

"That's what we're here to find out." Sybil paused as if listening for something.

"What are you looking for?"

"Shh." Sybil raised a finger to her lips. "Let me focus."

Tessa did as she was told. She hugged herself and rocked side to side as Sybil wandered—first in one direction, then another. The woman's forehead scrunched up as she concentrated.

"I've located his essence," Sybil said after a moment.

"How did you do that?" Tessa asked.

"Shamans learn to wander this plane," she replied. "It lets us manifest powers." She beckoned her. "Come on. We might not have much time before his venom wears off."

Tessa took off after the woman. Sybil seemed to glide through the landscape, her movements effortless and ethereal. The fog parted to let her through. Tessa found herself almost running to keep up.

"Don't listen to any voices," Sybil called over her shoulders. "We don't need any guides."

Tessa frowned. "What do you mean, *guides*?"

"They look like us," she replied. "Call them manifestations of our subconscious, if you will." She grunted. "I've never liked the mischievous buggers."

They hastened through the desolate, foggy Badlands. Tessa glanced at the black spiderweb of venom beneath her skin. Sybil's form shimmered as she strode ahead, each stride double that of her own. Tessa swore it was her imagination, but the woman's wrinkles had faded. A million questions ran through her head, but she forced them aside. All that mattered was finding Isiah.

Tessa scrambled up a crest and emerged on the edge of a wide canyon. The steady roar of a waterfall echoed from within. Sybil put her hands on her hips.

"He's nearby," she said. She scrunched up her face, then pointed to the waterfall. "Down there."

Tessa peered over the edge. A river snaked through the canyon far below. She cupped her hands to her mouth, but Sybil swatted them away.

"Don't do that," she warned. "You don't want to alert them."

"Alert who?"

"The creatures guarding the Sunstone fragment."

Sybil marched to a ridge that ran down the side of the canyon. "We can climb down to the river. Your friend must have found the ruin entrance . . . if he hasn't already been found by the Awakened."

Tessa's head swam. She tried to make sense of all the things Sybil was telling her. She hastily took the path down to the canyon floor with Sybil. Mist billowed in the air, making the rock slippery and damp.

"How are we going to get out of here?" she asked.

"I have the power to pull us out," Sybil said, "but I need time to make it work. If we're spotted, we'll have to run."

They kept to the canyon wall and approached the silvery water-fall. Tessa scanned the riverbank for any sign of Isiah. She stole another glimpse at the venom in her arm. *How much longer does he have?*

Sybil threw out a hand to stop her. Tessa jumped. Beyond, sprawled on the rocks behind the waterfall, lay Isiah.

"Isiah!" Tessa forgot her fear. Pushing past Sybil, she sprinted over to him and dropped to her knees at his side. She cradled his head and frantically searched for a pulse in his temple.

"Keep quiet," Sybil hissed.

Tessa hardly heard the woman. Her heart fluttered as she felt Isiah's weak pulse. She grabbed his wrist and checked it. A few blotches of dark venom were all that remained.

"We need to get him out of here," she said. "Hurry!"

Isiah groaned. His bloodshot eyes flickered open and stared back at her with a vacant expression.

Tessa leaned forward. "Isiah, can you hear me?"

Isiah's eye twitched. "Tessa." His voice croaked. He raised his arms and grabbed either side of her head.

Tessa jolted as a cascade of visions poured into her mind. First the Badlands and a group of Raiders, then the Royal Guards. The contents of her nightmare invaded her mind, just like she'd seen it a million times before. Her stomach churned at the all-too-familiar memory of crawling into the gutted corpse of her mother's eagle as the dragons closed in.

A man's gruff voice echoed, then the tense exchange with her trapped mother. After came the feeling of helplessness as the sabre dropped and a sickening thud sounded.

The visions should have ended. Tessa tried to pull away, but the scene kept unfolding. The face of the man who killed her parents glared at her.

Gaelon.

Tessa's heart stopped. She screamed and tore herself free of Isiah's grip. The boy's arms fell to his sides. He snapped awake as if shaken from a trance. Tessa crawled away and clutched her burning head.

A bellow echoed across the canyon.

"Get up!" Sybil ordered. "We have to leave before the Awakened find us."

"Tessa!" Isiah scrambled to his feet. Tessa curled herself into a ball, knees against her chest. Isiah shook her shoulder. "Let's go."

Tessa found it inside her to get up. The vision of Gaelon standing over her mother's corpse made her want to scream until her lungs were raw. Her entire world seemed to spin, making her dizzy and nauseous.

A second bellow sounded and a tall, gangly creature emerged from the fog.

"Run!" Sybil's shrill voice snapped her out of her shock.

The creature snarled from a gaping, toothless mouth and lumbered toward them. Several more bellows ripped through the canyon.

Tessa forced her legs to move. With Isiah on her heels, she bolted after Sybil. The closest beast crashed after them, jerking like a marionette on its twisted, spindly legs.

"We have to escape the canyon," Sybil said. Despite her age, the old shaman outpaced them.

Water exploded to their right. Tessa flinched as another one of the Awakened crashed through the river. Its skin rippled like a mix of dark obsidian and dusty sandstone. Piercing lights erupted from its hollow eye sockets.

Tessa skidded on the slippery rock. She flailed her arms for balance. Each thundering footstep behind her filled her with icy panic. More twisted figures emerged from the fog ahead.

"Use your magic!" Isiah cried. "It's stronger here!"

Tessa lashed out with her mind. A sandstone wall burst from the earth, blocking off the approaching beasts. The illusion solidified and the creatures crashed into it. Each impact sent a shock through her spine.

The figure behind them kept closing. Sybil reached the path leading out of the canyon and paused to wait for them. Tessa fought for purchase on the slick ground. Her lungs gasped for breath. She spun around and channelled her magic.

A second wall erupted from the earth. One of the Awakened lowered its head to charge through it, but the wall solidified, trapping it halfway. It bellowed in fury and lashed out with a long spike of an arm.

Tessa rubbed her temples. "I can't keep this up for long!" The trapped Awakened strained against her illusion, making her brain feel as if it was being stretched.

Sybil and Isiah clambered up the trail toward the top of the canyon. Tessa ran behind them. She clenched her jaw, fighting to hold the illusion. The walls began to flicker.

Sybil and Isiah made it to safety. With a gasp, Tessa let the illusions disintegrate and sprinted the last few dozen feet to the top of the trail. Sybil took both of their hands. Tessa caught sight of Isiah's wrist. A single vein of venom remained.

"Close your eyes," Sybil ordered. "And don't open them, no matter what. I'll draw our minds back to our bodies."

Tessa squeezed her eyes shut. Bellows erupted from inside the canyon. Rocks clattered as the Awakened climbed after them. Tessa's nails dug into Isiah's hand. Sybil muttered a string of words under her breath.

The sound of grinding stone grew closer. Each bellow made her muscles tense. Every part of her body screamed at her to open her eyes. She swore the creatures had almost reached the top . . .

A roar sounded a few feet away. Tessa screamed, then her body became weightless.

The rough, scratchy surface of a rug pressed into her cheek. She became aware of muffled voices talking. She opened her eyes a crack to see muted sunlight shining through the walls of Sybil's tent.

Tessa sat up so fast she almost passed out. "Isiah!"

Isiah stirred. He swore and clutched his head.

"You made it!" Myla cried. She wrapped her arms around Isiah's neck.

"I know where the missing Sunstone fragment is," he said in a hoarse voice.

"That was a close shave, boy." Sybil dusted herself off. "But it was another successful extraction."

Gaelon smiled. "I knew you could do it."

Gaelon. Tessa's heart dropped. The relief at saving Isiah melted away, replaced by a white-hot fury building inside her . . .

"I saw what you did," she spat.

Gaelon's smile faded. Tessa fought for words. The cold, smug expression Gaelon wore when he killed her mother was seared into her mind.

"You killed my family." Her throat tightened, making it come out as a whisper. The emotions she'd locked away in the dark recesses of her mind came flooding back. She wiped a hand across her eyes. "You stole everything from me."

"I know you must be hurt," Gaelon said. "Let me talk to you about it—"

Tessa staggered to her feet. There were so many things she wanted to say. She wanted to yell at him, to tell him about the relentless nightmares, about the years spent hiding in the alleys of Alcabaza with her brother. Somehow, Gaelon's calm, apologetic face filled her with even more rage.

Tessa stormed from the tent. Isiah called after her, but she ignored him. She had to get away. She couldn't spend another moment in front of her parents' killer without feeling like she was about to ex-plode.

She blinked back her tears and ran.

Murderer

TESSA SAT ON A BOULDER, HER KNEES DRAWN TO HER CHEST. She stared out across the Badlands. The nomad camp lay behind her, along with the tent that contained Isiah and Myla.

And the man who killed her parents.

Tessa furiously ran a sleeve across her teary eyes. A fire burned inside her. She cursed herself for running off and not giving Gaelon a piece of her mind. She'd dreamed of finding her parents' killer for so long.

Someone coughed behind her. Tessa swivelled around to see Gaelon making his way up the trail toward where she was sitting. She crossed her arms and turned away.

"I can't undo the past," Gaelon said as he approached, "but I can hope to make amends for it."

"Go away." Tessa's voice hardly sounded like her own. She wished Lazaro was by her side.

No, she thought. *You're too old to rely on him.*

Gaelon sat on a rock a few feet away. He rested his elbows on his knees and sighed. "How did I hurt you?"

"You shot down my parents," she said. "You killed their eagles. My mother was trapped. She couldn't do anything to harm you!"

Gaelon looked at his feet. "I remember that patrol," he said slowly. "I couldn't get it out of my head for months."

"Good," Tessa shot back. "How do you think I feel?"

"I don't want you to suffer any more than I've made you already," he started.

"It's too late." She whirled on him. "You don't have to live with the nightmares I do." She clenched her fists so hard she thought her nails would pierce her skin. "You ripped our life away from us!"

"I did a lot of things I regret while I was a Royal Guard," Gaelon said. "I know that *sorry* doesn't begin to cover it."

"Royal Guards don't feel remorse," Tessa snapped. "That's what Lazaro always said."

Behind her, in the nomad's camp, Vyrro ruffled his feathers. Part of her wanted to grab her eagle and fly far away.

"Do you want to know why I left the Royal Guards?" Gaelon asked.

Tessa held her tongue. She glared into the distance.

"I thought I was doing the right thing," Gaelon started. "Patrolling the border, keeping my precious Paradon safe from the hordes of vicious Raiders and thieving merchants. I saw it as my sacred duty to protect my homeland."

"By killing us?"

"The Raiders showed us no mercy when we were shot down or captured, so I figured that I should do the same." Gaelon shook his head. "Until I was ambushed. I'd pulled ahead of the rest of my patrol. I wanted to prove myself. Then a Raider gang caught me by surprise."

Gaelon unwound his turban and ran a hand through his hair. "I guided Enzo toward a valley so we could escape the Raiders. He hurt his wing in the crash. I was sure we were going to die to gorgons until a group of nomads appeared."

He paused. "They took me in. They treated my injuries and splinted Enzo's wing. When the next Royal Guard patrol came along and rescued me, they melted into the Badlands as if they had never even been there." Gaelon closed his eyes. "I realized why. They were scared of us."

Tessa refused to look at him. *He's lying*, a voice in her head told her. *He's still a murderer.*

"That experience stuck with me," he continued. "And I started to wonder if maybe we'd got things wrong about the people here. I realized I couldn't keep fighting for Paradon. But you can't just leave the Royal Guards. You swear allegiance for life."

Gaelon gestured to the camp, where Enzo was resting. "So I took Enzo and we escaped in the dead of night. I flew deep into the Badlands to become a hermit. The nomads here showed me how to survive. The spirit world helped give me answers."

"You can't take back the people you killed," Tessa said. "You'll never undo what you did to me."

"You're right." Gaelon stood. "But I can try to stop you from suffering more than you already have."

"I want revenge." She clenched her jaw. "Paradon *has* to suffer."

Gaelon shook his head. "I don't think that will make you feel any better."

"You don't know that!" Tessa jumped to her feet.

Gaelon raised a hand in surrender. "Isiah needs you," he said. "He has to recover after his journey into the spirit world. How about you come back and talk to him?"

Tessa folded her arms and sank back down onto the rock. "I'm going to stay here for a while. I have to think."

"You know it wasn't my intention to put either of you in danger…" Gaelon started.

Tessa refused to make eye contact with him. Gaelon hesitated for a moment, then she heard his footsteps as he walked away.

Tavern

"ARON!" MARIE CALLED. "THERE'S SOMEONE HERE TO SEE YOU."

Aron rubbed his eyes. He slung one leg out of the hammock and stumbled out of the house Valerie had given them. Marie beckoned him toward the open-air tent that formed their headquarters. Above, eagles circled in the pale morning sky.

Aron made it to her side. "Who is it?"

Marie pointed to an alleyway, where Heather was being escorted by two of Valerie's Raiders. She saw Aron and ran over.

"What are you doing here?" Aron asked.

"I heard about your visit to the roosts," she said.

Aron frowned. "How?"

She shrugged. "A Scavenger must have spotted you. Maybe you're not as careful as you think." She waved him away. "But it doesn't matter." She held a hand to her mouth and lowered her voice. "I know how you can destroy the storehouse."

Aron raised an eyebrow. "I'm listening."

"My Raider gang hates Mauriel as much as anyone else," Heather said. "If you find a way to destroy her only food store, the panic should be enough for us to launch an attack."

"That's what we thought," Aron replied, "but we still have to figure out how to avoid being blown apart." He told her about the beggar he'd seen.

"Poor Doug." Heather shook her head. "I warned him not to do that. He was convinced he knew where the explosives were hidden."

"What gave him that idea?" Aron asked.

"He watched us laying them in secret," Heather said. "Mauriel's Raiders dug up the plaza around the storehouse and forced us Scavengers to place the mines." She shuddered. "Some exploded while we were laying them. I lost a few friends."

Aron swore. "If you know how we can get even, I want to hear it."

"I remember where a few of the mines are hidden," Heather continued, "but I know how you can find them all." She checked over her shoulder. "Mauriel has a map."

"A map? Where?"

"She keeps it in her quarters up in the roosts," Heather said. "I heard that it shows the location of every mine, in case the Raiders ever need it. Makes sense, right?"

Aron rubbed his chin. "So how can we get it?"

"Mauriel and her gang are living in one of the taverns," Heather explained. "When they're not terrorizing the locals, they're draining the last of the kegs dry. I can arrange for my friends to let you inside."

"A stealth mission, ey?" Aron said slowly. "That could work."

"You still remember how to be a thief, right?"

Aron grinned. "It never left me."

"Good." Heather broke away. "I'll meet you in the roosts tonight."

Aron watched her go. He ran over everything she had told him. A familiar thrill bubbled inside him, just like when he used to pickpocket for Enrik's gang.

He nudged Marie. "I told you I missed Alcabaza."

* * *

Helen's eagle slipped through the night. It silently ascended on the air currents toward the roosts. Shadows shrouded the city, broken by small clusters of orange light that shone through windows hidden among the jumbled buildings. Helen guided the eagle toward one of the rooftops on the outskirts of the roosts.

"You don't have to do this if you don't want to," Aron said to Marie. The girl sat behind him, with her arms around his middle. "I could go in alone."

"No," she replied. He caught the quiver in her voice. "I want to help you."

After Helen had left, he'd told Lazaro and Valerie about his plan. They had agreed, and Helen volunteered to fly them to the roosts that night. Stealing the map was the best chance they had of undermining Mauriel's grip on Alcabaza.

As they flew, a building caught Aron's eye. It sat off to the side of the roosts, jutting from the mountainside and sporting a wide dome for a roof. Aron let out a low whistle. "That must be the observatory Edith told us about."

"Do you really think the two Sunstone fragments are inside?" Marie asked.

"I believe Edith," he replied. He felt a pang of sadness at their frantic departure. He tore his eyes away from the observatory. "But we have to deal with Mauriel first."

They approached the edge of the roosts. Helen directed the eagle to land.

"I'll wait for your signal," she said.

Aron braced himself as her eagle landed silently on the rooftop. They climbed off and he surveyed the tavern. It was built into the mountainside, with an exterior façade made of sandstone and a sloping rooftop. He recognized it as the same place that the Raiders had met before he'd been exiled.

"We'll locate Mauriel's room, sneak in, steal the map, then get out," Aron said. "Getting inside should be easy."

"Be careful," Helen warned. "If you get into trouble, I might not be able to help you. Mauriel is dangerous."

Aron grabbed the low wall that surrounded the rooftop and vaulted off. He landed silently on the street below. He paused for Marie to climb down after him, then they slipped into the roosts.

Sticking to the shadows to give them cover from any Raider sentries who might be lurking around, they followed the streets toward the tavern. They passed rows of pens with sleeping eagles. A few handlers leaned against the gates, their heads bowed as they slept.

Muffled talking and laughter wafted over from the direction of the tavern. The doors swung open as a couple of drunk Raiders staggered into the night, arm-in-arm. Aron pulled Marie into the shadows.

"Where do we go now?" she asked.

Aron spied a door embedded in the side of the tavern. A couple of Scavengers loitered nearby. Heather was among them. "There."

He hastened over. Heather saw him and perked up.

"Right on time," she said. She patted the door. "This will take you into the cellar. From there you can make your way up into the tavern and through to the rooms." Her nose crinkled. "Mauriel is using Scavengers as servants. You'll blend right in."

The other Scavengers unlocked the door. It swung open to reveal darkness. Aron thanked Heather, then entered.

A cold stone staircase led down to the cellar. Aron hugged the wall, careful not to slip on the rough-cut, uneven steps. Marie's breath tickled the back of his neck. Ahead, candlelight gave off a soft glow.

He reached the cellar. Rows of barrels were lined up against the walls, many missing their stoppers. Puddles of liquid stained the floor, and a low table was covered with jugs.

Aron grunted. "Heather was right when she said the Raiders are drinking the place dry."

Another door branched off, leading up toward the tavern itself. Aron took a breath to still his shaking hands, then climbed up it.

The light grew brighter. Talking and laughter echoed down the stairwell. The stairs made a sharp turn, and as he entered the tavern, a wave of light and sound washed over him.

A fire burned bright in the fireplace, basking the room in warmth. Raiders hunched around tables, playing cards and dice. A couple of Scavengers scurried about with handfuls of mugs. Several Raiders were slumped over, unconscious and drooling.

Marie gripped Aron's hand. They weaved through the tables, keeping their heads down to avoid drawing attention to themselves. He spotted the doorway that led further into the building.

The Raiders cheered as the door flew open and Mauriel sauntered into the room. She grinned and extended her arms. They lifted their cups as she strolled onto a small wooden stage and stopped before a podium. Her long dreadlocks—studded with dragon teeth and eagle talons—bobbed as she went.

"Today is a good day, Raiders," she announced. "The merchants stuck at the foot of the mountain have sold us a new shipment."

The Raiders hollered and clapped.

"Our storehouse is stocked to the roof," Mauriel said. "Those traitorous gangs think they can starve us into submission? The whole city will die before we do!"

Aron and Marie inched their way toward the door. He watched Mauriel out the corner of his eye. She gripped the edges of the podium and leaned forward as she spoke.

"As soon as we've cleared out the last gangs from the streets, we'll have complete control over Alcabaza. We'll rebuild the Raider's Oath, and it'll be stronger than it has ever been before."

Another round of cheering. Aron reached the doorway and paused. None of the Raiders seemed to notice him. They were all watching Mauriel.

"So drink the night away, because the city will soon be in the palm of our hands." Mauriel lifted a mug to them. "To our gang, and the future of Alcabaza!"

The Raiders gave a toast. Mauriel stepped down from the stage and headed for the doorway—walking straight towards them.

Aron twisted away so she didn't see his face. He leaned against the wall and fixed his eyes on the floor. Marie huddled next to him. His muscles tensed as Mauriel approached.

"Who told you to stop working, Scavengers?" she said. "We don't pay you for nothing."

Aron forced himself to speak. "Of course, ma'am." He prayed she didn't recognize his voice. Every muscle in his body screamed at him to run before she realized who he was. Mauriel grunted in satisfaction, then disappeared through the doorway. He breathed a sigh of relief.

Checking to make sure none of the Raiders were watching, they slipped through the door and silently hurried after her. Mauriel strode along a hall, past a row of doors. She reached a staircase at the far end and ascended. Aron wrung his hands. "She must be going to her room."

They followed Mauriel up the stairs and to the second floor. She marched down a hallway, then opened a door and vanished inside.

Aron tiptoed along the hall, passing rooms filled with sleeping Raiders, and stopped in front of Mauriel's door. He pressed his eye to the keyhole.

Mauriel stood on a balcony that overlooked the city. A few chests and bits of furniture decorated the room, along with a large bed. Aron frowned. *The tavern never used to look this fancy.*

"How are we going to get the map?" Marie whispered. "Do we wait for her to go to sleep?"

"That will take too long," he replied. He watched as Mauriel left the balcony and stepped through a door into a washroom. Aron heard the clunk of a pump, followed by water filling a basin.

"Now's our chance," he said.

Marie gulped.

Carefully, Aron turned the handle and slipped into the room. The balcony door was open, letting breaths of cold wind ruffle the curtains. Aron scanned the room for any sign of the map.

It must be somewhere safe, he thought. Remembering his years of thieving, he quickly creaked open a couple of chests, then checked the writing desk. No sign of it.

"Aron," Marie whispered. "Over here."

Aron hurried to her side. She crouched beside the bed. A box poked out from underneath it. Aron pulled it out and lifted the lid. A rolled-up scroll was nestled inside. He unfurled it.

A diagram filled the scroll, drawn like a grid. He made out the storehouse in the centre, with the plaza and fence around it. A series of dots filled the diagram—the mines. He grinned. "This is it."

The pump creaked and the water stopped. Aron quickly tucked the scroll into his robes to hide it, then shoved the box back under the bed. His smile faded as the washroom door swung open and Mauriel appeared.

She spotted Aron and froze.

"What do you think you're doing in here?" she snapped. "Scavengers aren't allowed in these rooms."

Aron's eyes flitted to the door. Marie's fingers dug into his arm. "Sorry, ma'am," he mumbled. He inched toward the door.

"Wait," Mauriel said slowly. "I know you. You're Enrik's old Scavenger." Her eyes narrowed. "And Lazaro's."

Aron swore under his breath. He forced himself to stand tall. "And what about it?" He tried to hide the uncertainty in his voice.

"If you're back . . . that means Lazaro's here, too." Mauriel chuckled. "Tell me, Aron, where's he hiding? I'll have his head delivered to my door. I still haven't forgiven him for stealing that dragon. I'll turn the whole city upside down if I have to."

"You already have," Aron said. "You won't get away with controlling the roosts for much longer."

Mauriel smirked. "Alcabaza is mine. You're not here to kill me. Lazaro would never send you to do his dirty work." She cocked her head. "So what brought you here?"

Aron adjusted his robes. He resisted the urge to glance at the box under Mauriel's bed.

"It doesn't matter," Mauriel said. "The game is up, now. The entire tavern will storm this room at the click of my fingers."

"Nice try, Mauriel." Aron heard his voice quiver. "You don't scare us."

Mauriel laughed. "I have plans for Alcabaza," she said. "And I won't let the likes of Lazaro ruin it." She gestured to the room. "Do you like how I've decorated the place? The townsfolk have some nice furniture. They're more than happy to trade it for their weekly rations."

Aron turned up his nose. "What sort of sick scheme have you dreamed up now?"

"Alcabaza needs a leader," Mauriel said. "We were too weak and disorganized. That's what killed the Oath. The people here need someone who can take the reins and keep the Raiders in check."

He scoffed. "And I suppose you think that's going to be you."

Mauriel drew her sabre. "Exactly." She cupped a hand to her mouth. "Guards!"

Movement stirred in the other rooms. Mauriel moved to block the doorway. Aron grabbed Marie's hand and dragged her in the only direction left.

Toward the balcony.

Aron threw the curtains aside. The balcony hugged the front of the building, only a few feet across. Beyond the low wall, a sheer drop awaited them. Aron swore and searched for an escape.

"You're cornered," Mauriel taunted. She drew her sabre. "Nobody will save you now."

The tavern roof jutted overhead. Wobbling his arms for balance, Aron climbed onto the low wall and grabbed the overhang. Marie scrambled after him. They pulled themselves onto the sloping roof as footsteps thundered in the hall and Raiders reached Mauriel's room.

Mauriel stormed onto the balcony and lashed out with her sabre. Aron pulled himself out of range. Marie squeaked in panic. He caught her arm and pulled her up.

"After them!" Mauriel snapped.

Aron scrambled up the roof as the Raiders started to climb. He dug his fingers into the dust-coated shingles. Ahead, the roof met the sheer mountainside, sweeping up to its flat, tabletop peak.

"You're only making this harder on yourself," Mauriel called.

Aron drew his sabre and swung at the pursuing Raiders. They swore and hesitated. Aron fought to keep his balance. If he lost his footing, he'd plummet to the ground far below. Marie's panicked breaths sounded beside him.

"Aron." She stared at him with wide eyes. "Where are we going?"

"Hold on," he said. "You have to trust me."

Aron scanned the darkened roosts. The lights emanating from the tavern windows illuminated Mauriel on the balcony, casting a giant shadow on the ground below. He frantically waved his arm in the air.

The Raiders drew closer. Aron aimed a kick at one. His foot connected with the man's knuckles. The man swore and pulled his hand away.

"There's nowhere to run!" Mauriel yelled. "You're only delaying the inevitable."

Aron risked letting go of the roof to wave both hands. A dark shape flickered in the air above the roosts. The Raider he'd kicked drew his sabre and pulled back his arm, ready to impale Aron's foot. His mouth twisted into a cruel smile.

A shrill cry cut the night. An eagle materialized from the darkness, wings outstretched and talons bared. The Raiders screamed and tumbled off as the bird slammed onto the roof, flapping its outstretched wings for balance. Mauriel ducked as shingles rained onto the balcony. One of the Raiders plummeted to the ground and landed with a sickening thud.

"Grab on!" Helen called.

Aron wrapped his arms around the eagle's leg. Marie did the same. The mighty bird kicked off and swivelled around to fly into the night.

Mauriel swore. A Raider threw his sabre at them, but it fell uselessly to the street below. Aron clung to the eagle's leg as it soared over the buildings and into the city. They dropped to the streets and the tavern disappeared from view.

Aron's feet hit the ground and he sprawled onto the sandstone. Marie landed beside him with a grunt. Helen's eagle landed and she jumped off.

"That was a close call," she said. "Are you alright?"

Aron helped Marie up and dusted himself off. His knees ached from the impact, and a trickle of blood seeped from a cut on his leg. "I think so. Do you think Mauriel will follow us?"

"The night should give us cover," Helen replied. "We can sneak back to Valerie's territory before Mauriel's eagles come looking for us. Do you have the map?"

Aron fished around in his robes. He sighed to find it still there. He pulled it out. Their hectic escape had crushed it against his body, but the scroll was mostly undamaged.

"Good work," Helen said. "Let's get this to Lazaro."

'Consequences'

"WE NEED TO LEAVE," ISIAH SAID. He tried to sit, but Gaelon put a hand on his chest and pushed him back onto the rug.

"You have to rest," he said.

"No." Isiah fought to get up. "I'm strong enough to fly."

"Venturing into the spirit world is no easy feat," Gaelon replied. "It would be best to stay here for a few days and recover your strength." His voice took on a grave tone. "We almost lost you in there."

Isiah slumped back, defeated. He stared at the cloth ceiling above. The faint sound of nomads talking reached his ears from outside. Tessa had visited him briefly after she stormed out, but she'd left again once Gaelon returned.

"I saw what the Sunstone can do," he said quietly. The image of the weapon splitting the sky was burned into his mind. He could have sworn the smell of charred flesh lingered in his nostrils.

"It's a powerful weapon," Gaelon replied. "Now do you see why the Ancients buried it?"

Isiah nodded. "We need to stop Abaddon from using its power." The thought of Abaddon wielding the Sunstone filled him with dread. "He'll rule the Badlands if he gets it."

Sybil shuffled into the tent. "The Badlands will be ruled by *some-one*, no matter who builds their Sunstone first," she said. "Do you think that you can bring a weapon like that to light without any consequences?"

Isiah adjusted his weight on the rug. Sybil had given him another brew to help ease the fire in his veins from the scorpion sting. When he tried to lift his arm, it flopped uselessly back onto the bed.

"Some magic is better left buried deep beneath the earth," Sybil said. "The Ancients knew what they were doing when they broke their Sunstones up and locked the fragments away. I know what your people would do with it."

Isiah shook his head to clear the images of burning dragons and melting soldiers. He remembered what Tessa had said when they first learned about the Sunstone. *Imagine what we could do to Paradon if we had a weapon like that.*

"If we don't beat Abaddon to the last piece, he'll use the Sunstone anyway," he said. "We don't have a choice."

Sybil raised her hands. "I'm just warning you, boy, the Sunstone isn't something you can use once and then hide away. What you do here will have consequences."

Gaelon cleared his throat. "I trust their judgment."

Sybil turned her attention to an assortment of herbs. Isiah propped himself up on his numb arm.

"I'm sorry I showed Tessa what you did," he said. "I shouldn't have invaded your privacy like that."

"It's alright," Gaelon replied. "Perhaps it's better she did find out. Secrets don't make for good friends."

"Where is she now?"

"She's still on the outskirts of camp."

Isiah tried to roll off the rug. "I want to talk to her."

"She needs time to think," Gaelon said. "She has a lot she'll want to work through."

Isiah shook his head. "Let me see her."

Gaelon hesitated, then opened the tent flap. Isiah awkwardly got up and staggered out of the tent. The piercing sunlight forced him to squint. He wandered past groups of talking nomads, then a group of children washing clothes in the watering hole. He spotted Tessa sitting on the edge of camp.

"Tessa." He wandered over.

Tessa twisted around as he approached. She eyed the camp. "Where's Gaelon?"

"He stayed behind," Isiah replied. He plopped himself beside her. "Are you alright?"

Tessa ignored him. "You should be resting."

"I wanted to talk to you."

"I don't want to talk," she said. She wrapped her arms around her knees, then added, quieter, "I don't know what I want."

"I'm sorry you had to learn about Gaelon's past like that." Isiah scratched the back of his neck. "I don't know what I was thinking." He paused. "I never thought Gaelon could be a killer."

"He was a Royal Guard. What do you expect?" Tessa whirled on him. "Of course he killed Raiders. He's just like the rest of them."

"I–I think he's changed," Isiah said weakly.

"Changed?" Tessa's voice grew louder. "That won't bring my parents back. That won't undo everything he put me through!"

"I didn't say it would . . ."

"You're just siding with him because he promised to teach you."

He flinched. "That's not true, Tess."

Tessa stood. "I told you not to call me that."

Isiah threw out his arms. "What does it even matter at this point?"

"It matters because only Lazaro and my parents used that name," Tessa shot back. She choked up. "It's the only thing of them I have left."

Isiah caught himself. "Tessa, I'm—"

Tessa slumped as her anger deflated. "I want to go back to Lazaro."

"What? You can't! What about the Sunstone?"

"You don't need my help to find it," she replied. "You've got *Gaelon* to help you."

Isiah caught her arm. "You can't leave now. What happened to you being too old to run to Lazaro?"

"I can't live with my parents' murderer!" She pushed him away. "You don't understand, Isiah." Her words cut into him like a knife. Tessa slipped past him, avoiding eye contact. "I need time to think."

Isiah watched her go. It pained him that she thought he'd side with Gaelon over her. Didn't she see how much he cared about her?

"Isiah, there you are!" Myla sprinted toward him. "You're supposed to be recovering."

"I had to talk to Tessa," Isiah said, still unable to tear his eyes off her.

Myla put an arm around his shoulders and started guiding him back to the tent. "You can't help anybody until you're better," she said.

Isiah let her escort him back to the tent. When they entered, Gaelon and Sybil had disappeared. Myla helped ease Isiah onto the rug that made his bed.

"That's better," Myla said. She waggled a finger at him. "Don't you go wandering off again."

Despite himself, Isiah smiled. "What are you? My doctor?"

"No, but I'll *drag* you back in here if I have to." Myla laughed. It filled him with a bubbly sensation. He hadn't heard her laugh since the night Abaddon attacked the Hidden Citadel.

Myla sat back and brushed a curl of hair off her face. "Tessa's taking it rough, isn't she?"

Isiah nodded. "She is."

"I can't imagine what she's going through," Myla said. "I never knew what happened to *my* parents."

Isiah remembered her story of arriving at the Hidden Citadel. Solomon had rescued her from the merchants after they'd destroyed her home.

"After Solomon freed me, he took me in and . . . well, you know the rest."

Isiah stiffened at the mention of the man's name.

"You keep doing that," Myla said. "What's wrong?"

Isiah sighed. He debated telling her. "It's just . . . I thought Solomon was different. Nobody else understood my Mark like he did. I felt like I could tell him anything." He hung his head. "I can't believe he betrayed us like that. It feels like I can't trust anyone."

"Do you trust Gaelon?" Myla asked quietly.

"I–I don't know."

She lowered her voice. "Is that why you're having trouble with Aegon?"

Isiah remembered what Gaelon had told him while flying. *You don't trust her. Something is holding you back.*

Myla sidled closer. "Well, you can trust me."

Isiah squeezed her hand. "Thank you."

She leaned in. "You know, when you first arrived at the Hidden Citadel, Solomon told me to get close to you. I guess it was because he wanted me to try and draw you away from your friends so that you wouldn't miss them as much when they *disappeared*." Her finger traced circles on his arm. "But that's not why I did it."

Isiah's mind flashed back to their day spent flying with Solomon in the Badlands, when Myla had kissed him. His gaze flitted up to her deep chestnut eyes.

Myla's breath tickled his face. Her hand slipped beneath his collar and traced his Mark. Their foreheads touched and Isiah wrapped one arm around her body.

Their lips met and all his worries about Tessa slipped from his mind.

Tessa

TESSA TOSSED IN HER MAKESHIFT BED. HER FOREHEAD creased in her sleep. She gritted her teeth as images flashed across her dreams.

Her mother's eagle plummeted from the sky. Her heart flew into her throat as they hit the ground in a plume of dust and skidded across the empty mesa. Her throat tightened as she crawled into her eagle's corpse. Hot, putrid air invaded her nostrils. Her terrified breathing swirled in her eardrums.

Gaelon's smug, smiling face filled her with rage.

Tessa jolted awake. The soft sounds of the Badlands greeted her. She gasped for air, holding a hand to her thundering heart. She wiped the sweat from her forehead as the lingering effects of her dream faded back into the recesses of her mind.

Tessa clenched her jaw. *Another nightmare.*

She stood. Sybil's wheezing breaths echoed from the far side of the tent. Isiah slept nearby, with Myla curled up by his side. They had both been asleep by the time she returned to the tent. She hadn't had the chance to ask them what they had been doing.

Gaelon had volunteered to sleep somewhere else. The thought of sharing a tent with her parents' murderer made her feel sick. Tessa calmed her shaking hands and tugged on her collar. Her skin was slick with a cold sweat.

This is his fault. Her blood boiled. *He did this to you.*

Tessa pulled on her robes and wandered out of the tent. A few crickets chirped from the watering hole nearby. Further off, she spotted the hulking, scaly beasts that the nomads used as pack animals. They grazed on a crop of grass with beak-like mouths, the hump of their shoulders taller than her head.

She craned her neck to the sky and tried to steady her ragged breathing. The image of Gaelon floated before her mind's eye, taunting her. She squeezed her eyes shut. *Go away!* she screamed in her mind.

Even worse was his calm, apologetic expression.

He destroyed my life, she thought. *We were forced onto the streets because of him.* And after all that, he didn't even try to make excuses. He didn't argue with her or say her parents deserved it.

He just apologized.

Someone has to suffer. Tessa marched through the camp. *The nightmares will never end until I get my revenge.*

She passed the two totem-pole figures of their sleeping eagles, then Aegon and Enzo. Sybil had given Gaelon a spare tent on the edge of camp. The highland nomads had agreed to let them stay until Isiah had recovered.

Tessa approached the tent. She didn't know what she was doing, but her legs carried her there as if with a mind of their own. The image of her mother's corpse stuck in her mind. When she tried to shove it away, it refused to leave. The memory of the dead eagle's bloodied body made her throat tighten and her eyes water. She felt like she would never be able to wash off its filth.

Tessa pushed through the tent flap. Gaelon lay sleeping on a rug, his expression peaceful. Her face darkened.

It's not fair, she thought. Why could he sleep so easily after everything he'd done? Her nightmares would never give her that privilege.

Tessa's hand shakily fell to her sabre.

I have to avenge them, the voice in her head told her. *Or I'll never be free.*

Tessa slowly drew her sabre. She gripped the hilt with both hands to calm her trembling arms. She feared the rattle of the blade against the scabbard would wake him. The turmoil inside her made her want to throw up.

She pulled the sabre free and clutched it with white knuckles. The silvery moonlight shone through the open tent flap behind her, reflecting off the wickedly curved blade. Tessa raised it above her head, poised to plunge it into the sleeping man's throat . . .

Tessa hesitated. Her muscles locked, freezing her in place.

You wanted this, the voice told her. She'd spent years fantasising about finding the Royal Guard who wronged her and making him suffer. Sometimes the dream of revenge had been the only thing that kept her going on those cold nights spent in the alleys of Alcabaza.

Then why couldn't she do it?

Enzo growled a warning. Gaelon stirred and opened his eyes. He blinked and raised a hand to shield his eyes from the moonlight. "Tessa?"

Tessa remained poised, her sabre above her head.

"Put the sabre down, Tessa," Gaelon said slowly. He reached out a hand. "You know this won't help you."

Tessa wobbled, her face set in determination. "How do you know what will help me?" she spat.

"I know you must be hurt." Gaelon's voice took on that same quiet, apologetic tone that drove her mad . . .

"Stop saying you're sorry!" she yelled. She didn't care if her voice woke up the entire camp.

Gaelon sat up. "I know you want a reason to hate me," he said. "I had enough reasons to hate myself before I left Paradon. You want me to justify you getting revenge, don't you?"

"You don't know what I want." Tessa fought to keep from choking up. "I'm sick of these nightmares!"

Gaelon reached out a hand and brushed the point of her sabre away. "I know a lot about hanging onto the past," he said. "I can't tell you to let go—but you have to believe me that I don't want you to suffer anymore."

"I'll only stop suffering when I avenge my parents," she snapped.

"Will killing me make you feel better?" Gaelon asked. "Will it suddenly solve your problems? Will you find peace? Will it erase your pain?" His words hung in the air.

Tessa gripped the sabre so tightly she thought the handle would snap. Gaelon took her arms and slowly brought them down until her sabre hung uselessly at her side.

"I learned something about your people when I crashed that day," he said. "You're not senseless killers. I was wrong to fight you—so I did the only thing I could."

Tessa gritted her teeth. "I'll never forgive you."

"I'm not asking you to forgive me," Gaelon said. "Not for my sake, at least. I'm asking you to do it for yours."

Tessa whirled away and marched from the tent. Tears welled in her eyes, but she angrily wiped them away. She sheathed her sabre and ran to Vyrro.

I have to leave. She couldn't stomach being around Gaelon for a moment longer. She had to go back to Lazaro. He would know what to do.

Vyrro startled awake. Tessa tightened the straps of his saddle and climbed on. He shook his head and his neck feathers puffed up.

"Come on," she ordered. "We're going."

Vyrro protested, but he took flight. Tessa lowered her head and they ascended into the night together.

All That Matters

ISIAH STIRRED. HE OPENED ONE EYE A CRACK, straining his ears for what had woken him. Myla lay curled against him, her head resting on his chest. Isiah glanced around the tent. Tessa's rug lay empty.

She must have gone on another one of her night-time walks, he thought.

The thought sent a pang of guilt through Isiah's chest. He played over their argument in his mind. *I should apologize for upsetting her.*

Carefully slipping out from beneath Myla's head, he dragged himself to his feet and stumbled from the tent. Fatigue gripped his muscles from his time spent in the spirit world. He dragged his legs along like dead weights.

The moonlight cast a silver sheen across the nomad camp. Isiah searched for any sign of Tessa. He knew she couldn't have gone far.

Aegon lay curled asleep on one side of the camp, near Enzo. Gaelon had taken a separate tent. *To give Tessa some space*, he'd said.

Isiah's gaze drifted to the sleeping figure of Myla's eagle. He froze when he noticed Vyrro missing.

No, he thought. He hurried over as fast as his tired legs would allow. *She can't have gone. Vyrro must have wandered off.*

He skidded to a halt by Myla's eagle. Vyrro's tracks were etched in the dirt. There was no sign of the bird.

"Aegon," Isiah hissed. The dragon grumbled and one eye slid open. He tugged on her wing. "Get up."

Aegon raised her eel-like head and huffed. Twin plumes of smoke and mucus erupted from her nostrils. She unfurled her tail and reluctantly dragged herself to her feet.

"I know you don't want to," Isiah said. "But this is important."

Aegon tilted her wing and let Isiah climb onto her back. He gripped her with white knuckles, willing his fatigued body to hold on. Every movement felt clumsy.

"Take it nice and slow," he said, more to himself than to her.

He spurred Aegon into motion. The dragon relented, lumbering through the camp and taking flight. Isiah tried to figure out which way Tessa had gone.

She must be going to Alcabaza, he thought. He steered Aegon in the direction he thought the city was. The stars above gave him a rough idea of where to head. He leaned forward, hugging Aegon's frill as she powered them through the sky.

The minutes ticked past. Isiah didn't know how long it had been since Tessa left, but he knew he would catch up with her. Dragons flew faster than eagles.

A shape materialized in the distance. Isiah leaned forward. He balanced his weight on Aegon, all too aware of the empty drop on either side of him. The shape was too small to be a skyship. He cupped a hand to his mouth and yelled Tessa's name. His voice came out hoarse.

"Leave me alone, Isiah!" Tessa's voice drifted back.

Isiah urged Aegon forward. The dragon easily closed the gap. Tessa kept her eyes fixed ahead.

"I can't stay with Gaelon any longer," she yelled. "You'll have to find the Sunstone fragment on your own."

"Let's talk about this, Tessa," Isiah pleaded.

"I can't do this anymore!"

Aegon bore down on Vyrro. The eagle shrieked in protest and puffed up his feathers.

"Isiah!" Tessa fought to control the bird's reins.

"I want you to land," Isiah said.

Aegon forced Vyrro to fly lower. The dragon's wingspan stretched out on either side of him, preventing him from pulling away. They descended to the rocky, arid terrain below.

Tessa yelled in frustration. Vyrro landed and Aegon swept overhead, before circling to block the way.

"Stop chasing me," Tessa said. "I've made up my mind."

"Alcabaza is days of flying away," Isiah replied. "How will you reach it without any supplies?"

"I don't need supplies. I'll figure something out."

"And what about the skyships?" he said. "They're bound to spot you. I won't risk letting them hurt you."

Tessa folded her arms. "If you really cared about me, you'd let me go."

Isiah grabbed her shoulders. "Forget about Gaelon. This is about us."

Tessa averted her gaze. Isiah steadied his breathing. The hectic flight had left him dizzy. He wobbled on his feet.

Tessa caught him to stop him from falling. "You shouldn't be here."

"Me?" Isiah gave a weak laugh. "You're the one who shouldn't be here. I'll chase you all the way back to Alcabaza if I have to."

"Stop it." Tessa helped him sit. "I won't let you put yourself in danger anymore."

"Then come back with me," Isiah said.

Tessa fell silent. The wind whistled through the landscape, stirring her hair. Isiah's eyes flitted over her face.

She hugged herself. "It's my fault you saw the truth about Gaelon," she said quietly. "If I didn't pressure you into looking for the Sunstone fragment faster, you wouldn't have gone into the spirit world."

"It was my choice too," Isiah replied. He squeezed her hand. "And you saved me from it."

"You could have died." She looked at her lap. "Then what would I do?"

The adrenaline from the flight wore off. Isiah watched as Tessa's shoulders slumped. The anger left her eyes.

"Hey," he said. "We're in this together, alright? I won't put anyone else between us—dragon rider or not."

Tessa managed a weak smile.

"So, will you come back?"

She sniffed. "I guess so."

Isiah managed to stand. Tessa helped support his weight as he hobbled to Aegon. Before they parted, she pulled him into an embrace.

"You were right," she said. "I don't need to run to Lazaro."

"I'll deal with Gaelon," Isiah replied. "You don't need to talk to him if it will upset you more."

Tessa pulled away. Her expression hardened. "I'll never forgive him, you know."

"You don't need to," Isiah spoke slowly, careful not to say anything that would anger the girl. "Focus on stopping Abaddon. That's all that matters."

Tessa rejoined Vyrro and they flew after him. Isiah watched the horizon for any sign of the skyships. He tried to imagine the Sunstone's deadly beam cutting the tranquil night sky. The image of the burning Hidden Citadel was seared into his mind.

He couldn't let Abaddon get his hands on the last piece.

The Ruin

Sybil shook Isiah's shoulders. "Get up."

Isiah groggily sat up. Sunlight flooded through a widening hole in the tent roof. As he regained his senses, he realized that the nomads were dismantling the structure.

"What's going on?" he asked.

"We're packing up," Sybil replied. "We've stayed here long enough." She rolled a rug and carried it under one arm. Isiah scrambled out of the tent as the nomads dragged the material off the long wooden poles. Others carried out boxes of Sybil's things.

Isiah rubbed his eyes. Soft blue painted the heavens, the sun already creeping into the sky. Since convincing Tessa to return with him, they'd spent several more days at the highland nomad camp for him to recover.

Aegon grumbled a welcome and slithered over to him. Isiah spotted Gaelon beside Enzo. Tessa and Myla tended to their eagles. Tessa kept her back to the man.

Isiah approached Gaelon. "Are we leaving now?"

He nodded. "If you're strong enough, we can head for the ruin you found in the spirit world."

Around him, the nomads collapsed their tents and secured them to the flanks of their hulking, scaly pack lizards. The animals huffed and clawed at the ground as nomad children jumped between their backs. Isiah couldn't help but feel a pang of sadness.

"I'll miss these guys," Myla said. "I liked it here."

"It's time for them to melt back into the Badlands," Gaelon replied. "And not a moment too soon." He pointed to the sky. A few dark blobs hovered on the horizon.

"Skyships," Isiah said.

"Exactly." Gaelon slung a pack onto his shoulders. "I've gathered all the supplies we'll need to loot the ruin." He turned to Isiah. "Are you ready?"

Isiah took a deep breath to steady himself. He flexed his muscles, testing them for any weakness. The wind ran through his hair, blowing away the last of the mental fog that had lingered after visiting the spirit world. "I am."

Sybil's tent collapsed in a pile of poles. The old shaman emerged, dusting herself off. "I have one last thing for you before you leave," she said.

She shuffled to their side and pulled off one of her many rings. "While you were asleep, I returned to the spirit world," she explained. "This ring is linked to the Sunstone's magic."

She pressed it into Isiah's palm. The milky-white stone embedded in it was cold to the touch. "The stone will light up when you're near a Sunstone fragment. I made it as strong as I could."

Isiah took it and held it against his chest. "Thank you."

Sybil's voice took on a grave tone. "Remember what you saw in the spirit world, boy. The Awakened are dangerous—and that's not to mention what will happen once you bring the Sunstone to light."

"Why are you helping us?" Tessa asked. "I thought you said the Sunstone is better off buried?"

"It is," Sybil replied. "We nomads swore to protect the Badlands' secrets." She shook her head. "But we're not fighters. I trust you with it more than I trust Abaddon."

She shuffled past him and hugged Gaelon. "Look after them," she said. "And no more brews without my permission."

Gaelon returned her embrace. He chuckled. "Yes, shaman."

The highland nomads finished packing up and rallied their animals. Their lizards pitched from side to side as they walked, each footstep producing a puff of dust. A few scrawny mules and goats followed in tow. Sybil put a hand on Isiah's shoulder.

"One final piece of advice," she said. She lowered her voice. "While the Awakened slumber, their minds wander the spirit world. If you want to leave with the Sunstone fragment, *don't wake them.*"

Isiah gulped. "We won't."

"They'll sense your presence the moment you touch the Sunstone fragment. The Ancients built a failsafe into the fragment's chamber." She tapped the ring. "Place this ring inside the plinth and it will deactivate the Awakened long enough for you to escape."

Isiah turned over the ring. "Got it."

Sybil shuffled away. "There's a haboob brewing on the horizon. I can feel it. The dust will give us the perfect cover to slip away from Abaddon's skyships. Make sure you're far away from here when it hits."

Isiah climbed onto Aegon's shoulders. With Tessa and Myla on their eagles, they ascended into the sky alongside Gaelon. Isiah watched as the nomads grew smaller and smaller below. The skyships hovered in the distance, slowly drifting across the Badlands.

Gaelon cupped a hand to his mouth. "Lead the way, Isiah!" he called.

Isiah focused. He tried to imagine the canyon where the ruin was hidden. The site of his scorpion sting throbbed. The sensation grew stronger when he pointed it in a certain direction.

"I think it's this way," he said.

Taking the lead, Aegon soared over the Badlands. Isiah kept his arm extended in front of him, acting as a compass. They flew in silence. Tessa's face was set in determination. Isiah spotted the haboob Sybil had warned them about in the distance, no more than a yellow smear amid the rising heat.

They flew for a while, until a river materialized from the Badlands. It cut through the rugged terrain, then plunged into a canyon in a glittering sheet of water. Isiah's pulse quickened.

They descended toward the canyon. The roar of churning water echoed off the walls. Mist billowed from the foot of the waterfall, reflecting the light in a shimmering rainbow. Far from the foggy, barren canyon in the spirit world, greenery hugged the riverbanks.

Aegon dropped into the canyon and glided along its length. Isiah directed her to land a few hundred feet away from the waterfall. She touched down with a flurry of wingbeats on the riverbank.

Isiah jumped off. His boots crunched on the loose rocks. Vyrro landed nearby and Tessa joined him. She stared at the waterfall.

"Where are the Awakened?" she asked. "I don't see any."

Isiah studied the canyon; she was right. "They must be inside the ruin," he replied. "Sybil said they were sleeping."

Tessa's hand curled around his. "My magic might not be strong enough to help us again."

"I prepared for something like this," Gaelon cut in. He rooted around his bag and pulled out a stout crossbow. "This thing is strong enough to puncture armour. Whatever is in there doesn't stand a chance."

Isiah hoped he was right. Aegon rumbled and nuzzled him with her snout. He stroked her. "Wait here," he said. "I won't be gone long."

Leaving their dragons and eagles behind, they picked their way along the canyon toward the waterfall. As they approached, the roar of water climbed in volume until Isiah could barely hear himself think. A fine mist settled on his eyelashes and made his robes damp.

He carefully climbed the slippery rocks and made it around the waterfall. The water caught the sunlight like a prism, scattering it across the rocks . . . and the gaping doorway that led into the earth.

Isiah swallowed. The darkness seemed to draw him in with a magnetic pull. He tentatively touched the broken remains of the sandstone door, half-expecting to be greeted with more visions.

Nothing happened. Isiah stepped through the doorway and into the blackness.

Gaelon pulled a handful of torches from his bag. "These will give us a couple of hours' worth of light," he yelled over the roar of water. He struck a firestarter against one and it sprang to life. The light flickered across a damp sandstone entry hall.

Gaelon passed the torches around. Isiah raised his and wandered into the tunnel. A staircase led into nothingness. Calming his shaking hands, he ventured down it.

The footsteps of his friends echoed behind him. As they went, the waterfall's roar grew muffled. Rough, bumpy stalactites protruded from the ceiling.

"You can still see the bricks," Tessa said, her voice echoing. She ran her fingers over the grooves in the sandstone slabs that made up the wall. "This ruin has been well-preserved."

"How old do you think it is?" Myla asked.

The staircase levelled out into an open hall. Thick pillars, engraved with murals and patterns, supported an arched ceiling. Tessa craned her neck and stared at it, open-mouthed.

"Old, I take it," Gaelon said.

Doorways branched off the room, leading in several directions. Isiah slipped on the ring that Sybil had given him. He held his fist aloft and waited for it to light up. Nothing. His face fell.

"We must not be close enough yet," Gaelon said.

Tessa examined the doors. Thick sandstone blocks formed the frames, each one intricately decorated. "This place is so . . . ancient," she whispered. She turned to them. "I've never seen anything like it."

They selected the most ornate door and began down it. Rooms branched off—some blocked off with bricks, others open. Stone sarcophagi dominated the rooms.

"These must be their burial chambers," Tessa said.

They wandered through passageways, delving deeper into the ruin. Isiah searched until he lost all track of time. He strained his ears for any sound of the Awakened, but the passageways were eerily lifeless. Their torches crackled, slowly eating through their fuel. Smoke pooled on the ceiling above, staining it black. Isiah wondered how much longer they had left.

Myla caught his arm. She pointed at his hand. "Look at your ring!" she exclaimed.

Isiah checked it. He'd almost forgotten he had it. A faint glimmer played across its surface. Tessa and Gaelon crowded around.

"The Sunstone fragment must be around here somewhere," Gaelon said. "See if you can give us a direction."

Isiah slowly turned, holding the ring out in front of him. As he went, it grew dimmer. He swivelled around the other way and it grew bright again.

"This way." He took the lead. The ring's soft, silvery light danced across the tunnel walls. Gaelon fitted a bolt into his crossbow. Isiah exchanged glances with Tessa. Her hand rested on the hilt of her sabre.

The light guided Isiah down the tunnel. The sandstone bricks melted into one another as the tunnel began to warp. Its square sides smoothed out to form a natural cave. The faint trickle of water echoed from ahead.

Isiah stopped before a sheer drop. He leaned over and tried to spy the bottom. The ring's light reflected off water far below.

"It looks like an underground river," Tessa said. "It must have eroded this whole chasm."

"How are we going to get down?" Myla asked.

Gaelon fished around in his bag. "I've got us covered."

He produced an armful of rope, then let one end drop into the chasm. He took a stout hammer and secured it to the rock with a metal peg.

Isiah watched the rope swing in empty air. The subterranean river snaked along, winding out of sight. The smooth chasm walls were painted in bands of orange and yellow. Gaelon secured two more ropes and let them drop.

"Strap yourselves in," he said. He handed a pair of harnesses to Isiah and Tessa. "We'll rappel to the bottom."

Isiah clipped the harness on and secured himself to the rope, then handed his torch to Myla.

Gaelon went first, leaning back and then walking down the smooth chasm wall. Isiah copied him. The rope went taut and he dug his boots into the rock as best he could. He hoped the metal pegs would be enough to take their weight.

"It's just a short climb," Gaelon called. His voice bounced off the walls.

Isiah gripped the rope with both hands as the harness cut into his body. He grunted with the effort. The seconds seemed to drag on.

Tessa swore and fumbled with her rope.

"Take it easy," Gaelon warned.

"I'm fine," she said. Her body twisted as she fought to regain control.

"Let me help you." Gaelon kicked off the rock and landed closer to her.

"No." Tessa pulled away. "I don't need your help."

Isiah hesitated, unsure whether to say anything. His muscles strained from gripping the rope.

"Your harness is twisted," Gaelon said. "Let me untangle it. You have to trust me."

Tessa swatted him away. "I said I'm fine!"

Her foot slipped. She gasped and clung to the rope as she slammed against the wall. The metal peg creaked in protest.

Gaelon lunged toward her and wrapped an arm around her middle. Holding Tessa against his chest, he gripped the rope with his spare hand and rappelled toward the ground.

Isiah hurried after them. When he reached the bottom, he unclipped himself and rubbed his sore arms. Tessa pulled away from Gaelon.

"I would have been fine on my own," she snapped.

"You were in trouble, and I didn't want you to get hurt," Gaelon said. He shook his head. "Wait here while I help Myla."

Tessa unclipped her harness and let it drop. She faced away from them and crossed her arms. Isiah tentatively put a hand on her shoulder.

"He's looking out for you, you know," he said.

Tessa sighed. "I don't want to talk about it. Let's just find the Sunstone fragment and get out of here."

They waited until Gaelon had helped Myla rappel down, then followed the subterranean river. The cold water lapped against Isiah's chest, seeping into his robes and chilling his skin. Stalactites hung from the ceiling like crooked teeth.

He used Sybil's ring to light the way. Gaelon held their only torch—they'd been forced to leave the others at the top of the chasm. It gave them just enough light to see where they were going.

"We must be close," Gaelon said.

They waded through the river until they reached a bank. Another doorway was carved into the rock. Two statues stood guard on either side, their features scuffed with age. Isiah pointed the ring toward it and the crystal glowed even brighter. His breath escaped him in a rush.

"This is it."

Failsafe

Isiah cautiously approached the door, squinting into the darkness. A single thought played on his mind.

Where are the Awakened?

Murals decorated the interior of the room, depicting tall figures in various poses. More thick pillars held up a curved ceiling. Isiah quelled the butterflies in his stomach. The Sunstone fragment seemed to beckon him from somewhere beyond.

They wandered through the room. Isiah's gaze flitted over the murals. The figures sported long, spindly legs that supported their tall bodies. Their stretched arms ended with sharp points. Toothless mouths gaped wide. He gulped.

Tessa drew her sabre. She gave him a knowing look. Isiah put a hand to his ear, listening for any noises coming down the tunnels.

Gaelon adjusted his grip on his crossbow. He narrowed his eyes. "Where are they?"

They passed more murals. Sybil's ring led them on, past doorways filled with sarcophagi. Isiah lifted the ring to get a better look at one of the figures embedded in the wall.

"Isiah," Tessa whispered.

Isiah hardly heard her. The figure seemed to protrude from the wall, as if it was embedded and not carved. He fought the urge to reach out and run his hand over it.

The figure twitched.

Isiah stifled a cry. Gaelon grabbed him and dragged him into a doorway as the figure's leg ripped free from the wall. The scrape of stone echoed through the tunnel. Isiah crouched behind the doorway, clutching the ring to his chest to dim the light.

A thud sounded, then another. The scraping stopped as the creature finished pulling itself free. A low, guttural moan made Isiah's skin crawl. Tessa's shallow breathing swirled in his ear. Myla clamped a hand to her mouth.

Isiah's muscles tensed as the Awakened's slow, heavy footfall sounded on the other side of the wall. From his position, he could peer through the open doorway to see a sliver of the tunnel. Three orange beams of light illuminated it.

The freed Awakened stepped into view. Isiah held his breath. The light he'd seen shone from the creature's face. It walked with the same jerky, awkward motions that he'd seen when in the spirit world. He prayed the creature wouldn't turn around.

The seconds ticked past. The Awakened hobbled away from them along the length of the tunnel. The light from its face grew dimmer.

"What do we do now?" Tessa hissed. "It's going the same way we are."

Isiah racked his brains. He sensed the Sunstone fragment further down the tunnels. It seemed to reach out to him, reeling him in . . .

"We have to follow it," he said.

"What? Why?"

"It's heading toward the Sunstone," he replied. "I–I can feel it."

"If you're sure about this . . ." Gaelon said. "But we can't use Sybil's ring. The light will alert it."

Isiah stuffed the ring into his pocket and they were plunged into darkness. Isiah felt his way into the tunnel. The faint light from the Awakened shone further down.

"What if it turns around?" Tessa hissed.

"Can't you do anything with your magic?" he asked.

"What am I supposed to do?" She paused. "Wait, I've got an idea."

Tessa scrunched up her forehead and a cloud of darkness materialized around them, swirling like a thick fog. Isiah pulled out Sybil's ring. The darkness smothered its light.

"Good thinking," Gaelon said.

Tessa grunted.

They crept along the tunnel, following the Awakened's jerky silhouette. Isiah wrung his hands. He prayed the other Awakened wouldn't be woken by their presence. Tessa grimaced as she maintained the illusion around them.

The Awakened they were following stopped at a doorway. Intricate lines and markings covered its sandstone surface, and a round hole was set into the wall beside it. Isiah held his breath as the Awakened inserted its long arm into the hole and the door slowly ground open.

Isiah's muscles tensed. The Sunstone fragment called him from within. The creature took a few lurching steps into the room. Myla gripped his arm. Sybil's ring glowed so hot it burned his finger.

The Awakened's light washed over the Sunstone fragment. It sat atop a stone plinth in the centre of the room, glowing with a warm gold colour.

"What now?" Tessa whispered.

Isiah gulped. He waited for the creature to turn around. It stood in front of the fragment, motionless.

"Do we wait until it leaves?" Myla asked.

"What about the door?" Tessa replied. "It might lock the room behind it." She rubbed her temples. "I can't hold this illusion for much longer."

"Maybe I can sneak inside," Isiah said.

"What? No way. It'll see you."

"We have to do something." Isiah fought to keep his voice under control. The Sunstone fragment commanded his attention. Visions from the spirit world lingered in his mind. He became aware of the other Awakened sleeping in the walls, their minds roaming the spirit world, waiting for someone to touch the Sunstone fragment and bring them to life . . .

Isiah's gaze fell to the base of the plinth. There was an indent in the stone, just like Sybil had told him about.

The failsafe.

Isiah broke away from his friends and crept toward it.

"Isiah!" Tessa hissed. Isiah ignored her. She swore and cast her illusion to follow him.

Isiah slipped through the open doorway and approached the plinth. The Awakened stood hunched, its back turned to him. Despite its rounded shoulders, the creature towered over his head.

Isiah fixed his eyes on the indent in the plinth. The light erupting from the creature's face reflected off the Sunstone fragment, filling the room with a golden hue. Its deep, slow breathing made Isiah's hair stand on end.

He carefully slipped off Sybil's ring. To fit it into the plinth, he'd have to reach through the creature's sharp, angular legs. They shone like smooth marble, glossy black like obsidian.

The Awakened adjusted its footing. Isiah slowly extended his arm, reaching toward the plinth. Beads of sweat ran down his forehead. His arm trembled so much that he feared he would bump into the Awakened's leg and alert it.

His hand left Tessa's illusion and the ring's piercing light flooded the room.

The Awakened bellowed and whirled around. Isiah scrambled away to avoid being impaled on its spear-like feet. The ring flew from his hand and clattered across the floor.

Tessa's magic evaporated, leaving him exposed. The Awakened loomed over him, pinning him down with its empty gaze. He raised a hand to shield himself.

Gaelon leapt from cover and raised his crossbow. A bolt whistled through the air. It struck the Awakened's chest and left a dent. The creature snarled and spun on him.

Isiah scrambled to his feet and drew his sabre. The beast's cavernous mouth dropped open and it let out a blood-curdling bellow. The tunnels came to life.

Isiah's heart skipped a beat. Gaelon swore and loaded another crossbow. Tessa turned and threw up an illusion wall to block off the tunnel.

"I can't hold this for long!" she cried.

The echo of scraping stone reverberated down the tunnels as the Awakened ripped themselves free from their murals. The one that Gaelon had shot lashed out at Isiah with its arm. Isiah leapt aside to avoid it. He hit the ground and rolled. The impact sent a shock through his forearms. He scanned the floor for the ring.

Gaelon fired another bolt. This one ricocheted off the creature's shoulders. It shrugged off the impact and spun around. Isiah's friends scattered as its arm struck the stone where Gaelon's head had been moments earlier. A plume of dust and rock exploded from the impact site.

"Get to cover!" Gaelon ordered. Myla grabbed Tessa and they scurried to the far side of the room. Tessa's face contorted as she held the illusion. Footsteps thundered down the passageways as the rest of the Awakened closed in.

The attacking creature swung its arm in Isiah's direction. He staggered away and held out his sabre. He aimed a strike at its mouth. The blade missed and glanced uselessly off its stone face. Gaelon readied another bolt.

Isiah spotted the ring on the floor. The Awakened moved to corner him. Its right arm flashed through the air. Isiah pulled away and it missed him by inches, slamming into the wall. He tried to duck beneath its legs, but something caught his robes.

He twisted around to see the Awakened's arm impaling the material.

The creature seemed to smile. It raised its left arm and stood poised, ready to drive the long spike through Isiah's chest. Its gaping mouth filled his vision, burning like a red-hot furnace. Isiah braced for the inevitable.

A bolt struck the Awakened's head and broke off a chunk of its cheek. It bellowed and flinched as if in pain. Isiah seized the distraction. He plunged his sabre deep into the creature's throat. Its bellow turned to a scream.

The Awakened reeled away. One of its feet hit the ring and launched it across the room. Isiah threw himself toward it.

"My illusion is breaking!" Tessa yelled. Her face twisted in pain. The wall blocking the tunnel flickered.

Isiah scrambled across the floor. He fumbled for the ring and his fingers closed around it. The attacking Awakened thrashed around with jerky, distorted movements. It grasped at the sabre protruding from its throat. Isiah dodged past it and made a mad dash for the plinth.

Tessa's wall dissolved. A flood of living statues stampeded toward them. Myla screamed. Isiah collapsed in front of the plinth and jammed the ring into it.

Their attackers froze. An explosion ripped through the room as the closest one blew apart. Dust and chunks of rock pelted Isiah's shoulders. Isiah waited until the dust had settled before slowly raising his head.

The remaining crowd of Awakened were petrified mid-lunge. The lights in their eyes and mouths were dark. The closest one was frozen mere feet away, poised to drive its arm into Isiah's chest. All that remained of the beast that had attacked them was a crumbling pile of obsidian. Isiah's sabre lay in the middle of it, the blade tinged red with heat.

Isiah gasped. He dragged himself to his feet and faced the motionless crowd.

"It worked." Tessa laughed.

Isiah rubbed his ringing ears. The sudden silence made him aware of the frantic thump of his heart. He scooped up his sabre and turned to the Sunstone fragment.

It sat on the plinth, adorned with the same lines and carvings he'd seen on Abaddon's fragments. He reached out and touched its warm surface. It seemed to hum with a life of its own. His friends crowded around. Isiah felt Tessa's hand curl around his. He tried to speak, but no words came.

Stone crunched behind them. Isiah whirled around, his sabre at the ready. Gaelon raised his crossbow.

Sybil shuffled between the lifeless Awakened. Isiah lowered his sabre. "Sybil?" he asked. "What are you doing here?"

Sybil gave them an apologetic look. Isiah's smile melted as Abaddon stepped into view, the tip of his sabre pressed against her back.

"Hello, Isiah," he said.

Monster

"I TOLD YOU WHEN I SPOKE WITH YOU ON MY FLAGSHIP," Abaddon said, "I *will* finish my Sunstone, whether you help me or not."

"How did you find us?" Tessa snapped.

"When I saw a pair of dragons, I knew it had to be you," he replied. "I had my crewmates follow you at a distance and see where you landed." He motioned to Sybil. "I took a detour myself to pick up a nomad."

Isiah balled his fists. "What did you do to them?"

"Nothing, yet," Abaddon said. Around him, a dozen crewmen picked their way past the Awakened. "When I threatened to destroy them with my fleet, their shaman accompanied us willingly."

"You won't take the Sunstone fragment." Tessa puffed up her chest.

Abaddon laughed. "You don't have a choice. My crewmates outnumber you, and your dragons can't help you down here." He gripped Sybil's collar. "Fight us and she dies."

The crewmates advanced. Isiah's nostrils flared. He gripped his sabre hilt so tightly he thought it would break. He desperately searched for a plan.

"One step closer and I'll pull out the ring," Tessa announced. "The Awakened will come back to life."

Abaddon chuckled. "You'd die too. You're not that reckless."

Tessa narrowed her eyes. "Try me."

"Tessa, don't." Isiah put out a hand. "He's right."

Abaddon nodded to him. "Smart boy."

The crewmates pushed past them and pulled the Sunstone fragment off the plinth. They wrapped it in a cloth, then placed it inside a crate and carried it to Abaddon.

"This will complete my collection," he said. "Thank you for leading us to it."

"You're a monster," Myla spat.

"If that's what it takes to save my people and take revenge on Paradon, so be it," Abaddon said coldly. His crewmates carried the crate with the Sunstone fragment down the tunnel and out of sight. More crewmates produced a long metal lever.

"I learned a lot about these creatures from looting other archaic ruins," Abaddon continued. He ran his fingers down one's face. He stood nearly as tall as the beast itself. "While inactive, they're in stasis. Until they realize the truth, if you remove that ring and they awaken, they'll still think the Sunstone fragment is in there." He smiled. "With you."

The crewmates fitted the metal lever into the hole beside the door. Isiah's eyes widened as he realized what they were going to do.

"You called me a monster," Abaddon said slowly. His expression hardened. "I'll prove you right."

Sybil gasped as Abaddon shoved his sabre into her back and it burst through her chest. Isiah froze as he shoved the woman and she collapsed into the room. Abaddon flicked the blood off his sabre and motioned to the crewmates. They turned the metal lever and the door began to grind shut.

Gaelon roared and fired his crossbow. Abaddon ducked as the bolt flew overhead. Gaelon vaulted over the plinth and sprinted toward the rapidly closing door. The crack narrowed and the door slid shut.

Gaelon slammed his palm against the stone. "Damn you!" he spat. He dropped to Sybil's side and cradled her head. The shaman wheezed as blood oozed from the hole in her chest.

"Is there anything we can do?" Myla asked.

Gaelon shook his head. Sybil clutched his hand as the colour drained from her face. Isiah watched helplessly as the old woman's life slipped away. Gaelon closed his eyes as Sybil's body went limp. The light from the ring flickered.

"Abaddon is carrying the Sunstone fragment out of the ruin," Gaelon said. "The ring will start going dark." He scooped up the remains of his smouldering torch. "We need to find a way out of here before we run out of light."

Tessa felt the edges of the door. "There has to be a way to open it from the inside," she said. "Right?"

Swallowing his panic, Isiah examined the walls. Gaelon rooted around his bag and pulled out the hammer that he'd used to secure the ropes they'd rappelled down. He gripped it with white knuckles and struck the door. Each impact echoed across the room.

"It's too thick," he said after a minute. "The hammer will break before I get anywhere."

"What if we use the Awakened to get out?" Myla asked. "They can open the door, right?"

Gaelon gestured to the frozen figures trapped in the room with them. "They'll rip us to shreds before we can escape."

Isiah felt his way along the wall, probing for any weaknesses. He tried to fight the growing sense of hopelessness. The shadows lengthened as Sybil's ring lost its light.

The rush of water caught his attention. He pressed his ear against the wall. "I hear something!"

Gaelon and the others rushed over.

"It sounds like the subterranean river," Gaelon said. "It might have eroded the wall enough for us to get through."

Isiah stepped aside as Gaelon let out a guttural yell and slammed his hammer against the wall. The veins in his forearm bulged as he attacked it, over and over. His voice echoed through the room. The sandstone cratered and cracks snaked across it.

Water began to seep through. Gaelon fell to his knees and ripped the rubble away. The trickle of water intensified into a gushing torrent. Gaelon's chest heaved and he dropped the hammer.

"You were right," he said. He wiped a hand across his bright red forehead and calmed himself. "Sorry."

"How are we going to get through?" Myla asked.

"I'll go first and see if I can find where it leads," Gaelon said. "Then you can follow."

"Wait." Tessa held up her hands. "What if we get stuck? We could drown!"

"Do you see any other options?" he shot back. His voice took on a softer tone. "I'll go with you if you're worried."

Tessa folded her arms. "I didn't mean that I needed your help."

"Whoever goes last will have to take the ring with them," Gaelon said. "It's our only source of light."

Isiah cast a nervous glance at it. Shadows cloaked the corners of the room as the Sunstone fragment grew more distant.

Gaelon sucked in a breath and disappeared through the hole. Isiah anxiously waited. The water seeped into his boots. Myla wrapped a curl of her hair around her finger. When Isiah met her gaze, she gave him a weak smile.

An eternity seemed to pass, until Gaelon re-emerged. Isiah helped drag him out.

Gaelon coughed. "I found a way." He spat the water from his mouth. "This section is a narrow channel, but it opens up and there's air further along. We should be able to find a path to the surface."

The light from Sybil's ring continued to dim. Isiah cleared his throat. "Who's going first?"

"I will," Myla said. She nervously shuffled toward the hole. "You're sure it's safe, right?"

"I'll be with you the whole time," Gaelon replied. "Follow me."

Gaelon disappeared through the hole. Isiah gave Myla a brief hug. "Good luck."

Myla crouched and went after the man. Her legs vanished and she was gone. Tessa stood off to the side, her arms wrapped around herself.

"I know you don't trust Gaelon," Isiah said. "But can't you see he's looking out for us?"

Tessa eyed the rushing channel. The water in the room lapped against their knees. "You know I don't like narrow spaces."

"I'll be right behind you." He tried to sound encouraging. His own heart hammered against his ribcage.

Tessa stole a look at the door. "Are you *sure* we can't take our chances with the Awakened?"

"Tess." Isiah took her hands. "You've got to trust us this time."

Tessa's face set in determination. "Okay."

She knelt and climbed through the hole into the subterranean river. Her feet disappeared as the current swept her away. Isiah hurried to the plinth and took hold of the ring. The closest Awakened was poised to strike. He prayed he'd have enough time to reach the hole.

Here goes nothing, he thought.

Isiah yanked the ring free and leapt away from the plinth. A chorus of bellows sounded as the Awakened sprang to life. The closest one jolted forward and crashed into the plinth with an explosion of dust. Isiah scrambled to his feet and sprinted toward the hole.

A clunk sounded and the door began to grind open. Orange light flooded into the room. Long arms burst through the widening crack, straining to reach him. The Awakened already inside the room charged.

Isiah filled his lungs and threw himself toward the river. A torrent of water rushed past. His heart leapt as footsteps thundered toward him. He put his head down and dived into the current.

The cold shocked his body. Bubbles streamed in front of his face. The light from Sybil's ring bounced off the rough, narrow walls of the channel. Isiah kicked, powering himself along as the torrent carried him away. A crash sounded as one of the Awakened struck the wall. Their bellows grew muffled behind him.

Isiah sped into darkness as the current carried him. He bounced against the ceiling and a bolt of pain flew through his shoulders. The river slammed him against the walls as if trying to shake the air from his lungs.

Isiah gritted his teeth against the pain and swam as hard as he could. The cold sapped the last strength from his muscles, numbing his fingers.

Hands plunged into the river. They caught him and dragged him from the torrent. Water streamed from his robes. He wiped his eyes and gulped in the thick subterranean air.

"Good work," Gaelon said. "If we're fast, we should have enough light to make it out of the ruin."

Isiah took a moment to regain his senses, then he hurried down the subterranean river with the rest of them. He fought to keep Sybil's ring from losing any more light. They found a doorway that led into the ruin and ran along its passageways. Isiah willed his tired legs to keep moving. After what felt like an age, the roar of the waterfall met his ears.

Isiah burst into the light. The waterfall greeted him. He collapsed against the canyon wall to catch his breath. As his friends emerged behind him, he put a hand to his forehead and squinted against the harsh sunlight.

Abaddon's skyships hovered over the canyon, slowly drifting away.

* * *

Isiah hastened along the riverbank. He scanned the canyon for any sign of Aegon. He breathed a sigh of relief when he saw her emerge from a cave in the wall. *Abaddon didn't spot them.*

Isiah skidded to a halt at Aegon's side. The adrenaline from their escape left him lightheaded and dizzy. He leaned against her flank for balance. Tessa and the others picked their way along the riverbank toward him.

"What are we going to do now?" Myla asked. "Abaddon has the final piece of the Sunstone."

Isiah fought the sense of despair. "We need to go after him," he said.

"How are we going to do that?" she said. "You saw his fleet."

Isiah racked his brains. "I don't know, but we can't let him use the Sunstone against the Badlands."

"You're right," Tessa cut in. "There has to be some way to stop him."

Gaelon dumped his bag at his feet. "We can't do anything right now. We have to rest."

Isiah gave into his aching limbs and collapsed on the riverbank. Tessa sat nearby with her knees drawn to her chest. He studied the sky where the skyships had disappeared.

"They'll be flying back to their flagship now," he said. "Maybe we can intercept them before they make it."

"We don't have the strength to face Abaddon," Gaelon replied. "At least now we have the element of surprise. As far as he's concerned, we're still stuck in the ruin. If he sees us, we'll lose that advantage."

"We can't hope to fight his flagship," Tessa said. "Once he finishes the Sunstone, we're done." She kicked the ground. "Don't you want revenge?"

"I do." Gaelon clenched his fist. He raised an eyebrow at her. "But I won't let it cloud my judgement."

"Maybe we can infiltrate the flagship," Isiah cut in. "If Abaddon isn't expecting us, we could sneak inside and smuggle the Sunstone out."

"He'll hardly let us walk out with the entire thing," Tessa replied.

"We only need one fragment." Isiah stood. "Think about it. If we stole it back, Abaddon's Sunstone would be unusable, and we could fly to Alcabaza and finish our own."

Gaelon scratched his chin. "The haboob Sybil warned us about is approaching," he said. "It would give us perfect cover."

Isiah paced about. His mind buzzed as their plan began to unfold. "Exactly! You can drop us off with Enzo, and then you'd stay behind to pick us up once we've stolen the Sunstone fragment."

"All this sounds good enough," Gaelon started, "but it's dangerous. Abaddon has an entire fleet. We're not in a position to fight him." He added, quieter, "And I gave that life up a long time ago."

"We don't have a choice," Isiah said.

Tessa climbed to her feet. "Isiah is right. The Badlands is depending on us."

Gaelon ran a hand through his hair. He sighed. "If you're sure about this . . ."

"When do you think the haboob is going to hit?" Isiah asked.

"It should reach us by tonight."

His brow hardened in determination. "Then let's do it."

"For Sybil," Myla added.

"Okay," Gaelon said. "For Sybil."

Aron

ARON KICKED HIS LEGS IN THE EMPTY AIR. He was perched on the edge of a sentry tower, watching the dark streets of Alcabaza. A few clusters of light illuminated the mountainside city, but most of the buildings were dark. Raiders patrolled around the border of Valerie's territory, no more than murky shadows in the dimming light.

Aron exhaled. "I never thought the city would turn out like this."

Marie and Heather sat next to him. After returning from their mission to retrieve the map, Lazaro and Valerie had begun devising a plan to turn the city against Mauriel's gang and drive them from the roosts.

"It shows you how much the Raider's Oath was holding us together," Heather said. "Without it, we're at each other's throats."

A few eagles circled in the darkening sky. Aron knew that at the foot of the mountain, merchants were selling their wares to the Raiders to transport into Alcabaza. But without access to the city, he knew that it was only a matter of time before the last bazaars ran dry and people began to starve.

"The city is falling apart." Aron watched his legs dangle. "Even if we defeat Mauriel, how are we ever going to get the Raiders to work together again?" He was reminded of what Mauriel told him in the tavern. "We need a leader."

"Valerie says she'll send her gang to fix the elevators once we have control of the roosts," Heather replied. "As soon as the merchants can get in, we won't be at risk of starving anymore."

"The merchants are only half of it." Aron gazed up at the roosts. "What's going to happen when Isiah and Tessa find the Sunstone?"

Heather shrugged. "We'll fight Paradon, I guess."

Aron had seen the Sunstone fragment Edith had given them in Lazaro's quarters. The Raiders were careful not to let word of it spread to other gangs.

"Without something to hold us together, who's to say the Raiders won't devolve into constant in-fighting?" He shook his head. "Whoever controls the Sunstone will rule the Badlands."

Marie sidled up to him. "It's better than letting Abaddon use it, right?"

"I guess." Aron sighed. "It's almost like we need him to invade just so we have something to unite us."

"We've got enough problems here," Heather said. "Leave your friends to worry about this Abaddon fella."

They fell silent. The first stars glimmered overhead, peering through shreds of pale cloud. The silhouettes of rickety sentry towers rose over the city streets. Aron made out the figures of young sentries climbing between rooftops.

"I swore to uphold the Oath when I became a Scavenger," he said quietly. "I thought it was the only way to maintain peace. After Enrik broke it by capturing Isiah, I knew I had to do something."

"Is that why you betrayed him?" Marie asked.

Aron's hand instinctively went to the scar on his chest, where Enrik had run him through. "Marked or not, Isiah was part of the Raiders.

I nearly died because of it." He lowered his head. "It almost feels like everything we did to get rid of Enrik was for nothing."

"Hey," Heather said. "Don't talk like that. We've still got a chance to pull Alcabaza back from the edge." She stood and stretched. "We should sleep. You've got an important job coming up."

Aron bid her goodnight and they left the sentry tower. He wandered through the open-air tent that formed Valerie's headquarters. Marie walked alongside him. She wrung her hands.

"Are you really sure we can do this?" she asked. "What if something goes wrong?"

"I trust Heather," Aron replied. "She knows her stuff. All we need to do is move some explosives. Valerie will do the rest."

Marie bit her lip. "I keep thinking about that old man we saw . . ."

Aron put an arm around her shoulders. "Nobody's ending up like that on my watch," he said. "We Raiders look out for one another around here."

"Do you think I've got what it takes to be a Raider?"

"I know it," he replied. "You helped me steal Mauriel's map. That was very brave."

Marie managed a weak smile. "That makes me feel better."

Laughter caught Aron's ear. He turned to see a group of Raiders leaning against a wall, next to a makeshift fire on the street. Lazaro stood among them.

"Aron," he said, wandering over. "I didn't expect to see you still awake."

"I needed to think," Aron replied. He raised an eyebrow at the other Raiders. "Are you still planning our next move?"

"We are." Lazaro raised a cup, and his words slurred when he spoke. "But the drink is getting to our heads. The rest of the gang has already retired." He glanced over at the others, then leaned in. "Don't tell them I said it, but these guys aren't so bad."

Aron cracked a smile. "So they don't have any more bones to pick with you?"

Lazaro shrugged. "With the situation like it is, we've got bigger rivalries to deal with." He lowered his voice. "Valerie even talked about us moving back into the roosts once all this is over."

Aron high-fived the man. "That's more like it."

"Yep." Lazaro nodded to himself. "I like the sound of being back in the roosts. It's been years since Tess and I lived there." He paused. "I still hate the idea of her being out there on her own."

"If I know Tessa, she can handle it," Aron replied. "Besides, she's got the others to look after her."

"All I know is, the sooner she returns with the last piece of our Sunstone, the better." Lazaro took a swig from his cup. "We're going to change things around here forever."

Infiltration

ISIAH CLUNG TO ENZO'S BACK. GAELON SAT IN FRONT OF HIM, guiding the dragon through the sky. Tessa's arms were wrapped around his waist, with Myla behind. They glided across the darkening Badlands, silent on the wind.

"Abaddon's flagship is just ahead," Gaelon said. "I'll fly to the lower sails, then you can climb up to the ship itself."

Isiah nodded. He'd mentally gone over the plan as they waited for nightfall. To his left, a wall of murky dust slowly crept towards them. Enzo slipped through the night, flying low to mask his serpentine form. They had left Aegon and the eagles behind to await their return.

Isiah's hand fell to his pocket, where Sybil's ring sat cold and dull. The light would guide them to wherever Abaddon was keeping the finished Sunstone.

Enzo growled. A shape loomed from the darkness ahead. Its masts seemed to stretch across the heavens. Further away, the skyship fleet was moored to the ground. A shiver ran down Isiah's spine.

"In and out," he said. "Abaddon will never even know we were there."

"He may have guards," Gaelon warned.

"But we have the element of surprise," Tessa replied.

Isiah took a breath to steady the turmoil in his stomach. The wind tugged at Enzo's wings and whistled through the valleys below as the haboob drew closer. The skyships rocked as the wind ran through their masts and battered their weathered hulls.

"I'm dropping you off now," Gaelon said. He directed Enzo to ascend. The dragon flew toward the sails that hung from the underside of the flagship. Isiah prepared himself for what he was about to do.

Enzo slowed his flight as they reached the sails. The masts hung above their heads, intertwined with a mess of ropes and pulleys. Isiah reached up and grabbed one.

"He can't stay still for long," Gaelon warned. Enzo wobbled as he fought with the air currents to remain stable.

Isiah gripped the rope and heaved himself into the rigging. Tessa and Myla climbed alongside him. Enzo's tail twitched as he glided in place.

"I'll wait for your signal," Gaelon said.

Enzo soared away, leaving them alone. Isiah steadied his footing on a narrow wooden beam, all too aware of the empty drop beneath him. The wind raced through the rigging, making the ropes quiver.

Isiah grunted as he began to climb toward the flagship's hull. Tessa and Myla climbed nearby. The sails were drawn, leaving the masts bare. Isiah focused on making slow, methodical movements. He gritted his teeth and kept his gaze fixed on the ropes in front of him. He refused to glance at the shadowy Badlands far below.

Ropes creaked and groaned in protest. Isiah tested his weight before making each move. The flagship's hull slowly grew closer. Tessa climbed above him. A torch was tucked into her belt—their signal.

The masts grew thicker as he climbed. Isiah threw a leg over a beam and steadied himself, catching his breath. Tessa and Myla reached the wide, sweeping underbelly of the flagship.

"Where do we go now?" Myla whispered.

Isiah's gaze drifted to the protruding, wing-like masts that stretched from the ship's sides. "We'll have to climb around the hull."

Carefully, they shimmied along the beams, rounding the hull of the flagship and then clambering toward the deck. As they approached the railing, Isiah paused to listen for any sign of movement. Silence cloaked the ship.

Isiah gripped the railing and hauled himself over. He collapsed onto the deck. *Made it.*

Tessa and Myla joined him. They crouched in the shadows. Beyond, the haboob loomed over them like a wave about to come crashing down. The wind whipped across the deck, lashing Isiah's face.

"They must have locked the ship down," he said. "It's deserted."

"Let's get out of the wind," Tessa replied. "We can't use your ring here. It's too exposed. We'll be spotted."

Keeping to the railing, they navigated the length of the flagship, heading toward the room where Abaddon had shown them the Sunstone.

The growing storm tugged at the rolled-up sails and blew Isiah's hair into his face. They climbed the stairs to the room where he'd first seen the Sunstone. He tried the door and it creaked open.

An empty room greeted him.

"Where has it gone?" Tessa asked.

Isiah stepped inside. The carved blocks of sandstone were still there, along with the maps and books, but the Sunstone itself was missing.

"Maybe Abaddon moved it," Myla suggested.

Isiah fumbled with his pocket and drew out the ring. It gave off a faint glow. "It's still on-board," he said. He slowly spun around, trying to locate the direction the Sunstone was in. His heart sank when he lowered it to the floor and the ring grew brighter.

"It must be inside the hull somewhere," Tessa said. She swore. "How are we going to find it now?"

"The ring will guide us," Isiah replied. "We can't leave empty-handed."

He paused to listen for any sound of crewmates, but all he heard was the steady creak of the vessel. He crept along the passageway into the belly of the flagship.

As they wandered deeper, the sounds from outside became muted. Isiah passed doorways and long halls that snaked through the ship's interior. The faint sound of snoring emanated from some, betraying the crewmates within. They passed the meeting room that Abaddon had taken them to and kept going.

"Where do you think he's hiding it?" Myla asked.

Isiah shifted his footing. "It must be somewhere safe," he said. "Maybe his own quarters."

"That would make sense," Tessa replied. "But where would that be?"

Isiah checked the ring again. It pointed toward the far end of the ship. Stepping lightly on the creaky wooden floor, he kept going.

Footsteps sounded ahead. Isiah pressed himself against the wall and froze. He slowly peered around the corner. A crewmate wandered towards them. The man rubbed the back of his bald head and yawned.

"Someone's coming," he hissed.

Tessa swore. She darted to a doorway and waved them over. Isiah and Myla hurried to her side. She scrunched up her forehead and formed an illusion. It blocked the doorway, making it blend in with the surrounding wall.

"What if he notices something is wrong?" Myla asked.

Tessa gritted her teeth. "Then we'll have to fight."

They held their breath as the footsteps approached. The crewmate whistled as he walked. His footsteps rounded the corner and kept going. Isiah sighed.

They waited until the sound had faded, then resumed their search. As they wandered the interior of the ship, the halls became more decorated. Long rugs covered the floors, and paintings hung from the walls. Isiah passed a narrow slit-like window and gazed out at the shadowy Badlands beyond.

"This must be the back of the ship," Tessa said.

Isiah checked his ring. It flooded the hall with light. "We're close."

He hastened ahead, letting the carpet muffle his footsteps. His pulse quickened in anticipation.

"Wait up," Tessa whispered.

Isiah hardly heard her. The Sunstone seemed to reach out to him, just like it had in the ruin. He could almost feel its presence . . .

"Hey!" a voice yelled behind them.

Isiah spun around to see a pair of crewmates round the corner. His hand flew to his sabre, but Tessa threw up an illusion to cut him off.

"Haven't you heard the ship is on lockdown?" a crewmate said.

Isiah strained to hear what was going on. Tessa's wall cut off the passageway, blocking his view. The footsteps stopped on the other side.

"Thought you could sneak off and wait out the haboob some-where nicer, did you?" the crewmate said. He scoffed. "Just because you have those fancy robes doesn't mean you're above all the others. You belong in the hull with all the rest."

Isiah pressed his ear against Tessa's wall. He heard the crew-mates marching Tessa and Myla away.

"Behave yourselves and we won't report this to Abaddon," one of the crewmates said. "Otherwise you can spend the night tied to the masts!"

Tessa's wall dissolved, revealing an empty hall. Isiah wrung his hands. He started to go after them, but the Sunstone called out to him from somewhere behind.

I have to save them, he thought. He wobbled on the spot. *But the Sunstone is so close.* He cast a look in its direction, then clutched Sybil's ring to his chest. Once he found it, then he could help them.

Isiah followed Sybil's ring until it led him to a door. A metal plaque told him who the room belonged to: *Abaddon.*

Isiah pressed his ear against the door. No sound came from within. Holding his breath, he gripped the handle and entered.

Lantern light illuminated the space. A writing desk stood against one wall, with a scroll and a pot of ink on it, next to a large bed. Twin rows of glass windows stretched from the floor to the ceiling, giving a sweeping view of the Badlands.

The Sunstone leaned against the wall.

Isiah slowly approached it. Magic hummed through the golden disk, reverberating through his bones. Its intricate markings seemed to shimmer, reflecting the lantern's light. The visions of burning armies flashed through his mind. His awe transformed into a gut-churning dread.

Isiah gripped one of the four fragments and tugged. A magnetic force held the Sunstone together. He gritted his teeth and pulled again. The fragment began to slide out.

The door creaked open behind him and Abaddon ducked through. Isiah whirled around. He searched for somewhere to hide, but it was too late. Abaddon saw him and froze.

Isiah reached for his sabre, but Abaddon was faster. He yanked his blade free and aimed it at Isiah's throat.

"Step away from the Sunstone," he said coldly.

Isiah gulped. He inched away from the golden disk. The tip of Abaddon's sabre hovered level with his neck.

"You escaped the ruin," Abaddon said slowly. "Clever." He closed the distance in one stride and wrenched Isiah's sabre from its scabbard. He flung the blade across the room. Isiah's eyes darted to it.

"Don't even think about it," Abaddon snapped. He prodded Isiah with the tip of his sabre. "Or I'll run you through like that old shaman." He drew a length of rope from his belt. "Put your hands behind your back. You're coming with me."

The Hull

"I'M TELLING YOU, YOU'RE MAKING A MISTAKE," Tessa said. "We're *supposed* to be out here."

"And I'm telling *you* to keep quiet," the crewmate replied.

Tessa strained against the man's grip. He marched her along the hall, away from Isiah and the far end of the ship. His companion walked nearby, holding Myla by the arm.

"You know what Abaddon's orders are," he said. "*All* of you are to stay in the hull until the haboob has passed."

Tessa racked her brains for a plan. Her gaze dropped to her sabre. She tried to imagine pulling it free and killing the crewmate before he could raise the alarm. Her fingers twitched, inching toward the hilt.

The crewmates turned abruptly and herded her down a narrow staircase. The hiss of pipes echoed from ahead. As they reached the bottom, they passed a doorway. Tessa caught sight of a mass of pipes, which were wrapped around several long cylinders.

That must be what keeps the flagship afloat, she thought.

"In here." The man shoved her toward a door. Several other crewmates sat on chairs nearby, their heads drooping as they slept. *Guards,* Tessa thought. The man unlocked the door and shoved her inside. Myla bumped into her from behind.

"Next time we won't be so charitable," the crewmate said. He slammed the door shut behind them.

Tessa waited for her eyes to adjust to the dim light. A few candles lit the room. Figures sat in bunk beds and on benches against the walls. Some turned to look at them, but most ignored her. The steady creak of the vessel rose above the hissing of air valves. The flagship shuddered as the haboob approached.

"I don't blame you for trying to sneak out," one of the youths said. "It sounds like this storm is going to be a big one. What I'd give to find some comfortable hole to crawl into."

Tessa hardly heard him. She tried the door handle. As she expected, the crewmate had locked it.

Myla lowered her voice. "Do you think Isiah is going to be able to find us?"

Tessa rubbed her arms. "There are crewmates out there. He'll have to find a way past them." She fought to quell the turmoil inside her. The candles flickered as the wind crept through cracks in the hull.

"Maybe we can blend in until the haboob has passed," Myla suggested.

"It will be too late by then," she replied. "Abaddon will have noticed the fragment missing." She rattled the handle again. "We need to find a way out *now*."

The door banged. "Keep it down in there," a crewmate said.

Myla paced about. "If we don't return, Gaelon will know something's wrong. He'll have to come looking for us."

Tessa's nose crinkled. "Gaelon won't help us, you know. We're on our own here."

"Gaelon cares about us, you know," she said. "I think Isiah's right about him."

"Isiah wasn't right about Solomon."

Myla flinched at the harshness in Tessa's words. "You were fooled, too," she said. "We all were. Isiah still feels guilty about what happened."

"I told you to keep it down!" the crewmate yelled.

Tessa collected herself. "Forget about Solomon," she said. "I can't trust Gaelon. I *won't* trust him. You don't understand what he did to me."

"He said he's changed," Myla said quietly. "And I believe him."

"He was a Royal Guard. He's a killer. He'll never make up for what he did." Tessa fought to keep her voice under control. Several of the youths were staring, but she ignored them.

"Solomon was a monster, too," Myla said. "But that's not all I remember him as." She looked at her feet. "He was a good man until he started his experiments. He took me in—he took all of us in."

Tessa crossed her arms. "He was still evil."

Myla seemed not to hear her. "I wondered for ages how he could do such a thing. Edith said it was because he was desperate. He thought he was doing the right thing—like Gaelon."

Tessa huffed. "He was wrong. They both were."

"But Gaelon realized that," she said. "I can only remember Solomon before he became a monster, but Gaelon is trying to make things right."

"No." Tessa shook her head. She angrily wiped a sleeve across her eyes. "He needs to pay for what he's done."

"What makes you think he hasn't already?"

Footsteps sounded outside the door. A hand slammed against it. "Right, I warned you!"

A key turned in a lock and the door flew open. A crewmate stepped through and brandished a whip. "If you can't keep your mouths shut, you'll have to learn the hard way."

The youths scattered as he grabbed Myla. Panic flashed in her eyes and she tried to pull away. The man shoved her against the wall. "Let this be a lesson to the lot of you," he growled.

The crewmate raised the whip above his head. Tessa's hand flew to her sabre. She yanked the blade free and plunged it into his armpit. The crewmate screamed as her blade pierced his flesh.

Youths cheered as he dropped the whip and collapsed, writhing in pain. Several more crewmates appeared in the doorway.

The lead man's face twisted into a snarl. "You're dead meat."

Tessa levelled her sabre at them. "Come and get us." Myla drew her sabre and stood beside her. The youths cheered.

"You show 'em!" one said.

"Shut up," a crewmate ordered. "Or we'll whip the lot of you."

The youths rallied around Tessa. The man raised his whip, but this time they didn't back off. The crewmates faltered.

"We won't let you push us around anymore," one of the youths said. He turned and raised his fist. "Mutiny!"

A chorus of voices echoed his call and the youths surged forward.

Tessa fought to stay on her feet as the mob carried her through the doorway. Panic flashed across the crewmates' faces as the youths swept over them and wrestled the weapons from their hands.

The crewmates struggled to break free of the mob. One tripped and fell. A youth grabbed a metal pipe and brought it down with a sickening crunch. Myla covered her mouth and looked away.

Tessa found her voice. She thrust her sabre into the air and let out a battle cry. The youths stole the crewmate's keys and unlocked several more doors, freeing their companions. Others flooded down the halls.

"This is our chance." Tessa grabbed Myla's wrist. "Let's go find Isiah." She hesitated. "And Gaelon."

Graveyard

Isiah stumbled as Abaddon shoved him. Ropes bit into his wrists, and the tip of the man's sabre pressed into the small of his back.

His mind raced. The thought of Tessa and Myla being locked away in the hull filled him with dread. He stumbled as Abaddon gripped a handful of his hair and forced him up a flight of stairs.

"You're a thief," Abaddon said. "And on my ship, we don't take kindly to thieves."

Isiah winced against the pain. "Where are you taking me?"

"You'll see." Abaddon marched him toward a door. As they went, the roar of the haboob grew louder. He yanked it open and the wind hit Isiah full in the face.

"Out," Abaddon barked.

Isiah stumbled into the haboob. Dust stung his eyes and whipped into his face. He wobbled to keep his balance. The raging cloud of murky yellow reduced visibility to only a few feet.

Abaddon pushed his head forward. "Move."

Isiah blinked back tears as his hair yanked on his scalp. Abaddon marched him to one of the wide masts that protruded from the centre of the ship.

"Stand against the mast," Abaddon ordered.

Isiah did as he was told. He frantically searched for any kind of escape. The wind raged around him, making it feel like he was about to be swept off the deck. Abaddon sliced his binds and then secured him to the mast with his arms spread out.

"If *you* survived the ruin, that means your friends did too," Abaddon said. "I know you won't sell them out easily."

Isiah strained at the ropes biting his wrist. His cheek pressed into the rough wood. He strained his neck to see what Abaddon was doing.

Abaddon sheathed his sabre. The end of his headscarf flapped in the wind, and particles of sand stuck to his beard.

"What was your plan, boy?" he asked. "To sneak into my vessel and steal a piece of my Sunstone?" He laughed. "You're too late. I should throw you from my ship and let you fall to your death. But that would be too easy."

He pulled something from a rack next to the sail. "Do you want to know how we punish troublemakers?"

Isiah tensed. He tried to quell the panic building inside him. Abaddon dangled a long whip with multiple strands.

"A bit of old-fashioned discipline keeps the crewmates in check," he said. A cruel smile crossed his lips, but his eyes were empty. "Now tell me where your friends are."

Isiah held his tongue. He matched Abaddon's gaze.

Abaddon shrugged. "Suit yourself."

The man grabbed Isiah's collar and pulled down his robes. The wind lashed Isiah's bare skin—and his Mark.

Abaddon's jaw clenched. "You're from Paradon," he spat.

Isiah flinched as Abaddon lashed out the whip and cracked it against his back. He gritted his teeth against the stinging pain.

"Do you have any idea what your people put us through?" Abaddon said. He brought the whip down again. "You slaughtered my family and drove us from our homeland!"

Isiah gasped in pain.

"You burned our cities to cinders and killed everyone we held dear," Abaddon said. "These ships are all we have left!"

The whip flashed again. Isiah bit his tongue to keep from crying out.

"I have nothing to do with Paradon!" Isiah blurted out. Stinging pain rippled through his muscles from each blow.

"Nonsense," Abaddon spat. "You ride dragons just like them. You're even working with their spy!"

"He's not a spy," Isiah pleaded.

Abaddon ignored him. "Paradon and its people must suffer for what they did to us." He grunted as he brought the whip down again. "This Sunstone will finally let us have our revenge."

Isiah strained at the bonds around his wrists. He felt the warm sensation of blood oozing down his back.

"My armada needs a new home," Abaddon said. "And I won't let a bunch of filthy Raiders stand in my way." Abaddon flicked the whip. Flecks of blood stained the deck. The wind stung Isiah's back, filling his wounds with sand.

Abaddon stepped forward and grabbed a handful of Isiah's hair. "You don't appreciate the magic like we do," he said through clenched teeth. "Raiders are only interested in profit. You and the merchants don't understand what you're living on top of."

Isiah winced as Abaddon gripped him tighter.

"You're nothing more than flies, picking over the bones of the Ancients' long-dead empire. Only *my* people know how to treat this graveyard as it deserves." Abaddon stepped away and readied the whip. "Where are your friends?"

Isiah grimaced against the pain. "They're already stealing the Sunstone," he lied. "I was just a distraction." He gasped as the whip lashed across his back again. With his ear against the mast, he made out a faint commotion reverberating up from inside the ship.

"You *will* tell me," Abaddon said, "or I'll tear your flesh until your Mark is nothing in comparison!"

The commotion grew louder. Voices yelled, rising above the storm. Abaddon paused. The metallic clang of alarm bells rang out into the storm.

"Wait here." Abaddon dumped the whip on the rack and marched into the haboob.

Isiah let his breath escape him. Every second spent in the storm made his back ripple with searing pain. He gripped the binds securing him to the mast and pulled. The ropes creaked, but they held fast.

The noises inside the ship rose in volume. Crewmates screamed and metal clashed. Isiah focused his attention on escaping. The rack reached up to his waist. He placed one foot on it and balanced his weight. The ropes grew slack as his head came level with his binds. The rough rope was frayed at the edges. Gripping it between his teeth, he started working himself loose.

The seconds dragged past. His back itched as the blood dried to his skin. He ignored the pain and tugged on the knots with his teeth. They gradually began to loosen.

With panic driving him on, he wriggled his wrists until the ropes loosened enough for him to pull his hand out. He untied his other hand and dropped to the deck. He scanned the deck in the direction Abaddon had gone.

The Sunstone fragment.

Pulling his robes over his bloodied torso, he ran into the flagship. Isiah slammed the door behind him and the roar of the wind grew muffled. Shouting echoed from somewhere beneath him. Crewmates barked orders. Boots thundered as dozens of feet stampeded through the halls.

Isiah pulled out Sybil's ring and retraced his steps into the belly of the flagship. Metal clashed from somewhere to his right as a fight unfolded. The steady sound of the warning bell rose above the chaos.

Isiah ran over his plan. *Find the Sunstone fragment, then help Tessa and Myla.* He winced as his robes rubbed against his wounds. Every movement made his skin feel like it was being stretched and distorted. Fresh blood oozed down his back and made the material stick to him.

Isiah made it to the far end of the ship and located Abaddon's quarters. He prayed Abaddon wouldn't be waiting inside. He peered through the keyhole.

Nothing. Eager to get out of the hall before anyone could stumble on him, he opened the door and almost fell inside.

The Sunstone remained against the wall where he had last seen it. His sabre lay nearby. Isiah sheathed it in his scabbard and then grabbed one of the Sunstone fragments. He placed a foot against the golden disk and pulled.

The fragment slipped free and hit the floor with a bang. The chaos from the unfolding battle masked the sound. Isiah grunted as he lifted the Sunstone fragment in his arms. He hobbled out of Abaddon's quarters and tried to find his way back to the deck.

He rounded a corner and stumbled into a mob.

Isiah fought to keep his balance as a crowd of youths swept him up, carrying him like a surging current. They thrust their boarding pikes and makeshift weapons into the air, yelling at the tops of their lungs. A gang of crewmates stood at the far end of the hall, brandishing whips and sabres. The youths slammed into them with the scrape of metal.

Isiah struggled to free himself from the crush of bodies. He ducked as a whip cracked overhead. Crewmates wrestled with the crowd of youths as they fought to re-establish order.

"Tessa!" Isiah yelled. He strained to hear anything over the din of voices. He pushed his way to the edge of the crowd and slipped down another hallway.

A staircase led to a higher level of the ship. Tucking the Sunstone fragment under one arm, he took it. He reached the floor above and ducked aside as a gang of crewmates thundered past. Isiah followed them.

The wind howled as doors flew open to the deck. The youths spilled out, clashing with the crewmates in a disorganized surge. A crewmate screamed and went down, clutching his side. Youths scattered as his comrades brandished long whips. Isiah scanned the crowd for any familiar faces.

"Isiah!" Myla's shrill voice caught his attention. He spotted her alongside Tessa, bouncing and waving her hands.

Isiah hastened toward them. None of the crewmates seemed to notice him. He reached Myla's side. "What's going on?"

"They're having a mutiny," Myla replied. She frowned. "Are you hurt?"

"Abaddon found me." Isiah waved her away. "It's nothing." He tried to hide the pain in his voice.

Tessa grabbed his hand. "Come on. I'll signal Gaelon."

Ignoring his aching body, Isiah waded through the crowd until he made it to the fringes. The battle faded behind them and they reached the prow of the ship.

"Are you sure this will work?" he asked.

Tessa pulled out the torch. "It has to."

She used a firestarter to light the end and then held it aloft. The torch sprang to life, hissing as it pierced the haboob with deep-red light. She leaned over the railing and waved it in the air. Isiah adjusted his grip on the Sunstone fragment and they waited. He glanced over his shoulder in the direction of the battle. His injuries throbbed with a dull, lingering pain.

A shadow loomed from the haboob. Isiah stumbled away as a bellow sounded and Enzo materialized. Wood splintered and creaked as he landed on the railing. Gaelon clung to the dragon's back, his turban pulled over his mouth like a scarf.

"Pass me the Sunstone fragment," he said. "Hurry."

Tessa and Myla helped Isiah lift the Sunstone fragment and slide it into an empty bag hanging from Enzo's side. The dragon lowered his wing so that they could climb on. His sides heaved with laboured breaths.

"This haboob is giving us trouble," Gaelon said. "We can barely stay airborne."

Tessa dropped the torch as she and Myla scrambled on behind Gaelon. The man reached out a hand to help Isiah up. "Come on!"

A whip cracked behind him. Isiah spun around to see Abaddon marching from the storm.

"Get back here, Isiah," he snarled. Crewmates materialized around him, armed with boarding pikes. His face darkened when he noticed the Sunstone fragment poking out the top of the sack. "You filthy thief!" He motioned to the crewmates. "Kill the dragon."

The crewmates threw their pikes. Enzo roared and twisted away. The pikes struck the wooden railing and clattered across the deck. Isiah watched helplessly as Enzo took flight and melted into the haboob.

Abaddon cracked the whip again. "We're not finished yet."

Isiah scanned for an escape as the crewmates moved to block him off. Gaelon's muffled voice echoed somewhere above him. He backed up against the splintered railing and sharp wood pressed into his skin.

"My crewmates have the mutiny under control," Abaddon said. "And your dragons can't help you in this weather. Give it up."

Isiah burst into a sprint. The crewmates threw themselves toward him, but he managed to slip through a gap between them.

"After him," Abaddon ordered.

Isiah kept running. Crewmates and gangs of youths materialized around him like murky figures. A blast of fire illuminated the sky for a split second, betraying Enzo's position. The dragon rocked on the wind, fighting to stay airborne.

The mast materialized ahead of him. Rigging ascended into nothingness. Without thinking, Isiah grabbed it and began to climb. Abaddon reached the mast below him.

"You can't escape me, boy," he yelled. He dropped the whip and yanked his sabre free. "Enough games."

Isiah clung to the rigging with white knuckles. The full force of the haboob battered him, as if trying to rip him free and send him plummeting to the deck. The ropes creaked in protest as Abaddon began climbing after him.

A new surge of panic powered Isiah on. The deck faded into the storm below. Another flash of fire illuminated Enzo circling the flagship. Isiah waved to try and catch their attention. "Gaelon!" His hoarse voice was lost to the haboob.

The rigging jerked as Abaddon gained on him. The man gripped his sabre between his teeth. Isiah scrambled up to the crow's nest near the top of the flagship. Gripping a handful of the bunched-up sails for balance, he pulled out his sabre and began sawing through the rigging. The rope began to fray—but not fast enough.

Enzo circled the mast. Flashes of fire illuminated the terrified faces of his friends. The flagship rocked from side to side. Isiah fought to keep hold of the rigging. Abaddon's cold, empty eyes burned into him.

A new roar split the storm. Isiah's heart leapt as Aegon materialized. He yelped as Abaddon's sabre bit into the mast below his foot.

"You're trapped," Abaddon said. "There's nowhere left for you to go!"

Isiah pulled up his legs and climbed into the crow's nest. The small, circular basket tossed about like they were at sea. Aegon tried to fly closer, but the wind threatened to throw her against the ship and tangle her in its ropes.

"Isiah!" Gaelon yelled. Isiah strained to hear him. "Jump!"

Isiah's face paled. His muscles locked up as he hugged the crow's nest. "I can't do that!"

"Trust . . . Aegon," Gaelon's voice sounded again.

Aegon soared past. Abaddon pulled back his sabre and pierced the underside of the crow's nest. Isiah yelped and pulled away as the tip punctured a hole inches from his foot. He searched for somewhere to go. The only thing above them was the tattered flag that crowned the highest point of the ship.

Isiah steadied his shaking hands. He tried to focus on his bond with Aegon. Gaelon's words echoed in his head. *Aegon trusts you. Why can't you trust her?*

He jumped.

His stomach climbed into his throat he flew past Abaddon and plummeted toward the Badlands. He opened his mouth to scream, but his throat locked up. He squeezed his eyes shut and called out to Aegon in his mind.

His body jolted as Aegon's feet closed around him. She snatched him mid-fall and soared through the haboob. The rush of her wings echoed in his eardrums. Her jaws cracked open and she let out a cry of victory.

Isiah gripped her legs with all of his strength. Empty air rushed past below him. Aegon's long talons dug into his shoulders as she carried him away from the flagship and toward the Badlands far below.

Isiah's head rocked. The adrenaline surging through his veins made him lightheaded. Darkness crept into the edges of his vision.

His grip went slack and he slipped into unconsciousness.

Observatory

HEATHER CROUCHED IN THE DARKNESS. "ARE YOU READY?"

Aron nodded. He patted his chest, where the map was safely hidden under his robes. Ahead, the makeshift wall that bordered the roosts blocked the way. A couple of sentry towers—their guards on break—were silhouetted against the night.

Heather leapt from the market stall she was hiding behind and darted toward the wall. Aron took a deep breath, then went after her. Marie followed close behind.

Keeping to the cover of the shadows, Aron made it to the wall and began to climb. The pile of jumbled wood and stone offered plenty of handholds. He scrambled over the top and dropped to the other side. Heather was already waiting for him.

"The storehouse isn't far from here," she said.

Aron wiped his palms on his robes. He knew that somewhere behind them, Valerie and the other Raiders were waiting for their signal to strike. She'd convinced several other gangs to join them on their assault of the roosts. But everything came down to him.

Heather took the lead, slipping down a deserted street toward the plaza that held the storehouse. Aron strained his eyes for any silhouettes standing watch on the rooftops. Since he'd infiltrated the tavern, Heather said Mauriel had grown more paranoid. Aron hoped she hadn't discovered the map missing.

Ahead, the street ended, opening to reveal the plaza and its low wooden fence. The storehouse lay quiet. Aron stuffed his shaking hands into his pockets.

"Be careful not to set any of the mines off," Heather said. She slung a coil of fuse off her shoulder. "Once we pile them in the storehouse, this fuse will give us time to get out before it blows."

Aron hardly heard her. He fumbled with his robes and pulled out the map. He raised it, trying to catch the moonlight. Each dot betrayed a grisly death. He tried to forget the beggar's screams.

He pointed. "The first mine is there."

Heather ducked under the fence and carefully stood on two sandstone slabs. She lifted a third, revealing a round metal disk. She pulled it out and placed it beside them.

Aron leaned away. "Be careful with that thing."

"They don't go off when you step on them," Heather said. "That's the trick. You think you're safe. But then you lift your foot and—" she clicked her fingers "—bang!"

Aron shuddered. He exchanged glances with Marie. She gave him a shaky smile.

"How many do we need?" he asked.

"Enough to give us a clear path to the storehouse," Heather said. "Now, come on."

Slowly, Aron ducked under the fence and entered the plaza. He balanced his weight on a sandstone slab. He wobbled his arms to keep his balance.

Heather studied the map. "There's another one there."

Aron picked his way toward it. He winced as he made every step. He knelt by the slab Heather had pointed him to and inched it off. A metal disk greeted him, with a pressure plate on top. Aron wiped the sweat off his forehead and added it to the pile.

"Good job," Heather said.

Aron swore under his breath. "I'd rather handle desert scorpions than these things." The mines gave off a faint acrid odour of explosives.

They inched across the plaza, locating the mines and placing the loose slabs as a makeshift path. The pile steadily grew. As they worked, the tremble in Aron's hands began to subside.

The moon dipped behind a cloud, forcing him to squint at the map. "Where's the next one . . ."

Something clunked.

Aron's heart skipped a beat. He looked down, and the sandstone slab beneath his foot had dropped an inch. Heather's face paled.

He swore. "What am I supposed to do?" Every muscle in his body screamed at him to jump away, but he knew he'd never make it before the explosives detonated.

"Don't panic," Heather stammered. Her eyes darted about. "Stay there."

"There's not much else I can do." He laughed, all too aware of the tremble in his voice.

Heather rubbed her temples. "There has to be a way to disarm it."

"You mean you don't know? I thought you laid these!"

"We did," she shot back. "But Mauriel never told us how to turn them off."

"What if we transferred the weight?" Marie asked. "It won't go off as long as there's something on it, right?"

"It's too risky," Heather replied. "It could go off and kill us all."

"Well, we have to do *something*." Aron fought to keep his voice low. The sandstone slab wobbled, balanced atop the mine. He focused on keeping his weight atop the pressure plate.

Marie picked up a slab. "What if we stacked them?"

"It might not be heavy enough," Heather said.

"It's the best chance we've got." Aron shifted his foot to the side. It gave enough room for Marie to place the slab next to him.

"We need a bunch," she said. She grabbed two more and shakily placed them atop one another. Aron tugged at his collar. The memory of the screaming beggar and his bloodied stump of a leg swirled around his mind. Marie placed several more slabs, forming a lopsided tower.

"Careful not to crush it," Heather said.

Aron eased his weight off slightly. He tensed, waiting for the deafening explosion. Marie's shallow breathing was the only sound in the silence.

"Go," Marie said.

Aron gritted his teeth. He lifted his foot off the mine and they all backed away.

Nothing.

Aron sighed. He wiped his forehead and tried to quell the dizziness. He hugged Marie. "Thank you."

"It's like you said," she replied. "Raiders look out for one another."

"There aren't many more to go now," Heather said.

Aron returned to work. They cleared the last few mines and reached the storehouse door. He tried the handle. Locked.

"I'll try the roof," he said. He scaled the wall to the flat rooftop and located the trapdoor he'd seen the Raider use. It swung open and he climbed into the storehouse.

Piles of crates and sacks filled the room, reaching to the ceiling. Loose grain crunched beneath Aron's feet as he picked his way over to the door. He unlocked it and swung it open.

Heather let out a low whistle. "Mauriel's gang has been busy."

Aron nodded. "She wasn't lying when she said the city would starve before they did."

She broke away. "Let's get the mines inside."

They returned to the pile of mines. Heather grabbed a few and walked along the now-cleared path to the storehouse. They placed the mines in the centre of the building, beneath the stairs. Aron counted at least several dozen mines.

"If one of these is strong enough to blow a man's leg off, imagine what all of them can do," Heather said. She unravelled the fuse and placed a small stick of explosives down. "This will get them started. With any luck, they'll blow the whole building apart."

"How much time will we have?" Aron asked.

"Enough to get away," she replied.

They unravelled the fuse, retracing their steps along the cleared path through the plaza. Heather connected the end of the fuse to a small detonator. She pushed down the plunger and the fuse lit up.

"Let's go," she said.

Sparks hissed as the fuse burned, snaking its way toward the storehouse. Aron sprinted along the street, eager to get as far away as possible. He braced himself for the explosion. Heather and Marie ran into the darkness.

A force slammed into him and sent him sprawling.

"Got you!" a gruff voice said. Aron writhed as a pair of hands dragged him to his feet. "Mauriel warned us you might be back."

Aron twisted around to see a pair of Raiders.

"Where's your little friend?" the first Raider spat. "Mauriel will want to see you."

"Let me go." Aron struggled to break free of their grip. He tensed, waiting for the storehouse to blow . . .

"No chance," the Raider started.

An explosion ripped through the roosts.

A blinding flash split the night as a plume of fire rose above the storehouse. Aron ducked and covered his head as the shockwave erupted down the street. The Raiders released him and staggered away in panic.

Aron sprinted for cover as bricks and chunks of stone pelted the street. He pressed himself against a doorway and curled into a ball. Chunks of stone as big as his head ricocheted against walls and bounced down the road. Eagles shrieked in panic in their pens.

A battle cry went up from Valerie's forces. Aron staggered into the dust-filled air, coughing. One of the Raiders who'd grabbed him clutched his head. The man locked eyes with him and his expression darkened.

"What did you do?" one of them snarled. Blood oozed from a cut on his head. He fumbled for his sabre.

Aron ran.

Eagles broke free from their pens and soared into the night sky. Raiders spilled out of Mauriel's tavern, still clutching their cups. A glance over Aron's shoulder revealed the two Raiders giving chase.

Aron emerged in the plaza with the storehouse. Grain and chips of stone crunched underfoot. The broken silhouette of the storehouse loomed from the dust.

Aron held a sleeve against his mouth and kept running. The explosion had set off some of the hidden mines, leaving holes that pitted the ground. He rounded a corner and looped back toward the growing battle cries of Valerie's forces. He prayed Marie and Heather had made it back safe.

The Raiders rounded the corner behind him.

"You'll pay for this, boy!" one yelled. They closed the gap between them.

Panic flared in Aron's chest. He reached a building and scrambled up its side, using windowsills as handholds. He clambered over the low wall and onto the roof as the Raiders reached the bottom. They swore and started after him.

A piercing shriek split the sky. Aron ducked as an eagle swept overhead, dust billowing in its wake. More eagles circled the tavern. Mauriel's Raiders ran to the eagle pens, but most of the birds had broken free and fled. The Raiders' panicked cries carried on the wind.

A hand appeared on the low wall. One of the Raiders grunted and pulled himself up. Aron drew his sabre and levelled it with the man's chest.

"Mauriel is finished," Aron said. "Surrender while you still have the chance."

The Raider laughed. "This fight ain't over yet, boy."

Aron cast a glance behind him. Part of him urged him to jump to the street below . . . but the fall threatened to break his ankle.

The Raider swung his sabre. Aron parried the blow and stepped out of reach. The back of his legs met the low wall.

"No more running," the Raider said.

Aron flicked his sabre at the man, forcing him to parry. The scrape of steel echoed as their blades met. The point of the Raider's sabre hovered a few feet from Aron's throat.

The Raider lunged. Aron sidestepped instinctively and the blade brushed past his ear. The second Raider climbed onto the roof and moved to corner him.

Aron's sabre wobbled. Valerie's Raiders had reached the tavern, but the street behind him was deserted. The dust settled to reveal a cloud of eagles wheeling about in the sky.

The Raider darted forward. Aron parried his blow, but the man lashed out with his foot. It connected with Aron's stomach and the wind exploded from his lungs. He staggered backwards and collapsed against the wall, clutching his ribs. He fought to suck in wheezing breaths. Each one sent a stab of pain through his chest.

"You should have stayed an exile," the Raider spat.

A shadow fell across the roof. The Raider screamed as talons dug into his back. A blast of air whipped into Aron as an eagle plucked the man from the rooftop. The man writhed as it carried him high into the night sky—then let him drop.

The eagle turned on its wing and glided toward the rooftop. The second Raider vaulted over the low wall and ran for cover. Aron leaned his weight against the wall and climbed to his feet. The eagle flapped its wings as it gently landed.

"Do you need a ride?" Helen asked.

Aron bit back the pain in his ribs and smiled. "Good timing. Are Marie and Heather alright?"

"We picked them up during the attack," Helen said. "The plan went off without a hitch." She beckoned him. "Come on."

Aron hobbled to the eagle. Helen helped him into the saddle and they flew into the night sky.

* * *

"Line them up," Valerie ordered.

Aron watched the line of captured Raiders. They knelt on the ground in front of the tavern, hands on their heads. Valerie's forces had confiscated their sabres and knives. Darla and Antony stood guard as the last of Mauriel's Raiders were marched out of the tavern.

"Aron!" Marie ran over and threw her arms around him. "I was worried about you."

Aron winced as she crushed his sore ribs. "I knew the others would have my back."

Lazaro and the others crowded around. He raised the cloth sack. "I have the Sunstone fragment."

Aron's expression hardened. "Then let's go to the observatory and check it out."

They left Valerie and followed a narrow path away from the tavern and the eagle pens. As they reached the observatory, a pair of Valerie's Raiders opened the doors for them.

"Are the two pieces in there?" Aron asked.

One of the Raiders nodded. "Just like you said they'd be."

Aron hurried past them into the building. A series of large telescopes dominated the main room. Maps and intricate charts of the sky adorned the walls, except for one side of the dome. A circular inlay was built into the wall, containing half of a golden disk.

Lazaro pulled out the third Sunstone fragment and cradled it in his arms. The others crowded around as he carefully lifted it and slotted it into the inlay. Aron held his breath. A magnetic hum sounded as the fragment slid into place. A shiver ran down his spine.

"Three down," he said. "One more to go." The Sunstone seemed to command his attention. His eyes flitted over its many markings and symbols.

"It's down to Tess and Isiah now," Lazaro said.

Aron looked out the window across the dark, empty Badlands. "Let's hope they get here soon."

With the third Sunstone fragment delivered to the observatory, they left the building and headed back to the tavern. As they approached, a commotion went up from the building.

"Lazaro!" Valerie called. "I found somebody for you." She dragged Mauriel out of the building. The woman's arms were bound behind her back, and her dreadlocks flopped about her face. Valerie forced Mauriel to her knees.

"We found her hiding in the back of the tavern," she said. "I guess she thought she was too good to join the fighting after she declared herself queen of Alcabaza."

Lazaro smirked. "Well, Mauriel, look who's had the last laugh."

"You should be dead!" she spat. "You're banished."

"And you're the most hated Raider in Alcabaza." He drew his sabre. "I've waited a long time to get even with you after you got us exiled."

"It was your own fault," Mauriel replied. "You can't help but get into fights with everyone you meet."

"Look around," Lazaro said. "Who caused this mess? I'm here to set things right."

Marie gripped Aron's arm. Lazaro's hand twitched on the hilt of his sabre.

"Go on," Mauriel said. "Kill me. Show all these Raiders that you're nothing more than a lowly Oath-Breaker!"

Lazaro exchanged glances with Valerie. The woman stood with her arms folded. She shrugged. "What's one more Raider dead?"

Lazaro turned to Mauriel. "You ruined the Oath when you stole the roosts," he said slowly. "And I've come to realize that the Oath is the only thing that will hold Alcabaza together."

"Don't lecture me," Mauriel shot back. "You're no better than I am."

Lazaro sheathed his sabre. "Get out of our city."

Two Raiders pulled Mauriel to her feet. She struggled against them. "What?"

"You heard me," Lazaro said. "You're banished. Leave Alcabaza and never return."

Mauriel scoffed. "You can't do that without the other Raiders' approval."

"I think you'll find they agree with me." Lazaro turned to the captured Raiders. "If you agree to abide by the Raider's Oath, we won't punish you for Mauriel's power grab."

"I never agreed to that—" Valerie started.

"You have our vote!" one of Mauriel's Raiders yelled. "I never liked this whole idea anyway!"

"Traitor," Mauriel spat.

"You're the only traitor here," Lazaro said. "Alcabaza belongs to us." He motioned to Valerie's Raiders. "Put her in the prison. She'll be banished at dawn."

The Raiders dragged her away.

Antony clapped Lazaro on the shoulder. "That was honourable of you."

"I wanted to execute her," Lazaro admitted. "But this feels more fitting. And it's better for the Oath, too." He nodded to himself. "Alcabaza is more important than revenge."

Valerie clapped her hands together. "Raiders, wrangle the escaped eagles and gather the last of our food. We'll work on fixing the elevators at dawn."

A cheer went up from her gang. Heather gave a whoop. Aron found himself joining in. It made his lungs ache, but he didn't care.

Alcabaza was theirs again.

Armada

ABADDON MARCHED ALONG THE DECK. HE STUDIED the row of youths out the corner of his eye. They sat against the railing, heads down and knees drawn to their chests. Several held rags to their wounds, while others tended to lashes from whips.

"So, you decided to mutiny," Abaddon said slowly. "What did you hope to accomplish? Did you think you'd kill my crewmates and seize control of my flagship? What then?" He laughed. "This armada is the only home you have!"

The youths averted his gaze as he passed.

"Your precious Paradon won't save you here," Abaddon spat. "And those of you from the Badlands, the gorgons will pick your bones clean if you try to escape. No—we're in this together."

He turned on his heel and kept walking. "A mutiny is a serious offence," he said. "The penalty is death, or a hundred lashes—if you can survive it."

Several crewmates cracked their whips. Others levelled boarding pikes and sabres at the youths. The haboob continued to rage around them, making ropes creak and the hull groan.

"I should weed out the ringleaders and throw you over the railing," Abaddon said. "I won't tolerate your disobedience on *my* ship."

The crewmates muttered in agreement. Abaddon's eyes flitted over the faces of the youths. None raised their heads to challenge him.

"But I'm willing to overlook your infraction," he said.

The crewmates paused. Some of the youths risked exchanging glances.

"You can't be serious," Ramah cut in.

"The thieves who infiltrated here today stole part of our Sunstone," Abaddon replied. "And we need to get it back. If you man your stations and steer this ship, I'll pardon your mutiny and let you all go without punishment."

A murmur went through the youths. Some risked standing.

Ramah stepped forward. "Captain, the ship is locked down," he said. "We can't fly in weather like this."

"And we can't afford to let those thieves slip away!" Abaddon whirled on the man, then caught himself. "We've worked for *years* to build that Sunstone. We must pursue them immediately if we want to get it back, else they'll slip into the Badlands and we'll have lost our chance."

Abaddon motioned to the youths. "Get up. Unfurl the sails and keep the vessel steady." He pointed to another. "Ring the bell and send word to the other skyships. I want the whole fleet following us."

Some of the youths sprinted off and climbed the rigging. Others held back.

"But . . . the wind is too strong," a girl said. "The masts aren't safe. We'll be blown to our deaths!"

"You're welcome to *jump* to your death, if you'd rather refuse my offer," Abaddon replied. "Now, go, before I change my mind."

The remainder of the youths went to work. Sails dropped and filled with wind. The flagship lurched into motion. A bell rang out across the storm.

Abaddon nodded to himself. The prow swivelled in the direction Isiah had disappeared. Crewmates broke away and started giving out orders. A chorus of bells responded to the flagship's call. Skyships materialized from the haboob and drifted past.

Abaddon marched to the prow and looked out into the storm. "You thought you could rob me of my Sunstone, did you?" he said under his breath. "I'll chase you to the end of the Badlands!"

Returns

THE ROAR OF THE HABOOB ASSAULTED ISIAH'S SENSES. The wind tugged at his clothes and stung his face. He groggily spat out a mouthful of sand.

He pulled himself into a sitting position. The eagles stood like statues, their heads pulled in and their wings drawn close to their bodies. Aegon and Enzo sheltered beneath an overhang. Beyond, a murky yellow wall obscured the rest of the Badlands.

"That was quite the scare," Gaelon said. He knelt by Isiah's side and passed him a waterskin. "You did well, trusting Aegon like that."

Isiah rubbed his sore shoulders where Aegon had grabbed him. He downed the waterskin and felt the warm water soothe the dryness in his throat. "Where are we?" he managed to ask.

"A short flight away from the flagship," Gaelon said. "I hoped we would be able to slip beneath their notice."

"And we can't?"

Gaelon shook his head. "Abaddon's skyships are searching for us."

Isiah collected himself. The adrenaline of their escape left his limbs weak and shaky. "Do you have the Sunstone fragment?"

Gaelon nodded to the sack that hung from Vyrro's saddle. "Safe and sound." He paused. "As safe as you can be out here, at least."

Tessa and Myla appeared from behind Vyrro. They both ran over.

"Are you okay?" Tessa asked. Worry creased her brow.

"I'm fine." Isiah waved her away. "We need to fly to Alcabaza."

"We have to go *somewhere*, that's certain," Gaelon replied. "Abaddon will find us if we stay put."

"Vyrro doesn't like this weather," Tessa said.

"And he'll like it even less if Abaddon arrives."

"Can't we escape the haboob?" Isiah asked.

"We may be able to pull ahead of the storm if we fly quickly," Gaelon said. "It's better than trying to wait it out. Abaddon will scour the Badlands looking for us. If the haboob clears, we'll be sitting ducks."

Aegon left the overhang and slithered over to Isiah. He wrapped his arms around her scaly neck and pulled her close. Her large, dark eyes reflected his face back at him.

"You did well out there," Isiah said to her.

"You both did." Gaelon stood. "The sooner we take off, the better chance we have of outrunning the haboob—and Abaddon."

"Wait," Isiah said. "What about our dragons? The Raiders will attack us."

"We'll have to work it out as we go," Gaelon said. "We don't have time."

"Can't you pretend you're a Raider?" Myla asked. "Surely *someone* from the Badlands must have bonded with a dragon at some point in history, right?"

Gaelon shifted his weight. "It'll be a hard sell, but maybe we can convince them to believe us."

"Once we show them the Sunstone, they'll *have* to accept us," Tessa said. She bit her lip. "I hope Lazaro is safe."

He climbed onto Aegon and she swivelled in the direction of Alcabaza. Tessa and Myla took the lead on their eagles. They kicked off and ascended into the haboob, flying low to the ground to avoid the worst of the wind.

Isiah clung to Aegon's neck. The hectic escape from the flagship had sapped the strength from his muscles. A dull, stinging pain radiated from his back where his robes rubbed against his raw skin.

They flew in silence. Aegon shook her head and coughed. She squinted against the sand-filled air. Vyrro's tail twitched as he fought to stay aloft on the wind.

A horn echoed from somewhere behind them. A dark shape materialized to their right. Isiah's heart sank as a skyship's prow sliced through the haboob.

Gaelon swore. "Try to outrun them."

Isiah urged Aegon to fly faster. The skyship's sails strained as they filled with wind. Ropes creaked and the hull groaned as it fell into pursuit. Crewmates yelled and ran to the crossbows mounted on the deck.

"It's just a scouting vessel," Gaelon said. "The wind will tear up their sails if they're not careful."

Youths strained against the wind as the skyship gained on them. One of the smaller sails ripped free of its mast and spiralled off into the storm. The youths retracted other sails and the skyship began to slow.

"They're still gaining!" Tessa called.

A series of loud pops sounded as the skyship fired a volley of bolas. The chains arced toward them—but they fell short.

Aegon dropped toward a valley. Enzo and the two eagles flew ahead, weaving between the cliff walls. The skyship fired another round. Bolas struck the cliffsides and spat up rocks, but none came close to hitting their mark.

Aegon swivelled her head around and unleashed a burst of fire. The skyship pulled away as flames lashed its hull.

"Be careful!" Gaelon yelled. "The light will guide Abaddon right to us."

Isiah fought to revive his mental link to Aegon. After a moment, the fire in her chest died. The skyship giving chase lost several more of its sails. One of its wooden wings grated against a butte and splintered. Another burst of bolas erupted from the prow. Aegon twisted aside as they flew past. The ship fell away and the haboob consumed it.

Tessa pumped her fist and cheered. Isiah patted Aegon's flank.

"Abaddon knows the direction we're going," Myla called. "He'll follow us."

Isiah bit his lip. "You heard Gaelon. Abaddon will find us if we hide. We need to finish the Sunstone before that happens."

"You're right," Gaelon said. He lowered his voice. "Let's just hope it's enough."

* * *

"I see something!" Myla called.

Isiah leaned forward to peer over Aegon's head. The haboob lay behind them in the distance as a long yellow wall. Since escaping Abaddon's ships, they'd flown for as long as they could, escaping the haboob's grip and stealing quick rests to let their dragons and eagles recover. Isiah squinted and made out a line of people wandering through the Badlands.

"Do you think they're nomads?" he asked.

Tessa frowned. "They don't look like nomads. Where are their animals?"

One of the people pointed up at them and waved. The others crowded around, joining in.

"Let's see what they want," Gaelon said.

Tessa twisted around to look at the haboob. "We're not that far ahead."

"It will only take a moment," Gaelon replied, "and we have a couple of hours before the haboob catches up to us, by my reckoning."

They dropped toward the Badlands and landed near the crowd. People rushed over.

Myla gasped. "I recognize them." She covered her mouth. "They're from the Hidden Citadel."

Tessa bit her lip. "Oh no . . ."

An old woman shuffled through the crowd. Myla jumped off her eagle. "Edith!"

Isiah joined her and they ran over. They reached Edith's side and she leaned against them.

"What happened?" Myla asked. "Why are you here?"

"Abaddon ruined the Hidden Citadel," Edith replied. "There wasn't enough water left for us." Her voice came out hoarse. "We were forced to take the last of our things and leave." She shuddered. "The gorgons took so many of us. Others set off for different cities, but I thought we could reach Alcabaza."

Tessa hurried over with a waterskin. Edith thanked her and took it.

"Alcabaza isn't far from here," Isiah said. "You should come with us."

Edith waved him away. "We've lost too many people. I can't abandon the rest."

Myla took her arm. "You're in no position to walk anymore. The others can follow us."

Edith protested, then relented. As Myla spoke to the rest of the townsfolk, Tessa helped the old woman climb onto Enzo.

"It's only a short flight now," Tessa said. "I recognize this landscape."

With Edith safely behind Gaelon, they took flight and hastened toward Alcabaza. As they approached, the Badlands fell away to reveal a flat, open plain. Despite himself, a tired smile crossed Isiah's face.

He adjusted his seating on Aegon's back as the city of Alcabaza materialized, its lone mountain rising above the fields. Aegon gave a low rumble of recognition.

"Where do we land?" Isiah asked. "The Raiders might attack us."

Tessa put a hand to her forehead. "The longer we stay in the air, the more time they have to get suspicious. Let's land in the roosts. Royal Guards would never do that."

Isiah guided Aegon toward the top of the mountain. Vyrro gave a piercing cry as they descended on the roosts. As they drew closer, Isiah spotted the rows of eagle pens—and the Raiders.

Vyrro landed and ruffled his feathers. Raiders stumbled away as Myla's eagle touched down. A chorus of shouting went up when they spotted the dragons. Isiah took a deep breath. Aegon landed and took a few lumbering steps. Raiders scattered for cover, while others drew their sabres. Isiah's breath caught in his throat as one drew a bow.

"Stop!" Tessa waved her arms. Vyrro puffed up his neck feathers and spread out his wings. The eagles in their pens shrieked in panic as

Enzo landed and made the ground tremble. Gaelon slid from his dragon's back and raised his hands.

Handlers rushed to calm the birds. Others hung back, peering out from behind buildings. Raiders massed around them, watching with suspicious eyes. Aegon's nostrils flared and Isiah stroked her neck. He tried to ignore the tension in the air.

"We're Raiders," Tessa said. Her voice wobbled. Raiders grasped their sabre hilts. "We're with Lazaro's gang."

The Raiders exchanged glances. Isiah tensed, waiting for an arrow to fly. Enzo growled and clawed at the ground.

A voice rose above the crowd's muttering. Somebody pushed their way through. Lazaro stumbled into view. He locked eyes with Tessa and a smile broke out on his face.

"Lazaro!" Tessa jumped from Vyrro's saddle and sprinted over to him. The other Raiders backed away as he wrapped her in his arms and spun her.

"Tess," he exclaimed. He put her down and surveyed the dragons, then stepped in front of the crowd and raised his arms. "It's alright. We can trust them."

Tessa frowned. "What's been happening here? Have the Raiders accepted us back?"

"You could say that," Lazaro replied. "Do you have the Sunstone fragment?"

Tessa hurried to Vyrro's side and untied the sack. As Lazaro pulled the final Sunstone fragment out, Darla and the rest of the gang pushed through the crowd.

Isiah slipped from Aegon's shoulders. The reunions faded to a blur on the edge of his awareness. He watched the approaching haboob.

He swore he could almost make out the silhouettes of Abaddon's armada ...

Darla clapped him on the shoulder. Isiah winced, the wounds from his lashes still fresh. "I knew you would do it!" She let out a low whistle. "And just in time, too."

"Abaddon is coming," he blurted out.

Lazaro lowered the Sunstone fragment. "What?"

"He followed us," Isiah said. "He wants the Sunstone fragment."

A murmur went around the Raiders. Several exchanged confused glances.

"Nobody ever told me about an *Abaddon*," a woman said. The other Raiders stood aside to let them pass. "Who are these people?"

"Valerie," Lazaro said, "this is the rest of my gang. I told you they were looking for the final Sunstone fragment."

Valerie's nose crinkled. "You never said they had dragons."

"They won't hurt you," Isiah said quickly. "You can trust them."

She narrowed her eyes. "We'll be the judge of that."

Gaelon stepped forward. "We don't have time for this," he said. "Isiah is right about the armada." He turned to the Raiders. "A fleet of flying ships is approaching inside that haboob. They're coming for the Sunstone."

"Flying ships?" a Raider scoffed. "Sounds like nonsense."

"How do we know you're not from Paradon?" another said.

Edith hobbled over. "It's true," she said. "They attacked our settlement and destroyed it."

The woman scowled. "So you've led them right to Alcabaza?"

"With this fragment, we have a finished Sunstone," Gaelon said. "The fleet won't stop until they use it to control the Badlands. Fighting them is our only hope."

Lazaro frowned. "And how do you know so much about them?"

Gaelon exchanged glances with Tessa.

"He's a friend," Tessa cut in.

"We must finish the Sunstone," Gaelon said. "We don't have much time before the haboob reaches us."

Lazaro took the Sunstone fragment and they hurried into the crowd. Isiah hesitated.

"Stay here," he said to Aegon.

He helped Edith after Lazaro and the others. They crossed the roosts and entered a large building with a dome for a roof. Isiah found Gaelon standing before the Sunstone embedded in the wall. Three quarters were there. Only one was missing.

Isiah held his breath as Lazaro lifted the final fragment. He felt Tessa's hand loop around his own. The pain and fatigue of their journey melted away as Lazaro slid the fragment into place and made the Sunstone whole.

A low humming sound emanated from the disk. Isiah's bones trembled as he approached the Sunstone and placed a hand on it. Energy coursed beneath his palm, rippling through the detailed lines and markings. It seemed to pulse with a life of its own.

"So how do we use it?" Lazaro asked.

"It requires magic," Edith said. She rubbed her hands together. "I still remember my studies."

Isiah stepped aside as Edith placed her hands on the Sunstone. She closed her eyes and bowed her head.

"The Ancients took care to prevent anyone from firing this weapon," she said. "Abaddon must have spent years studying their mysteries."

The Sunstone began to glow. A deep pulsing sound reverberated through the room. Lazaro and the others backed away as a rhythmic pattern of light rippled across the Sunstone's surface.

Edith gritted her teeth. The pulsing grew faster, louder. Isiah peered out of the window. The sunlight seemed to grow stronger, illuminating the observatory so brightly that it forced him to squint. The visions from the spirit world played across his mind.

The Sunstone fired.

A blast of light erupted from the far side of the disk. Isiah covered his ears as it tore a hole in the wall and erupted into the sky. The cries of panicked eagles sounded outside as the Sunstone seemed to puncture the heavens. He winced as a wave of heat washed over him.

Edith hissed and yanked her hands away. The beam flickered, then went out. She staggered backwards and wiped a hand across her forehead.

Isiah caught her. "Are you alright?"

Edith put a hand over her heart. "It works," she said quietly.

"What was that?" a voice called. Footsteps thundered outside. Several Raiders sprinted into the observatory and skidded to a halt. They stared at the Sunstone with gaping mouths. The observatory wall was charred black.

"That," Lazaro said, "is the magic we'll use to destroy Abaddon's fleet."

Edith wobbled. Tessa grabbed her arm and helped her sit.

"It's a powerful weapon," she said. "I see why the Ancients buried it."

"Do you think you can destroy Abaddon's flagship?" Isiah asked.

Edith nodded. "I'll try my best." She paused. "But I won't be able to see him inside the haboob. The skyships are hidden."

Tessa swore. "We'll have to lure him out of it."

Isiah shifted his weight. "That will take too long. If he reaches Alcabaza, he'll destroy it."

"All I need is someone to signal where to aim," Edith said. She climbed to her feet. "Like your dragon."

Isiah hesitated. "What do you mean?"

"If you use your fire to light up the skyships, I can harness the power of the Sunstone to shoot them down," she replied. "It'll be too dangerous to use the Sunstone once the skyships reach the city. We need to destroy them before they start dropping their explosives."

"That sounds like a plan," Gaelon said. He turned to Isiah. "What do you say?"

Isiah's expression hardened. "I'll do it."

"If you're going, I'm going with you," Tessa cut in. "It's too dangerous on your own."

"There must be dozens of skyships in Abaddon's fleet," Lazaro said. "That means you'll need help. We'll go with you."

"What about the other Raiders?" Gaelon asked.

Lazaro scratched his chin. "Leave them to me."

Isiah and the others followed Lazaro as he left the damaged observatory and marched into the roosts. A crowd of Raiders had gathered, staring at the sky where the Sunstone had fired. They caught sight of Lazaro and erupted into a frenzy.

Valerie raised her arms to calm them. "*That's* your Sunstone?" she asked. "I've never seen anything like it!"

"Nobody has," Lazaro said. He raised his voice. "It's a weapon unlike anything we've seen in hundreds of years."

A murmur went around the Raiders. Tessa sidled closer to Isiah. She puffed up her chest and beamed at Lazaro.

"We need your help," Lazaro said. "My friends are right. An armada is coming to steal this weapon from us." He pointed to the haboob. "And they're hiding inside the storm. The dragons can light up the skyships to betray their positions, but they can't do it alone."

"Can't you just fire blind?" Valerie asked. "You saw how powerful the Sunstone is."

Lazaro shook his head. "Edith can't manage that. She needs to know where to aim. If the armada reaches us, they'll destroy Alcabaza. I've seen it happen. The Raider's Oath was made for times like this."

Valerie folded her arms. "What do you want us to do?"

"Pretend that it's Paradon invading."

The Raiders muttered among themselves. The seconds dragged past. Isiah wrung his hands.

"Well, Lazaro," Valerie said, "if you'd shown up a few months ago and given this speech, I'd have called you crazy. But you were right about the Sunstone—and the Oath." She put out a hand. "My gang is with you."

"Thank you," Lazaro said. "Anyone else?"

Another Raider stepped forward. "To hell with our differences. If Alcabaza is really in danger, I'll fight to protect it."

Several Raiders drew their sabres and joined him.

"This has been a chaotic few days," Lazaro said. He turned to the haboob. "And it's going to get much worse before it gets better."

Haboob

Isiah jogged toward Aegon. Gangs of Raiders exited the tavern and ran to their eagles. Handlers hurriedly secured the birds' saddles and swung open the gates. Gaelon sat waiting atop Enzo's back.

Isiah put a hand on his stomach to quell the turmoil. They had stopped to rest and prepare before the battle, but he hadn't been able to bring himself to eat. Tessa climbed into Vyrro's saddle and took his reins.

"Be careful," Isiah said.

She cracked a smile. "I always am." He caught the unease in her voice.

Lazaro and the others readied their eagles. Marie had volunteered to stay behind and watch over Edith in the observatory. Aron took a seat behind Tessa on Vyrro. Around him, the other Raiders spurred their eagles out of their pens. Isiah felt Aegon stiffen as she sensed the tension in the air.

Aron gave Isiah a salute. "Watch yourself out there," he said. "We'll try and help if you get into trouble."

Gaelon had explained the skyships to the Raiders. He'd warned them about their bolas and the way Abaddon's ships fought.

"The haboob will hurt the skyships' aim," he said. "But don't underestimate them. Fly low and avoid getting tangled in their sails. Once the ships are burning, they'll be an easy target for the Sunstone."

Isiah focused on his connection with Aegon and urged her forward. His stomach lurched as she broke into a run and launched herself from the roosts. The ground dropped away below him. Enzo roared and the Raiders fell into pursuit.

Isiah twisted around. Rows of eagles took flight, soaring away from Alcabaza and forming a thick cloud. Isiah spotted Tessa among them, along with Myla and Lazaro's gang. Ahead, the haboob loomed into the heavens. Isiah searched the rolling cloud for any sign of Abaddon's fleet.

Gaelon pulled a scarf over his mouth and nose. Tessa and the other Raiders did the same, until only their eyes were visible. Isiah fumbled with his scarf, slipping it over his nose to give him some protection from the stinging dust and sand.

The haboob drew steadily closer. Raiders gripped their eagles' reins. Aegon flexed her talons as dark shapes materialized inside the haboob. Isiah lowered his head as the storm washed over them.

The fury of the wind blasted him from all sides. Isiah fought to cling onto Aegon's back. A series of deep, metallic clangs echoed from the haboob as skyships sounded their bells. Aegon cracked open her jaws and unleashed a blast of flame.

The fire pierced the murky, swirling gloom, illuminating the prow of a skyship. It raced over the hull and forced crewmates to scatter for cover. Behind him, the Raiders entered the haboob and were lost to view. Isiah searched for any sign of the flagship amid the storm.

A series of loud pops sounded to his right. Aegon twisted away as bolas whipped past. They spiralled into the storm as a second skyship materialized. Eagles appeared as flashes, diving toward the decks and ripping crewmates from their perches.

Another volley of bolas arced through the air. Aegon climbed higher, fighting with the wind. The bolas flew past, narrowly missing them. Several struck the skyship on the opposite side. Crewmates yelled orders and the vessel veered toward them. Its sails loomed overhead, and its long hull filled Isiah's vision like a vice about to close.

Isiah urged Aegon into a dive. She folded her wings and dropped in altitude as the two skyships collided. Isiah ducked instinctively as the gap closed above them. The grinding of wood filled the air as masts snapped and hulls scraped.

Aegon flew beneath the skyships and emerged behind them. Isiah pressed his heel into her flank and she swivelled around. An orange glow welled in her chest as she soared toward the sails.

Her jaws cracked open and she unleashed a stream of fire. The sails, dried from the relentless wind, burst into flame. The eagles scattered. Crewmates desperately tried to cut the sails loose, but the wind fanned the flames until it became a swirling inferno.

Aegon pulled away. The second skyship dislodged itself from the first and drifted away, its left mast hanging like a broken wing. The burning sails cut through the gloom, revealing several more skyships sailing in the storm.

A deep humming noise made Isiah's bones rattle. His muscles tensed as he felt the Sunstone charging.

Crewmates screamed and threw themselves from the ship as a blinding pulse of light ripped through the haboob. It struck the skyship's hull and tore a hole through it. Aegon roared as the ship exploded, launching wood and masts high into the air. Isiah shielded his eyes and turned away as a wave of heat washed over him.

The remains of the skyship plummeted to the ground. The beam flickered and went out, and the haboob swept back in. Isiah struggled to get his bearings.

Where's Abaddon? he thought. Somewhere further away, another fireball pierced the storm as Gaelon and Enzo attacked. Aegon wobbled as she fought to stay aloft on the raging wind. Isiah's heart leapt into his throat as the flagship's massive prow appeared ahead of them.

Aegon turned on her wing and went into a dive. The flagship's golden figurehead ploughed past where they had been moments earlier. Bolas whistled past, striking buttes and ripping apart chunks of rock. Isiah struggled to keep his grip on Aegon's back as she dodged the deadly projectiles.

A bola flashed through the air in front of them. Aegon made a sharp turn and reeled away. Isiah's leg slipped and his heart flew into his throat.

"Aegon!" he made a desperate grab for her neck, but it was too late. The momentum ripped him from her back and sent him plummeting through empty air.

Isiah's stomach backflipped. Aegon disappeared into the haboob. The dark, sweeping underside of the flagship hovered overhead. Another flash lit the sky like lightning as the Sunstone fired again somewhere further in the storm.

Isiah hit the ground and the air was knocked out of him.

The world became a blur. He rolled down a slope, legs flailing. Sand stung his eyes and filled his mouth. An explosion of pain made him gasp as he struck a rock. The slope ended and he dropped several feet into a narrow gulley.

The spinning stopped. Isiah's head swam. He gritted his teeth and clutched his side. Tears sprang up in his eyes as the cuts from Abaddon's whip re-opened and trickles of warm blood seeped out. Fighting to draw breath, he dragged himself to his feet, leaning against the gulley wall for balance.

"Aegon!" His voice came out hoarse. The gulley offered him a moment of protection from the howling wind. He searched for any sign of her in the sky above. He tried to focus on their bond, but the pain made it hard to think.

The flagship floated above him. A flash lit the sky. Isiah waved his arms and yelled, trying to attract Aegon's attention.

A barrel dropped toward him and a surge of fear flooded his veins.

Isiah covered his head and ran as the barrel struck the side of the gulley and exploded. Rock and earth pelted his shoulders. He staggered away as more barrels dropped. One landed a few dozen feet away. Then another.

A series of buttes materialized ahead. Isiah fought to stay on his feet as he sprinted toward them. The flagship's bottom mast extended dangerously close to the ground. The sails bulged with air, powering the vessel forward.

Another explosion sent up a plume of rock and earth. The impact shook him to the bones. He waited for the flagship to pull up to avoid the buttes. Instead, it kept coming.

The mast collided with the buttes and cracked like a gunshot. Beams splintered and collapsed. Sails broke free and spiralled into the haboob. The underside of the flagship grated against the rock until it crumbled and fell. More barrels dropped from its sides.

One exploded nearby. Isiah stumbled and fell as the impact slammed into him like a punch. The fireball illuminated the mass of ropes and broken masts dangling from the underside of the vessel.

Isiah propped himself up on his knees and held his hands to his ringing ears. The sounds of the haboob were muffled and distant. His muscles tensed, waiting for another explosion. He desperately delved into his mind and cried out to Aegon in his thoughts.

A roar sounded. With the last of his strength, Isiah climbed to his feet and ran under the flagship, retracing his steps. He poured the last of his energy into his link with Aegon.

I'm over here! he called out in his mind. *Come and find me.*

Aegon roared again. A shape emerged from the storm. Aegon landed on the gulley and bounded over. Isiah collapsed against her flank.

"You came back," he managed to say. Despite the pain that came with each breath, he laughed. He climbed onto her shoulders and they hurriedly ascended into the haboob.

"We have to bring down Abaddon's flagship," he said. The massive vessel loomed ahead of them. A bell sounded and it began to turn. Isiah's scarf flapped uselessly in the wind. Sand clung to his eyelashes and irritated his nostrils. He pulled the scarf free and tied it over his eyes.

"I hope Gaelon was right," he said.

Isiah gripped Aegon's neck as she raced toward the flagship. He channelled his energy into feeling her movements. The scarf rendered everything dark, but he could have sworn he saw the vague outline of the flagship ahead. Heat burned in Aegon's chest as she closed in for another attack.

257

Crewmates loaded more bolas, but they were too late. Aegon launched herself upwards, releasing a stream of fire that bathed the central mast. The heat baked Isiah's face, causing sweat to form on his brow. Aegon pulled away as a cloud of smoke enveloped the flagship.

Another volley of bolas fired. This time Aegon was ready. She folded her wings and the chains flew past. She opened her jaws and bellowed in victory. Isiah let out a whoop and their voices merged into one.

A low, bone-chilling hum invaded Isiah's senses. He caught the panicked cries of crewmates through Aegon's sharpened ears. The air pressure dropped and the hair on the back of his neck stood as the Sunstone unleashed its fury.

Blinding light pierced Isiah's blindfold as the devastating beam ripped a hole through the flagship, puncturing the balloons that kept it airborne. The flagship groaned and lurched to one side as an explosion erupted into the sky. The vessel collided with a butte and scraped against it. Sails and ropes tangled around the hunk of rock and it lurched to a stop.

A cloud of Raiders appeared, closing in on the vessel. Enzo and Gaelon materialized, leading the charge. Crewmates stumbled about on the broken deck. The flagship groaned as one of its wings collapsed.

Isiah pulled off his blindfold and Aegon soared toward the flagship. Burning tatters of sail wafted through the air, and the wind whipped the blackish smoke into a billowing cloud. Raiders landed on the uneven deck and leapt off, sabres at the ready. Several youths fell from the vessel's ruined wings and plummeted to the ground below.

Isiah braced himself as Aegon crashed onto the deck. The force made the vessel shudder. Wood ground against stone as the flagship hung over empty air. He slid off and scanned for Tessa and his friends.

Crewmates took up arms and collided with the Raiders with a clash of steel. Eagles flashed through the sky above, visible through breaks in the smoke. Crewmates collapsed with cries of pain.

A gang of crewmates charged toward him. Isiah fumbled for his sabre. Aegon released a burst of fire and made them scatter. Youths ducked between the fighting and ran for safety. Isiah spotted Enzo and sprinted toward him.

"Gaelon!" he called. He reached their side and doubled over.

"Good job, Isiah," Gaelon said. "The rest of the skyships are panicking, but the wind stops them from turning back. They're sitting ducks."

"Where's Tessa?" he asked.

"She was flying with me," he replied. "They can't be far."

Isiah scanned the deck. He spotted Tessa with Myla and Aron in the chaos. He called out to them and they sprinted over.

The flagship lurched and tilted to one side. Several crewmates lost their footing and slid off the edge. The wind stole their screams as they plummeted out of sight. Other crewmates tried barricading themselves inside the flagship, but they couldn't halt the Raiders' advance. The flagship lurched and dropped a few feet.

"The flagship is barely holding on," Gaelon said. "We ought to get out of here before the ropes come loose."

Raiders returned to their eagles and took flight. Embers and bits of charred sails dropped from above. A couple of singed crewmates advanced. Aron drew his sabre and helped Tessa repel them with the clash of steel.

"What about Abaddon?" Isiah asked.

"Without his flagship, he's done for," Gaelon replied.

"No." Isiah shook his head. "We have to be sure. If he escapes with his Sunstone fragments, he could still finish it."

He hurried toward the far end of the ship. His friends came after him. Gaelon called Isiah's name, then abandoned Enzo to give chase.

Crewmates dropped ropes from the side of the flagship and slid out of sight. Bodies lay crumpled on the deck, their blood staining the wood red. Several Raiders dragged away their injured.

Isiah skidded to a halt as Abaddon emerged from a doorway. Two Sunstone fragments were tucked under his arms. He locked eyes with Isiah and let them drop. His face twisted into a snarl.

"You did this!" he roared. The end of his headscarf was singed, and his eyes blazed like glowing coals. He drew his sabre and marched toward them.

Gaelon stepped in front of him. "Give it up, Abaddon. You've already lost."

"There's still time for my revenge," he spat. "Against you *and* the boy."

Abaddon lashed out with his sabre. Isiah leapt aside as Gaelon parried it and the scrape of metal rang out. Abaddon batted Gaelon's sabre aside and whirled on Isiah.

"I should have killed you when I had the chance," he said.

Isiah raised his blade in defence. Abaddon towered over him. His sabre reflected the inferno above and gleamed with a cruel light. Isiah inched away, trying to keep his footing on the slanting deck.

Gaelon swung at the man. Abaddon parried the blade and swept his foot out. Gaelon slipped and landed on his stomach with a grunt. Abaddon aimed a thrust at him.

"No!" Isiah darted forward. His sabre glanced off Abaddon's middle, slicing through his robes. Abaddon hissed in pain and clutched his side as a red line formed.

Gaelon scrambled to his feet. Enzo roared and tried to lumber towards them. The flagship groaned and shuddered harder. One of the masts collapsed, covering the deck in a wall of fire.

"You can't do anything without your dragons." Abaddon launched a flurry of blows. Gaelon wobbled and retreated. Behind him, the deck ended in empty air.

Gaelon's chest heaved as he parried Abaddon's blows. His movements grew clumsier. He gritted his teeth as Abaddon landed a cut on his arm. Abaddon flicked his sabre, staining the deck with blood.

"Let's see if you can fly, Royal Guard." Abaddon planted his foot on Gaelon's chest.

Gaelon's eyes widened as he pitched backwards. His sabre flew from his hand. He twisted his body and caught the edge of the deck.

A bolt of panic flew through Isiah. He scooped up one of the Sunstone fragments and raised it over the edge. "Abaddon!" he yelled.

The man whirled on him. His eyes narrowed when he saw the Sunstone fragment. "You wouldn't dare."

Gaelon gritted his teeth as he clung to the edge of the ship. Isiah forced himself to stand tall. "Try me."

Abaddon broke into a run. Isiah dropped the Sunstone fragment and it plunged into the storm. He turned and ran toward the rear of the ship.

"Tessa!" he called over his shoulder. "Help Gaelon!"

Tessa hesitated. Gaelon gripped the deck with both hands. His feet dangled over empty air. Blood oozed from the wound on his arm. His face contorted with the effort.

Tessa threw herself forward and slid across the deck. She grabbed his wrists and splayed her legs out to try and gain purchase. "Help me!" she called. Myla and Aron sprinted over and grabbed Tessa's ankles.

Abaddon marched after Isiah. "I don't need that fragment," he said. "There are ruins all over the Badlands. I'll find more, then I'll bring you all to your knees."

Isiah ducked behind a mast as Abaddon swung his sabre. The blade bit into the wood.

He yanked it free. "I'll flay you alive," he snarled. "You'll suffer like I did when Paradon ripped away my home."

Isiah jumped onto a lower deck as Abaddon's sabre sliced the air where his head had been. Below, Tessa grunted as she slowly hauled Gaelon onto the deck. Every second seemed to take an eternity. Aron gritted his teeth and leaned back with all of his weight.

"I'm slipping," Aron hissed between clenched teeth. Gaelon's legs swung uselessly in empty air.

Isiah flinched as Abaddon's sabre bit into a railing. "I'll never forgive your people for what they did to us." He swung again. "I'll kill every last one of you."

Isiah parried Abaddon's attack. The impact sent a shockwave down his arm. His eyes widened as a loud snap sounded. The blackened blade, already damaged by his fight with the Awakened, snapped in two.

Aegon roared as she flew past the flagship. The mess of burning sails and tangled ropes blocked her from getting any closer. The flagship jolted as it dropped several more feet. Tessa screamed as she fought to keep hold of Gaelon.

Isiah ducked beneath Abaddon's blow. The man's chest heaved, and veins bulged in his neck. Isiah gripped the broken half of his sabre. Abaddon grabbed a railing as the flagship lurched again. The last Raiders fled the vessel as the deck tilted at a sharper angle. Myla and Aron jammed their feet against the last of the railing.

"I'll get my revenge if it's the last thing I do!" Abaddon threw aside his sabre and lunged. Isiah's arm jolted as his broken blade sank into the man's flesh. Abaddon seemed not to notice. He wrapped an arm around Isiah's neck and pulled them toward the drop.

"We'll go down together!" he yelled.

Panic flared in Isiah's chest. He caught a passing railing and latched on. His muscles screamed as they lurched to a stop. Isiah gritted his teeth as a searing pain coursed through his arm. His shoulder felt like it was about to be ripped from its socket.

Abaddon grunted. Blood oozed from the sabre wound in his stomach. He placed a hand on the railing and pushed. His other arm wrapped around Isiah's neck like a vice. Isiah's palm was slick with sweat. He felt his grip slipping.

With a desperate cry, he yanked his broken sabre free and brought it down on Abaddon's hand.

Abaddon screamed. Isiah's blade sliced clean through his fingers. With the last of his strength, Isiah wrestled free. Abaddon wobbled, then he toppled backwards and plunged off the edge of the flagship. His scream echoed in the wind.

Isiah dropped his broken sabre and hugged the balcony. His lungs heaved. Ropes snapped as the flagship began to pull free of the butte.

"Isiah!" Tessa called.

Isiah pushed off the railing and hobbled to her side. He collapsed to his knees and took hold of Gaelon's arm. With the help of Myla and Aron, they dragged the man onto the deck and then scrambled away from the edge.

"The flagship is about to break free," Gaelon said. "It's too late to fly off. Aegon landing might be enough to dislodge it."

"Where do we go?" Myla asked.

Gaelon pointed to the butte. "Over there. Hurry."

Burning masts collapsed onto the deck. Flames ate at the ropes until they snapped. Isiah clawed his way up the deck and reached the butte that the flagship rested against. Gaelon found a narrow ledge and they all joined him. The man wrapped his arms around the two girls. Tessa clung to him as she pressed herself against the rock.

The flagship jolted. Wood splintered and cracked. Isiah tightened his grip against the butte as ropes cracked like whips overhead. Then the flagship gave way.

Isiah closed his eyes as the burning masts dropped past. The butte shook as the flagship plummeted to the ground and crumpled with a deafening crash. Smoke and embers billowed in the air. Isiah adjusted his footing on the narrow ledge, all too aware of the dizzying drop just a few inches beyond.

The haboob raged around them. Somewhere beyond, Aegon roared. Isiah crouched with his friends in the storm as the murky silhouette of a dragon materialized.

He willed himself to peer over the edge of the drop. Far below, the flagship lay in ruins.

At Peace

Isiah lost track of time. He huddled on the ledge, drifting in and out of consciousness. They waited as the haboob lost its power and the dust began to settle. As the wind died, Aegon lifted them from the ledge and carried them to the Badlands below.

Isiah picked his way over the broken remains of the flagship. The vessel lay sprawled like a dead whale, a mass of shattered masts and charred wood. Aegon nuzzled him and gave a low rumble.

A deathly calm lay across the Badlands. Shafts of sunlight began to peer through the dust cloud, illuminating the broken bodies of sky-ships. Movement stirred as Raiders and their eagles emerged from caves and gullies in the earth. Isiah tried to ignore the corpses littering the battlefield.

Vyrro spotted them and flew over. Tessa wrapped her arms around his neck. As Alcabaza became visible in the distance, Raiders took off toward it.

"Is it over?" Myla asked.

Isiah nodded. "Abaddon is dead." His voice came out hoarse. The madness in Abaddon's eyes was burned into his mind.

Gaelon put a hand on Tessa's shoulder. "I want to thank you for helping me," he said. "I would have fallen if not for you all."

Tessa rubbed her shoulders and grimaced. "I can't forgive you for what you did." She hesitated. "But maybe I can put it behind us."

Gaelon smiled. "All I want is for you to be at peace."

Isiah climbed onto Aegon and settled into the groove in her shoulders.

"You did well," Gaelon said. "I saw you take down the flagship. You trusted her."

Isiah patted Aegon's neck. Her head swivelled around and she gave him a look of recognition. "I remembered what you said."

"Does this mean you don't need a teacher anymore?" Myla asked.

"I don't know," he replied. "Gaelon *did* say Royal Guards took years to train." He turned to Gaelon. "Are you returning to the highlands after this?"

"I won't run off just yet," Gaelon said. "I thought I'd stick around for a while. If I'm welcome here, that is," he added.

A smile upturned the corner of Tessa's mouth. "I think you are."

"We still need to keep the Sunstone safe," Isiah said. "Everybody will know about it now."

"You're right," Gaelon replied. He bowed his head. "Sybil would have wanted me to look after it."

The haboob rolled past Alcabaza, becoming a hazy smudge in the distance once more. Coils of smoke rose from smouldering fires.

"Do you think any of the skyships escaped?" Isiah asked.

Gaelon shrugged. "Without their flagship—or the Sunstone— there's not much they can do to hurt us. Any last ships will be easy pickings."

They took to the skies and wearily flew to Alcabaza. Downed skyships littered the ground behind them.

"There must be a lot of treasure from all the ruins they looted," Tessa said. "And magic."

They reached the city and landed on the roosts. Handlers tended to eagles and treated the injured. Raiders carried their wounded comrades to troops of medics. Lazaro appeared, holding a bandage to his shoulder.

"Tess!" He threw his good arm around her. "That was some good flying out there. Abaddon never stood a chance."

Tessa grinned. "We wouldn't have been able to do it without the dragons." She grew more serious after a second. "Is everyone else okay?"

"They made it back safely," he replied. "Valerie asked me to help with the wounded."

Tessa exchanged glances with Isiah. "Does this mean you're not still angry with them for banishing us?"

Lazaro raised his hands. "The past is the past. We've got an Oath to repair."

"Isiah!" Marie called. Isiah turned to see the girl waving her arm as she helped Edith shuffle along the road.

Isiah hurried over as fast as his aching body would allow. Edith huffed and eased herself onto a bench.

Tessa and Aron joined them. Tessa's brow creased in concern when she saw Edith. "Are you alright?"

"The Sunstone took a lot out of me," Edith replied. She coughed. "But I think I'll be fine."

Isiah's gaze went to the observatory. Part of the wall was blackened from the Sunstone's magic. From the city, he made out the smoke rising from the battlefield.

"If any skyships slipped past us in the haboob, they'll be carried straight to the border with Paradon." Edith managed a hoarse laugh. "I'd like to see the looks on their faces when they realize that."

"Abaddon said it was Paradon's fault they had to leave," Isiah said suddenly. "He was trying to save his people. They had nowhere left to go."

Tessa folded her arms. "They ruined their chance for peace when they attacked the Hidden Citadel. The Badlands belongs to *us*."

"And now we've got the Sunstone to protect it, right?" Marie asked.

"From Paradon, yes," Edith said, "and any other threat that challenges Alcabaza." She shuddered. "But I've felt its power. I know what it could do if it fell into the wrong hands."

Isiah grimaced as he remembered the visions he'd seen in the spirit world. "But we'll protect it. It'll be safe here."

"For now, yes," Edith said. "The power of the Ancients is nothing to be trifled with." She brightened up. "But don't let my ramblings get you worked up. Go and rest. You deserve it."

Isiah bid the woman goodbye and broke away. He walked with Tessa back toward the tavern. As they went, she looped her fingers through his.

"Does this mean you're not angry with Gaelon anymore?" he asked.

Tessa looked at her feet. "Maybe I was wrong about needing revenge," she said. "I was only hurting myself." She dropped her voice. "And I don't want to turn out like Abaddon."

"That won't ever happen." Isiah squeezed her hand. "You've got us looking out for you."

"It'll take time," she said, "but I can feel the weight lifting."

"Will you tell Lazaro?"

Tessa paused. "Not yet. He's got the Raiders to deal with. I don't want to say anything that will ruin that for him." She glanced in his direction. "He was hit just as hard by our parents' deaths—even if he doesn't like to show it."

Isiah stopped. "Does this mean that we're here to stay?"

Tessa shrugged. "I guess so." She looked at her feet. "I always liked it here."

Tessa sidled closer and her eyes darted to his. Her breath tickled his face. She leaned forward and her lips met his.

Isiah cracked a smile. "What was that for?"

"I don't know . . ." Tessa stepped away. "It felt right." She dusted the sand off his shoulders. "Let's go into the city. I want to see our old house."

Isiah scratched the back of his neck and grinned. "Whatever you say."

Get a Free Book!

He dreamed of killing a dragon. Now he has to save one.

A single dragon pelt could buy Cole a life outside the slums—but when he joins a band of outlaws to seek his fortune, the hunt doesn't go the way he thought.

Because dragons aren't the monsters he believed... and the moment he refuses to kill it, he becomes the prey.

Stuck with a wounded dragon and with rival hunters closing in, Cole has one chance at survival:

Keep it alive long enough to escape the wilds.

Grab your copy now at: www.morganclasperauthor.com

Acknowledgements

I'm always excited to expand on a book series and take the lore and characters in new directions, and this novel was no exception. From the powerful sunstone, inspired by ancient Aztec artefacts, to the spirit world and the mystical source from which the magic in this universe springs, writing Nomad's Ruin was great fun.

I particularly enjoyed getting a chance to delve into Tessa's character and explore her conflicts – and unresolved trauma – in more detail. I'm also happy that I had the opportunity to bring the cunning Raider Mauriel back and incorporate her into the bigger picture. Speaking of villains, I'm also grateful that I finally had a reason to introduce flying ships (something I've always wanted to do in a book!) with Abaddon's armada.

With another novel comes another list of people to thank. As always, the invaluable advice and guidance of my editor Darcy Werkman helped make Nomad's Ruin what it is today. And of course, where would I be without the beautiful book cover from my talented cover designer Fabrice Bertolotto? I'd also like to thank my illustrator Marina

Baskakova for once again providing a selection of breathtaking ink illustrations that help bring the Badlands to life.

As of writing this, Nomad's Ruin is my seventh published novel, and I've learned a lot along the way. I'd like to thank every reader who has given both this series and the Frostwing Quadrilogy a go. Without your readership and feedback, this wouldn't be possible. Seeing so many people enjoy these adventures inspires me to continue writing and dreaming up new ways to expand on Isiah and Tessa's adventures. I hope to see you all again in the next novel!

- Morgan

About the Author

Morgan Lee Clasper is a fantasy author and freelance copywriter who has over seven years of experience in the publishing industry. As a copywriter, he's worked with New York Times, Wall Street Journal, and USA Today bestselling authors to craft beautiful book blurbs, engaging author bios, and eye-catching sales copy.

Morgan is the author of the YA fantasy series The Frostwing Quadrilogy and the Chronicles of Alcabaza. When not writing, he enjoys studying philosophy, existential psychology, and Christian and Orthodox theology. For more information (and a free book!) visit:

www.morganclasperauthor.com

feet. The sticky sensation of blood crept down his skin from dozens of thorns. He shrugged off the stinging pain and turned back the way he had come.

Being stranded alone at night is suicide. He knew this place was gorgon country. He tore up a nearby sapling and stripped its leaves to form a walking stick. Leaning his weight against it, he gritted his teeth and began to walk.

He just had to make it to Alcabaza before the killers found him.

Aegon

"And if you lean to the side like this," Isiah told Tessa as he braced himself against Aegon's scaly flank, "you tell her to turn."

The Badlands sprawled below, illuminated by the vivid hue of the blue-white sun overhead. The light reflected off his dragon's scales in a dazzling display, forcing him to squint.

"And what about when you want to go down?" Tessa asked. Her arms were wrapped around Isiah's middle. "I still don't understand how you do it without reins."

"It goes deeper than that," Isiah said. "Ward always said that after you bond, they can sense what you want them to do."

"So it's like magic, huh?" Tessa asked.

Isiah shrugged. "I guess so."

Aegon turned on her wing, spiralling around a rock formation. Isiah shifted his weight, settling into the swell of her wingbeats. Without Ward or any of the Royal Guards to train him, he'd spent weeks figuring out how to fly with her.

"Well, we need to land," Tessa said. "My legs are getting sore."

Isiah guided Aegon into the safety of the rocky spires that had become her home. The cave appeared and he braced himself as she

landed. Tessa let go of his waist and slipped off the dragon's back. She winced and stretched her lower back.

"You need a saddle," she said. "It's nothing like riding an eagle."

"You just have to get used to it," Isiah replied. He gave her a nudge. "*You* were the one who wanted to go flying today."

Tessa rolled her eyes. "You can walk back to Alcabaza with that attitude, wise guy."

She ran her hand down Aegon's flank. A shimmering mix of silver scales adorned the dragon's body, giving way to intense blue and purple where the sun touched her. Thick hind legs supported her weight, while her wings doubled as arms with long talons. Aegon let out a plume of hot breath and gave Isiah a knowing look.

"Hey, I've got to deal with her all day," Isiah said. Tessa folded her arms, and Isiah raised his hands in mock surrender. "Kidding, kidding."

She smiled. "You've got the Raider spirit," she said. "I'll give you that."

Isiah laughed. Ever since they'd defeated Enrik and his gang of Raiders, he and Tessa had grown closer. Getting away from Lazaro's house and the stuffiness of the city let him relax and lower his guard. Due to the risk of Raiders spotting them, they often went out to fly Aegon across the Badlands under the cover of night.

Tessa sighed after a moment. "Lazaro will probably be wondering where we've got to."

Isiah groaned. "Lazaro would come with us if he could."

Since Aron had told the Raiders the truth about Enrik's plan to sell the oasis water to the nobles at Paradon, the Raider groups had allowed Lazaro to remain in Alcabaza. Isiah knew the Raiders hadn't

apologized for arresting them and trashing their house, but he was thankful for their unspoken truce.

"At least Lazaro is looking out for us," Tessa replied.

Isiah feigned offence. "Does he still not trust me?"

Tessa winked at him. "He doesn't trust you not to get up to no good." She turned and beckoned him. Her dark hair swished behind her, and her colourful robes matched the reds and oranges of the Badlands.

Isiah gave her a sly grin. "So I need a chaperone now, do I?"

He said goodbye to Aegon and took off after Tessa. They exited the cave and followed a narrow, rocky path to a nearby spring, where Vyrro sat waiting. The giant eagle perked up when he saw them. He ruffled his feathers and marched over.

"There you are," Tessa said. She patted his scaly leg. "How about we head back to Alcabaza?"

Isiah stopped by the pool and filled his waterskin, before clambering up behind Tessa. Vyrro kicked off and took to the air with a series of wingbeats. Isiah took one last look over his shoulder at Aegon's cave, before the rocky landscape stole it from view.

* * *

The Badlands fell away and the city of Alcabaza came into view. Isiah raised a hand to shield his eyes from the sun as the massive mountain materialized. A grassy plain, coated in a sea of maize, sprawled around the mountain's feet. Its flat peak, squared off as if cut by a huge knife, broke the skyline. Eagles, no more than dark silhouettes, spiralled around it.

Vyrro lowered his head and picked up speed, sensing their home was near. The city hugged the mountainside, divided into three terraces cut into the rock. Hundreds of squat, flat-roofed buildings sat piled atop one another, fighting for space and spilling over the edges. Near the foot of the mountain, a lattice of beams and scaffolding supported wooden elevators that lifted merchants into the city.

Vyrro folded his wings and dropped onto a landing pad near the mountain's peak. Beyond, Raiders streamed past the eagle pens, heading further into the roosts.

"What's going on there?" Isiah asked.

Tessa furrowed her brow. "I don't know."

Luca emerged from the crowd. He bounded toward them, his golden hair flapping wildly.

"I'll take Vyrro for you," he said. He grabbed hold of the eagle's harness as Isiah and Tessa slipped off.

"What's with the commotion?" Tessa asked.

"A Raider meeting," Luca replied. "You know how well Lazaro gets on with the other Raiders. He skipped it and sent me here instead."

Tessa smiled. "That's like him alright." She cocked her head. "What's it about?"

"Nothing important, yet," Luca said. He started leading Vyrro away. "I'll let you know if anything interesting happens."

The pair bid Luca goodbye, then Tessa led Isiah away from the mountaintop and down a staircase into the city itself. Isiah pushed through the crowd to keep up with her. No matter how long he spent in the city, he was sure he'd never find his way around.

Streams of people jostled him back and forth through the narrow streets. Some ducked into twisting alleyways, while others crowded

around merchant stalls. Dust spiralled into the air from hundreds of shuffling feet. Occasionally the sound of a donkey rose above the chatter.

Isiah tightened his cloak and hastened after Tessa. They passed a bazaar with its brightly coloured tarps and suffocating incense, then past a row of houses with clotheslines strung over their flat, walled roofs. Isiah caught glimpses of the plain far below.

"Is it me, or has it got busier here?" he asked.

Tessa mulled it over. "It's a good season for merchants. Nobody stays in Alcabaza for long." She paused. "Except us Raiders."

They made it down to the lowest terrace. The streets here were wider, and the steady grumble of machinery sounded in the direction of the elevators. Wooden platforms extended off the mountainside, with staircases disappearing to meet the elevators. Caravans of merchants and nomads entered the city, their mules straining under the weight of goods. Taverns, carved into the mountain itself, stood open to receive them. It reminded Isiah of when he'd first arrived at the city with the nomad Reuben.

They passed the entrance and navigated to the edge of the terrace, where Lazaro's house sat alongside a row of others, jutting over the edge. Windows—a few boarded up—looked out over the street, while a sturdy door was set into its dusty sandstone walls. Tessa produced a key from her cloak and let them both in.

The bright colours and deafening sounds of the city faded as Isiah ducked inside. A cool shadow washed over his skin, driving away the heat from the searing midday sun. Tessa poked her head into the dining room that jutted off the entryway.

"Lazaro, we're back," she called.

"Lazaro went out," Aron said. "He's avoiding the meeting. Told me to keep an eye out for you." He wandered into the hall and cracked a mischievous smile. "I thought you'd invite me flying with you."

"Hey, Aron." Isiah nodded at the boy.

Aron clapped Isiah on the shoulder. "How did training go?"

"We're getting somewhere," he replied. "It would go faster if Ward was still alive to teach me."

Tessa pushed past them and dumped her gear on the dining room table. Lazaro had managed to replace most of what had been destroyed in Enrik's raid with the money they'd earned from the ruin. A few windows remained boarded-up, but the place was almost back to normal.

"At least you have something to fly," Aron said. "I don't know the first thing about *eagles*, never mind dragons."

While Aron fell into a conversation with Tessa, Isiah climbed the creaky staircase to the cramped storeroom that he slept in. Lazaro had moved a few of the barrels and crates out to make room for a second bed. Aron's gear lay in a pile nearby. Isiah stepped over the mess and placed his sabre on his bed.

He cast another look at Aron's side of the room. Ever since Enrik died and his Raiders had scattered, Aron had been without a home. Tessa had offered to let him stay with them—a proposition that Isiah was beginning to have second thoughts about.

A small window let a shaft of sunlight into the storeroom. The heat from outside made Isiah's skin itch. He wandered to the washroom and studied his reflection in the small, cracked mirror. He peeled back his cloak to reveal his warped, disfigured skin. The scarring stretched

from his chest over his right shoulder and upper back—the sign of being Marked.

Isiah gave the rusty hand pump a push and waited until water appeared. Cupping it in his hands, he doused his Mark to relieve some of the redness and itching. It sapped the heat away, giving him momentary relief.

Isiah let the pump run dry, then readjusted his cloak to cover his Mark. It felt bumpy to the touch—like a melted candle. He pushed the thought out of his mind and exited the washroom. When he returned downstairs, Aron was leaning against the table, still chatting with Tessa.

"Have you been keeping tabs on the other Raiders?" Tessa asked.

Aron nodded. "Nobody has a clue about Aegon. If anyone starts spreading word of a dragon, I'll be the first one to know."

"Good," Isiah said. "It feels wrong leaving her on her own like this. She must be lonely."

"She'll be fine." Tessa put a hand on his arm. "She's in a good hiding place. No Raiders ever fly near there."

"Unless they find a ruin or something," Aron said.

Isiah shifted his footing. "Then let's hope they don't."

"If I hear any whispers from the Scavengers, I'll tell you," Aron said. "But keeping a dragon hidden isn't an easy job, you know."

Tessa tilted her head and peered out the window. "I think I see Lazaro."

She broke away from the table. Isiah went after her, relieved for the distraction. Tessa opened the door and Lazaro stepped in.

"You're back, are you?" He nodded at Isiah. "You're supposed to tell me before you run off."

Tessa rolled her eyes. "Relax. We had Vyrro with us."

Lazaro ran a hand through his short-cropped hair. Stubble clung to his tan skin, and his nose slanted to the side from an old scuffle. "Then maybe you can put him to use and find a ruin for us." His nose shrivelled as he looked around their still-damaged house. "Those damn Raiders trashed everything."

Lazaro filed inside, followed by the twins Darla and Antony. Tessa started to close the door, but Isiah caught someone running down the street.

"Hold on," he said.

Luca pushed through the crowd. He skidded to a halt in the doorway, doubled over.

"Luca!" Tessa's brow crinkled. "What's wrong?"

"Something is going on at the meeting," he said between panting breaths. "You guys should see this."

Lazaro stepped into view. "How serious is it?"

"I ran as fast as I could." Luca beckoned them. "Come on. We'll miss it."

Lazaro adjusted his sabre. "This better be good."

They followed Luca deeper into the city. As they ran, Isiah fought the welling unease in his gut. They ran up the terraces and reached the eagle roosts. Isiah's lungs strained at the thinning air. As they drew closer, a commotion reached his ears. It came from the direction of the Raider meeting he'd seen earlier.

He ran past the eagle pens and their colourful tarps, then skidded to a halt on the edge of the group. Lazaro craned his neck to see into the ring. Shouting erupted from inside.

"Get in there." He gave Isiah a push. "See what's going on."

Isiah put his head down and shoved his way into the crowd. Tessa and Aron came after him. He neared the front of the crowd where he could get a look at the source of the noise.

"My eagle crashed in the Badlands," a Raider said. Bandages covered his torso, and his clothes were torn at the edges. Cuts crisscrossed his exposed arms. "The gorgons almost found me before I could get here."

Frenzied conversation rippled around the crowd. Raiders shifted their footing and cast suspicious glances at one another.

"What are they saying?" Isiah asked.

"Shh," Tessa replied. She craned her neck to try and get a closer look.

"Did you see who they were, Keegan?" another Raider asked. "Even a small glimpse?"

Keegan shook his head. "It was too dark—and they were wearing masks. They didn't want to be identified."

The frenzy grew louder. Isiah spotted Lazaro and Darla pushing into the crowd.

"They weren't Royal Guards," Keegan replied. "They had eagles."

One of the Raiders narrowed his eyes. "So you're saying we've got Oath-breakers among us?"

"Nobody has ever committed such a blatant attack," one of the Raiders said. A few strands of grey hair poked through his beard. He lowered his voice. "Except maybe for Lazaro's gang. They've always been a wild card."

Isiah glanced over his shoulder at Lazaro. He saw the man's fists tighten. Darla grabbed Lazaro's arm.

"Whoever it was, they clearly planned it," Keegan said. "Who says they won't do it again?" He spread out his arms, then winced at the pain. "It could be any of you."

Several Raiders dropped hands to their weapons. Groups huddled closer together. Lazaro broke away from the crowd, and Tessa pulled Isiah after her. They made it out of the crowd and reunited with Lazaro and the others.

"Someone else broke the Oath?" Isiah said. "Why would they do that?"

"To deal with a rivalry, perhaps," Tessa replied. "There are more than a few feuds that have fallen short of blood because of the Oath. But now that Enrik broke it . . ."

Lazaro scowled at the Raiders. "The nerve of them to accuse us. I should have given him a piece of my mind."

"Not here," Antony said under his breath. "We don't need another fight."

They wandered away from the group, back in the direction of their house. Isiah let the sounds of the crowd fade to the edge of his awareness. The Raider's Oath was the only thing stopping anarchy. "What happens if someone else decides to break it?" he asked, but he already knew the answer.

"Then the whole of Alcabaza could fall apart," Tessa said.

"Do you see why I called you?" Luca asked. "The Raiders are scared. I hear it from the handlers when I'm caring for the eagles. They figure if someone as popular and influential as Enrik could be a traitor, secretly working with Paradon, who else could be hiding secrets?"

Isiah tightened his cloak. He tried to ignore the ever-present feeling of his Mark. Whenever he was in the city, he could feel people's eyes washing over him. All it took was for one Raider to get too suspicious.

They left the roosts and entered the lower levels of the city.

"What do we do now?" Darla asked.

"Nothing, yet," Lazaro replied. He slammed his fist into his palm. "If they think they can pin this on us, they've got another thing coming."

"We're just an easy target," she said. "After what happened with Enrik and all. The Raiders realized their mistake. We're not Oath-breakers."

"There are still more than a few of them who want to see us hanged," Antony replied. He turned to Tessa. "I don't know about Lazaro, but I don't like the idea of you flying Aegon at night with these attacks going on."

Isiah faltered. "What do you mean?"

"I mean if you keep sneaking off at night, you're going to end up running into trouble," Antony replied.

Tessa folded her arms. "It was only one group. For all we know, Keegan got into a scuffle with another gang and they wanted revenge."

"Antony's right," Lazaro said. "You know how I feel about you associating with dragons. I won't have you endangering yourself like that, Tess."

"Then we'll be careful," she shot back. She glanced at Isiah. "Right?"

"No nocturnal flights," Lazaro repeated. "If whoever is out there wants our blood, then they'll have to go through me."

Tessa huffed.

"He's only doing what's best," Antony said.

"What about scouting, then?" Tessa asked.

Lazaro's nose crinkled. "Scouting is different."

"Oh yeah, how?"

"Nobody is being attacked in the day, for starters," Darla cut in. "Just hold off on your nocturnal escapades, okay?"

They reached their house and Lazaro ducked inside. Isiah's head swam. The sight of Keegan and his injuries was burned into his mind. The idea of rogue Raiders hunting the Badlands made his skin crawl.

"We'll sneak out," Tessa said under her breath. "We can look after ourselves."

Isiah shook his head to clear the thoughts. "Maybe flying at night isn't such a great idea."

Tessa rolled her eyes.

"You know he means well," Isiah said.

She sighed. "I know, you're right." She checked that nobody else was listening. "But sometimes I wish he'd leave us alone."

Keegan's Ruin

ISIAH ADJUSTED HIMSELF ON VYRRO'S SADDLE for the hundredth time. Tessa's body pressed against his front, and Aron clung to his back. Isiah squirmed as the straps of Vyrro's harness cut into his legs.

"Vyrro isn't designed for three people," Tessa said. "They should know that."

Antony had insisted the three of them go out when scouting for ruins. *For extra security*, he'd said. Lazaro had forbidden them from travelling close to the area Keegan had been attacked.

"You know, it makes me wonder what Keegan was after that was so important," Aron said. "I mean, why did those mystery Raiders attack *him*?"

"I told you," Tessa replied. "It must have been a rivalry."

"But to go to all that trouble? Why not attack him inside Alcabaza? It would take much less effort."

"Are you saying we should go and check it out?" Isiah asked.

"Well," Aron said, "I don't want Lazaro to kick me out, so *technically* no. But all I'm saying is Keegan must have been going somewhere."

"Or he was scouting," Tessa replied.

"At night? Come on, Tessa. You don't scout for ruins at night." Aron leaned closer, further squishing Isiah. "You *raid* them at night, so nobody can see where you went and follow you." He pointed to the horizon. "I recognize the place where the attack happened. I reckon I can guide you there."

Tessa dug her leg into Vyrro's side. The eagle responded by pivoting on his wing. His tail feathers opened to act as a rudder. Isiah shielded his gaze from the twin suns above. The blue-white sun baked the Badlands in heat, while its reddish cousin sat off to the side.

"Lazaro doesn't trust us," Aron said. "You know we won't find any good ruins unless we push the boundaries a bit." He nudged Isiah. "What do you say?"

Isiah tore his eyes away from the Badlands below. "He has a point."

"And if we get there first, we can clear out any good stuff before Keegan is the wiser."

"Fine," Tessa replied. "We'll take a look." She spurred Vyrro on. "Nobody can ambush us in the day. You can see for miles here."

"Exactly." Aron grinned. "I thought *you* were the adventurous one."

Tessa spurred Vyrro on toward the area where Keegan had been attacked. The spires that sheltered Aegon's home sat on the horizon.

"I want to check on Aegon," Isiah said.

"What about the ruin?" Aron asked.

"We can do that after." He craned his neck to get a better look at the spires. "We could even use her for protection."

"You know flying her in the day is a bad idea," Tessa replied.

19

Isiah wrung his hands. "I know that. It's just . . . I feel bad for leaving her so much."

Vyrro flew toward the spires. After a few minutes, he entered their shadows and neared the cave where Aegon lived. A rocky trail led up to her cave, which was carved halfway up the side of the spire. Vyrro flapped his wings and landed on an outcrop with a cry of greeting. Isiah slipped off as Aegon's serpentine head emerged from the cave.

Isiah's Mark gave a twinge as the dragon laid eyes on him. He brushed it off.

Aegon unfolded her wings and glided down to meet them. The dragon dwarfed Vyrro. She lowered her wing for Isiah to climb on.

"How about we go flying?" he asked her.

"Stay low," Tessa told him. "The landscape will make you harder to spot."

Aron scanned the sky. "Do you see anyone around here? Raiders never visit this place."

"You're right, Tessa." Isiah settled into the dip between Aegon's shoulders, and she prepared to launch herself. "I'll be careful."

The dragon and eagle took off and cleared the spires, soaring toward the place where Keegan was attacked. Aegon hung close to the ground as Tessa had suggested, weaving between mesas and over flat patches of scrub.

Around them, craggy rocks and boulders concealed dark hollows and caves. A dead eagle, no more than a pile of feathers and picked-clean bones, lay where it had fallen. A couple of fat vultures turned their heads to watch Vyrro drift overhead.

Tessa's nose crinkled. "He was right about the gorgons."

A patch of stone caught Isiah's eye, almost invisible against the rocky backdrop of cliffs. "There's the ruin."

Aron rubbed his hands together. "See? I knew we were onto something."

Tessa pulled on the reins and Vyrro slowed, circling around the site in a wide arc. Aegon tailed the bird. Tessa leaned over his flank and studied it. "That's a ruin, alright."

"Maybe we should check it out," Isiah suggested.

"We'll tell Lazaro," she replied. "We can raid it together."

"If he doesn't flip out on us for disobeying him," Aron said. "We're not supposed to be here, remember?"

Tessa fidgeted in her seat. Aegon flew closer to the ruin, giving Isiah a better view. Sandstone bricks were cut into the rock, forming a doorway that disappeared into darkness. A rocky overhang shielded the ruin from above, making it near-impossible to see from the sky.

"Looks like a good one," Isiah said.

"Look at you," Aron replied. "We've got an expert on ruins here." He gave Isiah a playful grin. "You've only been a Scavenger for a few months."

Isiah ignored the embarrassment. "I mean, nobody will have found it before us, right? We should go before any other Raiders come looking."

"The Oath is broken," Aron said. "The other Raiders might not respect Lazaro's claim. Keegan might have even got here first, for all we know. That means it's technically *his* ruin to loot. We'll miss out."

"Alright." Tessa pulled on Vyrro's reins. "Then let's be quick."

Vyrro descended into the shadow of the cliffs and landed with a thud. Isiah braced himself as Aegon did the same, coming to rest on a patch of bare ground. Isiah climbed off and stretched his legs.

Tessa approached the ruin. "We don't have any torches—or rope, or anything."

Isiah scanned their surroundings. Low, dry bushes hugged the sandbanks and dried-up ponds around them. "We can use these."

He collected a stick and, after carefully splitting the top with his sabre, stuffed it with grasses and foliage. "A few of these will give us enough time to check it out, right?"

Tessa put her hands on her hips. "It might be empty for all we know."

"Then we'll have saved Lazaro coming out here to be disappointed."

As Isiah and Aron made the torches, Tessa led Vyrro away and hid him behind a rock formation. "Just in case anyone else is flying by," she said. "You should hide Aegon too. There's an overhang nearby."

Aron scoffed. "Good luck hiding anything that big."

Isiah ignored him. He put his hand on Aegon's neck and willed her to follow him. He took her around a corner to a rocky overhang.

"Wait here," he instructed. Aegon let out a puff of hot air from her nostrils and nuzzled him.

Tessa grabbed an empty bag from Vyrro's saddle. "We don't have much room for loot."

"Then we'll take the best stuff and leave," Isiah replied.

They returned to the ruin and, after lighting their torches with a fire-starter, cautiously ventured inside.

"Scavengers first." Aron stepped aside.

"We're *both* Scavengers," Isiah said.

They descended into the tunnel. Sand and dust coated the floor, and cracks riddled the stonework from earthquakes. As they went, the air grew colder. It clung to Isiah's skin, making his hair stand on end. When Tessa coughed, the sound echoed into the darkness.

The passageway began to narrow, forcing them to duck. Isiah saw that Tessa's breathing was quickening. He lowered his voice. "Are you sure you're going to be alright?" He remembered her claustrophobia at being trapped inside a ruin once before.

"I'll be fine," she replied. After a moment she reached down and squeezed his hand. "But thank you."

After a minute, the passageway widened into a room. Their torches pushed away the shadows, revealing old pillars and piles of rubble. Isiah kept his free hand on the hilt of his sabre.

"Stick together," Tessa said. "In case we run into a gorgon den."

They ventured deeper into the ruin. Isiah broke away from the others and raised his torch to survey the walls. Murals, faded and covered in sand, stared back at him.

"What do you think this place was?" Aron asked. His voice bounced off the walls.

"It looks like a tomb," Isiah replied. "Remember those murals in the ruin Enrik was excavating?" He abandoned the murals and tentatively checked one of the many branching passageways. The dust, disturbed by his footsteps, swirled in the air and tickled his nose.

"You were right," Tessa said. She motioned to a row of stone coffins stacked atop one another. "It's like a burial ground or something."

Aron rubbed his hands together. "I wonder if there's any magic. There's usually magic in tombs."

They picked a tunnel and started down it. Isiah scanned for the faint glimmer of gold. A few low stone tables sat in alcoves, along with more coffins.

"Maybe we've got to find the rich people's burial chambers," Aron suggested.

Tessa's nose crinkled. "Or it's already been looted."

Isiah beckoned them. "Come on. Let's look a bit further."

Tessa and Aron hastened after him. Isiah checked a few more small rooms that branched off, but nothing of value presented itself. His heart sank when he spotted another table. Wooden cups and goblets were scattered across the floor around it.

"Somebody has been here," Tessa said, echoing his thoughts.

Isiah wiped his fingers across the surface of the table. The dust was disturbed, as if somebody had haphazardly swept things off the table. "Maybe they were in a hurry. There might be something left behind."

Tessa tugged on Isiah's arm. "Then we'll come back with Lazaro. We'll get lost if we stay down here for long."

Isiah glanced at his torch. It had begun to burn low. He sighed. "You're right."

He went after Tessa and Aron. They navigated their way back to the ruin entrance and began up the sloping tunnel to the outside. After a moment, a glimmer of light appeared ahead. Isiah hastened toward it, but Tessa caught his arm.

"Wait," she said.

Isiah paused. Over the sound of their breathing, they could hear a noise from beyond the entrance.

Wingbeats.

They backed away from the entrance. The wingbeats grew louder, followed by a few thuds as eagles landed. Muffled talking reached Isiah's ears.

"Get those eagles unloaded. Who knows if we'll find something good."

Tessa swore under her breath. She grabbed Isiah and Aron's arms and pulled them after her. "Don't let them see your torches," she said.

Isiah pressed himself against the wall of the main cavern. "They're blocking the entrance."

"Who are they?" Aron hissed.

"Someone must have had the same idea you did." Tessa craned her neck to peer down the tunnel. "They'll be here in a minute."

"What if we make a lot of noise?" Isiah asked. "It could scare them off if they know there are already Raiders here."

"Or they could mistake us for nomads," Tessa replied. "I hid Vyrro. We've got no eagles to prove we're Raiders." She lowered her voice. "And we can't let them know about Aegon."

Isiah racked his brains. The Raiders' voices grew louder. "What if we confront them?" he asked.

Tessa shook her head. "It's too risky. Without the Oath, who knows what they'll do if they know we're alone down here."

"We have to do *something*," Aron said.

Tessa broke away from the wall. "We can hide." She nodded to herself. "We'll wait for them to start exploring and we can slip out while nobody is looking."

Without waiting for their reply, she took off. Isiah stumbled after her. His torch faded to a bundle of glowing embers, casting barely enough light for him to see the way ahead. "If we don't get lost in here," he said.

From behind them, the Raiders filed into the main entryway. Their voices climbed above the hammering of Isiah's own heart.

"Fancy Keegan thinking he could sneak off at night like that. There must be something good down here for him to do that," one said.

"Keep your wits about you," another replied. "Who knows if those rogues aren't lying in wait for us. Do you think they've got the guts to show their faces around Alcabaza after what they did?"

Isiah rounded a corner. He skidded to a halt to avoid bumping into Tessa. She looked around and swore. "Where are those rooms we found?" she asked.

"You must have taken a wrong turn," he replied.

The voices sounded again. "Split up, groups of three. Holler if you see anything strange."

Isiah wrung his hands. "Keep going."

They followed the tunnel for a minute longer, before the tunnel came to an end. The floor dropped into darkness. Isiah raised his dying torch to illuminate an empty chasm.

"It's a ravine," he started.

"And a dead end," Tessa replied.

Aron pointed to the ground. "Look at that."

A metal pole protruded from the earth, with the end of a rope tied around it. Isiah and Tessa exchanged glances.

"It's the only way," Aron said. "Unless you want to risk going back and running into them."

26

Tessa gave the rope an experimental tug. "It's recent. It must be from the same Raiders who looted it."

"You're the lightest," Aron said. "You go first."

Tessa clenched the handle of her dying torch between her teeth and grabbed the rope. She carefully lowered herself off the edge and, gripping the rope, began to climb down. Isiah leaned over the edge to watch her.

The seconds ticked past. Aron cast a nervous glance behind him. "She's taking too long."

Tessa's torch flickered across sheer rock walls. Beyond its faint glow, darkness extended. The voices behind them grew louder. Isiah prayed she'd make it to the bottom soon.

The rope snapped.

Isiah's heart flew into his throat. The metal pole lurched as the rope tore free and flew into the darkness. Tessa's torch went out. Aron grabbed Isiah's arm and pulled him away from the edge.

"We have to hide," he hissed. At the far end of the passageway, light peeked around the corner. Aron threw his torch into the chasm and crouched behind one of the many stone coffins.

Isiah hesitated. His muscles were locked. He snapped himself out of his trance and quickly followed Aron's lead. He crouched in the darkness behind a coffin, trying to ignore the image of Tessa's light snuffing out. She hadn't even had time to scream.

The Raider's torch flooded the tunnel in firelight. Shadows danced across the walls as three figures marched past. Isiah caught glimpses of them, but he didn't dare raise his head over the lid of the coffin.

One of the Raiders swore. "What is this supposed to be?" she asked.

"Looks like a ravine," another replied. "Or a fissure from an earthquake, maybe?"

"Or whoever built it couldn't be bothered to make a bridge."

Isiah risked peering out to see one of the Raiders lean over the edge.

"Nothing," he said. "Waste of time." He broke away. "Come on. There's nothing down here but bones and dried corpses."

Isiah waited until their footsteps had faded, before crawling out of cover to the edge of the chasm. He squinted, searching for any sign of Tessa. As the light from the Raiders faded, darkness swept in until it was impossible to see.

Aron grabbed Isiah's cloak. "Careful. You'll fall in."

"We have to find her," Isiah said. He fought the urge to call Tessa's name. "What if she's hurt?"

"We can't do it in the dark," Aron replied. "We need more torches. Come on—we can't help her if we can't see."

Fighting every fibre in his body, Isiah tore himself away from the chasm and then felt his way along the wall. With every step, nausea gnawed at his gut. Tessa was down there somewhere.

And the Raiders were still blocking their escape.

Chasm

TESSA'S BODY JOLTED AS THE ROPE SNAPPED. Her stomach lurched as a feeling of weightlessness seized her, before she plummeted into the chasm. She opened her mouth to scream and her torch flew into the darkness. She braced herself to hit the ground.

A couple of seconds passed until her feet connected with the earth and a bolt of pain coursed through her ankle. Her foot twisted and she collapsed onto her side. The torch clattered and went out, plunging her into darkness.

Tessa clutched her ankle, gritting her teeth as a throbbing pain coursed through her leg. She choked back the urge to make a sound in case the Raiders heard her. She probed her ankle, searching for any breaks.

Nothing. Tessa breathed a sigh. It was only twisted. She suppressed the icy panic and tried to survey her surroundings. A shallow layer of sand had broken her fall. Beneath it, smooth rock formed the bottom of the chasm. She felt about and found the rope lying in a pile nearby where it had fallen—but no torch.

Calm down. She forced herself to take a deep breath. The familiar sensation of being unable to breathe began to creep up on her, but she expelled it. *Not now.*

Tessa crawled about, searching for the torch. Her ankle hurt to move, but she ignored it. The torch had to be nearby. If she could light it again . . .

She paused. A faint glow caught the corner of her eye. Cautiously, she crawled toward the source. As she went, the rock beneath her palms turned to sandstone bricks. The light grew stronger, emanating from the far end of the chasm.

Tessa looked up at the darkness above. Isiah and Aron's torches had gone dark. She hoped the Raiders hadn't found them.

They'll find Lazaro, she told herself. *He'll know what to do.*

The light grew brighter. It shone with a faint purple hue, seeming to beckon her. Tessa dragged herself to her feet and hobbled over.

Sandstone bricks covered the floor and walls, stretching into darkness. A few doorways disappeared into the rock. In the centre of the space, looking out across the floor of the chasm, stood an altar.

Tessa's breath escaped her in a rush. She'd heard stories from Lazaro about the things Raiders found in tombs. Her mind raced, and for a moment she forgot her pain.

Could it be some kind of magic?

Tessa tentatively reached out and touched it. A totem, its features worn away until it was no more than a vague shape, sat in the centre of the altar. Coloured rocks formed its eyes, radiating the soft light she had seen.

A plaque sat beneath the figure. She leaned over and blew on the inscription, trying to clear the dust and sand. She squinted in the dim light. *Still illegible.*

Tessa glanced around. Shadows shrouded the chasm. Without her torch, she knew she'd never find a way out. Her gaze returned to the totem.

She swallowed to clear her throat. "You don't mind being moved, do you?" Her voice came out shaky. Lazaro had warned her not to mess with things in ruins—and after she'd seen the power the oasis had . . .

Tessa took the totem in both hands. She gave it an experimental tug. The scrape of stone echoed as it budged. Gritting her teeth, Tessa placed one foot against the altar and pulled.

The totem came free with a jolt. An electrical shock erupted through her body like a bolt of lightning. A flash of pain stabbed Tessa's palms. She gasped and dropped the totem. It hit the floor and split apart. Tessa clutched her hands to her chest as the totem's eyes grew brighter. They split the darkness, flashing across the chasm walls.

Tessa stumbled away. She raised an arm to shield her eyes. The light seemed to stab her, shining through her eyelids and piercing at her brain. It washed over her skin, pricking her with heat. Her injured ankle gave way and she collapsed.

The totem exploded into dust. Its eyes bounced across the sandstone. Tessa lay motionless, arm still clamped across her eyes. The shock faded, leaving a weird nauseating sensation in her gut. She rolled onto her side and fought the urge to throw up.

The totem's twin eyes lay in the sand. Their light dimmed, before they went dull. Dust from the totem swirled in the air, making Tessa's

eyes water. She staggered to her feet and leaned against the wall. Her mind spun.

Calm down, she told herself. Her throat tightened in panic, and the familiar suffocating weight of the earth seemed to close in on her from all sides. She sucked in a deep breath and tried to focus on Isiah. Her pulse began to slow.

Isiah's face flickered in front of her. Tessa paused. She could have sworn she saw his messy hair and bright eyes. She squeezed her eyes shut.

Get a grip, she scolded. *Now you're imagining things.*

The twin stones still gave off a glimmer of light. Tessa scooped them up and placed them on the altar in front of the inscription. The language was too old for her to understand. She cracked open her bag and carefully placed the plaque with the inscription inside.

Helen will know, she thought. Helen was good at reading old stuff.

Beyond the altar stood two doorways, bordered by sandstone bricks. Holding the twin stones ahead of her, Tessa inched her way toward them. The darkness swirled around her. She prayed the faint light wouldn't go out and plunge her into pitch-black.

If they go out, I'll never find my way back.

One of the doorways led to an old staircase, its steps rounded and chipped by time. With one hand on the wall to keep her balance, Tessa began to climb. Her shallow breathing bounced off the passageway, deafening in the silence. The air, thick and filled with dust, tickled her nose and made it hard to draw breath.

The minutes ticked past. The staircase continued to climb, unending. Tessa clutched the stones to her chest, squinting in the shadows to make out each step. She strained her ears for any sign of Isiah and Aron.

Or the Raiders.

The staircase ended at another doorway. A tunnel intersected it. Tessa tried to get her bearings.

I must still be in the ruin, she thought. *I can't have gone far.* She hoped she was right.

The plaque with the inscription seemed to weigh her down. She still felt the dim stinging sensation in her palms. Her gut churned at the thought of what she'd found.

Movement sounded ahead. A stone clattered. Tessa heard Aron curse.

"Aron?" she whispered. She didn't dare raise her voice in case any of the Raiders were within earshot. "Isiah?"

"Tessa?" Isiah asked.

Despite herself, a wave of relief washed over her. She hurried to the source of the noise and bumped head-first into Isiah. Their foreheads met and he grunted in pain.

Tessa rubbed her head. "How did you find me?"

"We were looking for another way down," Isiah replied. "The Raiders almost found us, but we slipped away."

"Are they still around?" she asked.

"I don't know."

"They must be distracted by now," Aron said. "We should make a run for it."

Tessa bit her lip. "Do you remember the way back?"

"I think so," Isiah said. "But we don't have any light."

"Use this." Tessa pressed one of the stones into Isiah's palm.

He furrowed his brow. "Where'd you get this from?"

"I found it," she lied. "At the bottom of the chasm. It doesn't matter."

Tessa followed the boys as they retraced their steps towards the exit. Part of her wanted to tell them about the altar, but she kept her mouth shut. Whatever magic she'd found, telling Isiah would only worry him. She rubbed her palms against her clothes to ease the throbbing sensation.

I'll tell Helen first. She'll know what to do.

After a few minutes, they neared the exit. A glimmer of daylight, only visible because of the near-total darkness, beckoned them. They paused at the entrance to the main room and waited.

"I don't hear anyone," Aron said. "Do you think they left already?"

"Maybe," Tessa replied. "Let's not push our luck."

They broke from cover and ran toward the tunnel. No Raiders confronted them as they jogged toward the daylight and finally emerged in the open. The bright sunlight stabbed Tessa's eyes, forcing her to raise a hand to shield them. Further off, the Raiders' eagles stood waiting.

Aron laughed. "Made it! Those Raiders will be none the wiser." He clapped Tessa on the shoulder. "For a moment there I thought we'd lost you."

Isiah turned to Tessa. "Are you hurt?"

She forced a smile. "No. It'll take more than that to do me in."

Her smile faded as boots crunched on stone. The subtle sound of a sabre being drawn met her ears.

"What do we have here?" a gruff voice asked.

Lazaro's Lot

ISIAH'S HAND FLEW TO HIS SABRE. HE WRENCHED it free and spun in the direction of the noise. A Raider stood atop a pile of rock, sabre in hand. A pipe poked between two rows of yellowed teeth.

"Fancied stealing someone else's ruin, did you?" he asked.

Tessa and Aron drew their blades. Isiah took a few steps back as the Raider jumped down from his perch. His colourful robes flapped in the breeze, camouflaging him against the rock.

"It's a good thing I stayed behind to watch the eagles," he said. He nodded to the trio. "Empty your bags."

"Cool it," Aron replied. "We only flew out here to see what Keegan was after. We're all Raiders here."

"Really?" The man looked over his shoulder and whistled. A second Raider trudged over a crest. "Then where are your eagles?"

"We hid him," Tessa cut in. Her eyes darted between the pair. "To stop anyone from stealing him."

The second Raider waltzed over. "I know you," he said slowly. He wagged a finger at Tessa. "You're Lazaro's lot."

The first Raider's mouth twisted into a sly smile. "Then nobody will notice if they go missing."

Tessa adjusted her grip on her sabre. "The Oath still stands."

"That's up for debate," the Raider replied.

Isiah cast a look in the direction they had taken Vyrro and Aegon. The two Raiders were close, but if he could reach his dragon in time . . .

Aron raised his hands. "Look," he said, "we're all not supposed to be here. This is Keegan's claim. How about we all agree to look the other way?"

The Raider's smile dropped. "Keegan's a friend of mine." His voice took on a hard edge. "He even sent me over here to look out for thieving rats like you."

Isiah caught Tessa's eye. She nodded in the direction of Vyrro. His muscles coiled, ready for a fight. The handle of his sabre felt slick with sweat.

"Here's what's gonna happen," the Raider said. He and his friend circled them, like predators waiting to strike. "You'll give us your valuables and we'll march you into Alcabaza to face the Raiders for violating Keegan's claim. Or"—he lowered his voice—"I call for the rest of my group and we bury you inside the ruin."

Isiah and Aron took a step back. The Raiders pressed in, cornering them against the cliff near the ruin entrance. Their sabres gleamed with a cruel light. Isiah fought the urge to make a break for it. He knew Aegon was painfully close. He could almost feel her presence.

"This ain't a fight you want to take," the Raider snarled. He tapped his blade against the tip of Tessa's sabre. The metallic ring made Isiah's skin crawl. "Because the Oath ain't going to protect you no more."

An ear-splitting bellow cut him off. The Raider's heads snapped around to see a glittering shape erupt from the Badlands. Isiah's heart flew into his throat as he realized what it was.

Tessa seized her chance. She swung her sabre and batted away the closest Raider's blade as Aegon closed in. The dragon's enormous wingspan stirred the dust and surrounded her in a billowing cloud. The Raiders' eagles screeched in panic and pulled at their binds.

The Raiders swore and stumbled away. One of them fumbled with a whistle. An eagle broke free of its ropes and launched itself into the air.

Tessa grabbed Isiah's hand and yanked him away from the chaos. "Come on!"

Isiah recovered his senses and stumbled after her. "What are we doing?"

"They can't know the dragon belongs to us," she replied. She leapt over a pile of rocks and ducked through a crop of scraggy bushes. Isiah hastened after her, raising his hands to shield his face from the foliage. Behind him, panicked cries broke out as Aegon closed in on the Raiders.

Isiah's foot caught on a root and he was sent sprawling. He clutched his throbbing knees and peered out at the dragon.

The Raiders slashed the ropes to their eagles and the birds scrambled away. A smouldering heat welled in Aegon's silvery chest, before she cracked open her jaws and spat a trail of fire after them. The flames fell short as the eagles spiralled into the air.

"How did she know we needed help?" Aron asked. "Did she hear us?"

Isiah swallowed. "I don't know." He waited for his heartbeat to slow. Aegon glared at the retreating Raiders, before breaking away and slithering in their direction. Tessa made sure the coast was clear, then stepped out.

"That wasn't good." She folded her arms. "Who knows what those Raiders will tell the others."

Isiah pushed out of the bushes and reunited with Aegon. A blast of hot air baked his face. He stroked her opal flank. "They can't prove it had anything to do with us."

"That doesn't mean they won't tell stories about a wild dragon hunting in the Badlands," she replied. "Maybe they'll even try to blame Keegan's attackers on it."

Isiah's mind flashed back to when he first met Tessa while travelling with nomads. She'd been hunting wild dragons then.

"I *knew* we shouldn't have visited the ruin," Tessa said. "But *someone* thought it would be a good idea."

Aron raised his hands. "Now, now, let's not be too hasty here. How about we fly back to the dragon's hiding spot? We'll talk about this in Alcabaza."

Isiah cast a nervous glance at the tunnel entrance. "Good idea."

Aegon lowered her wing to allow Isiah to clamber on. As Tessa and Aron ran off to recover Vyrro, he guided Aegon to take flight. She kicked off and drifted low to the ground, taking shelter behind crags of rock. He stroked her flank and she returned it with a reassuring rumble.

"Thanks for helping us back there," he said, unsure if she could understand him. The dragon turned in the direction of the spires that marked her hidden home.

Isiah hoped they hadn't blown her cover.

Magician's Tricks

THEY FLEW BACK TO ALCABAZA IN SILENCE. TESSA KEPT her eyes glued to the horizon, waiting for the mountain that the city was built into to materialize. When it came into view, she spurred Vyrro toward it and the eagle glided toward the roosts. As they landed, she narrowed her eyes and surveyed the Raiders. She didn't spot the ones that Aegon had scared away.

"Do you think they'll say anything?" Isiah asked.

"They're bound to," she replied.

"No," he said, "I mean about us."

She mulled it over. "I don't know. I'll tell Luca to listen to the handlers. They always know what the Raiders are up to."

As she spoke, a couple of boys scurried up and offered to take Vyrro. Tessa slid off the bird, patted his flank, and nodded to the handlers. She led Isiah and Aron away from the roosts as the handlers took her bird away.

They navigated through the cramped, bustling streets of the city toward their home. After a while, they reached the house and Tessa let herself in.

Antony sat at the table, stitching a Raider harness. He looked up as they entered. "Did you find anything?"

"No," Tessa lied. She exchanged looks with Isiah and Aron. "We decided we needed some air, is all." She hugged the bag with the plaque tight and hid it from Antony's view.

Isiah and Aron excused themselves, leaving Tessa alone with Antony. She wandered to the table. "Is Helen home?" she asked.

"I think I saw her upstairs, on the roof," Antony replied.

Tessa thanked him, then hurried to the second floor. She passed Isiah and Aron's room, then turned at the end of the hall and took a narrow, rickety staircase to the roof. She found Helen there, hanging a bundle of robes on a clothesline.

Tessa wandered over. She clutched the bag with the plaque to her chest. The woman turned as she approached.

"Tessa," she exclaimed. "Good timing. Help me with this, will you?"

Tessa obeyed. Helen was a tall woman, with arms thicker than half the Raiders in Alcabaza.

"What brings you up here?" she asked.

"I found something while flying in the Badlands," Tessa explained. "I wanted you to take a look at it."

"Out there?" Helen laughed. "The only things to find out there are scorpions and gorgon dens." She put out a burly hand. "Let's have a look."

Tessa lowered her voice. "Don't tell Lazaro, okay?"

The woman furrowed her brow. "Just what have you been doing out there that requires so much secrecy?"

Tessa opened the bag. "We found a ruin earlier."

Helen put her hands on her hips. "A ruin? Why didn't you come back here and tell us? You know how dangerous it is alone."

"It wasn't my idea." Tessa started to protest, then stopped herself. "We only went inside for a moment. I think—I think I found some magic."

Helen's stern expression flickered for a moment. "What kind of magic?"

"It was an altar," Tessa explained. She recounted the story of finding the altar at the bottom of the chasm. She left out the part about falling while hiding from the other Raiders. She pulled the plaque out. "I remember you learned how to read stuff in tombs."

Helen took the plaque from her and squinted at it. She moved away from the low wall and the busy street beyond so that nobody could overhear them. "I've seen stuff like this before."

Tessa fumbled with her pocket. "I also found these." She pulled out the twin stones.

"Those look like they're used for rituals," Helen replied. "A lot of tomb relics have them. Merchants like to hawk them to nomads as protection charms." She scoffed. "Merchants are conmen." She patted the inscription. "But this . . . it's different."

Tessa wrung her hands. The memory of being hit by the magic made her insides roll. Ever since finding the totem, something had felt . . . off. She put a hand on her stomach to quell it.

Helen squinted at the inscription. "It's archaic," she said. "And faded. I'll have to take it to my room to study."

Tessa's shoulders slumped. "Can't you make out anything?"

The woman brought it close to her face and blew on it. Tessa coughed at the shower of dust. Helen scrunched up her nose.

"It says something about a mirage, I think. Like those ones nomads see when they get lost and wither away to dehydration."

Tessa pulled a face. "What sort of magic does that?"

The woman ignored her. "Then there's a word for a trick. No—deception." She traced her finger across it. "Then an old word for *eye*—or is it a sun?" She muttered to herself. "No, I was right. Maybe it's some old shaman's plaque." She grinned. "Or a magician's tricks. Does this help?"

Tessa forced a smile. "It does."

Before Helen could rope her into a job, she scurried away. She needed time to think.

She retreated to her room and slipped inside, closing the door behind her. It was next to Lazaro's room, with a raised bed beneath a window overlooking the plains. She hung her sabre on a rack and collapsed onto the bed. Part of her felt guilty about Lazaro forcing Isiah and Aron to share the cramped storeroom.

"Mirage, deception, eye," she repeated. She stared at the ceiling, where a few cracks in the plaster snaked across it. "What's that supposed to mean?" She lifted her hands and inspected her palms. Despite the burns, no sign of damage was visible. "And how is it supposed to even work?"

Tessa scrunched up her face and turned her hands over in front of her. *What do all these things have in common?* After a moment, she gave up and let her hands flop onto the bed.

"Maybe it *is* just some magician's tricks," she said. "An illusionist's spell, maybe." Something clicked in Tessa's head. She sat up. "What if . . ."

A knock sounded at the door. "Are you alright?" Isiah said.

Tessa stood and opened the door to find Isiah holding a half-eaten apple.

"You were acting kind of weird on the way back," he said.

Tessa stepped aside to let him in. "It's fine," she said. Her mind flashed back to when she had seen the image of Isiah's face in the ruin. "I want to try something."

She plucked the apple from Isiah's hand and placed it on her bedside table.

"What are you doing?" he asked.

"I found something when I fell," she replied. She sat on her bed and focused on the apple. "Give me a moment."

Tessa let Isiah's presence fade to the back of her mind. She furrowed her brow, concentrating on the apple. A small part of her felt like an idiot. She tried to recreate the feeling of being trapped in the chasm.

Slowly, a nauseating feeling welled inside her, the same gut-churning shock that she'd felt when she picked up the totem. The apple began to flicker. Tessa imagined it whole. For a moment, the bite marks disappeared.

"Tessa." Isiah's eyes widened. "How did you . . ."

Tessa's breath escaped her. She deflated and the apple returned to its former shape. She waited for the nausea to subside. "I found magic," she said. "I think it lets me cast illusions."

Isiah sat on the bed. He watched the apple as if expecting it to change again. "When did you discover this?"

43

"Just now," she replied. "Helen helped me." She hesitated. "Don't tell Lazaro, okay?"

"Why?" Isiah asked. He scooped up the apple and poked the part where the illusion had been. No trace of it remained. "That's so cool."

"I don't want to worry him," she replied. "And I don't want him knowing we snuck out."

"Okay." Isiah's gaze fell to his lap. "I'm worried about Aegon."

"She'll be fine," Tessa said. She put a hand on his knee. "She's a dragon, remember?"

Isiah's mouth flickered into a smile. "I guess. But I hope we haven't blown her cover. If the Raiders go looking—"

"They won't find her," she said. "The Badlands is a big place. There are so many ways to hide. Luca can keep an eye on the Raiders. We'll know if they're planning anything."

Isiah sighed. "You're right." He started to the door. "What are you going to do about your magic?"

"I don't know. Helen's looking at the inscriptions I found. Maybe she'll figure out how to make it work better." Her smile dropped. "But don't tell anyone, okay? Not even Aron."

Isiah gave her a reassuring smile. "Got it."

Her bedroom door creaked shut and he was gone.

Wild Card

Isiah sat at the dining room table. Soft candlelight flickered across the faces of the Raiders around him. Lazaro sat at the head of the table, his expression shrouded in shadow. Aron sat next to him, alongside Antony, Darla, and Helen. Only Luca was missing.

"Something's wrong." Tessa stepped away from the window and let the curtain fall back into place. "They're up to something. Where's Luca?"

Isiah wrung his hands. Several days had passed since their close shave at the ruin. They hadn't ventured out again, and he was beginning to miss his nocturnal flights with Aegon. That evening, he'd spotted the Raiders setting up torches. As night fell, Lazaro had grown increasingly twitchy.

Lazaro stood. "Let me have a look." He walked over to the window Tessa was standing at and pulled aside the curtain. Torchlight from the streets filtered through, making their shadows dance across the walls like twisted stick figures.

"What does it mean?" Isiah joined the pair at the window. Torches, their flames whipped by the wind, lined the streets. Darkness

shrouded the plains, wrapping the Badlands in a thick blanket. Clouds churned above, threatening rainfall.

"There are no celebrations on our calendar," Tessa said. "I checked. Do you think the Raiders are up to something again?"

Lazaro cocked his head. Outside, clusters of people navigated the streets, hunched together for safety. The shadowy figures of beggars were slumped in doorways and inside alleys. "Nobody told *me* anything."

Tessa caught Isiah's eye. He knew what she was thinking. *What if somebody found Aegon?*

A thud at the door made them jump. Lazaro crossed the room in three paces and ducked into the hall. Tessa and Isiah ran to the spot where Lazaro had disappeared and listened.

"Luca," Lazaro said. "What's the word from the roosts?"

"There's a meeting," Luca replied.

"Another?" Lazaro asked. "They had one not even a week ago."

"It's a big one," he said. "This ain't a small get-together."

Isiah could almost hear Lazaro scowl. "What is it this time?"

"They didn't say," Luca replied. "But every Raider in the city has been ordered to attend."

Lazaro scoffed. "Ordered? They don't boss us around. That's not how Raiders work."

"They weren't joking," Luca said. "They mean business."

An eternity seemed to pass. At last, Lazaro sighed. "Fine." He called over his shoulder, "Get your sabres. We have business to attend to."

Antony and Darla slipped from the table. Isiah tried to read their expressions, but their stony faces revealed nothing.

"A surprise meeting?" Helen said. "At this hour? Who do they think they are?"

Lazaro returned to the dining room. He adjusted his scabbard. "I don't know, but I'm keen to give them a piece of my mind."

"Keep your cool, Lazaro," Antony warned. "There's no need for us to make a scene. Let's tag along and see what the other Raiders have to say."

Isiah hurried to his room with Aron to grab their sabres. As they went, he fought the growing unease.

"What do you think it could be about?" he whispered.

"I don't know," Aron replied. "I've never heard of a meeting being called at night like this. Something's serious."

They collected their gear and rejoined the others at the front door. The Raiders were ready to leave. They spilled out of the house and began following the torch-lit road up to the eagle roosts.

Silence cloaked the city. A cold wind whistled through the streets, stirring the torchlight and tugging at the edges of their clothes. The alleyways and side streets were deserted, save for a few beggars huddled together to fend off the cold.

"I've never seen the place so deserted," Tessa said. Their footsteps crunched on the dusty stone street. Their breath formed a faint mist. Tessa's hand found Isiah's and slipped around it.

They climbed to the eagle roosts. As they went, the torches grew brighter, fighting against the relentless wind and leading toward a large building off to the side. Handlers scurried about the eagle pens. None turned to look as they passed.

"Where are we going?" Isiah asked.

"It's a tavern," Aron replied. "Enrik's gang used to practically live out of it. Raiders don't like mingling with the nomads on the lower levels."

Isiah's mind went back to the dark, cramped tavern he found while travelling with Reuben. As they drew closer, the Raiders' tavern appeared. A wooden façade covered the front of the structure, with a foundation of thick stone blocks. The structure melted into the mountainside, overshadowed by the eagle pens and landing platforms of the roosts.

Talking reached Isiah's ears from within. Firelight lit up the building's windows, and a few Raiders loitered in the entryway. Lazaro nodded at them as he passed.

"You're late," one of them drawled.

"We had better things to do," Lazaro replied. He pushed through the doorway and disappeared inside. Antony and Darla went after him. Taking a deep breath, Isiah followed.

The lights and sounds of the tavern washed over him, clearing away the night's chill. A roaring fire bathed the interior, and Raider groups sat clustered around the many tables. A bar stood on the far side, along with a small stage for hosting entertainment. A couple of stray dogs darted between tables, hunting for scraps.

"This doesn't look like a meeting," Tessa said.

"It is," Aron replied. He pointed to their empty tables. "Nobody's bought anything, see? They're here for something else."

Isiah rounded his shoulders, aware of the many pairs of eyes on him. He scurried after Lazaro and slipped into a seat. Despite the din of talking, the tension in the air made his skin prickle. He sensed it in his

gut, like the deadly calm before a storm. Behind the Raiders' bright eyes and fake laughs were cold, calculating stares.

"Listen up, you lot," a voice yelled. Something slammed against wood. The Raiders' heads turned to the stage, where a female Raider was waving her arms. Keegan sat in the front row, his limbs still bandaged. A walking stick leaned against his chair. The two men Aegon had chased sat nearby.

"You might be wondering why we brought you here on such short notice," the Raider stated, "and at this time of night, too. It's not to celebrate." She turned her head, surveying the crowd. Isiah shrank down in his seat as the woman's eyes passed over him. Her voice took on a serious tone. "Another group was attacked yesterday."

Her words rippled across the crowd. Some Raiders swore and slammed their fists. Others listened in silence.

"It was my brother and his gang, attacked near the outskirts of Alcabaza," the woman continued. Her dreadlocks, studded with eagle talons and trinkets, bobbed as she talked. A curved sabre swung at her side, its handle rounded and shaped like an eagle's foot. "I was scouting when I saw it. A black-clad group descended on them, felling their eagles and killing them all. My brother died before I could fly him back to Alcabaza."

A few pained cries rose from one corner of the room. Raiders muttered among each other.

"The Oath is dead," the woman said, "unless we root out the killer."

"We should raid Edward's house," one man shouted, pointing at his rival. "If we find the black outfits, then his gang is guilty!"

"Shut your mouth," Edward yelled. "This is all Enrik's fault. If he hadn't broken the Oath, none of this would have happened."

"You have a good point," the Raider with the dreadlocks said. She tilted her head back to peer into the far side of the tavern. "And somehow, Lazaro's group always manages to find themselves in the middle of it."

Lazaro pressed his palm against the table. "Don't try and pin this on us, Mauriel," he hissed. He ignored Antony's stern expression. "We have nothing to do with the killers."

Mauriel raised her hands. "I'm not pinning this on you," she said innocently. "But I do find it curious how you've fallen out with nearly every Raider gang in Alcabaza at one time or another."

A few Raider groups devolved into frenzied muttering. Chairs squealed as several men stood and started a shoving match.

Mauriel spun on them. "Keep your heads on straight! Let's not do the killer's work for him."

The Raiders ignored her. Isiah caught their suspicious glances. The stray dogs bolted from the room as the chattering grew more frantic.

Mauriel stepped down from the stage and waltzed toward Isiah's table. "And how do you explain your escape from our prison?" she asked. "You miraculously made it out of the city after being arrested on charges of Oath-breaking—and who can forget the time one of your Scavengers released a dragon that slaughtered a bunch of Raiders?"

Lazaro stood. Darla caught his arm. "That had nothing to do with me."

"Cool it," Antony warned.

"No," Mauriel said, "of course not. It just so happened that you found the one Scavenger who was secretly a spy for Paradon!" She turned her attention to Isiah, Tessa, and Aron.

"Leave them out of this," Lazaro ordered. Several Raiders looked up from their arguments as Mauriel's words caught their attention.

"But that spy escaped back to Paradon, so Aron told us," Mauriel said. "You broke out of prison on your own, fought Enrik, foiled his plan, and the dragon's escape was a mere coincidence."

Isiah squirmed in his seat. His Mark itched. He kept his head down so none of the Raiders could look too closely at him.

"How convenient it all was," she said. "It's also convenient that your Scavengers were present when a wild dragon chased some Raiders near the place Keegan was attacked."

Isiah saw the flash of surprise behind Lazaro's eyes. The pair of Raiders Aegon had attacked wandered over. One rolled up a sleeve. Behind the cover of the table, Darla's hand crept toward her sabre.

"We had nothing to do with that," Lazaro snapped. "We hate dragons as much as you do. Wild dragons are nothing new."

Mauriel twirled one of her dreadlocks. "It's only a coincidence, Lazaro," she replied. "Perhaps one coincidence too many."

The Raiders drew closer. Darla let go of Lazaro's arm and he rose to his full height. His nostrils flared. "I resent being accused of breaking the Raider's Oath." His spittle landed on Mauriel's forehead.

The woman slowly wiped her brow. "Oath-breaker or not, I think we can all agree that you and your gang have caused more trouble in Alcabaza than you're worth."

One of the Raiders made a grab for Lazaro. Lazaro shoved the table aside and swung a fist at the Raider. A sickening crunch sounded and the man spun away.

The Raiders burst into motion. Darla yanked on her sabre, but Mauriel grabbed her arms before she could free the blade. Shouting erupted as the Raiders closed in. Isiah staggered to his feet as his chair fell over. Lazaro slammed his fist into the man who had attacked him, but the other Raiders closed in.

Isiah wobbled, trying to keep his balance. His body was crushed against Tessa and Aron. Tessa fumbled with her sabre hilt, but the crush of people made it impossible to draw her weapon. She screamed and bit a Raider's hand as he grabbed her.

"Arrest them!" Mauriel ordered. She grappled with Darla. The woman lunged forward and slammed her forehead against Mauriel's nose, making her reel away.

Hands grabbed at Lazaro, catching his arms and wrestling him away. He grunted in pain as the bloodied Raider landed a punch to his gut.

A hand caught hold of Isiah's arm. He tried to wrench himself free, but the crush of people hemmed him in on all sides. Tessa cried out as more hands dragged her away. Isiah tried to reach her, but she was too far.

Something slammed into Isiah's back. A shock of pain ricocheted through his shoulder blades. He fell to his knees and the hands pinned his arms behind him. Somebody pulled his sabre free and confiscated it.

The crowd began to disperse. Chairs lay strewn across the floor. The Raider Lazaro had punched held a rag to his bleeding head. Mauriel wiped her bloody nose and spat on the ground.

"You've always walked a thin line, Lazaro," she said. "But the Oath tied our hands."

Lazaro glared up at the woman. He tried to wrench himself free, but the other Raiders held him tight. "You've got nothing on us," he snarled. "You need proof."

"Not to exile you," Mauriel replied. "I'm not going to throw you in prison to rot, or execute you for Oath-breaking." She pushed her hair out of her face. "The Raiders will hold a vote on your banishment. Until then, you can stay locked up."

A chorus of approval went around the Raiders. They began to drag Lazaro and the others away. The crowd parted to reveal Tessa and Aron. Tessa watched with wide, fearful eyes as Lazaro was pushed around by his captors.

"Troublemakers are thrown out of the city," Mauriel said. "And that doesn't only apply to sleazy merchants or drunken nomads." Her lips parted as she turned to Isiah, revealing a predatory grin. "But I know of a better way to use Scavengers."

The Raiders yanked Isiah to his feet. His arms were forced against his back, making his shoulders burn. Tessa called out to Lazaro, but the Raiders pulled her and Aron away.

"Put them in the cellar," Mauriel ordered. "We can't do anything with them right now."

An elbow in Isiah's back made him walk. Tessa writhed beneath her captors' grip, but her struggling achieved nothing. Isiah's captors forced him through a doorway and Lazaro disappeared from view.

"I'll deal with the Scavengers in the morning," Mauriel announced. She paused. "And after that, we have a dragon to hunt!"

Isiah's blood turned to ice. The Raiders pushed him down a flight of stairs and swung open a wooden door. A shove sent him sprawling. He landed in a pile next to Tessa and Aron. The door slammed shut, plunging him into darkness.

"See you in the morning, Scavenger," a gruff voice said. "Oh, and don't mind the rats."

Goose Chase

Isiah groaned and rubbed his aching arms. The muffled sound of Raiders talking filtered down from somewhere above, but he couldn't make out any words. He shifted his weight on the hard floor.

Tessa stood and stumbled to the door. She rattled on the handle. It didn't budge. She pounded it with her fist. Each bang echoed across the space.

"Are you alright?" Isiah asked. A lump formed in his throat.

"We need to get out of here," Tessa replied, rattling the door harder. She spun around. "Did you see if they had a key?"

Isiah cautiously stood, leaning against the wall for balance. In the shadows, he made out large wine barrels. The soft scamper of a rat emanated from somewhere beyond.

"They're taking Lazaro somewhere," Tessa said. "We have to break him out."

"You heard what Mauriel said," Aron replied. "They're holding a vote. Lazaro will be fine until the morning."

Tessa ignored him. She felt the door, probing the lock. "See if you can find anything that can help us." Her voice grew higher with each word.

Isiah leaned against the barrels, trying to collect himself. His shoulders still ached where the Raiders had pinned him. He steadied his breathing. "They're going to hunt Aegon," he managed to say.

"We'll worry about that later," Tessa replied. "We need to find a way out of here first."

"It's a cellar," Aron replied. "In a mountainside. There's not even a window to climb through."

"Then look for a bit of wire or something," she snapped. "We must be able to make a lockpick."

"And then what? Waltz out while every Raider in Alcabaza is sitting up there?" Aron's voice grew louder. He stopped himself. "We need time to plan."

Tessa stopped. She sank to the floor, her back against the door. "You're right." She slammed her hand against the stone. "I knew we shouldn't have come here. Lazaro was right to avoid meetings."

Isiah sat next to her. The cold stone sapped his body heat away. When he put his hand on Tessa's leg, she was shivering. "We have until morning," he said. "There'll be plenty of opportunities to get away."

"You don't know that," she replied.

"Lazaro can look after himself," Isiah said, more to himself than to her. "And so can we." His words hung in the air.

"He's right," Aron said after a moment.

Tessa sighed. She shuffled closer to Isiah and rested her head on his shoulder. "It's cold down here."

Isiah bit his lip at the thought of Aegon, blissfully asleep in her cave. She had no idea what the Raiders were about to do. "Once we get out of here and find Aegon, we'll be fine," he said. "We can reunite with Lazaro and we'll be safe."

Even as he said the words, a nagging voice in the back of his mind told him he was wrong.

* * *

"Good morning!" Mauriel's sing-song voice called.

The door lurched, knocking Isiah forward. He and Tessa scrambled away as light flooded the cellar. His limbs were stiff from the cold, and goosebumps riddled his skin.

Mauriel stood in the doorway with several Raiders. They marched into the cellar and dragged Isiah to his feet. One of the Raiders grabbed Tessa, but she pulled her arm away and stood herself. Further back, Aron rubbed the sleep from his eyes.

"Did you have a good night?" Mauriel asked.

Tessa glared at her. "Where's Lazaro?"

"I wouldn't worry about that," Mauriel said. "I told you I had a plan for you." She motioned to the Raiders, who grabbed Isiah's hands and pinned them behind him. The familiar bite of rope cut into his wrists.

"Remove their harnesses," Mauriel said. "We can't have them looking like Raiders where we're going."

One of the Raiders produced a knife and cut away the straps that pinned Isiah's robes to his body. The material hung loose, reminding him of the merchants and nomads who inhabited the city.

"Tie them together," Mauriel said, "and follow me."

The Raiders obeyed. Isiah found himself at the front of the line, being led up the stairs and through the tavern. The room stood

deserted. There was no sign of the previous night's brawl. Mauriel led him out of the building and into the bright Badlands sun.

"Where are you taking us?" Tessa snapped. She was behind Isiah, with Aron in the rear.

"You're not in a position to ask questions," Mauriel replied. Her dreadlocks swung as she walked.

The eagle roosts faded behind them. Mauriel fell into stride beside Isiah. She grabbed his hood and yanked it up over his head. His robes hung loose, concealing the binds around his wrists. The other Raiders closed in to form a tight-knit group.

"Let's not make a scene," Mauriel hissed. "We're just a normal Raider group out for a walk." As she spoke the words, Isiah felt the prick of a knife in his back. "You got that?"

Isiah nodded.

Mauriel beamed. "Good."

They walked further into the city, before making a sharp turn into a long, covered structure packed with colourful market stalls. Isiah's nose crinkled as the aroma of incense hit him in the face. Merchants hawked their wares as streams of nomads and city-dwellers funnelled past.

It's a bazaar, Isiah thought. Bright tarps and rugs coloured in deep red and purple hung from the rafters, and an arched roof protected them from the harsh sun. A donkey wandered past, led by a couple of merchants. Voices bartering and children laughing filled Isiah's ears.

Mauriel scrunched up her face. After a moment she exclaimed, "There."

The Raiders pushed Isiah and his friends in the direction of a merchant group. They loitered to one side, surrounding a band of a dozen people. Despite the dim light, Isiah made out the ropes connecting the people's wrists. Isiah's heart sank.

"The city-dwellers don't like the sight of labourers," Mauriel said. "They couldn't care the least about beggars, but how *terrible* it is for them to be reminded of slavery." She waved at the merchants as they approached. "But these bazaars give us the perfect cover from prying eyes."

Tessa gasped. "You're smuggling us out of the city."

"You're a smart one," Mauriel said sarcastically. She patted Tessa on the head. "And you'll be far away before Lazaro and his gang are set loose. What better way to rid him from Alcabaza than to send him on a wild goose chase to find his sister?"

"You're sick," Tessa spat.

Mauriel laughed. She reached the merchants and engaged in a hushed conversation. One of the men tapped his foot. Isiah strained to hear them.

"You kept us waiting," the merchant said. "What's so special about these ones, anyway?"

"They're Scavengers," Mauriel replied. "We caught them pickpocketing from their group."

"And you can't just disown them?"

Mauriel shook her head. "They know the city too well—and our roosts. They'll forever be a pest. Why not offload them and get them out of our hair for good?"

The merchant shrugged. "Fair enough." He produced a pouch of coins. "Our usual rate?"

"Hey!" Tessa cut in. "You can't sell us! I'm a Raider, not a Scavenger. We're with Lazaro. Ask around and you'll see for yourself."

Mauriel laughed. "You'll have to gag this one," she said. "She's such a convincing liar."

Mauriel collected the pouch and the Raiders pushed Isiah toward the group of labourers. The merchant—a short, bearded man with a dust-stained face—secured him to the rest of the convoy.

"Right, you lot," he ordered, "start walking. We're already late. I expect to reach our camp by noon."

Several labourers lurched forward and the chain began to move. Isiah found himself being dragged along with the crowd. Part of him urged him to resist, but he knew it would do no good. One of the other labourers was too slow, and a merchant repaid him with a strike from a long stick.

Mauriel gave them a little wave. The rest of the bazaar stole her from view. The merchants marched Isiah and his friends out and through the city. He kept watch for any sign of Lazaro, but deep down he knew it was hopeless. Tessa walked behind him, her head bowed.

The crowd parted to let the merchants pass. A flicker of pity crossed the faces of some, while others averted their eyes and hurried in a different direction. As they neared the edge of the city, the grumble of machinery became audible.

Isiah mustered the courage to speak. "Where are we going?"

The bearded merchant grunted. "For processing."

The machinery grew louder. The stone streets of the city gave way to wooden platforms that jutted over the distant plains below. A ramp led down to one of the elevators. Isiah remembered arriving with Reuben. He'd seen merchants with a crowd of labourers then.

"What does processing mean?" he asked.

The merchant scowled. "Keep walking."

Isiah flexed his wrists. The ropes cut into his skin, making his fingers numb. He mentally groped for a plan. "These binds are too tight."

The merchant brandished his stick. "You'll learn pretty fast to stop talking if you keep up like that."

Isiah fell silent. Pulleys squealed and ropes creaked as one of the elevators was lifted to the ramp. The labourers piled on. The elevator—no more than a wooden platform with waist-high sides—swayed as they boarded. A voice gave the all-clear and the elevator lurched into motion.

As it descended, the lattice of beams and supports that made up the city's underbelly drifted past. Pulley-boys, no more than shadows, darted between the ropes and winches, operating their elevator. Several other elevators lifted merchants and nomads to the city.

The elevator hit the ground with a jolt and one of the walls fell, forming a ramp. The merchants herded the labourers off.

"Get a move on," the bearded merchant ordered. He grabbed Isiah's collar and pushed him off the elevator. "Scavengers like you might be used to flying eagles, but the rest of us don't have that luxury. You'd better get used to walking."

A wide dirt path led through the plain. Run-down fences, separating fields of maize and wheat, bordered it. Farmers worked in the fields, tilling the ground with hand tools.

"Eyes on the path," the merchant snapped. Isiah winced as the stick connected with his shoulder. "Unless you want to be put to work alongside them."

The path led away from Alcabaza, cutting through the plain and then splitting off and winding into the Badlands. Isiah shot a glance over his shoulder at the city. A few silhouettes of eagles circled above it.

The labourers left the plain and climbed the steep bank into the mesas and gullies of the Badlands. Merchants bordered the line, guiding them through the terrain. *And making sure nobody tries to escape*, Isiah thought.

The merchant beside him fell back to bring up the rear. Isiah risked talking to Tessa.

"Where do you think we're going?" he whispered.

"It must be a merchant camp," she replied. "They spring up near the big cities." She crinkled her nose. "That's where they sort the labourers before they get marched off to different parts of the Badlands."

Isiah swallowed. His mouth, already parched from spending the night in the cellar, felt shrivelled. The lump in his throat had returned—but not from dehydration.

Aegon, he thought. He willed his thoughts to travel to her, but he knew it would do nothing. *Where are you?*

The line of labourers snaked through a gulley and passed into the shadow of overhangs. Fallen rocks and loose scree littered the ground. Sheer, painted walls of stone hemmed them in. Beyond, a thin coil of smoke curled into the clear air.

Isiah rounded a corner and the merchant camp materialized. A palisade wall bridged the gap between the cliffs, each log sharpened into a crude point. Beyond, a series of tents stood, their peaks poking higher than the walls that surrounded them. A few more merchants stood near the gate, alongside mules laden with bags.

"Took your time," one of them said. "We were worried we'd have to set off without you."

"And risk our labourers dying on the trip?" the bearded merchant replied. "Pack your things. We'll depart at dawn."

The merchants ushered Isiah and the labourers through the crude palisade gates and into the camp. A large, white tent dominated the entryway, with tarps to shield the hard earth from the scorching sun. The cliffs around them provided shelter, protecting them from the wind—and the gaze of eagles who might happen to fly above.

Merchants, wielding their sticks, began untying the ropes that linked the labourers. One stopped in front of Isiah.

"And don't even think about making a run for it," he said. "We have ways of dealing with runaways."

Another merchant leaned in, grinning as he flashed a knife. "If you see anybody missing a few fingers or an ear, you know what happened."

The merchants began dividing the labourers into groups. Isiah strained his neck to keep sight of Tessa, but she disappeared into the crowd. Isiah ended up with Aron and the men on one side, with Tessa and the female labourers on the other.

"Get this lot processed," the bearded merchant said. "Then let them into the yard with the others. Everyone else can rest up and go over our planned route through the Badlands."

Wood creaked as the palisade gate shut, sealing them inside. Isiah eyed the sheer walls surrounding them. He'd never be able to climb those. But he didn't have time to think about escape.

The merchants began herding the women toward the tent. One gave Tessa a shove. She twisted around and met Isiah's gaze, before she was gone.

'New Life'

TESSA STUMBLED AS THE MERCHANT PUSHED HER. She gritted her teeth to keep from spitting an insult. Her binds cut into her wrists, making them ache, and the crush of bodies carried her into the large tent. The tent flaps closed behind her—the shadow of merchants betraying the guards.

"Line up," a female merchant snapped. She wore long, colourful robes that shielded her from the harsh sun and dust of the Badlands. Several other merchants stood around tables covered in rags.

The labourers all lined up against the far tent wall. Tessa poked the fabric with her foot, probing for a loose tent peg or any weaknesses. If only she could make it out of the camp . . .

The merchants stopped by each labourer and untied their binds. Unlike the labourers she usually saw, the people around her wore the robes of nomads and city-dwellers. The merchants paused whenever they found a gold earring or a ring.

"You won't need these where you're going," the merchant said. "You're labourers now, and it's time you got that into your heads."

Tessa waited as the merchants moved down the line. She tried to imagine punching one and causing a distraction. Her empty sabre scabbard bounced against her leg, seeming to mock her.

"Whether you're prisoners from the border, swallowed up by your debts, or you're petty criminals not worthy of living in Alcabaza, you're all here for a new life—whether you like it or not," the merchant said, strutting in front of the line. "We'll march you to the nearest city and put you to work. There's no shortage of ways for a labourer to be useful." A faint smile crossed her lips. "And for some of us to get rich in the process."

Tessa tensed as the merchants reached her. They inspected her for jewellery, then untied her hands.

"This one's got nothing," one of her captors said. She grabbed Tessa's scabbard. "But this is a fancy scabbard. Worth a pretty penny, by my reckoning."

The woman in charge grunted in satisfaction. She scooped up a bundle of rags from the table and dumped them in Tessa's arms. "Take it off."

Tessa clutched her hands to her chest protectively. "What?"

The merchant gestured to her robes. "We can sell those clothes of yours." She leaned in. "You're a labourer now, remember?"

Around her, the other merchants started handing out rags. Heat welled in Tessa's chest, but she swallowed her pride and slipped off her robes. The other merchants collected their shoes and bagged everything up.

Tessa pulled on her new rags and grimaced. The worn, rough material made her skin itch.

"Better," the woman said. She gestured to the tent flap on the far side. "Proceed to the yard. If you're lucky, we'll feed you before we depart."

The line of labourers marched into motion. Tessa wrapped her arms around herself and shuffled along with them. The Badland sun greeted her. She blinked, adjusting her eyes to it. The wall of palisade wrapped around, forming an open space littered with a couple of tarps and a few logs as makeshift benches. Labourers, all clad in the same faded clothes, sat huddled in the shade and against the walls. A few merchants patrolled between them and stood guard.

The female merchant and her cronies exited the tent and made their way to another structure. A voice called out from the other side of the tent. Tessa's stomach dropped as she realized Isiah was among them.

His Mark, a voice in her head told her.

Tessa scanned the yard. A low bench sat against the tent wall. She quickly took a seat next to a line of labourers. She racked her brain for some kind of plan. If the merchants saw Isiah's Mark, she dreaded to think what would happen.

A few holes pitted the tent wall. Blending in with the other labourers, Tessa pressed her eye against one. It gave her a view of the interior of the tent. Isiah and Aron were marched in alongside their group. The merchants began untying them and checking them for valuables.

"You haven't earned the right to wear anything more than rags," a merchant said. He passed out the same moth-eaten cloth she'd been forced to wear. "Time to swap."

The merchant stopped in front of Isiah. Tessa saw him falter.

"What do you mean?" he asked.

"I mean, give us those fancy robes of yours," the merchant replied.

Isiah swallowed. "Now?"

The merchant sighed. "Yes, now." He pushed the robes against Isiah's chest. "Like everyone else."

"I—I can't," Isiah stammered.

"Why not?" the merchant said. "Are you squeamish?"

"I—I've got a skin condition," Isiah lied. His eyes darted about. "These robes were made special."

"I don't care if your head is falling off," the merchant replied. "Either you get changed now or I'll beat you within an inch of your life."

Tessa's pulse quickened. Her mind raced as she desperately tried to find a plan.

"Hey, you," a voice snapped. Tessa pulled away from the hole to see a merchant staring at her. "Stop spying."

A few of the other labourers laughed. Tessa waited until the merchant wasn't paying attention, then put her eye back to the hole. Isiah fumbled with his collar. Many of the other labourers were already done. The remaining merchants closed in on him.

Tessa held her breath. She focused on Isiah's Mark, willing it to change. She conjured up the image of the apple in her room. A familiar unsettling feeling welled inside her. Isiah pulled his robes off.

"See?" the merchant said. "Was that so hard?"

Isiah studied his shoulders with wide eyes. Tessa gritted her teeth, willing the illusion to last. He hurriedly pulled on the rags and dusted himself off.

Tessa pulled away from the hold and slumped against the material with a sigh. A minute later, Isiah's group filed out of the tent. She caught his arm as he passed and pulled him toward her.

"Isiah," she said.

He collapsed on the bench next to her. "Tessa." She caught the slight tremble in his voice. "You won't believe what happened."

"I know," she replied. She leaned in and lowered her voice. "I used my magic."

Isiah faltered. He pulled up his collar and inspected his Mark. "How did you—"

"Like in my room, remember?" she asked. "I was watching you."

Isiah nodded slowly. His expression dropped. "Wait, does that mean you saw me . . ."

Tessa covered her mouth so he couldn't see her smile. "It worked though, didn't it?"

"Guys." Aron sat opposite them. "I overheard those merchants say where they're gonna take us. They say we're marching at dawn for some salt mines on the other side of the Badlands. It'll be a week before we even reach the halfway point."

"Damn Mauriel." Tessa kicked the ground. "She must have had this all planned out from the beginning."

"They're stopping at a couple of settlements along the way," Aron added. "Maybe we'll be dropped off there." He put a hand to his mouth and leaned in. "Or we can escape on the way."

"What about Lazaro?" Isiah asked. "Won't he come after us?"

"There are tons of merchant trails that stretch all over the Badlands," Aron replied. "How will he know which one we followed?"

"And he won't recognize us," Tessa added. She bit her lip. "Without our robes, we'll be impossible to spot from the air."

Aron stood. "I'm sick of sitting about and waiting," he said. "I'm gonna take a look around. Maybe I can learn something useful." He turned to Isiah. "You coming?"

Isiah joined him. He adjusted his rags to make sure his Mark was covered.

"Be careful," Tessa warned.

The pair melted into the crowd of labourers. Tessa stayed put, watching the merchants as they patrolled around the camp. She tried to count the number of guards and what weapons they had.

"Who's Lazaro?" a voice asked.

Tessa jumped. She turned to see a girl on the edge of the yard. She peered out from beneath a makeshift hood that shielded her from the sun.

"Oh," Tessa said. "He's a friend." A nagging voice told her to keep quiet.

The girl shuffled over. She brushed a few loose strands of hair from her face. "I thought labourers didn't have friends."

Tessa sighed. "It sure looks that way."

"Are you from Alcabaza?" she asked.

"How did you guess?"

"I saw your robes when you came in with the others. You were a Scavenger, right?"

Tessa checked that none of the merchants were listening. The nearest labourers were engaged in their own hushed conversations, or staring aimlessly at the ground. She leaned in. "I'm a Raider."

The girl frowned. "You can't be a Raider. How'd you end up here?"

"It's complicated," she replied. "What about you?"

The girl drew her knees to her chest. "I don't want to talk about it."

Tessa shrugged and let the matter drop. She resumed watching the guards, trying to figure out when they changed shifts. A few mules

leaned against the palisade wall. She wondered if she could spook them and cause a commotion.

There has to be a way out, she thought. *All I have to do is find it.*

* * *

"Get up!" a merchant barked.

Tessa shifted and opened her eyes. The twin suns peered over the horizon, casting long shadows across the camp. Despite how early it was, the Badlands was already beginning to heat up.

Tessa propped herself up on her elbows and took a moment to collect herself. Her face fell as she remembered where she was.

The other labourers woke up and then ordered themselves into a line. A few merchants passed out wooden bowls. Tessa brushed the dust off her rags and hurried to join them. She strained her neck to spot Isiah and Aron.

"Eat quickly," the bearded merchant ordered. "Either we make good ground this morning, or you'll be marching under the midday sun."

Tessa collected her bowl. It contained a watery broth, but her aching stomach didn't complain—not that the merchants would listen to her protests, anyway.

The girl she'd spoken to the previous day stood off to the side, on the far end of the line. The merchants finished handing out the bowls and then several departed to load their mules for the journey ahead. As soon as the labourers had finished, the merchants re-bound their wrists and connected their ankles with ropes.

To stop us from running, Tessa realized.

Beyond the white tent the merchants used for processing, the palisade gates creaked open. The merchants spurred their mules and began herding the labourers toward it.

Tessa caught sight of a few large, hulking beasts beyond. Scaly flanks protected their large bodies, and saddles laden with bags hung from their hump-like backs. They had short, stumpy heads tipped with beak-like mouths and short tails that wobbled as they walked. She recognized the creatures as some of the pack-beasts that the nomads often used.

The line lurched into motion. Slowly, they trekked out of the camp and into the Badlands beyond. The merchants rode their mules at intervals, keeping the labourers in order and brandishing long sticks at anybody who lagged behind.

Tessa winced as her bare feet met the hard, rocky terrain. The ropes around her ankles restricted her movement so that she couldn't take a full stride. The bright, shimmering blue sun above warmed the rock. She knew that by midday it would be blistering.

They rejoined the trail and left the camp behind. The steady trotting of mules' hooves and the thud of the pack-beasts' heavy feet broke the morning stillness. A couple of merchants fell into quiet conversation. Tessa strained her ears, but they were too far for her to hear.

As the twin suns crept higher into the sky, Tessa settled into a mindless shuffle. It let her mind wander. She flexed her wrists, probing her binds for weakness. Merchants weren't good fighters. Not like Raiders. If she got a sabre in her hands, she'd have a shot at escaping.

The sun beat down on her shoulders, the thin rags doing little to protect her. She tried to spot Isiah in the line, but everybody looked the

same. She hoped his Mark wasn't giving him trouble. Further back, one of the labourers stumbled, and a merchant swooped in with his stick.

"Get a move on," he snapped. "We have to make good time. We're already behind schedule!"

Tessa winced as they crossed a patch of sharp rocks. The sun neared its midday point, scorching the earth with its unrelenting glare. She remembered when she was a kid, when her parents would fry food on the rocks when scouting.

The labourer in front of her stumbled. Without arms to steady them, they collapsed to their knees. Tessa heard a girl gasp in pain.

"You!" the merchant barked. "You're slowing the whole line down."

The labourer twisted around. Tessa recognized the same girl she'd met in the camp. The merchant marched over, stick in hand. He grabbed the girl and yanked her to her feet.

"It was my fault," Tessa said quickly. "I bumped into her."

The merchant whirled on her. "Then don't be so clumsy."

He shoved Tessa forward and whacked her with his stick. Tessa clenched her jaw against the sting of the impact. She refused to give the merchant the satisfaction of a response. She blinked back the tears and kept walking.

When Lazaro finds me, she thought, *they'll wish they never crossed us.*

Mauriel

MAURIEL HUNCHED HER SHOULDERS AND HURRIED through the alleyway. She ducked from shadow to shadow, stepping over the unmoving forms of beggars and slipping past the closed shutters of houses. She neared the edge of the city, where the stone turned to wooden platforms and houses spilled out over the empty air.

She stopped at a dead end. Her hand hovered above the hilt of her sabre. She'd taken a risk leaving the roosts without her Raiders at night. Every shadow appeared to conceal a half-starved beggar with a knife or a gang of thieving nomads waiting for their next victim. She strained her ears, listening for any sign of movement. Boots crunched on stone.

"Did it go according to plan?" a voice asked.

Mauriel jumped and her sabre flashed into her hand. She sighed as she recognized the voice. "It went off without a hitch."

A figure stepped out of an alleyway. Black robes clad his body and a mask obscured his face—a necessary precaution, he'd told her. Mauriel was sure his eagle wasn't far away.

"You could have sent someone to the roosts," she said. "Instead of having me walk all the way out here. If anyone sees me with you, I'll be hauled off and killed as an Oath-breaker."

"Relax," the man replied. He gestured to the roosts. The faint moonlight played across his crooked metal hand. "The other Raiders are none the wiser, and soon I'll be out of your hair. I wanted to speak to you personally."

Mauriel folded her arms. "You killed my brother."

"He got in the way," the man said. "It was unfortunate, yes. But as soon as you've finished helping me, the killings will stop and your precious Oath can go back to the way it was." He paused. "Where is Lazaro?"

"He's cooling off with the rest of his gang in the prison," Mauriel replied. "I convinced the Raiders to vote against him. He'll be exiled and his house seized tomorrow morning."

"And Isiah?" the figure asked.

"Sold to the merchants, along with Lazaro's brat of a sister and that traitorous Scavenger, Aron. They'll be miles away by the time Lazaro is released. He'll be kept busy looking for them."

"Good work," the man said. "I should have dealt with Aron earlier. I always did question his friendship with Tessa." The man waved his hand. "But that doesn't matter now. What about the dragon?"

"The one that chased Keegan's friend? We're assembling a hunting party to find it."

"Make sure you do," the man replied.

Mauriel grunted. "I don't see why it's such a big deal. Dragons cross the border all the time. Why is this one so special?"

The man dropped his voice. "Because Isiah is the boy who freed the dragon from our arena."

Mauriel paused. "But Aron said—"

"Aron lied to you all," the man said, cutting her off. "Isiah was from Paradon all along. I saw it for myself. He's Marked." He stepped forward. "You have to kill the dragon. My Raiders don't have the numbers on our own."

"We've got the situation under control," Mauriel said.

"Don't underestimate it. The dragon didn't kill Isiah like it should have. I'll sleep easier once I know it's dead and there's one more loose end tied up."

"Alright." Mauriel rubbed her hands together. "A good old-fashioned dragon hunt. It'll be easy."

"See that you take care of it." He paused. "I'll return with your reward once this whole *situation* is cleared up."

Mauriel gave him a mock salute. "See you around, Enrik."

Enrik marched into the shadows. Mauriel waited a few moments until wingbeats echoed and a shape erupted from behind a row of houses. An eagle glided into the night sky and soared toward the Badlands. She watched him go, then turned and marched back to the roosts.

Gorgon Territory

DARKNESS CLOAKED THE BADLANDS. The last of the sun's rays dipped beneath the horizon and the scorching heat dissipated. The labourers sat huddled on the cooling earth, sheltered inside a winding riverbed. The merchant's fire crackled. The light danced across their hunched forms, casting distorted shadows on the ground behind them.

Tessa rubbed her aching feet. Her legs were sore from a day of walking, and her calves were caked in dust. The merchants had unbound her wrists, but she still wore the ropes around her ankles. Her sweat-drenched clothes stuck to her skin, chilling her as the warmth from the sun leeched away.

One of the merchants stood and waltzed over. "For some of you, it's your first night on the trail," she said. Tessa recognized her as the woman from the tent. "You might be wondering why you can't just loosen those binds on your ankles and make a break for it."

Among the crowd, Tessa caught Isiah's eye. The possibility had crossed her mind the moment the merchants had stopped to set up camp.

"But this is gorgon territory," the woman continued. "And you should know the stories of gorgon packs stumbling upon lost travellers and tearing them to shreds."

Tessa shivered—and not from the cold. She'd faced off with gorgons before.

"We're miles from the nearest settlement, deep in an arid and unforgiving wilderness," the woman said. "So keep that in mind next time you think about escaping. You wouldn't last a day out there."

She returned to the fire. A cool wind stirred Tessa's hair, bringing with it the aroma of whatever the merchants were cooking. Her stomach groaned in protest. Nearby, the merchant's mules and pack-beasts grazed on a patch of bushes.

The night grew longer, and as it did, the fire dimmed and the merchants drifted off to sleep. Several sat on watch. The labourers huddled together and leaned against boulders. Somewhere, soft sobbing reached Tessa's ears.

"Thank you for helping me," a voice said.

Tessa turned to see the same girl from before. She sat with her knees drawn to her chest, peering out from beneath her hood.

"Oh—it was nothing," Tessa replied.

"You distracted the merchant," she said. "You didn't need to." She hesitated. "Did you really mean it when you said you were a Raider?"

"I did—but they betrayed me." Part of her told her to keep quiet, but she found herself recounting the story of their capture by Mauriel.

The girl gasped. "But the Oath . . ."

Tessa scowled. "I guess they don't play by the rules anymore." She paused. "What's your name?"

"Marie," the girl replied.

They sat in silence. Marie twirled a lock of her hair. Despite the merchant's warnings, Tessa probed the knots that bound her ankles.

"I'm not from Alcabaza," Marie said suddenly. "I've been a labourer for a while. They picked me up from a farming village."

Tessa stopped tugging her binds. "What happened?"

"It was a bad year," Marie replied. "The crops failed and the families couldn't feed us. So when the merchants came in with an offer . . ." She trailed off. "They think I'm an apprentice somewhere."

Tessa shifted her weight. "I'm sorry that happened to you."

Marie motioned to Tessa's binds. "I gave up trying to escape."

"Well, I won't," Tessa replied. "Neither will my friends." She managed a smile. "And once Lazaro finds us, we'll free the rest of you, too."

Marie returned her smile. "I hope he does."

Tessa scooped up a pebble. "Do you want to see something?"

Marie nodded.

"Promise you won't tell anyone."

Tessa placed the pebble on the ground between them and focused. She tried to imagine what she did to help Isiah. A familiar sensation welled inside her—strange and nauseating. The pebble took on a shiny, black appearance. Tiny legs appeared, then a pair of antenna. It began to scuttle around.

Marie's eyes widened. "How did you do that?"

Tessa relaxed and the image of the beetle disintegrated, revealing the pebble. "It's an illusion," she explained. "Pretty neat, huh?"

"What else can you do?" Marie asked.

"I don't know," she admitted. "I'm not sure how it works."

"Well, I think it's pretty cool." Marie crawled closer.

Tessa spied Isiah and Aron on the opposite side of the camp with the male labourers. Part of her told her to sneak over and check on them.

"Do you mind if I sleep here?" Marie asked.

Tessa shifted to let Marie sit next to her. "Just keep what I showed you a secret, okay?"

Marie nodded. "You can count on me."

Merchant Den

"ALMOST THERE!" A MERCHANT CALLED. He spurred his mule across the arid terrain. "Don't stop now or we'll drag you the rest of the way."

Isiah forced his weary legs to keep moving. He lowered his head against the relentless heat and tried to keep his mind off his parched, swollen throat. The line of labourers cut through a dry river valley, heading toward a distant cluster of smoke on the horizon.

Loose, jagged rocks littered the earth, stabbing his feet. He stepped over streaks of blood where labourers had cut themselves. A thick layer of dust coated his calves and clung to the edges of his rags. His hair, drenched with sweat, stuck to his forehead.

The merchants had herded the labourers for several days, driving them through the unforgiving terrain to reach a distant camp. He'd had few chances to speak to Tessa during their journey. The thought of escape played on his mind, but the merchants always had someone keeping watch.

"I don't like this place," a merchant said. Isiah kept his eyes glued to the ground to avoid attracting their attention.

"What's so wrong about it?" a female merchant asked.

"I've heard the highlands are cursed," he replied. "Gorgons roam these hills every night. If you sit around the campfire and listen closely, you can hear their calls."

"We've got nothing to worry about," the woman said. "Gorgons don't attack groups as big as ours. They like hunting loners and small clans."

"Too many merchants have gone missing here for my liking." The merchant shivered. "Whole groups of labourers, too. They disappear into the hills, never to be seen again."

"Stop being so superstitious," she replied. "It's nothing more than a bunch of stories the older merchants like to use to scare you."

"Oh yeah?" the man said. "Then how come so many labourers go missing in these parts? It's cursed. I know it."

The woman sighed and spurred her mule on. Their words gave Isiah a flicker of hope—but he knew exchanging the merchants for a gorgon pack would be a sorry trade-off.

A few merchants headed to the front of the line, where they climbed over the ridge of the dried river and disappeared beyond. The smoke grew closer, coiling into the air from multiple sources. Flat-topped mesas and smooth boulders gave the landscape a strange, almost alien appearance. One of the merchants beckoned.

"Hurry those labourers along," he called. "A few more minutes and we'll be out of the sun."

Isiah pushed on with renewed vigour. The hope of rest and a drink gave him a new burst of energy. The sharp rock beneath his feet changed to sand and dusty earth as he climbed the riverbed and pushed into new terrain.

A merchant camp appeared ahead of them. An assortment of large tents and tarps huddled together in the barren landscape. As they drew closer, Isiah made out other groups of merchants. Their mules were tied to palisade fences nearby, alongside more hulking reptilian pack-beasts, and people in brightly coloured robes milled about inside the camp. A watering hole, brown and cloudy, let a few skeletal acacia trees grow nearby.

"There's our rest," a merchant said. "This has to be the most remote merchant den in the entire Badlands."

"Enjoy it while it lasts," the woman replied. "The boss wants us out of here tomorrow morning."

Isiah counted two dozen tents, all large enough to house multiple people. The merchants herded him into the shadow of tarps that were strung over the path. Several merchants broke off to tend to their donkeys.

"Over there," the bearded merchant barked. He pointed the labourers to a bare hillside on the edge of camp. "You can wait here."

Isiah's aching knees gave way and he collapsed on the hillside. As the rest of the labourers joined him, he made out several other groups in different parts of the camp.

"Watch them," the bearded merchant said to his companion. "Make sure they don't cause any trouble."

Part of Isiah urged him to ask for a drink, but he knew he'd only be rewarded by a strike from the merchant's stick. He resigned to sit in silence with the others.

"Isiah." Tessa's voice caught his attention. She crawled over to where he was sitting.

"Hey, Tessa." Isiah winced at the hoarseness of his voice. His tongue felt too big for his throat.

"Did you see Aron?" Tessa asked. She was with another girl, one he hadn't seen before.

"I lost him after we stopped last," he replied. "Did you have a plan?"

"Not yet," Tessa said. She paused. "Maybe we can do something tonight."

Isiah lowered his voice. "What about your magic? Can't you use an illusion or something?"

"I don't know," she replied. "It doesn't work like that."

One of the labourers swore. Isiah heard Aron apologize. He turned to see the boy crawling over.

"This is a big camp," he said. "There's a lot of trade going on. Maybe we'll get lucky and the merchants will get drunk."

Frenzied talking erupted from a nearby tent. A bunch of merchants sat around a low table. One shook a pair of dice in his hand and cast it across the table.

"No way," one of the men boomed. "You're cheating! Let me see those dice."

"I'm lucky, is all," his opponent replied. "Now, are we going again or what?"

One of the merchants stood. "I'm running out of coin to gamble," he said. "But I've got more than a few labourers to enter."

The merchants stood and wandered over to Isiah's group.

"What do I want with a bunch of labourers?" one of the merchants asked. A potbelly protruded from his robes, and his bare arms were awash with tattoos.

"You can sell them," his opponent replied. "You know there's a huge market for labourers all over the Badlands."

The potbellied man scoffed. He crossed his arms. "If they don't die on the journey." He waded into the group. "But I *could* accept them as payment."

He stopped in front of Tessa and leaned over. "This one would make a good maid for the nobles in the city we're headed to," he said. He grabbed her arm and squeezed it. "And she's in good shape, too." Tessa glared at the man. The man laughed. "But not broken in yet, I take it." He turned his attention to Isiah and Aron. "And these ones would make good gorgon hunters, by my reckoning. We get too many of them, where I'm from."

"Then I'll put them on my ledger," the other merchant replied. "If you win, you can have them."

The potbellied man grunted in satisfaction and the merchants returned to their gambling tent.

"What if we're separated?" Aron asked. "I don't like the look of all this."

"Don't worry," Tessa replied. "We'll be out of here before that happens."

As the merchants returned to their games, one of Isiah's captors came around with a waterskin and he took a swig. He didn't even care that the water was lukewarm and full of sand.

"Take it easy," the merchant said. "This has to be shared with all of you."

The merchants gambled and traded long into the afternoon. Isiah anxiously awaited the moment the twin suns would dip beneath the

horizon and they could plan their escape. The merchants kept a close eye on them to avoid any escapees.

"Here they are," a voice said. Isiah's stomach dropped as the bearded merchant wandered over with a group of others. The potbellied man was with them.

"Grab the ones I pointed out earlier," he said. "They'll put on a good show."

The other merchants began selecting labourers and dragging them off. Isiah tensed as the bearded merchant approached him.

"Get up," he ordered.

"What's going on?" Isiah asked.

"What have I told you about asking questions?" He grabbed Isiah's arm. "Do as you're told."

Isiah awkwardly pulled himself to his feet and the merchant marched him over to the other group. He found himself alongside Aron and a group of other similar-aged boys.

"They'll do good, alright," the potbellied man said. "I'll take them—if they can prove their worth."

"Then you'd better do it now," the bearded merchant replied. "I'm leaving at dawn, and I'm taking them with me unless you buy them."

"So be it." The potbellied man gestured to his companions and they began leading the labourers into the camp.

Isiah's mind raced. The merchants marched him into a new part of the camp, out of view of the hillside. Several tents stood around a hole in the ground. As they approached, nearby merchants poked their heads out of tents to see the source of the commotion.

"Stop there," the potbellied man instructed. He stooped and cut Isiah's ankle binds. He then untied Isiah's wrists and jabbed a thumb in the direction of the hole. "Get in the pit."

Isiah inched toward it. A large rectangle stood at the bottom on one side. Tarps covered it, obscuring its contents. At intervals around the pit's rim, sharpened wooden stakes protruded from the earth. Isiah hesitated. "What's in there?"

"Don't talk back to me." The potbellied man shoved him. "Either you go down there or I'll throw you in myself." He freed Aron and a couple of the other labourers.

Isiah sat on the edge of the pit and slid inside. He landed on the hard, cracked earth. The rim of the pit stood a dozen feet over his head—too high to reach. One by one, the other labourers joined him. With a sinking feeling, Isiah realized what was going on.

The potbellied man collected an armful of spears and chucked them into the pit. The labourers took one each. Isiah counted half a dozen of them in total, him and Aron included. He gripped the rough wooden shaft of his spear and held it close. Its crude, flattened iron head was shaped like a leaf. On the opposite side of the pit, a ladder descended and a merchant climbed in with them.

Something inside the cage lurched. A throaty growl sounded. The merchant grabbed the edge of the tarp and pulled it free. Isiah gulped as his worst fears were confirmed.

Three gorgons paced about the cage. They snapped at the merchant with their long jaws. Strings of saliva hung from their four sabre-like fangs. The merchant carefully undid the latch to their cage and then retreated from the pit.

The gorgons spilled into the arena. They snarled and paced about, as if unsure of their surroundings. Their short, dark fur stood on end, and their ribs protruded from their sides.

"Gorgons don't like the sunlight," the potbellied man said. Around him, a growing crowd of merchants peered over the edge into the pit. "But that doesn't make them any less dangerous."

The gorgons' beady eyes fixed on Isiah and the labourers. Their muscles, weak from starvation but still limber and strong, rippled beneath their thick skin. Short tails trailed behind them, and pairs of long claws protruded from their feet.

Isiah levelled his spear at them. He adjusted his grip on the shaft. He'd faced gorgons once before with Tessa, inside a ruin. The labourers huddled together, spears outstretched.

"They pick off stragglers," the potbellied man continued. "They like to hunt in packs. Their jaws are strong enough to snap bones, and their fangs can impale a man."

The gorgons advanced. Patches of fur were missing from their flanks, and their stomachs were hollowed, but that made them no less threatening. One made a mock lunge at Aron. Isiah forced himself to control his breathing. The crowd around the pit grew larger.

"And when they're desperate," the potbellied man said, "they become more aggressive."

The gorgons charged. The labourers broke form and fled in panic. Isiah stumbled aside as a gorgon flew past him. Its hot breath blasted his skin. One of the labourers fell and the beast clamped its jaws around his leg.

The labourer screamed and dropped his spear. The gorgon shook its head, dragging him across the floor. The other two closed in to finish

him. The labourer writhed in pain and beat his fists against the gorgon's snout. The merchants gasped and pushed each other to get a better look.

Isiah forced himself into motion. He raised his spear and thrust it at the gorgon's neck. The blade sliced through its tough skin and a shockwave reverberated through Isiah's arms. The gorgon barked in pain and wheeled away. Isiah dug his heels into the ground to avoid the spear being wrenched from his grip.

The other labourers collected themselves. The injured boy scrambled backwards and Aron caught his arm. The gorgon that had bitten him snapped at Isiah. Its head was level with his chest. Isiah kept his spear trained on its face.

The other gorgons circled, like wolves closing in for the kill. The labourers waved their spears, but the tremble in their hands gave them away. The injured boy gasped in pain and clutched his bleeding leg.

The lead gorgon charged Isiah. He jabbed his spear forward and stepped aside. The gorgon wheeled away at the last moment. Isiah readjusted his footing. He scanned for some kind of escape. The walls were too sheer for him to climb, and the stakes prevented the gorgons from escaping too.

"You'll never be gorgon hunters if you keep up like this," the pot-bellied man called. He stood with his boot-toes poking over the edge of the arena. "Get in there! Work as a team to corner one."

The injured boy leaned on his spear. Blood seeped from puncture wounds in his calf and stained the earth a deep red. Isiah swallowed. The gorgons pinned the boy with their gaze. He opened his mouth to call a warning, but it was too late.

The lead gorgon leapt at him. The boy screamed as the weight of the beast collided with him and bore him to the ground. The other labourers scattered as the gorgons closed in. The snap of jaws made Isiah's insides churn. The boy's screams fell to pained gurgles.

The merchants hollered. The potbellied man folded his arms and shook his head. Heat burned in Isiah's chest. A plan flashed into his head.

He pulled back his arm and threw his spear.

The potbellied man's eyes widened. The spear arced through the air and buried itself into his stomach. He screamed and clutched the shaft as he toppled into the arena. He landed on the stakes jutting from the wall and snapped them, before hitting the floor and driving the spear further into his gut.

The gorgons whirled on the screaming man. Isiah yelled and waved his arms at them, trying to appear as big as possible. Aron understood what he was trying to do and joined in.

The gorgons ran from the yelling boys. The screams of merchants spooked them. One leapt at the wall and scaled it.

Merchants scattered. The three gorgons crawled through the gap in the spikes and sprinted into the camp. Isiah and the surviving labourers sprinted to the wall.

"That was a brilliant plan!" Aron exclaimed. The potbellied man lay writhing on the ground. Aron kicked dust over him.

"We still need to get out," Isiah replied.

Aron knelt and cupped his hands. "I'll give you a boost."

Isiah stepped into Aron's hands and he jumped toward the stakes. Grabbing one, he clambered over the edge of the pit. One by one,

the other labourers followed. The last one turned and caught Aron's arms, pulling him up.

"Come on," Isiah said. "We need to help Tessa."

The screams of merchants echoed through the camp. With it came something else. Isiah's breath caught in his throat as the shrill call of eagles split the air.

The labourers ducked as shapes blasted overhead. Voices yelled battle cries as eagles spread out their wings and circled the camp. Aron pumped his fist in the air and cheered. Isiah squinted at the birds, trying to make out their riders. *Could it be Lazaro?*

Several eagles landed among the tents. The power of their wing-beats made the structures collapse. Merchants struggled under the material, desperately trying to free themselves. Nearby labourers charged their guards and overpowered them.

Isiah took off running. He ducked beneath an eagle's outstretched wing and ran in the direction he'd left Tessa. He rounded a corner to find the bearded merchant on the floor, clutching his sword arm. The labourers cheered as a pair of Raiders untied them.

Merchants fled into the surrounding wilderness. One of the gorgons chased after them. Isiah reached Tessa's side and doubled over, breathing heavily.

"Isiah!" Tessa's eyes lit up. "I knew Raiders would come help us!"

"Secure the camp," a Raider called. His companions finished freeing the labourers and rounded up the last of the merchants. They bound their wrists and forced them to their knees. One stood guard, sabre in hand. His companion came over.

"Did Lazaro send you?" Tessa asked. "Where is he?"

The Raider raised his hands. "Hold on, there. I don't know of any Lazaro."

Tessa's smile dropped. "What do you mean? Then who are you?"

"Save your questions," he said with a laugh. "We'll answer them in good time." He pulled a sack from his eagle's saddle and tossed it to her. "Pass out some water, will you? It's still a trek to our home base."

The labourers crowded around to get their fill from the water-skins. The Raiders sorted through the merchants' collapsed tents and carried out anything of value. Isiah approached the man who had spoken to them.

"You're Raiders, right?" he asked.

The man smiled. "Indeed we are." He extended a hand. "We're here to save you."

Lazaro

"GATHER YOUR VALUABLES AND THEN HAND over the key," the Raider barked.

Lazaro stood in front of his house. Darla and Antony waited beside him, sacks slung over their shoulders. Helen and Luca filed through the door with their own.

"We, the collective Raiders, hereby declare that Lazaro and his Raider gang are to be exiled from Alcabaza," a Raider said. He held out a yellowed scroll in front of him. Several others, all armed, stood around.

"Cut the speech," Lazaro snapped. "I've heard it before."

The Raider scowled and folded the scroll. "Get out, Lazaro. You're not welcome here anymore."

Helen adjusted the sack over her shoulder and produced the key to the house—his house. The Raider pocketed it.

A fire burned inside Lazaro's gut. How dare the Raiders throw him out of his own home? He'd worked for years with Tessa to afford that place. The shutters were loose and the mortar was cracking, but it was *their* place to live.

"We'll escort you to your eagles and then confiscate your pens," the Raider said. "If you return to Alcabaza after today, you'll be executed."

"I'd like to see you try," Lazaro spat.

The Raider stepped forward. "You're lucky we don't have a dragon to feed you to." The pair stood forehead-to-forehead. "And if you can't find anyone to fly your sister's eagle, we'll take him off your hands."

Lazaro shoved the man. He stumbled a few steps, then replied with a shove of his own. Lazaro lowered his head and charged him. His shoulder connected with the Raider's chest and sent him sprawling. Before either could do anything else, Antony grabbed Lazaro and pulled him away.

The Raider stood and dusted himself off. "I defended you from Enrik too many times," he said. "No matter how many fistfights you got into, I was always there to apologise on your behalf." He spat on the ground at Lazaro's feet. "Now get out of our city."

The Raiders marched away. Lazaro gritted his teeth and waited until they were out of sight, then kicked the ground.

"Who do they think they are?" he snapped. "They don't own this city. That house is *ours*."

"We can worry about that later," Helen said. "We need to get our eagles and go after Tessa. If we're quick, we can catch up to them. She can't have been taken far."

"I have every right mind to cut off Mauriel's head," Lazaro replied. "She thinks we're Oath-breakers? Then why don't we prove them right?"